RESURRECTING
MIDNIGHT

ERIC JEROME DICKEY

RESURRECTING MIDNIGHT

DUTTON

DUTTON
Published by Penguin Group (USA) Inc.
375 Hudson Street, New York, New York 10014, U.S.A.
Penguin Group (Canada), 90 Eglinton Avenue East, Suite 700, Toronto, Ontario M4P
2Y3, Canada (a division of Pearson Penguin Canada Inc.); Penguin Books Ltd, 80 Strand,
London WC2R 0RL, England; Penguin Ireland, 25 St. Stephen's Green, Dublin 2, Ireland
(a division of Penguin Books Ltd); Penguin Group (Australia), 250 Camberwell Road,
Camberwell, Victoria 3124, Australia (a division of Pearson Australia Group Pty Ltd);
Penguin Books India Pvt Ltd, 11 Community Centre, Panchsheel Park, New Delhi—110
017, India; Penguin Group (NZ), 67 Apollo Drive, Rosedale, North Shore 0632, New
Zealand (a division of Pearson New Zealand Ltd); Penguin Books (South Africa) (Pty) Ltd,
24 Sturdee Avenue, Rosebank, Johannesburg 2196, South Africa

Penguin Books Ltd, Registered Offices: 80 Strand, London WC2R 0RL, England

Published by Dutton, a member of Penguin Group (USA) Inc.

First printing, August 2009
1   3   5   7   9   10   8   6   4   2

REGISTERED TRADEMARK—MARCA REGISTRADA

LIBRARY OF CONGRESS CATALOGING-IN-PUBLICATION DATA
has been applied for.

ISBN 978-0-525-95057-8

Printed in the United States of America
Set in Janson Text
Designed by Leonard Telesca

PUBLISHER'S NOTE

This book is a work of fiction. Names, characters, places, and incidents either are the product
of the author's imagination or are used fictitiously, and any resemblance to actual persons,
living or dead, business establishments, events, or locales is entirely coincidental.

For Dominique

"Evil is the blemish of our species that will not spare even the best man."

—Immanuel Kant

RESURRECTING
MIDNIGHT

Chapter 1

on dangerous ground

And their war began.

The stretch limousine exploded, became a time bomb moving at eighty miles per hour.

I verified the detonation in my side-view mirror. Its beautiful fire lit up the express lane on a humid night, the deadly cacophony forty yards behind me on I-95. The energy from that blast rolled through me, rattled both sides of the interstate and adjacent roads like we were in a San Francisco earthquake. Brake lights came alive in an abrupt chorus. Behind me, beyond that fiery limousine, four lanes of interstate crowded with cars, trucks, and motorcycles screeched to a halt, too late for speed demons to swerve and avoid flying debris.

I kept going.

The target was dead. The impossible mission was completed in less than forty-eight hours.

The corrupt and elusive con man inside the limo had been living a life of caviar and champagne, bodyguards at his side, men who were paid well and trained to shoot to kill. He was a man who didn't hesitate to take his enemies to the swamps and feed them to the gators.

A grifter named Arizona had been one of his problems.

And the man named Hopkins had become one of hers.

All I knew was what she had told me. And that wasn't much. The less the better.

What mattered was that deadly situation had been rectified.

The remote trigger that had caused that blast was in my gloved hand. I dropped it, pressed down on the throttle, hit the century mark, moved from right lane to left lane to right lane, threaded traffic like a needle, became a fast-moving shadow vanishing down I-95.

In this gritty world, people called me Gideon. A biblical name made famous by an adjudicator in the Book of Judges. That Gideon was also known as Jerub-Baal. Destroyer. Mighty Warrior. I was Gideon. Not sent by God. Employed by those who thought they were.

I was a hired gun paid to do what people wouldn't do for themselves.

This has been my vocation since I was seven years old. Since I aimed a gun at an angry man they called Midnight. I had killed that man before I had been given the truth about what he was.

Since that day, I'd been on the run, reared in brothels, lived in red-light districts, had been taken into a world of retribution and learned more than two dozen ways to end a life, all for a price.

Using a block of C-4 and a remote control wasn't even high on the goddamn list.

Late evening, the darkness of my bike and clothing mixed with the cruelty in the night.

I accelerated and felt like I was moving faster than the speed of sound, then slowed when I caught up and mixed with the next wave of fast-moving traffic on I-95, became a law-abiding commuter as I signaled and faded onto the next exit, took the streets, rode toward the causeways, breezed through city traffic, engine rumbling, balmy night air on my skin. Gun inside my messenger bag. Riding a Streetfighter. Trellis frame. Huge fork clamps. Solid performance. I sped toward the area called Aventura, hurried to meet my sponsor.

The international grifter named Arizona had arrived in the U.S. and was somewhere down here in Florida. The Hopkins job was done, but now I needed her assistance, had to work out my own problems. Problems that if left unresolved could have me sleeping six feet under.

Four days ago, after vanishing for almost a year, Arizona had resurfaced and sent a message. A job offer. The message had been a cryptic text, had come from an untraceable phone and was delivered to a temporary account on Gmail, one of a dozen we had set up for communicating. That particular account hadn't been used since I'd seen her in London. I'd gone to the Apple store in Minnesota's Mall of America, the country's largest retail and entertainment complex. If the IP addresses were traced, it would lead to that store. I blended with the Mac heads, wore a baseball cap and shades, my face always down and away from the cameras.

I logged on to a laptop and checked my messages.

That con woman had sent me an encrypted message that gave me a location on the edge of Miami. Encryptions. Countersurveillance. Rendezvous points. Wire transfers.

It was the language and lifestyle of killers and cons.

Within the next few hours, I was on a flight heading to the land of gators.

When I had landed in Fort Lauderdale, Arizona had arranged what I needed. Ducati Streetfighter, black motorcycle helmet, racing gloves. All that and a messenger bag that was weighed down by a nine, two extra clips, a remote, and something that would blow my target's mind.

I took a deep breath, pulled up my face shield, and cruised.

Starbucks was on the corner of Biscayne Boulevard and Concourse Circle Drive. Inside a plaza dotted with palm trees and filled with BMWs, Hummers, Bentleys, and Benzes. This section of South Miami looked like a dealership for new and preowned luxury cars.

The competition of capitalism continued despite the economic downturn.

I circled the well-lit strip mall twice before I paused on that prime chunk of real estate.

It was a parking lot that covered all the blood that had soaked into the soil. More than a century ago, the Seminoles and the U.S. fought over this land, a bloody war that might have been the deadliest and costliest of the Indian wars, from the point of view of the U.S. of A.

The sound of gunfire and cannon booms had been replaced with the hum of cappuccino machines and the purr of extravagant automobiles. The scent of war was now the aroma of the perfect latte.

As soon as I headed inside, my cellular vibrated. It was a text message: FUNDS TRANSFERRED.

I deleted that message and moved on, looked out at a warm night that thieving man thought he would live to see. But someone with anger in their heart and money in their pockets had other plans.

Inside was like Antarctica, the AC blowing on high. The noise level was in the red, a dozen multilingual conversations being trapped by glass and walls. Cubans had conversations about one Castro in their homeland being replaced by another Castro, argued that the free health care and free education wasn't enough to make them remain a *Fidelista* and things needed to change in a land where Cubans couldn't own cell phones legally and computers were prohibited; the Cubans sipped five-dollar coffees and argued over the need to *defender el socialismo*. Next to them, groups of elderly Jewish men discussed a meeting for Holocaust survivors. There was a lot of noise: the nonstop whirr of the machines making lattes and cappuccinos, the din of jazz being piped in, and people yapping on cellular phones.

Hairs stood up on my neck. Like in London. It felt like I was being watched.

I went into the bathroom, had to. Outside I was cool. But anxiety clung to me, shook me like a winter's chill. For a moment it felt like I was about to lose control. Another daymare. I'd had a few since Antigua. Images that attacked me while I was wide awake. I saw the dead. Faces I'd been paid to put in the ground. And I saw the faces of those who had tried to do the same to me. Standing behind them all, in the shadows, his face unclear but his silhouette unforgettable, was the man I had killed when I was seven. He was nothing more than a shadow.

The mercenary they called Midnight. The first man I had killed. My father.

My life was a haunted house filled with many ghosts.

Somebody tapped on the door and I pulled the nine millimeter out of my backpack. I called out that the bathroom was occupied. Paused. Whoever was out there walked away. The police wouldn't leave. Neither would the FBI. Both would announce they had come for me.

I took out my iPhone. Dialed a number in Powder Springs.

I wanted to check up on Catherine and the boys, Steven and Robert. Catherine was the woman who had raised me. Robert's mother had been killed because of my vocation. Steven was the boy Catherine called her son. But I knew that was a lie. Everything had been a lie.

No one answered, but the answering machine kicked on.

I didn't leave a message. I blocked my number and never left messages, not there.

I splashed cold water on my face, wiped my skin down with a paper towel, and went outside.

The hunter had been hunted before, more than once.

I spied the room. Cubans sipping cappuccino. Jewish women doing the same. A teenaged guy wearing Dockers and black sandals was eyeing the olive complexion of a blond woman seated at the next table, her pink button-down shirt and ripped jeans not enough to mask a body that could lure most men straight to the gates of Hell.

I sat at a back table, my back to the wall. Darkness masked what had been blue skies and puffy white clouds. Nighttime humidity rose as I waited, my anxiety not betraying me.

A Maserati whipped up under the lights, pulled into the lot, and found an open space between my Streetfighter and a 7-series BMW. The GranTurismo was beautiful. Gray coupe, red leather seats. It was her. That was her mode. Had been her style since she was coming up as a grifter in North Hollywood, back when she was a neophyte in the con game. She'd come up from sleeping on the streets to sleeping in penthouses. Had moved from Hyundai to Maserati.

Every time I read about a major scam, it felt like it was her doing. Maybe I was just hoping it was her criminal mind in full swing. I kept telling myself that it didn't matter, but no matter where I was in the world, no matter what job I was on, no matter whose bed I was in, no matter who was in my bed, when all was said and done, my mind always went back to her.

I needed her for her connections to the conniving world of high-tech cons and criminals.

Someone out there knew about me, some unseen foe existed, someone who had tracked my movements around the world, someone who had sold my information to a problem I'd had in Detroit, and that information was then passed on to other killers.

Those killers were dead, but the information was alive.

Arizona eased out of her Maserati GranTurismo and I couldn't stop my schoolboy smile.

A part of me I couldn't control would always want her.

Arizona's back was to me at first, her right hand holding her cellular to her ear. Her hair was long and dyed light brown with highlights, hung over her shoulders. She glanced toward the boulevard and I saw she had on dark shades with wide lenses, shades that matched the dark brown blouse she wore, a blouse that probably had hints of her lacy bra showing hints of her soft breasts.

I spied out at the parking lot, made sure she wasn't trailed. Force of habit. Then I checked the room again. The teenaged guy wearing Dockers had made contact with the pretty blond woman in the pink button-down shirt and ripped jeans. He had scooted his chair closer to her table, smiled at her as she blushed at him.

Arizona kept her eyes on the boulevard.

She had on four-inch heels made by a designer who put red soles on all of his shoes. One glance at the Maserati and Louboutins and you'd think she had matriculated from one of the best schools in the country, maybe the prestigious Miss Porter's up in Connecticut.

Arizona glanced back toward the coffeehouse, a serious look on her Filipina flesh, a walking enigma who could break a man's heart or empty every dime he had in his portfolio. She looked extraordinary, possessed an otherworldly beauty. No one would know she was the queen of scams. Just looked like a woman men would want to marry and put in a case with the rest of their trophies.

I licked my lips, could never forget the five senses of her. I'd stop the world from spinning if she asked me to. I'd betray God the way Judas Iscariot betrayed His son.

Arizona kept her cellular up to her face. A moment later, mine rang. Area code 809. Good old 809 had been disgraced, used in many Caribbean area code scams.

I answered, my voice heavy and serious. "I'm inside."

Arizona closed her cellular.

It had been over a year since I'd seen her.

A lot had happened since then.

She reached inside the car and took out a black briefcase, added that to the purse she was carrying. She gripped the briefcase by its handle, turned around, and what I saw her carrying made me sit up straight.

My heart stopped beating. Then my heart restarted, began beating as fast as it could.

Between Arizona's breasts and waist, there was roundness underneath her blouse.

A roundness that told me she was at least in her second trimester.

Chapter 2

honor among thieves

Arizona was pregnant.

She held the briefcase close to her. As if she were guarding it with her life. I thought she would walk in and come straight to me, but she stepped into the coolness and got in line.

I stared at her baby bump, thinking that it might go away.

It didn't. She remained swollen, looked pregnant from all angles.

Queen Scamz had been ridden bareback.

A moment later, she had two cups of tea on a tray. I stood to help her, but the guy in the Dockers had left the beautiful girl he was chatting up and had beaten me to the task. Arizona didn't part with her briefcase, but she let him carry the tray with the cups. He came to the table, moved ahead of her and handed the tray to me, then walked away, hurried back to the table with the beautiful girl. I was frozen. Arizona stopped and grabbed napkins and sugars, then came to the back, the last bistro table before the bathrooms. I stood when she came toward me, briefcase in one hand, her D&G purse now over her shoulder, the sugars and napkins in the same hand.

She said, "*Nauuhaw?*"

"Tagalog."

"You haven't learned Tagalog yet?"

"Some. The basics. Yeah, I'm thirsty."

Arizona spoke at least four languages: Spanish, Japanese, pidgin, and Vietnamese. She had a least three dozen aliases, a dozen more aliases than the legendary con woman Doris Payne, and had done financial damage in Greece, France, England, and Switzerland. I was surprised to see her back in America. I had thought she had outgrown this crumbling market.

I didn't know if she was going to hug me or shake hands.

She did neither. She put the briefcase on the floor, eased it close to the wall.

She sat down. "Green tea okay?"

"Thanks." I sat back down. "Long time."

"Seems like yesterday. But it's been a while."

"Last time I saw you was an ugly day in London and we were on the Millennium Bridge. I was fighting thugs from Brixton. You were throwing knives and cutting people left and right."

"I was fighting for my life. Fighting for your life. I was protecting you."

"You killed that day. Your first kill, as far as I know."

"Three people. My first time killing. And I killed three. For you."

I nodded. "Yeah. You did."

She took one of the cups of tea. I kept the other and nodded as a thank-you.

She slid me two sugars. Remembered how I drank my tea. Arizona put one package of white sugar in her tea, stirred it, sipped, as relaxed as everyone else.

I said, "You're carrying a little extra weight."

"The elephant in the room."

"Figured I'd get that out of the way."

My throat became a desert while my palms became a river.

Arizona reached inside her purse. It was opened wide enough for me to see a package of Djarums inside. She took out a device about the size of a Palm Pilot, placed it on the table, then closed her purse. While she did that, another elephant appeared. One that caught me off guard. One I ignored. On the device, the light flashed green. That meant no one was listening in on us, no high-tech surveillance devices were pointed our way.

She said, "Turn your cellular off. Anything electronic you have, turn it off."

I took out my iPhone, did what the grifter known as Queen Scamz asked.

Arizona took out a second device about the same size as the first. She clicked it on.

I asked, "What does that slice of technology do?"

"This widget is sweet, lifts information on cell phones and Palm Pilots. Same for laptops. Any information stored on computers inside the cars in the parking lot, if that car is on, it's snatched too. Starbucks computers. Anything Wi-Fi is being snatched."

"Always on the grift."

"Read the news. The world is nothing but one fucking grift."

I hadn't seen her in a year and she walked in pregnant. Didn't know what I expected from her at this moment. Wanted to look in her face and see mixed emotions. She gave me eye contact and wasn't nervous. Not the slightest hint that she wished that baby could be mine. I didn't see any residual feelings for me. Nothing like I was feeling for her right now.

I sipped my tea. "Hopkins should be on CNN by now."

Her nose flared. "Lost fifteen million on that double cross. And he tried to shut me out."

"Guess sending him a red-trimmed late notice wasn't good enough."

"This is bigger than that. Bigger than the fifteen million I lost."

"How much bigger?"

"I can get back what I lost. Plus some. I'll get to that in a moment."

She sipped her tea. I sipped mine.

I tried to imagine what it would be like to have fifteen million to lose.

She said, "You wanted to meet."

I nodded. "I need your help."

Didn't want to ask her for help, but I didn't have much of a choice. My handler hadn't come up with an answer. Arizona used me to get what she needed. I had to do the same.

I told her someone had tracked me a while ago, for an enemy that

I'd had in Detroit. Tracked me from parts of North America to the UK and then down to the West Indies.

She sipped her tea. "Detroit is no longer an issue."

"That account is closed. But whoever did her work for her still has my information."

"That's not good. Not good at all."

"So far as whoever tracked me, I'm not sure who *he* or *she* or *they* are. Don't know what they would do with the information. I need you to find out what you can find out."

Arizona said, "I'm in the middle of something else, but I'll see what I can do. At cost."

Again I looked to the front of the coffee shop. Doors opened and closed, customers came and went. The teenaged guy wearing Dockers sipped his brew, again at the same table with the attractive woman in the pink blouse and ripped jeans, his grin nonstop.

I checked my watch, asked, "We done here?"

The queen of cons shook her head. "I have a couple more items to cover."

"Personal or business?"

"Business. Something that I have been asked to . . . tasked to re-mind you. I wanted to recuse myself from this next matter, but that won't be possible, not without creating more conflict."

"Go ahead."

"My friend that assisted you in London."

"I take it that the *friend* you're referring to is Scamz's tight-suit-wearing son."

"Yes. The man that served as my wingman. Scamz's son."

I almost frowned. Almost. He had been her lover in London. Obviously he still was.

I said, "Cut to the chase."

Her expression hardened. She had become Queen Scamz, her crimes her crown.

She said, "He saved your life."

"You saved my life."

"No. He did. I was incapacitated at the time."

"You killed three people. With a knife. He didn't do shit."

"He picked up the slack."

"My debt is to you. If anyone owes anyone anything, I am indebted to you, and you can be indebted to him. But if you ask me, it looks like that debt has been paid."

"What does that mean?"

"Nothing. Means nothing. Ignore that."

She tapped the table, shook off my comment before she said, "Reciprocity is in order."

In that moment I felt it, that plastic bag over my head, felt Death clawing at me no matter how hard I fought. It was her lover, the man she opened her legs for, who kept me alive.

She said, "Without reciprocity, there are complications."

"The way of the gun."

She nodded. "We have our own rules, none written down, yet all engraved in stone."

I sucked in air, released, then asked, "What does he expect as reciprocity?"

"Things are happening now. He needs you. When it's time, he'll get the word to you."

"How will your wingman, your shadow, your friend find me?"

Arizona reached in her bag, took out a phone, slid it to me. A small Thuraya satellite phone. An electronic leash that was good in more than one hundred and twenty countries around Europe, Africa, and the Middle East. From the high seas to the North Pole, no matter where I went, they could reach me.

I gritted my teeth. "This shit never ends."

"It ends. Just not the way most of us want it to end."

"Ends with us becoming part of the foundation at Giants Stadium."

"Or blown up on a fucking interstate."

I said, "I'd rather be part of Giants Stadium."

Arizona sipped her tea, then took a breath. "I need to say something."

"Business?"

"Personal. I hate getting personal, but I feel this is unavoidable."

"Be human. Let the emotions flow."

"Since London, once I knew you were okay, I lost contact. Intentionally."

"Any particular reason?"

"Us together, it's no good."

"That wall has gone back up."

"It never came down."

I adjusted myself in my seat. "Guess you let that wall down for somebody."

"Opening my legs doesn't mean a wall came down. Just means I opened my legs."

"I stand corrected."

Arizona was guarded, had been that way for more than a decade, since her abusive relationship with Scamz. He'd been dead for an eternity, long enough for the mourning to fade away. But with her, whatever she felt, whatever Stockholm syndrome she had suffered, the admiration never subsided. Loved him so much that she bedded the man's son, that DNA probably kicking in her womb now.

I'd tried to get inside her head but had only made it as far as her panties.

I said, "Well, I'll congratulate your friend. Scamz Junior or Little Scamz or Mini Scamz."

"Gideon."

"Glad to see that you and your Latin Brit have had a good year together."

"Pejoratives aside, you don't want to owe him favors."

I asked, "We done here?"

"One final matter."

"Personal or business?"

"Business."

"Whose business? Yours or the guy in the English suits?"

"There is a problem in South America. It piggybacks on this Hopkins job."

When she said that, in that moment, she changed. I saw what I thought was fear.

I'd never seen this grifter wear fear before. She didn't wear it long.

I asked, "Another limo needs to be retrofitted with a block of C-4?"

"This is different."

"What kind of different?"

"Recon."

"I don't do recon."

"Something was stolen."

"You might need to get a new profession."

"What does that mean?"

"You were ripped off in London. Now this Miami thing. Now South America. You're getting conned left and right. Sounds like Queen Scamz is about to lose her crown."

"I said it was stolen. Didn't say it was stolen from me."

"I don't do recon."

"I'll double the pay."

"Not about money."

"Everything is about money. Money is power. Everything is about power."

I paused, took a breath. "What did you lose?"

She paused. "Consider it my MacGuffin."

"Where was it last?"

"Montevideo."

"Uruguay."

"Based on the pattern that's been reported, they move it every forty-eight, maybe every seventy-two tops. They're keeping it mobile, making it difficult to locate. The longest it has been in one place is a week. They never keep it in one location longer than seven days. But I have a way of getting within range."

"It has GPS."

She nodded. "It will be in Buenos Aires as soon as tonight."

"Buenos Aires?"

"You know that part of South America?"

"Been to Buenos Aires a few times."

"Contracts?"

"Had contracts along the Amazon. Brazil, Ecuador, Bolivia, Colombia, and Peru."

"So you know your way around."

"I can manage. First time I was down there was right after I had met you in North Hollywood. Over a decade ago. This guy from Ecuador had me following some human cargo that had caused him a few problems. Tracked him and his partner through Salto Ángel to the End of the World. Had other businesses down that way. Been on both sides of the Andes mountain range. You get up around the Iguazú Falls, that land that borders Argentina and Brazil, I'm not good, geography-wise. Would need a guide that spoke Spanish and Portuguese."

"Buenos Aires is where the package is heading."

"City or province?"

"Either or."

"That widens the territory. Large population."

"Not like Mexico City."

"No, not like Mexico City. But not like Odenville, Alabama."

"Where is that?"

"My point exactly." I sipped my tea. "When will the needle drop in the haystack?"

"Next few days. Can you go down there now?"

"No."

"No?"

"I have something that I have to take care of."

"Another assignment?"

"Confidential."

"Can it wait?"

"No. Consider it my MacGuffin. And it can't wait."

She took a breath, enough irritation on her side of the table to make her baby kick.

I said, "And you're positive this MacGuffin is in South America."

"Yes. It has been moved through Brazil, Colombia, Bolivia, and, before that, Peru."

"A moving target."

"I have satellite images. Days ago. It was in Montevideo on 18 de

Julio. Men transferred the package from one vehicle to another. Bodyguards all around. There is a sensor inside. Reads longitude and latitude. If it doesn't change location every seven days the package will . . . render itself useless. Not sure what determines how far or where it has to be moved."

"Will it explode?"

"No idea."

"You said it was moved at least once every seven days. Why *at least* every seven days?"

"The originator figured if he was unable to move his part of the package once a week, then he was dead."

"His part."

"There is a second part."

"GPS on that part too?"

"Yes."

"Will I be asked to get that part too?"

"That part is taken care of. That part is what Hopkins wanted. I need you on this part."

"The part you're after? Show me what you have."

Arizona took out a picture, slid it across the table. It was the photo of a black briefcase. One of those numbers that required a fingerprint to open. One that might be booby-trapped.

I said, "That looks like the briefcase you're carrying."

She nodded. "It does."

"Is that part of this?"

"I have part of what was being tracked by Hopkins."

"And this other part?"

"It's being tracked by my team. The one I have, my team tracks it as well."

"The one you have, you said it was being tracked by Hopkins too?"

"No worries. Hopkins is dead. The big man is dead. I'm safe."

I sat on her words for a moment. "Give me a couple of days to think it over."

Her irritation grew. She tapped her fingernails on the table.

She asked, "What will it take for you to reconsider?"

I sipped my tea, became the cool one at the table, the one in control.

She said, "Name your price."

"Not about money. Not gouging you."

She pulled her lips in, irritated, stressed. "How many days before you are available?"

"Four."

"Four days could make it a brand-new ball game."

I took a deep breath, her irritation not motivating me in a new mental direction.

She said, "Okay. Four days."

"When do I get the package?"

"The official work order will come through Konstantin."

"Why the change in the way we've been doing business?"

Arizona smiled. It was an ugly smile on a beautiful face.

She took out another remote, aimed it at her Maserati, pressed a button, its lights flashing in the night. The car started. The engine revved, then calmed down.

She wanted to make sure her GranTurismo didn't explode.

That was the world we lived in. In that way, my world wasn't any different from hers.

She said, "Payment and details on Buenos Aires have been forwarded to the Russian."

"When?"

"It was sent to Konstantin an hour ago."

My jaw tightened. "An hour ago."

"Yes. Satellite photos. Everything we have so far."

"What made you think I'd accept the contract?"

She said, "You've never turned me down."

With that, Arizona gathered her things, then stood to leave.

I said, "Sit down."

"I have to go."

"Sit. Or I walk."

She did what I asked.

I asked, "Should I trust you?"

"Why the doubt?"

"You're all about money. And power. That's what feeds you. Money and power. Judas Iscariot betrayed Christ for thirty pieces of silver. If Jesus can get betrayed . . . who the fuck am I?"

"Have I ever betrayed you?"

I took a breath, felt paranoid and foolish. "You put your life on the line for me in London."

"My record speaks for itself. I killed three people trying to protect you."

I let the anger speak, asked, "What about the man who sent me the satellite phone?"

"He saved your life in London."

"You were on that bridge with me. That fucker was nowhere in sight."

"It's about reciprocity."

"Guess it's too late to send him a Hallmark card and a Strip-O-Gram as a thank-you."

Nothing was said for a moment.

I asked, "Is that his baby?"

She smiled a difficult smile. "You've been jealous of him since you knew he existed."

She was right. Jealousy ran though my veins. I had no right to be jealous. But I was.

I'd been inside her deep enough to feel her heartbeat throbbing against the tip of my erection. But somehow she had managed to get deeper inside of me. She knew she had.

I said, "I worked for his dad."

"I know you did. I knew why you were in North Hollywood. I knew what you did."

"Do you know about the South America job I did for him?"

"I know you went to South America."

"I went to the End of the World."

She asked, "Are we done here?"

I nodded. "We're done."

Arizona took a breath and stood. She motioned for me to remain seated, then came to my side of the table. She kissed me on my cheek, pressed her soft lips into my troubled flesh.

She said, "I still watch *Battlestar Galactica*. Still listen to Miles and Coltrane."

It only took a few words to throw a man off balance.

She picked up the high-tech briefcase, adjusted her purse on her other shoulder, and walked away. She didn't walk like she had just lost fifteen million and ordered a man blown up on I-95. She moved like a goddess, in control and entitled. Arizona paused in the night, looked around. She looked out toward Biscayne, stared like she had seen something. I looked that way, saw nothing. For a moment she looked jittery. Almost afraid.

She put the briefcase inside the Maserati first.

The woman who had been robbed of a king's fortune looked around again.

Her body language changed, became a lioness that had sensed a predator.

I stood up, hand inside my messenger bag, ready to rush outside.

But her look of concern, that expression that I interpreted as fear, it left Arizona's face.

Arizona eased back inside her Maserati. Headlights came on. Brake lights. Reverse lights. She slipped out of her space, eased out like a baby leaving its mother's womb.

Then she was gone, the umbilical cord that held us together severed. Her soft kiss had aroused me. A primal part of me would've fucked her. Would've fucked her from here to Buenos Aires. Would've tried to fuck that baby out of her and loved a new one in her womb.

My eyes went to the satellite phone Arizona had left behind. A phone that I couldn't see because of the other elephant that had been at the table, that was on my mind. On her left hand, there had been a platinum diamond ring. She had worn a platinum wedding ring.

The room had been robbed.

But I had been robbed too.

I dug inside my pocket and took out a BC Powder, an analgesic composed of aspirin, caffeine, and salicylamide. A pure white powder, customers probably thought I was doing cocaine, and that probably made their mouths water.

The blonde in the pink blouse was gone. Same for many others.

The teenaged guy was still here. The one who had helped Arizona carry her cups of tea. He was on his feet, staring at me. Then he hurried my way. His look was different. He seemed anxious. He was tall and fragile; his slew-footed walk a combination of bad posture and awkwardness. He stopped in front of me, stood so close I smelled the coffee on his breath.

He said, "Gideon."

He said my name and it felt like my neck was on a chopping board, a sword coming down at my throat. He said my name and stood in front of me with a shallow smile on his thin face.

Without warning, he extended something toward me, an object small like a stun gun.

My hand went inside my messenger bag, went to my gun.

A bucket of blood was about be added to the land of the Seminoles.

Chapter 3

hard target

Black cellular phone.

That was what he had extended toward me, that was what had almost gotten a hole blown in his latte-filled gut. Another fucking phone. Motorola, basic flip model.

The phone was closed.

My finger eased off the trigger, but my hand didn't come out of my bag.

I asked, "Who are you?"

He asked, "Is your name Gideon?"

He had said my handle twice. This was not a mistake.

The wrong people had uttered my handle in London. In Huntsville. In Antigua. Had walked up to me like they had balls bigger than King Kong's and looked dead into my eyes.

For many, my handle had been their last word before dying.

I was near the men's room, no one else on that side, even though the glass exposed us to the parking lot. I hit the guy with a rabbit punch, a shock to his temple, stunned him, then yanked his shirt before he went down and tugged him inside the empty bathroom, then slammed his head into the tiled wall, swept his feet from underneath him, and dropped him on the floor. He hit the floor like he'd been thrown face-first out of a third-story window. While he embraced his pain, I locked the door and pulled out my piece, aimed it at the door in case anyone else was on his team. They never came alone. Not anymore. They knew better.

Head and mouth bloodied, he scampered like a crab, didn't know which way to go.

My foot connected with the side of his head and he rolled over.

I said, "You want Gideon, you get Gideon."

By the time he stopped seeing stars, he was being yanked up again, eyes fluttering as he was bitch-slapped and shoved against the back wall, my forearm across his neck, cutting off his circulation. He twitched and opened his bloodied mouth, choked on saliva, struggled to scream.

I hit him again and he went down, terrified, moaning. I wanted to hit him over and over, beat his ass the way I wanted to grab Scamz's tight-suit-wearing son and slam his face into the concrete. Voices were outside the door. A woman on her cellular, heading toward the next toilet. I waited. Women were just as deadly as men, twice as conniving. She had moved on. I heard the door to the ladies' room open and close, then heard it lock.

I went back to the fool, patted him down, found no weapons, took another cellular phone out of his pocket, dug his wallet from his pocket, then, as he struggled to breathe, I checked his ID. He had two driver's licenses, both with the name Nicolas Jacoby. One was from Denver. The other was from Florida.

I slapped him conscious, then shook him. "Who are you?"

"She . . . she . . . she told me to bring the phone to you."

I hit him again. "What *she*?"

He was talking about the woman in the pink blouse, the olive-complexioned blonde who had a body like the devil. The type of woman who could send a dumbass nerd on a fool's errand by flashing a smile that promised nothing.

Again I growled and asked, "Who are you?"

"Nicolas Jacoby. From Denver. I'm from Denver . . . what did I do?"

I hit him again, slapped him like he was a simple woman. Then I introduced the side of his head to the butt of my gun.

"Last time," I spoke in a hard whisper. "Who the fuck are you?"

He cried, pulled himself into fetal position, and repeated the same name over and over.

I snapped, "Who was the girl?"

"I swear I don't know who she . . . oh, lord . . . oh, God . . . are you a psycho boyfriend or something?"

"You were with her a long time."

"We were just talking. Nothing between us. I asked her about her tats and we started talking. Just asked her who did the Asian tats on her arms. Was my first time seeing her."

I hit him again. "What did she say about me?"

"Said you were her ex. Asked me to take you the phone, said you left it with her when you and her broke up in Antigua. I don't know . . . was too busy looking at her tats . . . and her tits."

"Describe them."

"They were . . . nice . . . about this big . . ."

I hit him again. "I'm talking about her tats. What kind of body markings?"

"Lots of flowers and Zen kinda stuff."

I hit him again, asked him the same questions.

He told me the same story, that the girl had asked him to bring me the cellular.

"Why do you have two ID cards? One from Florida, the other Denver."

"Because . . . you can get away with having two driver's licenses in Florida . . . they don't report to other states . . . thought it was cool . . . if I get pulled over I show them my Denver ID . . . get out of a ticket . . . then I can use my Florida ID to get a bank account . . . and don't have to give up my Denver license . . . or . . . or . . . I don't know why I did it."

"The girl. Is she connected?"

"To what?"

I hit him again.

"Is she connected?"

"I don't know what—"

I hit him again. "Is she with the mob? Police? With some goddamn rappers? Talk up."

"I . . . I don't know anything about anything like that."

I raised the butt of my gun but didn't bring it down.

His voice was so small I barely heard him beg. "Don't hit me again, please."

"That's up to you."

"Oh, God. I shit my pants. You made me shit my pants."

"Tell me what she said. Tell me what she sounded like. Get it right this time."

He did, but the information didn't change.

There was a tap on the door. I was ready to fire shots that way. I called out that the bathroom was occupied. I paused, listened to the footsteps as whoever it was walked away.

I went back to the fool from Denver, growled, "Where did she go?"

"I don't know."

"*Who was she?*"

"Why you doing this to me, man?"

"I'll blow your goddamn head off if you don't keep talking."

"No idea. Her English was so-so, but her accent was . . . was . . ."

The business end of my gun touched his forehead. "What accent?"

"Middle Eastern."

"What did she say? Word for word."

"We were talking about clubs. Said she didn't know how many tattoos she had. Had tats behind her ear. Had some sort of slave bands tattooed on her legs, on her calves down to her ankles. Had flowers tattooed on her back. One on her back was done in London by some guy named Bugs. Had a heart tattooed on her ass. Said she didn't have tats on her breasts, but they were pierced. And . . . and . . . then . . . she said she worked out five days a week . . . and . . . and . . . yeah . . . she talked about clubs in Lebanon. Said they partied all night long in Lebanon, said the clubs never closed and people never went home, that all they did was party, party, party. Said they spent days and nights at the club. Then . . . after that preg lady left . . . she smiled at me and asked me if I would take you that goddamn phone. Said you had left it in Antigua."

He stopped talking, struggled to catch his breath.

There was another tap on the door. My heart wanted to explode.

Again I called out that it was occupied. Whoever was out there didn't respond.

Time wasn't on my side. With every breath, the bathroom became smaller.

I couldn't kill the guy. Would be impossible to get a body out of here. Leaving a body here, after Arizona had gone and taken her little devices with her, with the security cameras in the building back on, that wasn't a good idea.

I squatted and looked in the patsy's eyes. My whisper was strong. "You have a watch."

"You can have it."

"I don't want your goddamn watch. Stay the fuck in here for ten minutes. Forget about this. Forget about the girl. Forget about anybody you saw me with. And forget about me. You don't ever want to see my face again. Ever. I'll be the last one to see you alive, understand?"

"Yes, sir; yes, sir."

"Ten minutes. Wipe the shit off your ass. Wash your face. Walk out. Forget whatever you brought with you. Leave it. Walk out that door. Don't look back. Don't ever come back."

"Yes, sir; yes, sir."

"Forget my name. Never repeat it, not even in your fucking dreams."

"I will . . . I will . . . please . . . I'm sorry . . . whatever I did . . ."

"And that was all she said."

"She said you were . . . you were from Arizona."

Arizona.

I smiled and extended my hand, pulled him to his feet.

Then I jerked him around, pulled him into a choke hold.

He panicked and fought for a moment. Fought as I stopped the flow of blood to his brain.

Then he collapsed. He was sweating. Dead men don't perspire. I'd put him to sleep. His panic had changed into calm breathing. Couldn't chance him running out behind me and screaming bloody murder as I fled. I took the cellular and IDs, took calm steps outside, my right hand inside my messenger bag. I used my left hand to make sure the bathroom door was locked as I stepped away. There was a Cuban waiting to get inside. A man who had no idea he had almost been shot. A man who had no idea he could still catch some lead. I told him the toilet was filled with shit and overflowing, suggested he find a plan B. He thanked me and walked away. He wasn't with the Lebanese. Didn't look like anyone else in the café was either.

I dashed into the humidity, the well-built Middle Eastern woman nowhere in sight.

I stood in the parking lot, became a statue and listened. Searched for a break in between the clamor, searched for a hole between the oncoming train and overlapping traffic noises, inhaled carbon monoxide and gritted my teeth. I listened for the sounds that couldn't be masked by chatter in Spanish, Portuguese, and English. The increase and decrease of overlapping sounds, the phenomenon called the Doppler effect, was overwhelming. But I held still. Refused to let my heartbeat muffle my ears. Horns blared, that cacophony of terror becoming louder, not fainter.

Then I saw headlights moving fast, switching lanes.

The Maserati sped down Biscayne Boulevard. Arizona had made a U-turn, drove like she was Danica Patrick going for the checkered flag. She broke through the darkness and headlights, blew through red light after red light, ran for her life, her pace causing drivers to panic and swerve, created metal-on-metal collisions, accident after accident as she fled.

Two black SUVs were on her trail, both rampaging and trying to run her down.

With the tinted windows in those Excursions, I would've thought that was one of the alphabet organizations, only there were no red lights, no sirens, and they were gunning at Arizona as she fled. In the middle of a busy avenue and a busy city, a hit was in progress.

The Maserati cut left, went over the median and head-on into oncoming traffic, then swerved right, cut hard at the intersection, screeched, and headed down N.E. Miami Gardens Drive. The lead SUV sideswiped cars, more metal-on-metal explosions as they took out headlights, but they overshot the intersection. The SUV hit the front end of a midsized car, ended up nose to nose with oncoming traffic. While that SUV hit reverse hard enough to burn rubber, the second SUV made the hard right turn, took the lead, sideswiped cars as they headed over the railroad tracks, and roared after Arizona, sped west at the speed of sound.

Helmet on, face shield up, I started the Streetfighter, made it roar, left the parking lot burning rubber, a plume of terror in my wake.

I sped toward the sounds of a swelling psychosis.

Chapter 4

to hell with the devil

I sped out onto Biscayne, cut left in front of six lanes of ferocious traffic.

I was almost hit head-on, but I swerved and pursued the death chase, then white-lined traffic and made a harder right and bumped across railroad tracks. Barely made the turn ahead of a train, a train that would separate that squad from any other hired guns chasing Arizona, would keep them stuck on U.S. 1 for at least ten minutes.

They were a half mile ahead, their insane speed adding distance between us.

I couldn't shoot and ride at this speed; needed my gun hand to keep the throttle down; lose the throttle, lose acceleration. Had no idea what the fuck I was doing, but I was doing it.

My speedometer was close to the century mark.

I sped by Greynolds Park, by a fire rescue station, by palm trees and signs posted to beware of alligators. I bore down, forced my four-hundred-pound iron horse to fly like a Cessna, whipped past cars, changed lanes, passed automobiles that had been run off the road, cars that had crashed into walls and poles and each other.

I remained in the chase, passed condos and shopping centers, drug-stores, gas stations, ran raccoons into the shadows and startled pedestrians out of the crosswalks, sped by pizza shops, Subway sandwiches, and martial arts studios, ran lights in front of Skylake Shopping Center. Cars jumped in my way as they left Publix, forced me to whip around trucks pulling out at WaMu, met the same impediment at Wachovia.

The lead SUV rammed the side of a Mercedes leaving McDonald's, ran that car into a bus stop. The second driver created the same havoc on a Lexus across from Pizza Palace, forced that driver into a pole. Up ahead, Arizona whipped left and right, zipped into oncoming traffic, then cut back in the right lane before she had a head-on collision. She drove fast and furious. Cars screeched and blew horns, drivers startled to find themselves in a scene that looked like it was straight out of *Ronin*.

Light poles remained a blur. Horns blared. Curses flew.

I sped by the second SUV, my speed one-forty. I had caught up with the first load of assassins, but I slowed down, slowed way down, controlled my speed, and when the speed was right, used two fingers on my front brake, went into a front-wheel stoppie, made the back end raise up, then came to a stop with my back end paused in the air, shifted my weight and worked with gravity, made the bike turn and spin 180 degrees on the front tire, came down facing startled traffic and the rampaging SUV.

Duc rumbling in neutral, its heat between my legs, kickstand down, I dug inside my messenger bag, pulled out my nine millimeter, and as headlights zipped by me on both sides, ignored passing traffic and fired at the driver's side of the black SUV sheltering the assassins. I unloaded, gritted my teeth, fired as fast as I could, shattered glass, each shot more desperate than the one before, sprayed right to left as my salty sweat became my enemy and stung my eyes, fired from driver to passenger and back again, destroyed that windshield, fired as headlights clicked to high beam, fired as that brilliance teamed up with my sweat, compromised my vision.

Then my clip was empty.

The SUV barreled right at me, three tons of metal and fiberglass.

Nowhere to run.

No way to run.

I was trapped, four hundred pounds of Italian workmanship humming between my legs.

I'd killed many, but I'd died once. And that death had been a horrible death.

I'd been killed in London. And brought back to life.

I knew that, at some point, I'd die again.

We all died that final death.

Even the resurrected.

I gritted my teeth, looked Death in the eyes, braced for impact.

In that moment, I thought about Steven and Robert. Thought about Catherine.

X.Y.Z.

Wished I knew the truth.

The SUV lost control, swerved by me, missed by inches, came so close I thought I'd been knocked over. The out-of-control SUV bounced over the median, went up on its two left tires, hit the curb, careened and slammed square into a condo building.

I stuffed my nine inside my messenger bag, kicked into gear, and hit the throttle, burned around 180 degrees, took off like a cowboy on his reared-up horse. I put my iron horse down and raced after the madness, forced my Streetfighter to move like a 747.

Heartbeat gonging.

I feared I was too late.

More wrecked vehicles confirmed the direction the pursuit had gone.

I saw them as I approached I-95. I'd hoped Arizona had vanished onto the first on-ramp, sped north toward Fort Lauderdale, or gone under the overpass and hit I-95 South, vanished toward Miami.

She hadn't done either.

Arizona had stopped right beyond the northbound entrance, had come to halt with her Maserati facing the wrong way, had done a 180 herself, her headlights facing the trouble that had been chasing her. The other SUV had stopped, facing the exit to the north off-ramp for I-95, its bright lights on Arizona.

The Maserati was damaged, smoke rising from under the hood. It had hit cars and run over center dividers. It didn't look like the same luxury car I had seen two miles ago.

I zoomed by the SUV, braked hard, came to a dramatic stop in front of the Maserati, the scent of burning tire rubber rising up inside my nostrils as I kept the Duc under my control. I put myself between Arizona and those aggressors, slammed down my kickstand, used the bike as a shield. She had her gun in her right hand. But she wasn't firing. It was empty. She had shot her load. I got low and reached inside my messenger bag again, had to get out my nine, take out the spent clip, then reload.

Had to do all of that while a pregnant woman took shelter behind her car door.

Had to do that while bullets whizzed my way.

In the middle of all the conflict, cars, trucks, city buses, SUVs, and motorcycles rampaged up Miami Gardens Drive, not caring that they were driving through the epicenter of a war zone.

My shots silenced the killer who jumped out on the passenger side to run our way, his Russian-made weapon blazing. His lifeless body fell forward, dropped to the ground chin-first. Then the spray-and-pray Uzi he was holding hit the ground and skidded my way.

They were Spanish men. Well-dressed Spanish men. Professionals with good tailors.

The driver rushed to the back of the SUV, didn't leave me with a good shot. Then he reloaded, came back shooting. By then I had bolted and picked up the dead man's Uzi.

I returned fire, held my ground.

We had company.

Another car raced down I-95 north's off-ramp. A car that wasn't slowing down as it approached the intersection. It was a silver BMW 650i, its speed at least sixty and rising. A speeding car that had killed its headlights, it too moving with an unmistakable fury.

The hired gun that had jumped out of the driver's side of the SUV looked toward that car.

A silver chariot that wasn't going to stop until it trampled somebody.

There was death. And then there were horrible ways to die.

When anybody was hit head-on, two horrific things happened, and I saw that horror when the BMW assaulted the driver of the SUV. His legs snapped and threw his body forward. His hands slammed into the hood of the 650i. The hired gun's broken body snapped at the knees and was thrown forward into the windshield of the sports car. His gun took flight, flew to the other side of the boulevard, landed and skidded across asphalt. I had expected him to tumble forward as well, roll over the roof of the car, his body spinning like a top and landing behind the BMW, crashing into the oil-stained asphalt. But the unexpected happened, and the hired gun went into the windshield.

He went headfirst, cracked his face open as he shattered the glass. Came to rest with his broken body halfway inside the 650i, his waist the dividing point, his broken legs dangling and twisted.

On impact, the driver of the silver chariot hit the brakes hard, but not hard enough to prevent screeching across four lanes and slamming into the wall on the opposite side of the overpass.

The air bag exploded, attacked the driver. The world stopped and silence intruded, overtook the cacophony of madness. Palm trees swayed. Traffic sped by overhead. Dim streetlights covered us.

I moved toward that damaged vehicle, Uzi trained on the madman at the wheel.

The driver of the 650i shoved the air bag away, loosened the seat belt, and crawled out of the damaged vehicle, legs wobbling, battered and struggling to find her center of gravity.

The streetlight revealed that the driver of the German sports car was a woman.

She was stunned, staggered a couple of steps, but she pulled her disheveled hair from her face. Even with a helmet on my head, even though I was mostly silhouette, she knew who I was. And I knew who she was. I knew her history. I knew her crimes. I recognized her silhouette. She wore jeans and a short white blouse, one that had colorful sleeves, her Filipina face looking tanner than it was the last time I had seen her in Amsterdam, her black hair longer, at least a year's worth of growth added to what I remembered.

Her name was Sierra. Arizona's younger sister. A woman I'd been sent to kill more than a year ago. That was around the same time Sierra had put a hit out on her big sister. Arizona had done the same, had put a hit out on Sierra. Two broken sisters who had once wanted to slaughter each other now stood side by side. An angered queen and a pissed-off Pussycat Doll.

The killer was stuck in the windshield of the smoking 650i. One of his broken legs moved. He was standing on Death's front porch, but he refused to ring the doorbell.

Sierra took a remote out of her pocket, aimed it at the damaged luxury car.

The BMW burst into flames. All evidence on fire. The smell of death, fire, car oil, and human flesh came together and created a deadly smoke. A flash of heat licked across my face. The sizzle of that burning body startled me, the stink of burning flesh unforgettable. It stalled Arizona too, but not enough to keep her from going back to the damaged Maserati and pulling out that high-tech suitcase and her D&G bag, the latter containing her high-tech devices. That burning assassin did nothing to Sierra. Arizona put one of her hands over her swollen belly, held her unborn like a protective mother. An Arizona I had never seen before. Sierra stood like she was a Filipina demigod who'd killed Culann's fierce guard dogs.

And at the same time, a second car raced down the ramp Sierra had just taken. It was a Quattroporte. Another luxury sports car, this one with four doors. Four doors could mean four people, four brand-new kinds of trouble. That V-8 could do zero to sixty in a little over five seconds, and it topped out at about one hundred seventy-five miles per hour. The driver moved like they were stressing all of that car's features. It came off the ramp and made a dramatic stop.

The front windows were down and I saw him. Saw his Latin features. The same features I had seen when we met inside an elevator in London. Saw he still wore his hair slicked back.

He jumped out of the car, hurried to Arizona. He held her stomach, held his baby.

He was Latin by heritage, British by culture, a man who fit in with any nationality, especially the Spanish. Strong frame dressed in an Italian suit, a nine millimeter at his side.

He was the man who had saved my life and negotiated my freedom. The man I owed a debt. The man Arizona had opened her legs for, the grifter who had put a baby in Arizona's belly.

South America. End of the World. The land of fire. It flashed before my eyes.

The well-dressed man saw the flames and burning body, saw me, then he nodded as if he thought he was telling me I had done a good job, his nod the pat on the head of a pet. Uzi in hand, I moved the business end away from his direction. Wanted to gun him down, kill him the same way his father had been killed. Kill him the way I had killed my father. Wanted to add his body to the flames of the new hell that warmed us. Over Arizona. Or over a debt. It didn't matter. I just wanted that motherfucker to not exist. One Scamz had died a much-deserved death only to have another rise in his wake. A younger version. A taller version. A better-looking version, in clothing and jewelry that made Armani and Rolex seem like rags of the poor.

Another man was inside his car. In the backseat. That man jumped out too. Short and muscular, dressed in high-end linen, hair long and wavy, maybe Samoan, reminded me of Troy Polamalu of the Pittsburgh Steelers. The man yelled at the women, said things in Tagalog, words that made them hurry. Tagalog. Not Samoan. Filipino. He was armed with a nine. His wingman rode shotgun, his burner locked and loaded. Sierra limped toward the passenger side of the Quattroporte, still dazed from her crash. The Filipino man took her hand and pulled her, rushed her into the backseat, practically threw her inside. Arizona rushed toward the same car, abandoned her GranTurismo for the Quattroporte, tossed her briefcase and D&G bag inside.

That briefcase. A duplicate of the one in South America. Had to have a tracking device.

It was what the SUVs were after.

I tossed the Uzi inside the burning BMW, let the flames of Hell erase my DNA, then jumped back on my Streetfighter, four hundred pounds of Italian machinery revving once again.

Flames rising, a body burning, Arizona climbed into the front seat, next to her sperm donor.

Arizona's hand came out of the car window, a remote aimed at her Maserati.

The damaged GranTurismo burst into flames. Just like the BMW.

In the distance, sirens.

Capítulo 5

resucitando a Medianoche

The assassin known as Medianoche jerked awake, came out of a deep sleep with his fists clenched, ready to do battle with the enemy. A hurricane moved through his body, a muscular body he struggled to control. Darkness lived on three sides of his world.

There were flashes that lit up like premonitions.

On the fourth side, lights in the distance confused him, made him think of enemy fire.

African children wielding U.S.-made guns and firing on armed American soldiers. Middle Eastern women and children who had been turned into walking bombs racing toward them in the name of Allah. He had been places where oil, blood diamonds, and cocaine were the commodity used for trade. Places where the hardened male children carried automatic weapons, wore fatigue pants, flip-flops, and Michael Jordan jerseys, children who killed before they could bust a nut. For a moment, there were flashes. Memories speeding by. Flashes from the things he'd seen. Some of the flashes were painful, dead memories battling to come back to life.

His missing memory was struggling to reboot, fighting to come back online.

Three silhouettes crowded his bed, all naked, motionless, limber limbs intertwined.

Bodies left on a smoldering battlefield.

He inhaled, expecting the familiar scent of death. Then he exhaled and swallowed. The room smelled of alcohol, sex, and three perfumes.

And smoke. Blended with the scents was the aroma of Cuban cigar smoke mixed with smoke from Argentine cigarettes.

He was below the equator. In South America. In Buenos Aires. Where he had been for the majority of the last two decades. The land of *pato*, *fútbol*, and rugby. Where they had undying love for Gardel, Guevara, Perón, Borges, and Mafalda.

He reached for the patch over his missing left eye, did this out of habit. The scars on his face, he didn't mind. War wounds gave him character. But the missing eye. Where the bullet had shattered his sight and put him in a coma, a wound he wore and couldn't stand the sight of.

He closed his good eye, moved his mind, tried to think of something beautiful, someplace peaceful. Montserrat. The emerald isle of Montserrat. Balmy breezes. Sunny skies. Abundant nature. Rolling green hills, plunging coastlines, and a simmering volcano.

Then he frowned.

He couldn't think of Montserrat without thinking about his last ex-wife. He knew she was still living in Brades, working at her mother's restaurant, helping her father run a sea charter.

He looked at his bed.

One of the women stirred. The youngest. She had worked in Plaza Dorrego at Todo Mundo for a while. A good place for foreigners to lose their wallets and purses. President Bush's daughter had been robbed there while being guarded by the Secret Service. Medianoche's young lover said she had been robbed twice, once as she left Dorrego and walked up Defensa, the other time as she stood at a bus stop on San Juan. Both times by boys who were no more than ten years old, killers with guns. They had taken all of her money, knew that women had started carrying their money inside their bras, had reached inside her bra and taken all she had. The last batch of ten-year-olds tried to get her to suck their prepubescent dicks. She wanted to work in a safer area, maybe Plaza Cortázar in Palermo Soho. Until that happened, she improvised. She had a little girl, a kid her mother was keeping.

Medianoche had found her photo on one of the many business cards stuck inside the phone booths on José Antonio Cabrera in Palermo

Viejo. Cards for girls were inside every phone booth in Buenos Aires. Women dressed in thongs. Or school outfits. The colorful card she had posted said she had a big ass and was over eighteen. The first part was true, but he doubted the latter. She was a Lolita. Dark hair, just like the other women recuperating in his bed.

The second girl he had met at the Evita Museum. She had been a receptionist. She was the one who fed pigeons and went to mass at the San Isidro Cathedral, loved to hold hands and take trips to Amalia Fortabat Art Collection, Museo de Bellas Artes, and MALBA. The wannabe aristocratic one who spent her spare time reading novels and cooking *Porteño* dishes. The type who wanted to be rich so she could despise the poor for not being rich.

The third had been in the lobby of the Hilton in Puerto Madero, a haven for tourists. New in the city. From Peru. Divorced twice. Trying to get away from bad relationships along with the violence and drugs in her homeland and make a better life for herself. She had been in the sunlight of the lobby, wearing a beautiful green dress and high heels, sipping coffee and eating a croissant, looking for a man who needed some company, a generous man who needed someone like her. She had worked at a *lavandería* in Barrio Norte, on her feet washing and ironing clothes twelve hours a day, but her employer was a mean woman and the pay was for shit.

Sex would be for sale as long as there was one person in need of sex and another desperate for cash. Maybe it would be for sale as long as there were two people in need of sex. By the hour or by marriage. There was always a price. By the hour, the deal was more honest.

He stared at the beautiful women. Three shapely Latinas. Women built the way a woman should be built. He'd never cared for skinny women. Slender, but not skinny. He was with a skinny woman once. A woman so lean that if she were flat on her back or on her belly, there was no difference. A woman was supposed to have breasts and a backside to keep a man oriented. Either that or have a THIS SIDE UP stamp across her breastless chest.

He took a deep breath and stared at the clock. It was two a.m.

He had time.

Medianoche slapped one of the silhouettes on her ass. Slapped her hard.

He commanded, "*Despertáte.*"

She knew what that meant. She knew what she was being paid to do.

"*Vamos, despertáte.*"

She crawled to him, put her head between his legs, took him inside her mouth. He moaned and lost control. It pulled him away from the bad memories, this therapy the cure for any level of PTSD he suffered. Medianoche ran his fingers through her brown hair, massaged her scalp. She set him on fire. She was slow, meticulous, the best he'd had in a while.

He slapped a second silhouette on the ass.

"*Despertáte.*"

She stirred, mumbled something in Castellano, then asked, "*¿Que hora es, mi amor?*"

He said, "*Son las dos.*"

She mumbled that she was tired. He slapped her ass harder, made her skin turn red.

"*Despertáte.*"

He watched her as her drowsy frown changed to a generous smile.

She moaned, "*Cuando me pegás en el culo me ponés mojada.*"

She told him he was a devil in bed, made her orgasm many times. His expression remained stern, glad that even on the other side of being middle-aged, some things hadn't deteriorated, at least not as fast as other things. The knees that couldn't stand as much pressure, the aches from working out that lasted longer. But on a good day, he was still stronger and faster than most twenty-year-old men. She crawled to him, kissed his arms. He put his hand in her hair as she sucked his nipples. The third girl pulled her hair from her face and joined in without having to be woken from her sexual exhaustion. She joined in, smiling, attentive.

Still he slapped her ass anyway. It didn't matter if she liked it. He did. At times he could be as malicious, cagey, and wicked in his relations with women as they said Picasso had been.

She whispered, "*¿Qué pasó con tu ojo? ¿Y esa cicatriz en tu cara?*"

She asked him about his eye. Asked him about his scar.

He told her, "Never ask about my scar."

She said, *"No entiendo inglés."*

He repeated what he had said in Castellano.

He wanted to drag her to the patio and hold her over that railing, have her naked body dangling from the seventeenth floor while she cried and pissed on herself. Anyone else, he would have. She was curious, enthusiastic, competitive, wanted to earn a generous tip. Very beautiful. Beauty should not be defiled. Beauty should be embraced. He pulled her to him, kissed her, put her breast in his mouth. He bit her nipples, made her let out a sound of sexual pain.

"Ooo, papi."

He called them his Tres Marías. Tres Marías was a constellation of three stars in a row in the southern hemisphere. Appropriate name for women who kept him so close to heaven.

He put one on all fours, went inside her slowly, made her moan, gasp in amazement.

Latin girls could move on the dance floor. All of that waist action. But when that fuck hole was filled with a real man's dick, it didn't move the way it could when it was empty.

A second María kissed him, gave him slow kisses, while a third María sucked his nipples.

This was the fountain of youth. This was where he didn't feel his mortality.

When they were done, the silhouettes cuddled like girlfriends at a slumber party. They had been strangers but had grown used to each other over the last week.

He stood and went into the living room. His wall was decorated with glass-framed photos of tango dancers. Dancers in front of the colorful buildings in La Boca. Dancers in San Telmo. Dancers on 9 de Julio. And one other framed photo. A photo of Olaudah Equiano.

He went into the kitchen, took a piece of leftover steak. Argentina had the best steak in the world. Medianoche took a Quilmes Cristal out of the refrigerator, sipped his lager and ate as he read the *Buenos Aires*

Herald, an English-language paper, its front page telling this part of South America that the stock markets were falling like ninepins. The Spanish-language paper, *La Nación*, screamed: OTRO DÍA DE PÁNICO MUNDIAL: EN LOS MERCADOS CRECE LA DESCONFIANZA. Same message of panic and financial ruin, Russia among those with the worst loss ever.

They said that when the U.S.A. sneezed, the world caught a cold.

If that was true, the world was experiencing a case of international pneumonia.

Medianoche set the paper aside, washed down the beef as he opened the balcony door and stepped out into the brisk air. Cold air jolted him. He went back inside, opened the closet in the front room, took out his tenor sax. He carried the sax back outside, played "Last Night When We Were Young." A chilling rain fell on his naked skin as he played that Frank Sinatra tune. Judy Garland had done it too, but Frank was the man. He looked down eighteen floors on the *avenidas* and *calles*. The city was old. Darkness hid all flaws. Like New York, it looked better at night. Las Vegas was a monstrosity that looked better at night. He looked better at night. He stopped playing his sax, abandoned Frank and looked out at the city, restlessness in his bones.

His cellular buzzed. A text message. It was time.

He put away his sax and took another bite of his steak. He hadn't been big on steak, not before Argentina. He had gone to La Caballeriza. A place that was serious about their bovine. So serious that their menu described the cow, its breed and weight, told the bovine's diet, introduced his meal like he was going to take it out to tango the night away. Lean cows that were raised in open *pampas*, not given growth hormones like in the United States. In North America, most of the food had growth hormones, hormones that had created an obese nation. He had ordered, taken one bite, and now it was all about the Argentine steak.

He washed his face, flossed, trimmed the hairs of his nostrils, same on his ears.

He stared at his face.

He nodded, clenched his teeth. Remembered the last moments in Charlotte, North Carolina, when he didn't have a hole where his eye used to reside. Lost his fucking eye because of some motherfucking kid. He should've put a bullet in that whore's head as soon as he walked in the door. But he was the one who had been gunned down. He had come out of a coma in a hospital in North Carolina, his headache severe, his face in bandages, a bullet removed from his head, his left eye and a sector of his memory gone.

He went to his closet. Tailored clothing, all lined in Kevlar. High-fashion attire from Miguel Caballero, Limited, of Bogotá, Colombia. The most violent country in South America produced the Armani of bulletproof clothing. Inside his closet were tailored sports coats, raincoats, Windbreakers, and dinner jackets. The same clothing presidents, dignitaries, and paranoid executives wore. Trench coats, business suits, suede jackets, and denim casuals. An antiballistic polo shirt cost four thousand dollars and could stop an Uzi or a knife. Same for his leather jackets. Every article of clothing could be worn out to dinner or to a full-on battle. Comfortable. Fashionable. Flexible.

He put on his suit, dark shirt, and dark tie.

He stared out the window. He knew Buenos Aires, knew her rhythm. Knew that right now black-and-yellow taxis were speeding toward the swingers clubs, Reina Loba or Anchorena, where the masses would swap partners until sunrise.

There was a lot of swinging in Tango City.

He put on his dark trench coat, adjusted his black fedora, slipped his dark gun inside a darker holster. In the mirror he saw the reflection of the perfect gentleman.

A dozen years ago, his goatee was black with a few strands of gray hair.

Now it was gray with a few strands of black hair.

He opened the medicine cabinet. Took out a small container. Unscrewed the top. Stared at the white powder. It had been a long time. Too long. He put some powder in the web of his hand. Wanted that rush. But not now. Not when he was working.

Medianoche put the powder back inside the small container.

He took out another small box. Opened it. His eye looked down upon an eye. Ocular prosthesis. He stared at what he hated. That memory played like an infinite loop.

Losing an eye. Some surgeon digging around the inside of his head with a scalpel.

He removed his eye patch. Inserted the convex shell made of cryolite glass. He looked at himself in the mirror. Not since he lived on the isle of Montserrat had he worn an ocular prosthesis. Not since he was married. His third marriage, to Gracelyn Furlonge. Petite and beautiful, owning an Irish surname like most of the natives on the island.

He took the prosthesis back out of his eye socket, cleaned it, put it back in its box. He put his eye patch back on, adjusted it. Medianoche. Midnight. He moved on. Went into the living room. He opened an envelope and pulled out a stack of pictures. Pictures taken in Atlántida, Piriápolis, and the latest in Montevideo; the latter was a major slave trade port, where African slaves were unloaded, then sent to work slave mines in Peru and Bolivia. The men in the photos were white Uruguayans. Men walking through the Tristan Narvaja street fair. Those same men walking down 18 de Julio, the street that marked Uruguay's Independence Day. Not their widest street, but the most popular. *El paisito*. That was what some Uruguayans called themselves. Next photos were on the beaches of Punta del Este and José Ignacio. Most of the photos were shots of the men from Uruguay. The protectors and couriers of the package. In every picture was the black briefcase. This was what an American named Hopkins was paying to obtain.

Everyone was after the prize.

The Russians. The French. Jamaicans. South Africans. Middle Easterners.

Money had the scent of blood, and the sharks were in the waters.

Morality would never outweigh money. Money made the moral immoral.

Many immoral fucks had died trying to get their hands on the package.

Tonight would leave the undertaker busy.

More flashes inside his head. Again, dead memories battled to be resurrected.

No time for the past.

Medianoche tore the pictures into dozens of pieces, then headed for the door.

It was time to go to war.

Medianoche stepped into the hallway with his weapon holstered, tucked away.

Standing outside the door facing his condo was a man in his fifties. Stocky and muscular with carnivorous eyes. Hair black with irregular white patches, like a Tasmanian devil.

Dark Italian suit. Dark shirt and red tie. Dark trench coat.

He had a gun in each of his gloved hands. Guns fitted with suppressors.

An assassin.

He recognized the killer's face.

He saw La Bestia de Guerra.

Capítulo 6

el tercer hombre

La Bestia de Guerra. The Beast of War.

Medianoche's gun was holstered. He stared at the gunman, saw a killer known to hunt and do barbaric things to his prey, a hired gun who worked alone, or sometimes with other devils.

The killer returned Medianoche's deadly glare.

The Beast was a man many feared, had a face like Marciano and a punch just as devastating. A man who'd shoot you before he damaged his callused knuckles.

A man who would rather cut off your limbs and behead you than waste a bullet.

Medianoche asked, "You plan on shooting me?"

"Been thinking about it."

"I've been thinking the same."

The Beast looked Medianoche up and down, his frown intense, then pulled his coat back, slipped a gun inside a holster, then slipped his second gun into the opposite holster.

Medianoche said, "Hopkins have the money in place?"

"Deposit has been transferred to the offshore."

Medianoche asked, "Where is Hopkins? He here yet?"

"Stateside. He was after the other part of the package. He should have it by now."

"He's outsmarted all the con-men bankers." Medianoche grunted. "Rich fuck."

"Much richer when he puts the two packages together."

"What does that get him?"

"Gets him what Madoff and Stanford got, minus the jail time."

Another door opened. Another man stepped out. Dark Italian suit, dark shirt, dark trench coat, and fedora. Holding a silenced weapon. Dressed the same as the other man.

Only his tie was pure, virginal, as white as the cocaine Oliver North has overseen.

The man wearing the white tie addressed The Beast, then Medianoche.

Medianoche said, "Señor Rodríguez. Nice suit."

"Sir, thank you, sir."

Medianoche said, "You did that assignment down in Pinamar."

"Sir, yes, sir. Made it back an hour ago, sir."

"How is that area?"

"Sir, beautiful, sir. Like being on the beach in Cannes or in Malibu, sir."

"How did you dispose of the target?"

"Sir, tracked him to Ku nightclub. When he went to the bathroom to take a piss, went in behind him and broke his motherfucking neck, sir. Left the target sitting dead on the shitter, sir."

The Beast asked, "Get your dick wet?"

"Sir, yes, sir."

"Good. Keeps the edge off."

The final door opened. Electronic tango music spilled into the petite hallway. Tanghetto playing "Inmigrante." Three Argentine men hurried out of the apartment. Men dressed in jeans and sweaters, men who held their winter coats and umbrellas in their hands. Men who had perfect faces like the underwear models on the billboards plastered all over Buenos Aires.

The first of the men said, "*Buenas noches.*"

The second said, "*Buenas noches.*"

The last, "*Buenas noches.*"

The Beast didn't reply. Neither did Medianoche. Neither did Rodríguez.

The Spanish men lowered their eyes as they stumbled into a hallway filled with assassins. One extended a nervous finger and pushed the call button for the elevator. They stayed close to each other, kept their eyes to the floor and waited. They boarded the small elevator with their eyes still on the floor, didn't look up as the elevator closed.

Medianoche said, "We should've beat those fucks into the tile."

"Inmigrante" ended. There was a pause. Then "Libertango" played, the band now Ultratango. The song ended. "Baires 6am" by Terminal Tango began to play.

Medianoche frowned at that fourth door.

The Beast put a strong hand on his shoulder. Be patient.

Rodríguez looked at his watch, shook his head.

Seconds later, the door to the fourth condo opened again. There stood an Indian woman born in Mumbai, a woman who, from a distance, could pass for Madhuri Shankar Dixit. A woman who had seen the horrors in Iraq and Afghanistan. Dressed in a fitted black Italian suit, a green paisley tie, black men's shirt, black boots with no-skid bottoms and square heels. She stepped out, closed the white door behind her. Hair black and wavy. High cheekbones. Black lipstick. Gap between her front teeth. Marks on her face that looked like severe acne scars. But it wasn't acne. It was where shrapnel had entered her flesh and compromised her beauty.

She put her hat on, slid her gun inside the holster covered by her long black coat, adjusted her green paisley tie. The woman made Medianoche uncomfortable. She reminded him of someone. Her eyes reminded him of Montserrat. Not in her action, not in her vulgarity, in her eyes. The woman grinned. Not ashamed. Proud those three men had left her glowing.

This was the team. Identical uniforms. The only difference was the color of their ties. One tie was the color of drying blood, one the hue of a starless midnight, the third a paisley with green being the dominant color, the final tie white.

Medianoche stepped forward, adjusted his black tie, pushed the call button for the elevator.

The elevator opened on their silence, an electronic voice with a strong Argentine accent announcing the elevator was on *piso diecisiete*.

Seventeenth floor above the lobby at *piso cero*. The Beast entered first. Then the woman. Then Medianoche. Rodríguez entered and stood next to Medianoche. The woman was behind Medianoche. He felt her eyes on him.

The elevator was small, European in size, like everything else in Buenos Aires, barely big enough for four adults. He felt her bullet-proof vest bump against his back as the elevator descended. He didn't want her goddamn body touching him. Didn't need an Achilles' heel. Women in war were a regiment's Achilles' heel. Because men were men, men were protectors. Dick protected clit. Because dick wanted clit. He'd always see any creature with ovaries as a liability.

In the door's reflection, he saw her studying him.

She asked, "What are you looking at, Medianoche?"

"Looking at you, soldier. And when you address me, address me properly."

"And instead of staring at me, take a picture, leave a tip, and move on."

She had said that with disdain. Because of the shrapnel. Her deformity. People stared.

Medianoche said, "Amaravati Panchali Ganeshes."

"I don't use my birth name." Her tone showed no respect. "Don't use it again."

Medianoche hit the stop button.

He asked, "Is there a problem, soldier?"

"Only if you want it to be one."

Medianoche nodded. "Which handle are you using with our organization?"

"Was going to use Saint Raven. You know, Saint Louis, Saint Raven. Used that handle when I worked in Rome."

"Your reputation contradicts that name. You're no saint."

"Not interested in being one, either. Saints have too many goddamn rules."

"What's your handle?"

"Since I'm in South America, I want to be called Señorita Raven."

"Okay, Señorita Raven. Read the report on you. IQ of 147."

"On a bad day."

"Speak four languages."

"Five if you count ebonics, sir. Throw in pig Latin, I speak six."

"Your father is doing life for killing your mother and her lover at a fleabag motel."

"He gunned them down in the middle of the night. My mother was a weak woman. My dad, not a likeable man. Hated that fucker. He would've decapitated my mother if he could've."

"Religious extremist."

"Just crazy, if you ask me. Just plain crazy."

"You're a middle child, have two siblings. Your older sister was pregnant—"

"By a poor white-trash loser who didn't want any more child support, so he beat the baby out of her when she was in her second trimester and that left her unable to have any more kids."

Medianoche said, "Left her insane."

"Yes, sir. That pretty much sums up those wonderful happy times with the folks."

"You suffered a breakdown."

"That's not on my record."

"No, it's not on the official record. Happened after your dishonorable discharge."

"If it's not on the fucking record, it didn't fucking happen."

"You had severe depression. Medics and police came to your home on a 10-56A."

"It didn't happen."

"That's a suicidal-person call."

"Fuck you, you one-eyed fuck."

"Watch yourself, soldier."

"I read your report too, sir. IQ 130. Dishonorably discharged, like the rest of us. You were down in North Carolina, getting trained with a group of mercs at a tactical training facility, but you went out on a pussy run, then the report got vague, just said you got shot in the face."

"How did you gain access to my files?"

"You went to dip your manhood in a slag's hole and ended up with a foxhole where your eye used to be, and that left you in a coma for a few weeks, and when you woke up, that eye was missing and so was some of your memory. You don't know what happened; just know you got fucked up. Shot in the eye twenty years ago, left for dead in a whorehouse. Yeah, you got bull's-eyed in the head by a friggin' kid. By a little boy. That had to suck. All the work you've done, all the firefights you had overseas, and end up in a whorehouse getting shot by a kid."

"Answer me, soldier."

"You grew up in El Pueblo de la Reina de los Ángeles. Your father was a detached drunk and your mother was a Romanian actress who died in the Baldwin Hills flood back in 1963."

"*How did you get my goddamn classified files?*"

"Trying to fucking diss me. So screw you, you one-eyed sonofa-bitch. Just because you can piss standing up doesn't mean your old ass can fucking—"

Medianoche spun and grabbed Señorita Raven by her throat, his grip swift and tight, that flippant look that had been plastered on her face now a look of severe pain and deep regret.

She tried to reach for her gun, but he grabbed her gun hand with his other hand, was tempted to head-butt her, add a bloody nose to the shrapnel in her once beautiful face.

Medianoche growled. "There is a pecking order. Respect me. Or get out of my elevator."

She gurgled, "Yes . . . yes . . . sir."

"I don't think you do. Play 51-50 with everybody else, but that shit doesn't fly with me."

He choked her again. Choked her until she slapped his hand in surrender.

"You will respect me. Act 51-50 and I will make that 10-56A a fuck-ing reality."

Her eyes. He saw Montserrat in her eyes. He saw rejection and betrayal, saw no loyalty.

She took a swing at him but didn't have the reach, didn't have the wind, could only slap his shoulders. Medianoche choked her, pushed her head into the back of the elevator, stayed on her until her eyes bulged and her midnight-colored fedora tumbled from her head.

The Beast whispered, "Stop."

Medianoche eased up. Let her catch her breath. Then he choked her again.

There were only soldiers in a war. No men. No women. Only soldiers.

There was no surrender in war. Not in the kind of war he believed in.

Medianoche reached inside his pocket. Came out with a black Montblanc ballpoint pen. Aimed that piece of high-quality workmanship at Señorita Raven's right eye. Give her something to joke about. Horror covered her face. No longer 51-50. No longer wishing for a 10-56.

Medianoche aimed at her eye as she turned her face away. He struggled to find her eye until Señor Rodríguez grabbed his arm and wrestled the Montblanc away.

Medianoche didn't let up on Señorita Raven. Looked in her eyes for that arrogance.

The Beast put a soft hand on Medianoche's shoulder. Medianoche respected the chain of command, yanked his hand away from the neck of what he had frowned upon as being an arrogant wannabe-bitch-ass-feminist fool, let her collapse into the wall. Medianoche turned back around, adjusted his tie, his shirt, his hat, the patch over his eye, kept his eye on Señorita Raven's reflection. And her gun hand. She coughed back to life, coughed hard, like she was a child reborn, sweat sprouting across her face, a river of foolishness draining into her black suit.

Rodríguez reached around Medianoche, hit the red button.

The elevator descended.

The ThyssenKrupp elevator stopped on the ground floor, floor zero, steel doors opening on the lobby. All glass and concrete.

Medianoche remained up front.

The Beast stepped up, moved to his left.

Señorita Raven picked up her fallen hat, put it back on, her breathing heated and thick.

In a firm voice, The Beast said, "Everything settled?"

"I'm not the one with the problem."

"Not you, Medianoche. I was talking to Señorita Raven."

"Everything is settled, sir. For now."

Medianoche said, "Get on your knees and thank Señor Rodríguez you didn't end up with that pen coming out the back of your fucking skull. Next time you won't be so lucky."

"Well, sir. You just started something I hope you can finish."

"Arrogant bitch."

"When I need to be. Most of the time I'm a just a regular diva, sir."

"Diva is right. Dumb. Ignorant. Vulgar. Arrogant. A disgrace to your people."

"My people?"

"That's what I said, soldier."

"I'm American. Those are my people."

"You'll never be a true American. Not North America. Not the U.S."

"You're one eye away from being invited to a camp sponsored by Stevie Wonder."

Medianoche opened and closed his hands, made his knuckles pop. "That witty banter might work in a sitcom, but this ain't a fucking sitcom. You will respect me. One more snappy comeback and the last sound you will hear will be the snapping of your pretty little neck."

"Guess you expect me to kiss your ass. I'm not an ass kisser. I've never kissed ass. Well, once. He was cute. And I didn't like the taste of ass, so I gave up ass kissing right away."

He barked, "I'm not your goddamn equal, Señorita Raven."

"And being seventeen points behind in the IQ department, you never will be, sir."

"No matter what you scored, no matter what you think you know, I outrank you, soldier."

"In the military. This ain't the fucking military. Get off my case, Cyclops. If you lost that peeper in combat, yeah, I'd respect you and call you Sergeant Rock. You lost it over a piece of rental pussy? Shot by a kid in North Caro-fucking-lina? What kind of loser shit is that?"

Medianoche was about to go for her again. Rodríguez moved in between.

The Beast said, "Soldiers. Enough. Recess is over. Check your egos. Time to work."

They left the edifice and paused at the security gate. The guard was a middle-aged *Porteño* dressed in a white shirt and black security pants, standard uniform, his coat black, like a parka. He saw them and a moment later handed each a black backpack. Then they were buzzed out of the premises, took to the narrow street lined with cars, taxis, businesses, and dog shit, turned right and marched into the coldness and the rain.

Señorita Raven hiked her backpack up on her shoulder and asked, "Smoke and flash?"

Señor Rodríguez answered, "I ordered stun and flash."

"I'm partial to smoke, good for instant cover, good for distraction, good for decoy. Assholes always pop a few shots into a smoke and expose their position."

"Good for confusion in small rooms with tangos in it."

"Pop a smoke in, followed by a frag, they'll get stuck against each other trying to escape."

Medianoche led the team through a parking garage on the corner, connected with streets lined with cars, buses, and Radio Taxis. Medianoche marched a step in front of The Beast, led his warriors, the Book of Revelation come to life. The bringers of the end.

The Four Horsemen of the Apocalypse.

Capítulo 7

los Cuatro Jinetes

Medianoche led the charge.

The Four Horsemen arrived like a hurricane battling an earth-quake, contents of the backpacks removed, a combination of M84 stun grenades and flash grenades that exploded and disrupted their enemies' senses, blinding and deafening their adversaries for six seconds as they moved in with precision, guns drawn, military force exerted on all who stood in their way, shooting the blind and deaf like they were sitting ducks. It sounded like a reenactment of the Buenos Aires civil war, a battle between the *unitarios* and *federales*.

Medianoche and the rest of The Horsemen moved like a tsunami, as if trained by notorious firms like Blackwater in both technique and ethics. They fired like they were renegades operating above the law, as if they were clearing the way for diplomats to come into Iraq, moved like they were deep inside Fallujah, on a mission to rescue hostages.

Blackwater was paid up to ten times more than government employees, and The Four Horsemen of the Apocalypse made twenty times more than Blackwater.

To murder with impunity.

The seventh floor was a war zone.

A dozen bodyguards on the ground, a dozen left.

A battle ensued as the target fled the hallway, bullets flying as the man from Uruguay grabbed the black briefcase and ran. Gunfire in the darkness. Spanish screams. Shadows moving. Shadows running. Shadows shooting. More flash grenades.

Medianoche felt his heart racing. Life or death.

Then the generator kicked on.

Fluorescent lights revealed Spanish bodyguards who had been taken down, men dressed in all black, the gear of a Spanish militia. Pristine white walls and contemporary Spanish art were now stained in warm blood. Medianoche moved down the hallway. Señorita Raven moved with him, shooting anything that moved. Medianoche did the same, hoping the bitch caught one in the eye.

Señorita Raven, the arrogant soldier who ignored the pecking order. Medianoche fired on a shooter who had appeared off to Señorita Raven's side, gun aimed at her head, about to take her out. Medianoche blew that sonofabitch's head off, saved Señorita Raven's life without thought, then moved on after the target.

He disliked her, but she was a soldier. His instinct was to protect The Four Horsemen.

His goddamn instinct was to protect a woman. A dumb, ignorant, vulgar, arrogant woman. A woman who had eyes that reminded him of the love he'd had in Montserrat.

Rodríguez popped one of the Uruguayan men in the leg. Then popped the other in his knee. Both went down in screams and pain. The third Uruguayan. The briefcase was in his goddamn hand. That was what the mission was all about. The third man panicked, abandoned his fallen comrades and ran off without his bodyguards, fled like a halfback taking off without his blockers. Medianoche went after the package. This was where he was the most alive.

They had been outnumbered six to one. Within thirty seconds, it had been two to one. Now, another thirty seconds later, it was an even fight.

He had seen the third Uruguayan take the briefcase and run through an emergency exit. Medianoche was up front, in the best position to capture the object. Señorita Raven, Señor Rodríguez, and The Beast covered Medianoche as he ran after the package. Behind him, flash grenades and gunfire.

The target fled down another hallway, ran past the elevators, and took the exit to the stairwell, sprinted to the exterior metal stairway above the Sanatorio Güemes building, the chase high over the intersection of Figueroa at Cabrera. Down below was a trail of headlights and taillights, nonstop on every avenue. Traffic down below headed at a northwest angle, the whole city in grids, mostly one-way streets.

He felt like he was too old to chase his prey. In a cold fucking rain. On a slippery metal stairway. In his younger days, that was the fun part, being a hungry lion chasing a gazelle through a storm. He had tracked and chased men across fields in the UK, across rooftops in Brazil, had chased prey through rivers and deserts.

He had lived for the chase.

Twenty years ago, the easy kill owned no thrill.

Now it pissed him off.

Anything extra pissed him off. Every day he was a little more impatient.

The contract ran like an animal.

Medianoche chased, refused to let his contract flee to safety.

The target ran up the goddamn stairs, went against gravity instead of running down. Medianoche gritted his teeth, anger rising as rain fell, frustration a raging storm. He didn't know why the man from Uruguay ran upstairs. There was no escape. Unless there were others. But there were no gunshots. He didn't know what was up there; he only knew that he couldn't let that fucker get away.

The skies rumbled. Lightning flashed.

The target was almost on the thirteenth floor, maybe one hundred and fifty feet off the ground, high enough to look out over the rooftops and see the blackness of Rio de la Plata out in the distance, beyond the *rico* lives lounging in Palermo Chico, Recoleta, and Barrio Norte.

Medianoche was catching up with his target, less than a floor behind him. He saw that the man from Uruguay had stopped running, exhausted, and had begun crawling up the damp, metal stairs. When Medianoche caught up, he removed his earplugs and stood over his target, winded, rain dripping down over his fedora as he raised his gun, listening for sounds, teeth gritted as he searched for shadows above him, ready to fire on anything moving, then did the same behind him, before realizing they were alone. Just him, the man from Uruguay, the shadows, the sound from the rain, noises from the streets below.

His target panted, trembled, got his breath, and managed to say, "*Los Cuatro Jinetes.*"

Medianoche nodded. *Cuatro Jinetes.* Four Horsemen.

The Uruguayans knew who they were.

The man panted, "*Los Cuatro Jinetes del Apocalipsis.*"

Again Medianoche nodded. The Four Horsemen of the Apocalypse.

The man from Uruguay pointed at him and said, "Medianoche."

The man knew who he was.

"*Sí.*" He adjusted the patch on his eye and nodded. "Medianoche."

In Germany he was Mitternacht. In Italy, Mezzanotte. Along the Scandinavian Peninsula in northern Europe, in Sweden, he was Midnatt. Hours away from where he stood, in Brazil, he was Meia-noite. So many ways to say the same word, to feel horror because of one name.

In North America, in Estados Unidos, he had been called Midnight.

A man known for his preternatural talent in the field of assassinations.

The man from Uruguay begged for his life. "*Por favor, no me mates.*" *Please, don't kill me.*

Medianoche asked the man how he knew the Horsemen were coming. Asked if there had been a phone call. The man nodded. He asked the man who had called him, who had warned him. The man wouldn't say.

Medianoche put the barrel of his gun against the man's temple.

Lips loosened.

The man said he didn't know. He wasn't the one who took the call. Said they had come over from Colonia on a high-speed Buquebus they had rented and were the only passengers, had arrived in Puerto Madero less than four hours ago, told Medianoche that no one was supposed to know they were in Buenos Aires. Yet someone had known their every move.

He asked the man why he was running up the stairs.

The man said he didn't know, said the explosions had left him disoriented, confused.

Medianoche didn't believe him.

Next to his target was what had been weighing him down. A black briefcase. It was the briefcase their client wanted. A briefcase their client had paid plenty of money to obtain by the next sunrise. The man from Uruguay yelled, said the package would do them no good, said there were two parts to the package, and one part was no good without the other.

Medianoche didn't give a fuck. The mission was to retrieve the package.

He picked up the briefcase. Mission accomplished.

Then he grunted and reached for the Uruguayan, told the bastard to come with him.

The man was terrified.

The man from Uruguay got his wind and leaped at him. Medianoche was caught off guard. The man punched him in the face, the blow intended for his good eye.

Medianoche took the blow and frowned. He had seen battles in many lands, hand gone hand to hand with many men, had taken blows that could put a rampaging bull into a permanent sleep. Had survived being shot in his head. Not even Death had succeeded at claiming him.

Being hit like that was an insult. Like being slapped by a teenaged girl.

Medianoche cursed in English and dropped the briefcase, then reached his scarred and veined hands out and grabbed the target. He slipped on the metal stairs, lost his grip on the man from Uruguay, and struggled for his balance, but the momentum was too great. Gravity pulled, yanked him downward. He and the man from Uruguay tumbled. Medianoche pulled the malnourished target underneath him, rode the thin man down the flight of stairs, the ride bumpy and ugly. When the ride was over, Medianoche saw that they were both near the briefcase. Medianoche threw his elbow into the man's face, hit him over and over, then pushed him down another flight of stairs, sent him headfirst, let him ragdoll down to the next level. Medianoche picked up the briefcase and walked down the stairs, put the briefcase down again, within arm's reach, and went through the man's pockets, found his cell phone and put that inside his own pocket.

The man from Uruguay was unarmed. He was not a threat.

But he had information.

Medianoche grabbed the man by his collar and picked up the briefcase, headed down the stairs, dragging the man from Uruguay, his prisoner battered and bruised, in agony, yelling that his employers would kill him, would murder his family, would slaughter his friends for losing the briefcase. Medianoche didn't give a fuck, not his problem. He didn't have a family to lose. The man from Uruguay tugged, slipped out of his coat, then hit Medianoche with his fist. It was like a child striking an adult. Medianoche cursed, put the briefcase down, then grabbed the man and lifted his two hundred pounds up over his head.

The man from Uruguay kicked and clawed.

Medianoche grunted and held the man from Uruguay over his head, the task taking more energy and effort than it did ten years ago. Cloaked by darkness, the target's scream was muffled by rain and thunder. The man from Uruguay was slammed back onto the metal stairs, his body turning, once again flailing, his long legs moving like he was trying to run on the molecules that made up air.

The man from Uruguay made it to his feet, his face revealing his severe pain.

Medianoche reached for his gun, pulled it out with a quick, snapping motion.

But the man from Uruguay ran and jumped into the air, sprang up on the rail, did that with amazing agility, his bloodied face the epitome of fear, and without saying another word, lunged into the blackness, leapt like he was a bird about to take flight. His flight had grace and style, took him headfirst, his trajectory sending him out beyond the edges of the café, beyond the trees, into the streets. Didn't flap his arms like he had changed his mind. He just fell through darkness into the lights on the streets below.

The man almost landed on top of a city bus on the street in front of Torcisco Café.

Almost.

He splattered right in front of the city bus. An empty bus weighed twelve tons, but this bus was close to being full. The bus ran over his broken and mashed-up body before coming to a dragging stop. Gun in one hand, fifteen-pound briefcase in the other, Medianoche stood there, winded, wet, lower back aching, angry, staring down at the scene.

The man from Uruguay had chosen to kill himself rather than face his employers.

"Medianoche."

He let the package go, let it fall at his feet as he jerked around, gun drawn, rain thumping his hat, prepared to shoot into the shadows.

Señorita Raven was one landing up, gun in her hand, aimed at him.

His gun was aimed at her.

He snapped, "Stand down, soldier."

"Stop pointing your weapon at me, unless you plan on using it."

"Stand the fuck down."

"If I wanted to shoot you, I wouldn't have called your goddamn name."

"Last time. Stand the fuck down."

Señorita Raven had come from above him, not from down below.

In his head he was in the middle of a countdown, finger squeezing the trigger.

Three.

Two.

Señorita Raven lowered her weapon.

Medianoche did the same, kept it at his side, ready.

Señorita Raven. So uncontrollable. Her own woman. Hardheaded.

Down below. People walked by the scene. Few stopped. No one screamed.

Medianoche adjusted his eye patch again, adjusted his fedora, then adjusted his long coat. There was a sharp pain in his lower back. He knew his muscles would stiffen up by sunrise. That pain. The sign of aging. Of a slow-moving end. Twenty years ago he could bench three times his weight with no aftermath. There was nothing nice about aging. Nothing nice at all. And nothing that could be done to prevent it. Nothing stopped the march of time.

Jaws tight, he headed up the metal stairway as Señorita Raven headed down.

Señorita Raven asked, "Sir, you okay, sir?"

His scowl remained on her frown.

Medianoche grunted. "I'm fine, soldier."

"You were frozen. I thought you had been hit and were making peace with your maker."

"I wasn't frozen. I don't freeze."

Medianoche's knees popped when he squatted and picked up the black briefcase. He ignored the popping, looked at the package. Made sure it was the one they were after, that it somehow hadn't been swapped, hadn't been compromised. Something wasn't right, but it was the briefcase in question. This simple black briefcase was worth a man's life.

This was part of the key to the fortune that had brought out the evil in many.

Señorita Raven asked, "Package secure?"

He ignored her, positioned himself to keep her in his periphery. "Where is the team?"

"They have the other two men from Uruguay."

"Injuries to our team?"

"None that I know of."

"Good."

"I understand that what's inside is worth millions. Maybe close to a billion."

"That's not our concern."

"Lots of casualties. Made me wonder what's inside."

"Not our fucking business, soldier."

"I heard it was connected to the missing stimulus package money from the Bush admin."

"I don't care about rumors, soldier."

"A lot of that money vanished; some say it was tucked away, spread out over several accounts, and this is the key to consolidating those funds and cashing in on that lottery ticket."

Medianoche thought about gunning down Señorita Raven.

He grunted. "Might take a thumbprint to open the package."

"Whose thumb?"

"Maybe the Presidente de la Nación de Argentina."

"Cristina Fernández de Kirchner?"

"She is the president." He grunted. "She is the *woman* who runs the country. What's your point?"

"Is part of the mission to extract her fingers, sir? Do we have a plan to break into La Casa Rosada, the Residencia Presidencial de Olivos, and cut off the president's fingers?"

"We have to cut off her hand."

"We take her hand?"

"Soldier. At ease."

"Oh. Sarcasm. My bad."

"More than likely, the men from Uruguay know the key to opening the package."

Señorita Raven said, "We're not supposed to open it, sir."

"That's my point. And if we had the key, not our fucking business, *comprende*?"

"*Sí, comprendo.* I'm not that kind of soldier, sir."

"So whether it's worth a billion U.S. or two pesos in South America, it's not our concern."

"I doubt if anybody would go through all of this for two pesos. That's sixty cents, U.S."

What was inside the briefcase had cost more than a few dozen men, and just as many women, their lives over the last few months. And now a family man had lost his mind and gone kamikaze from the top of a building, committed suicide over whatever was inside. He had seen many men kill themselves with guns and cyanide to protect secrets. That was nothing new.

Curiosity rose up inside him, something that rarely happened.

I understand that what's inside is worth millions. Maybe close to a billion.

The package was locked. What looked plain and black, upon closer inspection, wasn't plain after all. It was a high-tech number. Solid material. A thumbprint was needed to open the case. Might've even had a sensor that would make the briefcase explode if compromised.

He stood, looked at Señorita Raven, then glanced at the path the man from Uruguay had taken. Thirteen floors below, traffic was at a standstill. The bus rested on top of the dead man.

There was a rumble.

He looked to the sky. A helicopter was coming in. It paused over the roof. A light shone down. Medianoche began firing. Señorita Raven followed his lead. His first shot killed the spotlight. The chopper fled, took off as fast as it had come. Now he knew where the man from Uruguay was running. A helicopter had come in, like a rescue chopper in Vietnam.

A rescue chopper, not a chopper carrying more warriors.

The man from Uruguay had lied down to his last breath. Had been loyal to the end.

Medianoche headed back down the metal stairway, his coat flapping in the wind, his hand holding his fedora on his head as he moved with quickness, blending with the storm, Señorita Raven behind him as they reunited with The Beast and Señor Rodríguez.

They were in the hallway. A hallway filled with the scent of war.

The remaining men from Uruguay were tied to chairs.

The Beast was in front of them.

The Uruguayans cried, were in too much pain to scream.

The Beast held an axe in one hand. The kind used by firemen. One of the men from Uruguay was covered in blood. His foot was three feet away from his body, cut off above the toes.

The soldiers stood and watched The Beast show how he had earned his moniker.

A man who despised the Geneva Conventions.

War should have no rules. Wars were about winning.

The Beast walked toward the remaining Uruguayan, gun in one

hand, dragging the axe by its handle, letting the noise of the bloody metal blade meeting tile terrify the final man.

The Beast smiled. "Talk, and I will not kill you. That is my promise."

The final man began talking. He told of a hacker in La Boca. A hacker who had broken into Hopkins's system and had information. Told how to get in contact with the hacker. He told The Beast the code to say to initiate business.

The information was about a hacker who worked for an American who used a name he could not pronounce.

But he could spell the name.

"Siete . . . César . . . Ana . . . María . . . Zulema."

Those words represented the letters *S-C-A-M-Z*.

The Beast said, "Scamz?"

The man nodded a dozen times, his dialect Uruguayan, unable to pronounce that word.

The Beast asked, "Is that an organization? What do those letters stand for?"

The Uruguayan cried out that was the word he heard, said that was all he knew as he looked toward his bloodied friend, blood draining as he lived in a misery worse than death. The Beast walked over to the suffering Uruguayan. Raised the axe high. Brought it down.

The Beast walked away. He nodded at Señor Rodríguez and Señorita Raven.

Both took out their weapons and walked toward the surviving Uruguayan.

The man screamed that he had been promised he would live if he told all he knew.

The Beast had only promised that *he* would not kill him. That promise was being kept.

Medianoche handed The Beast the package.

The Beast asked, "The other guy?"

"Threw the sonofabitch off the goddamn roof. Thirteen-floor swan dive in front of a bus."

"Hate I missed that."

Medianoche looked at the headless man. Then at the head that had no body. Then at the man who was screaming and crying, these his last seconds of life.

Señor Rodríguez frowned, eyebrows furrowed, nose flared, the expression of a rabid animal before attacking. Señorita Raven smiled like a saint.

A soldier and a psychopath. Both were loading fresh clips into their weapons.

Medianoche moved away.

The Beast moved with him, stood shoulder to shoulder.

The young soldiers stood in front of the crying man, became a two-man firing squad.

The sweet whispers of silenced guns muted the terrified man's screams.

When it was done, Señorita Raven holstered her gun and looked at Medianoche.

Nothing was said.

Medianoche led the way. The Four Horsemen became part of the night.

Chapter 8

the big con

Thieves and psychopaths had fled into the balmy night.

It was moments after the chase and battle on Miami Gardens Drive.

We left carnage in our wake, slipped inside the darkness, took separate directions.

Arizona's baby's daddy had shown up like a knight on an Italian horse and whisked her away. I did the work on Miami Gardens Drive, but he would take the credit for that save.

I rode my Streetfighter up I-95, then exited, took the streets, made a few turns, then doubled back toward Fort Lauderdale. I abandoned the Ducati in the parking lot at Chuck's Steak House, wiped away my prints, tossed the keys and my smoking hardware.

I went back to my deluxe lanai guest room at the Hyatt on S.E. 17th, off the intercoastal. Had been there the last two days. About ten minutes from Fort Lauderdale's airport and Port Everglades. Three minutes from the beach. Twelve minutes away from Aventura.

An old enemy had given way to a new threat. That meant I would need security to watch over Catherine and the boys until I could get this new problem sorted out. Or until this new problem put me in the ground. I used my iPhone, made a call to a friend who had an apartment in Lithia Springs, Georgia. Alvin White answered on the first ring, his Southern voice thick and powerful.

I said, "Alvin. It's me."

"Everything okay?"

"It's that season again."

Alvin White was the closest thing I had to having a best friend. The Alfred to my Batman. I told him I was off the continent. Then I told him contact had been made.

He knew what I meant. He knew I'd been waiting for bad news to show up.

He said, "I can load up a couple of guns and go watch the house."

"Thanks. I appreciate it."

"Want me to do like I did last time?"

"Do what you have to do."

"Me and my wife were looking at CNN a few minutes ago."

"Same here."

"Crazy stuff down in Miami." He paused. "You be careful."

I said, "Doing my best."

Alvin yawned. "I have some schoolwork to do anyway. I can pack up a snack and coffee, sit out there and work until the sun comes up. The schoolwork will keep me awake."

"The thing Catherine is helping you with, how is it going?"

"Hardest thing I've ever done. My wife saw this movie, *The Reader*. She saw me doing my work and she broke down crying. Can't thank you enough for everything you're doing for me."

"Glad I could help."

"Got this book. Might call you up. Read some things to you. Not much."

"Okay. Do that."

"I got my passport. The one you got for me. I picked it up. Gonna get another one, too. A real one in my name. My wife filled out the paperwork for me. Used some of that money you gave us and paid for it. Got me a passport. Never had one before. So I guess I can leave the country."

I didn't say anything. I knew what he was asking me.

He said, "That money you gave me, my wife done gone through most of it. I guess when a woman sees sixty thousand dollars sitting in the bank account, she gets to wanting things she's never had before. A lot of it was spent on the kids. But she went through that money like termites go through wood. Like I said, I have my passport. The one you got for me."

I said, "I'll pay you for this security detail. But what I do, you're not ready yet. To join this fraternity, you're not ready yet."

"I know. Just letting you know."

We said our good-byes.

I felt better knowing he was going to watch over Catherine and the boys, but I didn't feel one hundred percent secure. Mine was a rough business. Revenge and money. Alvin had captured two men for me before. Men who had been sent to kill the people I cared about. Men who would kill women and children, then stop at Baskin Robbins and get a vanilla ice cream. I didn't want to admit it, but Alvin was already in this fraternity I belonged to. The two bodies I had buried near the Chattahoochee in Georgia red dirt verified that.

I took to the shower, had to scrub rage and the stench of burning flesh off my body. As soon as I was soaped up, there was a sharp knock at my door.

My jaw tightened. I was on a high floor. And naked.

I left the shower on. Pulled a towel around my body. Wished towels were bulletproof. My gun had been dumped, but I had a backup at my side. A .380. I stayed inside the bathroom, out of gunshot range, then called out to whoever was knocking and lurking outside my door.

They replied, "Room service."

"I didn't order room service."

"Jean-Claude. It's me. Open up the stupid door."

That was when I recognized the voice. I came out of the bathroom, looked out the peephole, saw she was alone, then tucked the .380 underneath the mattress. I opened the door. She wore white pants and gold sandals. White wife beater over a brown bra. Keys in her right hand. She held a light green plate-shaped Tupperware container in the other hand, the hand with the engagement ring.

She gave me a wide smile and said, "Surprise."

She kissed me as she came inside the room, rushed in like she didn't want to be seen.

She said, "Nice towel."

Her name was Miki Morioka. A tight-eyed waitress I'd met at a strip club called Tootsie's Cabaret. I had met her a few months ago when I was down here doing a job for Konstantin. Miki Morioka had been my cover last night. I'd taken her to South Beach, used her to get close to my target, blended with the crowd, broke away from her long enough to attach the C-4 underneath his limousine, then brought her to the suite for an hour before she had to leave and go home.

She put the Tupperware down on the dresser. "I brought you some food."

I grinned. Now I was Jean-Claude from Montreal, Canada. The world traveler who had called her as soon as he landed at Miami International and offered to take her out on the town.

I said, "Food?"

"It's still hot. Said you hadn't had Japanese food for a while. So I broke out my family's recipe book, cooked for you, and brought you the real deal. Glad you were still here."

I opened the bag and set free the scent of Japanese fried chicken, rice, cauliflower. Potato croquette dipped in Japanese sweet sauce and shredded cabbage.

She said, "Wasn't sure what you might like."

I thanked her. Thought she would leave, but she kicked off her sandals. Miki Morioka took off the rest of her clothing. She was naked before I could say another word.

She had a beautiful body. Breasts to kill for. Real breasts, not manufactured in a lab.

I was done with her. Had used her for what I needed her for and sent her on her way.

The look in her eyes told me she wasn't done with me.

"Cho-dai," Miki Morioka moaned. *"Cho-dai."*

Inside the shower, she took my heat and I handled her heat in return.

I held her up, my hands underneath her butt, her legs wrapped around my body. She strained, bounced up and down hard and fast, one arm around my neck, her other palm extended toward the wall. Water ran like a waterfall over her face, through her hair. Water as warm as fresh blood. We kissed and moved against each other. The phones I had were left in the suite on the desk. The phone from Arizona. My iPhone. And the phone from the Lebanese. One of the phones rang. Couldn't tell which one, not with all the noises in the bathroom. Miki Morioka kept her legs wrapped around me while I stepped out of the shower. Kept her legs wrapped around me and moaned and moved while I walked her toward the dresser.

The phone stopped ringing.

Miki Morioka was intense. I sat down on an armless chair, had her straddling me. I slapped her petite ass over and over, battled with Miki Morioka, then hurried her to the bed, put my weight on her body and held down her hands, kept her nails away from my flesh, her engagement ring catching light the way I wanted my enemies to catch a bullet. Had to battle my way out of this room the same way I had fought my way out of Antigua.

"*I'm coming . . . ikuuuu . . . don't stop . . . ooooo . . . yamenaide . . . ikuuuu . . . ooooo.*"

I rolled away, left Miki Morioka on her back, talking in a mix of Japanese and English, smiling like crazy, her breathing deep and rapid as she cupped and rubbed her damp breasts.

Miki Morioka said, "Lightheaded. Seeing. Polka. Dots. Wicked. Penis. You. Have."

She panted some more. My ears were on the door, thought I heard a sound.

Miki Morioka said, "Oh . . . remember that Hopkins we saw in South Beach last night?"

"The rich guy."

"His limo blew up on I-95. Ain't that something crazy? It happened a few hours ago. My first time ever seeing somebody rich like him, and the next day *ka-boom*, some terrorist shit."

A cellular rang. I rushed to the dresser, but it wasn't mine. It was Miki Morioka's. She reached over to her clothes, pulled out a Black-Berry Bold, looked at the display, and groaned.

She said, "I have to go."

I sat up. "Work?"

"Off tonight. Have to rush back over on Dixie Highway and get my kid from the sitter. She's going out to dinner with some married guy. Could only watch my kid for a couple of hours."

"I have to get to the airport."

"Surprised you called me yesterday. Didn't think you would. Took you months."

"Was surprised you remembered me."

"Told you back then, you have charisma, panache, this unbelievable sexual energy."

She hopped off the bed and jogged to the bathroom. The shower was still running. She got back in. A minute passed. She ran back with a towel around her body, water draining from her skin while she used another towel to dry her hair. She dressed as fast as she had undressed.

I opened the Tupperware, went to her, fed her some of her home-cooked food. Miki Morioka moaned, thought I was being romantic. I was making sure she wasn't sent here to poison me. She ate a little, licked my fingers, then I walked her to the door, kissed her good-bye. Her kiss was powerful. She sucked my tongue almost hard enough to rip it out of my mouth.

She kissed me the way Arizona had kissed me in North Carolina and New York.

She pulled her wet brown hair back from her face and said, "*Saikou ni yokatta.*"

"What does that mean?"

"You're good. That was so good."

I told her. "You're damn good yourself. Tens on all scorecards, even the East Germans."

Miki Morioka smiled. "Anytime you're in Miami, look me up and hook me up. If you lose the number, look up Miki Morioka. Dixie Highway. Had the same number the last ten years."

"Maybe when I come back to town, I'll buy you another drink."

"Seriously, let me know if you're going to be close to Miami anytime soon. Can't find anyone who can make me come like you did. Get that crazy look off your face. I need a really good fix every now and then. And so far, you're the only one that is hitting that spot right."

"Why are you getting married?"

"To be married. To stop working as much. To stop sleeping alone."

"So your kid will have a dad."

"That too. Mainly for that. Not easy doing everything by myself."

I nodded. She shrugged.

She asked, "Whatever happened with you and that Filipina girl you were crazy about?"

"Ran into her today. After about a year."

"Cool."

"She's pregnant. At least six months."

"Ouch. Not cool."

"Yeah. Ouch. Not cool."

"Probably for the best."

"Yeah."

I wanted to ask her why she had a kid. What made her want to have a baby and bring it into a situation as complicated as hers. Wanted to ask her what I didn't understand.

Wanted to ask her what I wished I could ask my mother.

Another unknown in my world.

Miki Morioka said, "Don't forget to look me up so you can hook me up."

She jogged down the hallway, sandals slapping against her petite feet as she went to chase her own problems.

I looked at the food she had brought.

That was her barter.

The money she had left on the table.

I rubbed my temples, went to the dresser, looked at the phones.

One missed called on the phone left by the mysterious Lebanese.

My headache returned.

So did my urge to kill every enemy I could find.

Chapter 9

the devil inside

I connected to GOTOMYPC.COM.

That way I could connect to the cameras at the home in Powder Springs.

They knew there were security cameras outside, but they didn't know I could tap into the twelve security cameras I had installed around the house, or that I could tap into them from anywhere I had Internet connection.

I saw Alvin's car outside the house, two houses down. He was doing his job. I switched from the exterior to the interior cameras. Wanted to make sure Alvin didn't show up after trouble. The cameras inside the house were disguised as smoke detectors and motion sensors. The house was quiet. Everyone was in the bedrooms, areas I didn't have cameras.

I switched to a camera in the kitchen. Focused on a FedEx that was on the counter.

That was the box that had the DNA results.

That was the box that held the answers. That was my MacGuffin.

A while ago I had taken DNA samples from Catherine and the boy named Steven. Catherine had done it begrudgingly, but she had done it. The boy had no idea what I was doing. I had swabbed the inside of my mouth too and sent that package to DNA Solutions. I needed some answers. Had become obsessed with getting those answers.

Catherine had raised me. She was the French woman born in Yerres who had told me that my mother was murdered when I was too young to remember. She had told me my mother had been found dead in a Dumpster. Had said that my mother was a prostitute named Margaret. She made it sound like she was a savior whore, making sure the men who had abused and did her friends wrong were killed, taking in the children of dead whores to save them from the system. But then she changed that story, told me that my mother wasn't the whore left in that Dumpster. She took Margaret away from me. She wouldn't say anything after that. She had left me in limbo.

She had told me I had killed my father. She had told me so many things. Before she took the name Catherine she had been a whore named Thelma. That was who I saw whenever I looked at her. I saw Thelma. Thelma had been the one who had put a gun or knife in my hand and sent me to kill, did that before I had hair over my genitals, told me that some people deserved to die.

Back then I had backed down. I had come off a hard situation in Antigua, and the other boy who lived with Catherine, the African who now used the name Robert, his mother had been killed because of me. Everywhere I had stepped, I had left blood and heartache.

Back then, maybe I couldn't handle any more bad news.

Back then I had needed some happiness, even if it was false.

I'd been on the run for more than a year and I was fucking tired.

I lived with a level of irritation I couldn't get to subside, not for more than an hour.

Now I kept the camera focused on the FedEx box. I stared at that box as that box stared back at me. It taunted me. Had given me sleepless nights. Inside that FedEx box was what was important. Inside that box were the answers to X.Y.Z.

I should've opened it a long time ago. I should've put this mystery to bed.

X.Y.Z. represented the DNA swabs I had taken. One sample from Catherine. One sample from Steven. And one sample from me. I don't know why I swabbed myself. I was old enough that things like this shouldn't matter. But I knew why I swabbed Catherine and the boy. I did it mainly for the boy. No one had seen Catherine pregnant. She had lived among whores, and not one woman in the red-light district

I found her in had seen her pregnant, not one had seen a photo of her with a swollen belly. I didn't know any pregnant women who didn't photograph their first pregnancy.

There were no pictures of her with the kid as a small child.

I think Steven was stolen.

I believed she was raising a child she had stolen from some woman. Or the child of another dead hooker. If that boy's father was alive, that was where he was supposed to be. With his family. Not with Catherine. Not with the whore who had called herself Thelma and had stolen me from my dead mother. I believed that I had been stolen. And I knew that my father was killed by me, but he was dead because of her. And I didn't know who I was.

On the computer, Catherine walked into frame. She headed into the kitchen. She had on a summer dress, a modest number that flowed over her figure and stopped below her knees. Catherine was a beautiful French woman. Her features and expression, maybe because of the makeup she used to wear when she was a sex worker, used to be sly and espiègle. But she looked different now, like a brand-new woman. Stunning and motherly.

I felt guilty for playing Big Brother, but I did what I felt I had to do. I spied. Everything looked copacetic.

She held a cordless phone in her hand, but she wasn't on the phone.

I watched her the way the cameras in Central London watched its citizens.

She poured herself a glass of wine and then she sat down at the table, facing the FedEx box. She sipped her wine and stared at that box. She ran her hand through her hair and shook her head.

That was when I saw it.

I saw who she was when she was alone.

Saw the anxiety and anger in her face.

Saw bits of who she used to be.

I saw Thelma.

I stared at her and frowned. Years ago. She was a pedophile.

A pedophile who had two young boys in her care.

I turned off the monitoring program and dialed the number in Powder Springs.

Catherine answered on the second ring. Her accent French, her voice a song.

"Catherine, how are you?"

"Jean-Claude. It is great to hear from you."

"Checking in. Anything suspicious around the house?"

"Nothing suspicious. Is everything okay?"

"Let me know if you see anything strange. Keep your eyes open."

"I will. It worries me when you say that. It really worries me."

I cleared my throat. "How is Alvin's reading coming along?"

"He's doing fine, considering." Her voice owned apprehension. "Has a long way to go."

"Will you be able to help him? Or should I find a literacy program? He's too ashamed to go into a program without knowing anything. Need you to help him as much as you can."

"He won't be able to read *War and Peace* for a long time."

"Just the basics."

"It's strange. Teaching an adult to read. The boys are smarter than he is."

"Book smart."

"And world smart. Alvin has never been out of the South. This is his world."

"You're saying he's ignorant."

"I'm saying he is a very nice man who has a long way to go. He's smart in his own way, far from being a big oaf, but he is limited. He can build anything. He memorizes everything. Lack of education puts a person in a small box. He will never have many options. He is lucky that he has managed to support his family all these years. He is thankful for you. He told me you gave him a lot of money. Sixty thousand dollars. He's living off that money. He's lucky because he's not even qualified to seek employment at a Waffle House. I don't understand why people . . . never mind. He is a good man. A very nice man. It's a tragedy. His life is tragic."

"Well, I give you money too. I pay for everything."

"You do. I know."

"And your life has been tragic as well."

"Yes. Yes it has. I'm sorry. Did I offend you?"

I paused. "If there is a problem working with Alvin, let me know."

"There is no problem. No problem at all."

I reined in my thoughts.

She had earned her money on her back and Alvin had earned his standing up. She had no right to chastise. Lots of uneducated and undereducated people had fought in wars all over the world. Her words pissed me off. But I wasn't as concerned with Alvin as I was with the boys.

The one who used to be Andrew-Sven and now called himself Steven concerned me.

Steven told me he had shot a man. He had killed a man and saved Catherine. Steven was always on my mind. The way we had met in London. He had pointed a gun at me. Didn't hesitate to pull the trigger. Tried to kill me.

I asked, "How are the boys?"

"They are fine. They want to know when you will be back to visit."

"I'll be there in a couple of days."

"Tell them. Tell them so they will stop asking me the same question over and over."

She held the phone and called back to the boys, told them it was me, Jean-Claude.

Robert made it to the phone first.

He panted from his run, "When are you coming to take us roller-skating?"

He was African, but he had a strong British accent. That was where he had spent most of his life. In the red-light district on Berwick Street. Raised the bare-bones way I had been raised. Like a street urchin. We had all lived from hand to mouth, like street urchins.

"Yeah, when are you going to take us roller-skating like you promised?"

That was Steven. On a second phone. He still had that German clip to his accent.

I laughed and told the boys I'd be there soon. Like I had promised.

Robert asked, "What about the secret place on the other side of Woodstock?"

"We want to go to the other side of Woodstock with you and Mister Alvin."

I said, "Your mother . . . Catherine might not like that. She doesn't approve."

First Steven's German accent. "We won't tell my mum. Please?"

Then Robert's British one. "Please? I won't tell mum Catherine. I promise."

I said, "I'll think about it. No promises on that one."

I finished with them and got back on the phone with Catherine.

I said, "Everything is okay at the United Nations."

"United Nations?"

"You have French, British, and German accents, all underneath a Southern roof. Then when I show up, that's five accents. If Alvin comes by, then that's six. The United Nations."

Catherine laughed. She laughed a good laugh.

Just like that, Thelma was gone. There was no trace that she existed.

And at that moment, there was no trace that Gideon existed.

Not long ago, I was on Miami Gardens Drive gunning down a team of assassins, and now I was in a suite in a hotel, towel wrapped around me as I ate Japanese food, talking to my family.

We all had many faces. We all told many lies.

Our truth had been buried so deep. It was time to finish the excavation I had started.

I was over what had happened in Antigua. The gunshot wounds and jellyfish stings and blows from brutal hand-to-hand battles had healed. Enough time had passed since Robert's mother was murdered in London on Berwick Street. We could handle a new pain now.

I asked, "How is Robert holding up?"

"He still has nightmares."

"Same thing?"

"He had it real bad before he was brought to London."

Robert concerned me as much as Steven. He had grown up in Europe, London mostly, his African mother a working woman who was always on the move, but she had homeschooled him well, his education much better than the public schools in Georgia. That told me that she had once had a better life, had an education, and had been derailed. Before London, Robert had witnessed the horrors of Africa. His mother had traveled in areas occupied by non-Arab Darfurians, had seen armed Janjaweed—the devil on horseback—in government-issued military uniforms, places where the governments used rape and murder as the tools of terror. He'd told Catherine that he was hungry most of the time, depended on agencies for food, lived in a camp that was more like a prison than a place of comfort. Had told Catherine that he had seen a village burned by the Janjaweed, said he remembered the gunshots, the terror, his mother taking his hand and fleeing, being chased and caught. He'd witnessed his mother being dragged, her clothes torn from her body as armed African men wearing military pants and boots raped her.

That was part of the way Robert saw the world. As a place filled with devils.

He had moved from an area of murder and rape, had escaped a tribal warfare that, centuries ago, made black slavery possible. He was living a life his mother never had a chance to have.

I said, "Robert."

"What about him?"

"Any idea who his father might be?"

She paused. "His mother never said. Why do you ask?"

"Was wondering if he had family out there somewhere. I wonder the same about you."

"There is nothing to wonder about, Jean-Claude. I have no family. There is no reason to wonder. I have told you I have no family. Robert has no one. His mother was murdered by a madman. Robert is here because his mother was murdered. He had been left homeless, an orphan begging for money and food. What matters is that he is not living on the street."

She said that with controlled anger, as if everything that had gone wrong was my fault.

I asked, "Should I send him to talk to somebody?"

"I will let you know if that is what he needs. Right now he needs to adjust to his mother never coming back, to being in America, to the culture and isms that exist in the South."

"He should talk to someone. He's been traumatized."

"We've all been traumatized."

I was going to tell her it was time to open that FedEx box and close that issue.

She paused. "It was great to hear from you. We will see you soon."

I told her that I would see her and the boys soon, then we hung up.

I could travel around the globe, could kill without hesitation or remorse, but when it came to this, I had become passive-aggressive. I could gun down men on a crowded boulevard, but when it came to opening that box, I had created resistance, had become my own obstructionist, had become stubborn and let that stubbornness give seed to a new layer of resentments.

It was a defense mechanism.

I was trying to dodge an unpleasant mission the same way I had dodged many bullets.

That box was another Achilles' heel. That box added heat to my personal hell.

I'd stick to my plan. I'd do it the way I had decided it should be done.

I'd surprise Catherine. Wouldn't give her any advance warning.

We'd do it face-to-face. Wouldn't give her another fucking chance to lie.

Then the heat in my hell magnified.

The Motorola phone the blond Lebanese had left rang.

Capítulo 10

treinta y uno

Gun in both hands, Medianoche waited in the chilling rain. Thirty minutes had passed since the massacre that had ended in their favor.

Cars zoomed by, doing twice the speed limit posted on the highway. The car he'd been driving was parked on the side of the *autopista*, emergency flashers on.

The Beast stood at the opposite end of the car, weapons in both hands.

Señorita Raven and Señor Rodríguez weren't present, had been sent back to the apartments to await further instructions.

Medianoche looked down from the *autopista*. Smelled grilled beef, chicken, *cerveza*, and *paco*. Saw lights that were kept on by illegal electricity and poverty. The music that played was loud, sounded almost inviting, but the lyrics to the songs were as warm as a rap record back in the States. Lyrics about killing and fucking *putas* until they bled. It was the lyrics about killing that had Medianoche on guard, ready to do the same. Music like that disturbed the senses, disoriented the enemy, kept them off balance.

Guns in both hands, The Beast moved and stood next to Medianoche.

Medianoche had been instructed to stop at one of the fourteen shantytowns. A quarter of a million lived in slums in the Paris of the South. A quarter of a million squatters that had claimed abandoned buildings and land, had brought in bricks, tin, and cardboard and taken over. These were squatters who fought armed police, squatters who stood up to the same military that made people vanish, hooligans that refused to be bulldozed off the most valuable land in the city. They stood at the outskirts of the slum like they were on the border of another country.

The *villa* had been built on land and spread out until it literally touched the *autopista*. The barbed wire that was supposed to keep them from hopping the fence and running across the *autopista* was used to hang laundry. So as people drove by, there were miles of clothes flapping in the wind, and more clotheslines on the roofs of structures that stood three or four floors high, odd shapes and sizes, all improvised.

A hooligan no taller than five feet tall walked across a building.

He was no more than fifteen. Hair slicked back from the rain. He had on blue and gold, a Boca Juniors soccer uniform, the team of the working class. The boy carried an Uzi. He climbed over the unsteady roof of one of the tin and cardboard houses, made his way to the top of the fence, a section where the barbed wire had been removed with wire cutters.

The Beast said, "Junior."

"*Buenas noches.*"

"How is your father?"

"My father he is good."

"How's the drug trade?"

"It is slow. Not so good."

"It'll get better."

"*Sí.*"

"Your English is getting better."

"I take English class for the community center on some days."

"How is your girlfriend?"

"She is . . . she is . . . *¿Cómo se dice embarazada en inglés?*"

"Pregnant."

"She is pregnant."

"Congratulations."

"*Sí.* I will going to be the papa soon. In four years."

"Months."

"*Sí.* In four months."

"*Año* is year. *Mes* is month."

The Beast handed the boy the black briefcase. Told him to tell his father that he would call him with instructions. The boy nodded. The Beast gave the boy two one-hundred-dollar bills. U.S. money. That was his tip. The equivalent of more than seven hundred pesos.

For a kid who lived off three pesos a day, he was rich. A Slumdog Millionaire.

The Beast told him there would be six hundred U.S. dollars when he returned.

Medianoche stared out at the slums. Poverty that went on for miles.

He looked to his left, a mile away, high-rises, the richest of the rich.

Back on the seventeenth floor, eighteen floors above the concrete jungle, Señorita Raven and Señor Rodríguez were already inside their condos.

Medianoche followed The Beast, went inside his apartment door.

His flat-screen television was on. A black-and-white movie. Humphrey Bogart. Mary Astor. Gladys George. Peter Lorre. *El Halcón Maltés*. Spanish for *The Maltese Falcon*.

A servant entered from the small kitchen in a hurry, like a waiter rushing to a customer at a five-star café. A young Greek man dressed in a butler's uniform, English-cut tuxedo, and black bow tie. A young man who served and cleaned and cooked and took care of The Beast better than a personal concierge and a personal chef.

Draco Calamite Ganymedes. Draco was meticulous, head shaved bald, always dressed like a goddamn butler, always in a goddamn black tuxedo, face clean-shaven, not a flaw in sight.

He served drinks when The Beast was thirsty. Cooked when The Beast was hungry.

Medianoche never spoke to Draco. Never looked at him.

Draco took The Beast's wet overcoat. Took his guns and placed them on a table. Then removed The Beast's suit coat like he was taking the robe away from a king. If The Beast were KIA, the concubines and wives would mourn, but the servant would take the closest sidearm and, with a single bullet, follow his master into the great battlefield beyond the one that existed on this astral plane. The ultimate act of loyalty. The ultimate act of madness.

Medianoche didn't enter beyond the rug at the door, kept his wet clothing on the mat.

The Beast's apartment was meticulous, clean and up to military code, everything in place. The tiled floor sparkled. The swank apartment had walls as white as a museum and the luster of a world-class traveler. Flags, a half-dozen war trophies, awards, coins, DVDs on military training, books on military heroes, military magazines, warplanes, books on WWII, Civil War, Vietnam War. Cuban cigars. Stainless steel flask. Matching lighter. Weapons qualification badge.

The Beast asked, "Want to talk about Señorita Raven?"

"I can handle her."

"*Una guerra de egos.*"

"My ego is fine. Not a war when one side can squash the other like a bug."

"Let me know if you need me to put her in check."

The Beast's cellular rang. He looked at the number and took the call. The conversation lasted about ninety seconds before he hung up and faced Medianoche.

Medianoche nodded. "Let me get out of this wet uniform."

"Señor Rodríguez will handle the disposal detail. Anything you need trashed or dry-cleaned, get it to him by morning."

"Not Señorita Raven?"

"She has next detail."

"She should have every detail. Women like her should clean up behind men like us."

"She should. But she doesn't."

Medianoche nodded.

The Beast said, "I'll pass the onerous task to the subordinates. That call I just received was about another contract. Mind going to meet with the client?"

"No problem."

Medianoche remembered Señorita Raven's words.

Whatever was in that briefcase was the key to millions. Maybe billons.

They were in the middle of pandemonium, and The Beast moved

around his apartment at a stride that said he wasn't worried. As if each step he took helped the world rotate, pushed what he didn't want to see back behind him, brought what he needed closer.

He walked as if the world was his. Like he was Mussolini.

Medianoche asked The Beast, "Where will that kid hide that part of the package?"

"Somewhere in the *villa*. If we brought it here, we'd have another firefight within the next few hours. So I'll let it sit in the *villa* for a day or two. Those people are insular. The moment a stranger sets foot in that area, everyone knows. That, soldier, is security."

"The Russians, Jamaicans, Jews, Italians, and North Americans are after it."

"They won't go in there. They'd wait for it to leave, but they wouldn't go in there."

"We don't go in there."

The Beast chuckled. "And we're some bad motherfuckers."

"So it stays there until Hopkins arrives."

"Or until I say otherwise."

Medianoche nodded. "When Hopkins arrives, then what?"

"Then we exchange the package for the wire transfer."

Medianoche understood. Had always understood.

The Beast said, "You never asked this many questions before."

"I'm curious."

"Why the curiosity, my friend?"

"Since that package is so valuable, have to make sure I'm doing what needs to be done."

The Beast nodded. "You always do."

"Lot of money. You could move back to the U.S. and buy up some nice real estate."

"I can't afford to be rich in America. Taxes too high. Winners have to pay for losers."

Medianoche nodded.

The Beast looked at his watch. "Get to that next meeting."

Medianoche left.

Capítulo 11

enamorarse

An hour later.

Medianoche sipped American coffee at a local café.

She was out there. He knew she was. He had been in this business too long.

Medianoche waited for her to show her hand, or show her gun.

She was 51-50. She had tried a 10-56. She was dishonorable. She was a slag.

On the stairwell, she had come from above him. It didn't make sense.

His lower IQ and experience was better than her higher IQ and arrogance.

Books were only so good. Experience was where the rubber hit the floor.

He was killing before Señorita Raven was a sparkle in her father's Indian eyes.

She didn't belong down here. Not in The Four Horsemen. Not in the military.

Medianoche was at a small corner café near Avenida Honduras. La Peca. Cold place. Wooden tables. Tile floors. *Sólo efectivo*. Cash only. A café that was advertised as being clean of foreigners. Not on the door or on the tables, but in the local magazines. No two wooden tables were the same size or height. Antique lights and chairs hung from the ceiling. Nothing matched, yet it all went together. Even in the wee hours, the place was filled with people in their twenties, mostly couples, all touching and cuddled up as they shared food.

A sign over the counter said tequila cost six pesos. Tequila Cuervo was ten pesos.

Medianoche was alone, his Tres Marías at his apartment, waiting for his return.

He had on different clothing. Black turtleneck. Black Turpin shoes. Black leather bulletproof jacket. Different watch on his wrist, the limited edition Movado that was a tribute to Derek Jeter. Copies of *Diario Popular, La Nación, Buenos Aires Económico, Buenos Aires Herald, La Prensa, USA Today, Ámbito Financiero, International Herald Tribune, El País,* and *Clarín* at his table. His Peruvian waitress was a petite woman with dark hair and keen features. He ordered steak. She brought him chips and fresh guacamole as a starter. She left.

Medianoche sipped his coffee and thought about the briefcase.

He shook his head.

Fuck Hopkins and the package they'd retrieved for him.

Fuck how much money it was worth.

Fuck the thoughts Señorita Raven had put inside his head.

He read about what he cared about. Argentina.

The global economic crisis was killing Argentina's soy, meat, corn, and wheat exports, had drained government assets of billions of dollars. President Fernández de Kirchner was barely at a 29-percent approval rating, as popular as the second President Bush in his waning days. Youth unemployment was high, the penal code had collapsed, and the police were inadequate. Crime was exploding. And the message from the government told the people to learn to take care of themselves, to stop sleepwalking on the streets and realize they were living in a jungle.

The government called their country a jungle.

Medianoche nodded. The world was a jungle, and we were all animals.

A minute later, a woman walked through the doorway. Alone. Her hair was gray, pulled back from her face. She was at least fifty. She was beautiful, in a Sophia Loren kind of way. Loren back in the 1940s. Nice shape. She wore jeans, flat shoes, and a simple overcoat. She carried an umbrella in one hand and a tattered backpack in the other. The backpack looked heavy. She moved like she could dance the tango, as if she could dance the tango well.

Medianoche made eye contact with the woman. She came to his table.

She said, "It's a shame they let Madonna play Eva Perón in that movie. It was a disgrace to the country. We have many Argentine actresses who should have played that role."

That was the proper code. He stood and she kissed his cheek as if they were old friends.

She took to a wooden chair. He sat back down.

Medianoche nodded. "Your English is impeccable, Señora."

"Caprica Ortiz."

"No names."

"I want you to know my name. I am not afraid. I do not want to be invisible."

"Okay. Señora Ortiz."

"Caprica."

"Okay. Caprica. Your English is better than that of the people in the United States."

"I don't muddle my words. My father told me to never muddle my words. Told me that when I spoke to someone, look in their eyes and speak clearly. If you muddle your words and cannot look a person in the eye, then they will not respect you. And if they muddle their words and cannot look you in your eye, you should not respect them. Without respect, there is no trust."

"Wise man."

She cleared her throat. "I was educated in Florida. FAMU. Earned my Ph.D. in England. I was a young woman when my father disappeared. He was a journalist. As am I. My father was kidnapped in 1979 and assassinated by the military dictatorship after he protested the junta and their crimes against humanity. They did to him what was done to writer Rodolfo Walsh."

She looked around. Angry. Anxious. Definitely not afraid.

She stared at his scarred face. Comfortable. Not jarred by his roughness.

He said, "Would you like to have dinner?"

"*Gracias, pero no.*" She shook her head. "I have to get back home to my husband."

He nodded, a twinge of disappointment in his expression.

She gave him a nervous smile. "Maybe if we ever met again."

"Would you like a glass of wine?"

She paused, considered, then nodded.

Medianoche ordered a bottle of red wine. The waitress brought two glasses, poured wine in each, smiled, then walked away.

Medianoche sipped his wine.

Caprica did the same, then said, "Thank you."

"*De nada.*" He nodded again. "Okay, Caprica. Tell me what you need from my organization."

She reached inside her coat and took out a USB flash drive. She held it inside her hand, looked at it, turned it over and over a dozen times before she looked at Medianoche.

He nodded again. "Talk. If you have changed your mind, it's fine."

"I have not changed my mind. I just have a lot to say."

"You have the floor."

"There are about thirty thousand people who are lost or murdered, people who will never be able to speak for themselves, people who will never be able to see true justice. The poor never see justice. I want you to understand me. And know that I am here for justice. First, I must tell you about the most horrible period of my country's history. When the military junta seized power in a coup from Isabelita Perón's government."

"The Dirty War."

She nodded. "Started March 24, 1976, and ended on December 10, 1983."

"The bloodiest dictatorship in Argentina's history."

"Videla. Viola. Galtieri. All evil. Anti-Semitic. Racist. Hated educators. Hated doctors. Hated lawyers. Hated well-educated people. Hunted students like animals. Tortured many people at the Navy Mechanical School. Feet from where the president sleeps. Every time I drive past Navy Mechanical School, part of me dies. Part of me screams out murder. They terrorized and murdered us, and now that place of terror and murder will become a museum. Places of death and horror should not become tourist attractions. They should be torn down."

Medianoche nodded. "I agree."

She said, "In its place should be a monument honoring the missing and dead. Every name should be on that monument. Mothers. Nuns. Activists. Journalists. Children were abducted, taken from their mother's arms, babies stolen and given to other families as if it were nothing. I could say a lot about that time. When the generals thought they were gods."

She paused, sipped her wine.

Medianoche sipped his wine, waited. He knew the story, knew their history.

Caprica said, "Thirty thousand people, dead or missing. Only forty-four people convicted. Many of those convicts are being held in military units that are like luxury estates. An insult to the thirty thousand that have vanished. Five hundred and twenty-six murderers are still yet to see their day in court. Close to two hundred have died since 1983. One hundred are still on the run. We can't do anything about the ones on trial. The ones who might end up living in military luxury. Those animals don't deserve human rights. But the one hundred. We can find them. One by one. I have found four. They walk the streets of this world, return to this country and walk across our bloodied soil as if they have never done anything wrong."

"That is what this is about, I take it."

"Our criminals. Our once powerful, our once arrogant, our once murderous. But of the ones who committed the crimes against thirty thousand, as I said, one hundred are on the run."

"Okay."

"And I have found four."

"The men are here in this country."

"Old and still alive, therefore they still must answer for their crimes against humanity."

"You want these men captured and turned in to the authorities."

"I want them dead. No life of luxury inside a military jail. I want them dead."

"Just wanted to be clear."

"I want them dead. I want them dead."

Medianoche asked, "Did you bring what was discussed with my CEO?"

"Yes." She patted her backpack. "I brought what was agreed upon with your CEO."

Medianoche nodded. "How soon do you want this done?"

"Thirty years ago. I want this done thirty years ago."

Medianoche glanced out into the streets. Gun still on his lap.

Caprica finished her wine. "Do you have children?"

"Getting personal."

"I find you . . . interesting. Quite interesting."

He shook his head. "No kids."

"I didn't think so. I see it in your face, that thing that says you'd never want a child."

"You're good."

"Why no kids?"

"Never been interested in cloning myself."

"I have a son and a daughter. Children who will never interact with their grandfather."

He nodded.

She asked, "Are you *married*?"

"Divorced three times."

"How was your marriage? Well, your marriages."

"The first two were like a bottle of champagne. Good while they lasted."

"The third?"

"It didn't last long enough."

She nodded.

He said, "Too bad."

"What is?"

"Too bad you are married. And too bad we will never meet again."

"That was . . . forward."

"I know."

She nodded.

She asked, "And if you did happen to see me again?"

"We could have coffee. Or we could sit, share a *mate*, and talk about the weather."

"Let's be real. You wouldn't want to talk about those things."

"No, I wouldn't. But I would if it afforded me the chance to see you again."

"You are a dangerous man."

"In what way?"

She looked away for a moment, then back at him, the proper etiquette for having a conversation in Argentina. Eye contact was part of the culture.

She said, "Horrible world out there. I mean the way they murder without punishment."

Medianoche let her change the subject.

He said, "When there was only Adam, Eve, and their sons, Cain and Abel, one of them became a murderer. Even then, twenty-five percent of the population would kill."

"Not much has changed since biblical times."

"I still think twenty-five percent are capable of killing the other seventy-five."

They sat in silence. Medianoche handed her a napkin to wipe her eyes.

Soldiers did what they were instructed to do, and in the end, war brought many tears.

Then she whispered, "*Nunca más.*"

She left with tears in her eyes. Thirty thousand tears. She had left the USB flash drive on the table. And she had left her backpack behind. A backpack heavy with the cost of justice. The words *Nunca Más* were stitched into the worn material in thread the color of blood.

That woman reminded Medianoche that it was never too late for justice.

Never too late.

That woman had been angry most of her life. Would be until she died.

She was a strong woman. Not a girl. A woman.

He touched his eye patch. Daguerreotype memories played at ten frames per second, the edges dull, the images in black-and-white, blurry, like a hand moving back and forth in front of his face in fast motion. That hole in his head. That missing memory struggled to reboot.

Then.

Daguerreotype memories clicked off when motorcycle lights came on. Through the rain. Across the narrow street. The enemy was exposed.

Señorita Raven. Watching. Stalking.

Medianoche's jaw tightened as he put his gun on the table. Next to his steak. Underneath a newspaper.

The motorcycle pulled away, sped into the darkness and rain.

Señorita Raven vanished into the streets.

Whatever was between them was personal. Not The Four Horsemen's business.

However that diva bitch wanted to reconcile this matter, that was okay with him.

He moved his weapon to his lap. Eyes on the streets as he chewed his delicious steak.

He felt it in the air. A storm was brewing.

He didn't know if it was coming from France, North or Central America, London, Pakistan, Ireland, or within his group, but he smelled it in the air.

The scent of a new war. The scent of blood.

The scent of death.

Chapter 12

the devil's sister

Sixty minutes later.

I was checked in at the American terminal at Miami International Airport. In my hand, I had the Motorola phone the mysterious Lebanese girl had left behind. I waited for the second call. Knew they would contact me again in a matter of minutes. Trouble never waited long. The phone had GPS. So they knew my general location, could use cell towers to triangulate where I was, plus or minus a half mile. Could be more accurate than that, depending on the level of technology they had access to. Seconds later, the phone rang.

I flipped it open. The number was blocked. I pushed SEND, connected to my next issue, said nothing, listened for background noises, heard nothing that would reveal a location.

A static-filled, electronic voice said, "Gideon."

"That's what they call me."

"You're still in Miami. In the airport area. Miami International."

"Good old Global Positioning System."

"Of course. GPS is wonderful, don't you agree?"

"Still stalking me? How nice. Was beginning to think you didn't like me."

"So happy to have finally established contact."

They were using a filter, a cheap one at that, the voice more mechanical than human. Voice changers were no big deal. Any nickel-and-dime spy store sold those units. A Motorola phone could be picked up anywhere. A SIM card could be purchased on any street corner.

I said, "You have my attention."

"Let me get to the point."

"Do that. Make a long story short."

"My employer has information regarding your life and occupation."

"Write a book. Change the names to protect the innocent."

"No time for jokes."

"And I don't have time to bullshit."

"My employer is willing to sell this information to you."

"Cut to the chase. What's the bottom line?"

"Two million dollars."

I paused. "So, how do you see this going?"

"I'm aware of what you do. I assure you, that has been taken into consideration. I have no intentions of being at the receiving end of your fury."

Again I paused. "And if I don't have two million?"

"Then you would have a problem."

"I need to see the information."

"I'm afraid that's not possible."

"Then neither is two million dollars."

"Sure you want to play it that way?"

"Show me what you have. How do I know it's worth two mil?"

"She kept an electronic journal that would be easy to send all around the world. Scotland Yard. Interpol. CIA. FBI. NTSB. DHS. To every law enforcement agency in the islands and Canada. To every government agency that has ever been created. Could send that same information to every social networking site. To CNN. To local stations from New York to Tokyo. Same info could be sent to the BBC. They would love that story. The Internet is powerful. One click and . . . well . . . once that is done, you know it can't be undone."

"One click."

"Only takes one click and it's done."

I licked my lips, swallowed, my jaw tightening. "You said she. She who?"

"A very powerful woman in Detroit. It was a hidden file. It was encrypted, but I have the information deciphered. Files about hiring you to kill her husband. Information about how the money was transferred. About being double-crossed. About properties you owned. About bank accounts you had. Files that document her interaction with you up until her last night in Antigua. You were there. And you were probably the last person to see her alive."

Ghosts reached out to strangle me from beyond the grave. From Hell.

I said, "You sure you want to do this?"

"I'll be in touch."

"When?"

"Soon."

"Tell me where you are. I'll come to you, meet face-to-face and—"

They ended the call. Did that as if they didn't want to be traced.

I had looked around the room while I was on the phone. Saw no one watching. No one talking at the same time my brand-new threat spoke their words.

My hands opened and closed, my trigger finger in motion.

I took out my iPhone, was about to pull up the software that allowed me to play Big Brother and check on Powder Springs again, but my iPhone rang. Once again, area code 809.

Arizona said, "What can I do to get you to move the project up?"

My voice remained intense, on edge, just like hers.

I said, "Are you safe?"

"We're safe."

I put my personal issues inside my mental Dumpster and I pressed on.

I said, "Let's stop focusing on you and talk about what I need first."

"Power play."

"Not a power play. I need reciprocity. Somebody was on me at Starbucks."

"When I was being shadowed?"

"Came at me after you left. I was being shadowed by a girl. The Lebanese."

"She was across the room."

Like me, Arizona had taken in the entire room when she entered.

I said, "When you lifted information, she was there, so you might have something usable."

"I'll see what I have."

"Do the same for the name Nicolas Jacoby. He was in the room too."

"Who was he?"

"The rail-thin collegiate-looking guy flirting with her. He carried your tea."

"They were at the same table. Had to be together. How do you think they fit in?"

"Not sure if they were together."

"But you don't know for sure."

"That's what I'm hoping to find out."

"He needs you to get to South America ASAP."

I paused. "*He.*"

Arizona took a breath. "I need you to get there. ASAP."

I sat on bubbling emotions. "Put him on the phone."

"He's not here."

"Don't fuck with me. I'll cancel this order. Now put him on the fucking phone."

She put the phone down. I heard her speaking in Tagalog, a language I couldn't understand, not at the pace she was speaking. Then I heard a male voice with a British accent.

"Cheers, Gideon."

"Cheers. What should I call you?"

"Scamz."

I paused. "Like your father."

"The name worked for him."

"Scamz and Queen Scamz. Nice."

The last Scamz had been Arizona's abusive lover. She had spread her legs. Allowed the son of the dead man she couldn't let go of impregnate her. Greek tragedy to the bone.

I said, "Let's cut to the chase. Tell me about South America."

"As you have been informed, it would be lovely for you to leave for Buenos Aires today."

"I told Arizona what I could do. Four days."

"But you also need her assistance on another matter, from what I understand."

My trigger finger moved back and forth.

I said, "You can buy one day. Get me what I need and I'll move it up one day."

"What's your price to make it right now?"

"I can't make it right now."

"New information just came in. Things have changed since Arizona contacted you."

Again I cursed. "Details."

"Just got word. A team of mercenaries have obtained the . . . what did Arizona call it?"

"MacGuffin."

"Yes, the MacGuffin."

"A team of mercs was babysitting your precious cargo."

"It was hijacked. One part of it."

"How many parts are there?"

"Two. Two parts. I believe Arizona told you that much already."

"Just confirming."

"But the mercs have managed to obtain one."

"The part Hopkins and his crew were after. That was what Arizona was carrying."

"We have one part, yes. That was why there was so much interest in us earlier."

"How many mercs are babysitting part two?"

"Not sure. But Hopkins hired The Four Horsemen of the Apocalypse."

"Israelis?"

"No idea. They are led by an assassin who is known in South America as *La Bestia*."

"*La Bestia*."

"Spanish for 'The Beast.'"

"I speak Spanish."

"Argentine Spanish?"

"Castellano, the Spanish of Spain and the Spanish of Mexico."

"Most people are ignorant enough to think that Spanish is Spanish, that it's universal."

"Most people don't have as many frequent flier miles as I do."

"Didn't mean to insult your intelligence."

"You didn't."

He was speaking to me in Castellano. Testing me. I didn't like being tested.

Scamz said, *"Impressive. Your Spanish is very impressive."*

"The Horsemen. What do you know about them?"

"They've been around for twenty years, operate outside of America."

Aggravation controlled my tone. *"The job sounds like more than a simple recon."*

"Arizona speaks highly of you."

I didn't comment.

He said, *"You're good."*

"I'm one man. One. I'm not a team of mercs."

"You're Gideon. You're a legend. I know you can handle it."

"They told Custer the same."

"The building where the skirmish happened, they had surveillance. My connections in Buenos Aires tapped into their system, downloaded it before it was purged. A one-minute battle. It's not clear enough to make out faces, just explosions and gunfire."

"Send it."

"It's being enhanced. Will send as soon as I can."

"Send the video. Get me what you can on La Bestia and his crew."

"Okay."

"And this job, it might cost you more than I anticipated."

"How much more?"

"A lot more."

"Gouging."

"Negotiating."

"The new price?"

"First and last, on top of my fee, you and me will be squared away."

"Agreed. You will walk away debt-free and compensated for your endeavors."

"My price depends on what I need. On who I need. Will get back to you on that."

"Fair enough."

I'd had enough of being tested by that sonofabitch. I'd had enough of life testing me.

In English I asked, "Are we done here?"

"Would you like to chat with Arizona?"

"Nothing to *chat* about at this point."

"On the contrary. Based on her expression, I think Queen Scamz wants a word."

"Sure. Put your queen on the line."

"Cheers."

There was a pause, more talking in Tagalog.

Arizona came on the line. She said, "You're at the airport."

"Miami International."

"The noise gave that away."

"Sounds like you and your crew are at the airport too."

"We just arrived."

I said, "Back to my problem."

"The Lebanese."

"She left me a phone. Motorola. Flip number."

"SIM card?"

"Yeah, it has one. Should I get this to you before we part ways?"

"One step ahead of you."

"What do you mean?"

"What gate are you at?"

I told her.

She said, "Look for one of my employees within the next twenty minutes."

I pushed the END CALL button. I was done talking whether she was or not.

My eyes went to the news while I sat at the gate, sweating, unable to cool off. A wealthy Republican had been found dead a few hours ago. A powerful man who funded the conservative side of Prop 2, the amendment that would define marriage in Florida's state constitution as between one man and one woman. Looked like he had slipped and fallen, drowned in his bathtub. Room locked from the inside. I nodded. A different wealthy Republican had died last week in California, a man who had funded Prop 8, the West Coast's version of Florida's Prop 2. That one ruled an accidental overdose.

Neither of those were accidents.

The California hit had been my work. The best jobs were the ones that never made the news. Too much attention was bad news in my business. That shootout on Miami Gardens Drive had me feeling like a disturbed amateur and a fugitive. I took my iPhone out, pushed the POWER button. As soon as the power came up, the phone rang. It was Konstantin, my handler.

I answered, "Hello, my friend."

"Gideon. My favorite son."

Konstantin was Russian, one of the assassins who trained me in this business. He had worked as a hired gun for decades. Had decreased the population from Hollywood to Moscow and places in between. He was the one who taught me to be ruthless. He had a family and was battling cancer. That cancer was the assassin that was trying to take him out.

He verified that Arizona had put in her order and transferred half of the fee.

That was standard operating procedure. Half up front, nonrefundable, the second half on completion.

Whatever tools I needed to handle the job would be at the destination.

I said, "The residual from my old problems. They finally made contact."

"Any idea who is running the second half of the show?"

I told him about Starbucks, the scene in the bathroom, gave him the description that had been fed to me, the Lebanese woman decorated with extravagant body art, and the phone call.

It meant nothing. Simple blackmail that led to nothing yet.

I said, "I told Arizona about my concerns. Wanted to see what she could find."

"Arizona . . . you trust her?"

"I've known her awhile. A decade."

"That means nothing in their business. They'd double-cross their mothers to close a deal. They are cowards and they call us to do their dirty work. They are all shit."

"True. Friendship means nothing and family is expendable."

"That job you did for the first Scamz a long time ago, that verifies your last statement."

"Was on my mind."

"You've never talked about it."

"Try not to talk about work. Not the specifics."

"If something gets to you, you have my ear. Every now and then, it's good to talk."

"Sure. Thanks."

"The thing you did for Scamz. It was a job he wanted me to do. I think you vanished for a couple of months when the job was done. What happened after that?"

"After I did the South America job, he wanted me to go back to North Hollywood. Wanted me to work for him. Big conflict for me. So I cut him loose, stayed where I was. Wanted to go back to California, but that . . . it could've gotten ugly."

"Because of that Filipina girl."

"Arizona."

"She was trouble then. She was always trouble."

"I went back and rode the End of the World Train. Got a room at Tierra de Leyendas. Met an engineering student at the Universidad Nacional de la Patagonia San Juan Bosco. We Visited Antarctica. Looked at icebergs and penguins and whales and seals. Tourist shit."

"In other words, you met a beautiful young woman and enjoyed your youth."

"Best way to learn to speak Castellano is to immerse yourself in the language."

"And you immersed yourself."

"She was a nice girl. Should've stayed down there. But she started asking too many questions. Squares always ask too many questions. Always a problem messing with the squares. Was there two months. One day I went out for walk, never went back."

"That's the business."

"Yeah. I know."

"Sorry, son, but I think I might have to cut it short."

"Family?"

"In Saint Paul. And the target is in sight. Need to pop him in the next ten minutes."

"Later."

"One quick thing. Thirty more seconds."

"I'm listening."

"This job is from Queen Scamz, so I'll have to trust it's not a setup. I don't need another Antigua, not with some rogue out there shadowing you, so I'm sending you in the long way. Want you to fly into Brazil, from there I'll get you to Uruguay, then I'll slip you into Argentina by boat."

"Tell those condescending fucks I'm not flying commercial. They want me there, they fly me there, private plane, bring me in under radar. You're right. I'm not chancing another Antigua."

"They won't go for that. That would add close to one hundred to their tab."

"Pass it on to Scamz. And Arizona. And whoever else is on that side of corruption."

"I'll pass it on, but be prepared to catch the flight I arrange."

I said, "Ninety-six hours. Not a lot of time for something of this magnitude."

"Any other special orders, text me the list."

Then we disconnected.

Konstantin went to kill. I practiced staying alive.

The energy in the airport shifted. Hairs stood up on my neck.

Sierra walked through the bustling crowd, at her side the other muscle-bound Filipino who had been riding with Scamz. She had a purse over her shoulder. A small purse.

She was a small woman, bowlegged, her expression always the same, always serious. She looked ten years younger than she was, could pull her hair back into a ponytail and pretend she was young enough to audition for the sequel to *High School Musical*. She had a small nose and Angelina Jolie lips, kissers that would probably make Brad Pitt do a double take.

The original Scamz had had her and Arizona at the same time. Had them the same way I'd had two women in London. That was what I saw when I looked at Sierra. All of them together.

I wondered if the new Scamz had picked up where his old man had left off.

Sierra stopped in front of me, didn't say a word. First she looked me over, inspected my change of clothing, surprised to see me out of jeans and wearing swank linen. Her eyes told me what she wanted. I faced a woman Arizona had sent me to Amsterdam to kill not that long ago.

She extended her hand, palm up. I handed her the phone.

She sat two seats away from me and popped out the SIM card, inserted it inside a device that was connected to a computer she had taken out of her purse, a computer barely larger than the palm of my hand. While she did that, I looked at her escort. Long hair, wavy, like Troy from the Pittsburgh Steelers. A little below average height but he looked taller because he was all muscle. Had beefed himself up the way insecure short men did, maybe figuring width and bulk would create an illusion that compensates for vertical deficiency. He was dressed in Ermenegildo Zegna clothing and Christian Dior loafers. Despite looking like a billboard demonstrating where fashion met steroids, he looked strong. Maybe intimidating.

I had killed much stronger men. With my bare hands.

He extended his hand. "Nice to see you again."

"Who are you?"

"Sierra's brother."

I saw the family resemblance, the Asian influence strong.

I nodded, then I shook his hand.

He said, "We met once. North Hollywood. Big Slim's pool hall. Long time ago."

My guess was he was there the day I met Arizona. I had been so focused on her that I didn't notice anything else. Wished I could do that day over. Still I didn't know him from Jeffrey Dahmer. Didn't know him. Didn't want to know him. Didn't need to know him.

Sierra put the SIM card back inside the phone, then tossed me the Motorola.

She turned to leave.

I said, "Sierra."

She paused, looked in the eyes of the man who would've killed her to keep Arizona safe.

Arizona was beautiful, looked like love. Sierra was stunning, darker in complexion and disposition. She looked like rabid lust chained to a stake, growling, struggling to get free.

I handed her the two driver's licenses I had taken from Nicolas Jacoby.

I gritted my teeth and said, "Have Arizona run these."

She held her stare. Said nothing, her breathing smooth and sensual.

She walked away. Her brother left with her.

I stared at Sierra, monitored her and her brother until I couldn't see them anymore.

As soon as they disappeared, I saw someone else was spying on me.

Another assassin.

Chapter 13

if death ever slept

The assassin spied on me like a well-paid shamus.

Pink baseball cap. Blue jeans, black T. Backpack on left shoulder. Gun hand pulling carry-on luggage. I held her in my periphery. She found a seat two rows over, dug a yellow *Spanish for Dummies* book out of her backpack. She saw me spying and shifted, put her shades back, then went back to her book. Her leg bounced as she moved her hair to the side.

They called my flight. I stood with the rest of the impatient crowd of world travelers.

The woman who was watching didn't get up with the crowd. Again she glanced my way, saw my attention on her, then shifted and went back to her studies, crossed her legs and pulled her expensive and stylish cowboy boots back so impatient people could shuffle by.

After the privileged had boarded and the paupers in zone one were called, I headed toward the plane. I looked back at the television. The news was showing the limo that had exploded on I-95, then cutting away to the aftermath of the mayhem on Miami Gardens Drive. The people on the street called the men in the SUVs savages. People who had witnessed one SUV being gunned down called the man riding a black motorcycle the same name.

When I was settled in my seat, the last seat before the toilets, I waited.

She came down the aisle, backpack and carry-on in tow. She came to the last row. My row. Looked at her ticket while I took in her features.

Her skin looked Mediterranean and Native American, hints of greens and yellows tinted with a poolside tan. She gave me a small smile.

She said, "Gideon."

I nodded.

She said, "No one was watching you."

"No one was watching you, either."

Her hair hung below her butt, was burgundy with highlights. Her haunting green eyes pulled me into her current, a current almost as powerful as the undertow possessed by Arizona.

Her name was Hawks.

I got up and stuffed her carry-on inside the overhead bin, then eased back into my row, took the middle seat. While I was up she had hijacked my window seat. A moment later, I glanced at this woman with the hypnotic eyes. She had haunting eyes that always reminded me of Sharbat Gula, the Afghan girl who had been on the famous cover of *National Geographic* back in '85.

Hawks asked, "Who were the Asians chatting you up?"

"Filipinos."

"Cousins of the Asians."

"Business in South America."

"What's popping down there, Mister International?"

"Long story."

"You look STFO."

"STFO?"

"Stressed the fuck out."

Her cellular buzzed. She pulled it out. FUNDS TRANSFERRED flashed on her screen.

Hawks hit SEND and put her cellular up to her ear.

"Guess what, Daddy. I got my stimulus check and I'm going to the West Indies. Puerto Rico. *¿Como estás, jefe?* And I said *jefe*, not heifer. Means 'boss' and nothing derogatory. You're the *jefe*, Daddy. Going with that guy I told you about, the jerk I met down in Dallas, guy I told you I'd never see again, said Hell would freeze over before I was nice to him. Well, tell the Devil to get his skates. Anyway. I'm going to see Old San Juan, the forts, Bacardi Factory, dance and drink fancy drinks. I'll get you a fancy shot glass or something. And a magnet. *Adiós, mi jefe.*"

She hung up her phone. Laughed as she put it away. Then she looked at me.

She hadn't called her father. She'd called Konstantin. That was her way of checking in after her job, letting him know she would be out of the country for a few days, with me.

By then, I had my iPhone out.

I said, "Checking on Powder Springs before we hit the air."

"You get that DNA thing straightened out?"

"Not yet."

"That boy. Steven."

"I know."

"You really should fix that. If he has been kidnapped . . . and I think he was."

"I know. Something else happened."

"What?"

I said, "The fuckers who worked with my old Detroit problem, they made contact."

Her jaw tightened. She understood. "When?"

I told her the same things I had told Konstantin.

Hawks took a nervous breath. "Want to cancel this trip?"

"I was on the move for damn near a year. Was hunted like an animal."

"What are you saying?"

"I'm tired. I'm fucking tired. I'm not going Bin Laden. Not again."

"And that means?"

"Just because somebody is after me, I'm not going to keep living in a fucking cave."

She reached inside her backpack, took out an envelope. We had the back row to ourselves. I clicked on the overhead light and she opened the envelope. Photos. Personal information. I saw notes that had an address in the San Juan area. It was an assignment.

I said, "You have a job in Puerto Rico?"

"Two meetings in P.R. Couple more in other places."

Hawks took out another set of photos. One was of a beautiful twenty-five-year-old model. The second, third, and fourth photos were of the same woman. Her face looked so deformed, so horrible, it shocked me. Both eyes blackened, face bruised, eyes swollen.

Hawks said, "Her ex did that to her. He's a hockey player."

"She called the cops?"

"She kept it out of the news. Lied about the situation."

"Why would she cover for the man who beat her into the ground?"

"Didn't want to ruin his career. Was in love. Who knows why she was so stupid."

"Those are major injuries."

"She had to sneak to Brazil and get plastic surgery because of that asshole."

"I take it he paid for the reconstruction."

"That he did. Put her on a private jet and got her out of the country."

"Good way to get her out of the public."

"And away from the paparazzi. She's down there now."

"So she has an alibi."

"Domestic violence makes my blood boil. I would've put Tommy Lee and Ike Turner down. Would've found the asshole that abused Halle Berry and put a sharp blade in his heart, and I don't care how young or famous or how well an asshole can sing or dance, that beautiful woman from the islands, if she had whispered the word, I would've done the work pro bono."

She took those pictures away, showed me a different one, one less personal.

I said, "This guy, the actor. His ugly divorce has been dragging out in the news."

"His wife has put a hit out on him. Not crazy about her, but it's a job. She wants to modify the settlement with a bullet to her husband's cranium. That's how she plans to upgrade her lifestyle. Her stimulus package. Her six-figure divorce settlement isn't enough. She wants one hundred percent. Greedy uneducated bitch. Hate greedy bitches too."

"Nobody ever has enough money. The rich will never be rich enough."

I reached over, took her hand.

She said, "We can cancel this."

"I promised. Have to keep my promise."

Hawks smiled. Then she closed her eyes. Put her head on my shoulder.

She had no idea how close this had been to not happening.

If Arizona hadn't been . . . pregnant.

I rubbed my eyes. Rubbed away that vision, only to settle on a different memory.

My mind returned to the End of the World.

Saw frozen blood in the land of fire.

Capítulo 14

la muerte es sólo un negocio

The Beast closed his cell phone. "That fucking fuck Hopkins is fucking dead."

Medianoche remained unfazed. "I assume it wasn't natural causes."

"Fucker fucked around and got blown the fuck up in fucking Miami."

"Did he get the second half of the package?"

"Fuck no."

"Now what?"

"We find the fuckers that took out Hopkins. My guess is they have the second half. If they don't, my bet is they know where the second half is located."

"We go to them?"

"Have to know where they are first. However they were being tracked, we need to get that information. We take it from there. Interesting position Hopkins has left us in."

"Sitting on the golden egg."

"Half the golden egg. And half is no good. Half gets us nothing."

"Any word on other interested parties?"

"Three Russians were killed last night."

"Where?"

"The *villa* where I left the package."

"The Russians were tracking it."

"It's in a safe place. Five Russians arrived two hours after we left the package. Twenty minutes after that, three were dead and the other two were running for their lives."

"Guess they didn't run fast enough."

"They weren't faster than speeding bullets."

Medianoche looked around the barrio. "Crowded out here."

"Damn tourists from all over the world."

"Only a few places in the world to go if you want to sit and wait and see everybody in the world. Times Square. Piccadilly Circus. Carnival in Brazil. And here. Everybody comes here."

La Boca. The land of the blue-and-gold hooligans. Home of Boca Juniors. Colorful homes painted with leftover paint from boats in the nineteenth century. An area that was dangerous at night.

It was noon.

Daytime. Several blocks were safe. The area was filled with busloads of tourists dressed in sweaters and coats, some wearing gloves, droves of credit card holders buying soccer and tango memorabilia. Historic area, placards all over, dwellings painted in Crayola colors: reds and yellows and blues and purples and oranges, commercial buildings painted the same, cafés and restaurants, outdoor seating, each with a tango show. This sector was energetic, but along the edges of the historic barrio, the bay smelled of sewage, was filled with trash.

Señor Rodríguez and Señorita Raven stayed behind them. Not a part of their conversation. Both the señor and the señorita were in jeans and military-style boots; both held motorcycle helmets and carried backpacks. Most tourists had backpacks.

Hopkins had been blown to hell. Hopkins had had presidential-style security.

Medianoche tugged at his gloves and asked The Beast, "Any idea who the other party is?"

"If all goes as planned, we will know who the fuckers are within the next fucking hour."

Medianoche nodded.

The Beast took a deep breath, looked at his watch, then said, "Let's walk."

Medianoche passed an armed policewoman, young and beautiful, gun inside a holster. Women and guns. The only real women left were the ones who wore dresses and danced the tango. Women with perfect hair. Makeup. Women who smiled, not hardened by disappointment and lies.

Things had changed overnight.

He had grown up in Los Angeles; inside the horseshoe-shaped Pacific Ring of Fire. He had lived in Baldwin Hills, before civil rights and the change in demographics. His family had lost everything when he was seven, when the Baldwin Hills aqueduct broke, that dam collapsing as the disaster was being shown live on television, broadcast by a helicopter on KTLA.

An unforgettable day. December 13, 1963.

More than 380 million gallons of water were sent crashing down a hillside, cars pushed down the streets a dozen at a time, current strong enough to rip away the walls and wash away their home, a home that had no insurance. The intersection of Coliseum and Cochran became a river. They lost more than a house and a '57 Chevy that day. His mother, killed when she was swept into an excavation hole. He remembered the mud. All the goddamn mud.

Village Green was the hardest hit of the villages. The scavengers and looters, opportunists who took advantage of others' misfortunes, they were there before the raging currents died. What the floods didn't destroy, the looters stole.

They had stolen his toys. Three boys older than him by at least ten years. His mother was dead and fucking asshole looters had swum upstream and stolen his toys.

Twenty years later, Medianoche returned to Los Angeles. Went to visit the boys who had stolen his toys. Now grown men with families. Walked up to their doors. Knocked. And when they answered, he had killed them. Three houses. Three hits within a two-hour period.

He was a man who never let things go.

Medianoche moved at a hurried pace next to The Beast.

Then.

He saw Thelma.

The prostitute from North Carolina. The whore from Yerres. The woman who had cost him his eye. She was in the crowd. A dozen tourists with her. Medianoche regarded The Beast, was given permission to break formation and he hurried back to that swarm. To that woman.

She and her friends were speaking in French. Thelma was French.

His angry frown changed into a charismatic smile as he tapped her shoulder.

She turned and was startled. The ruggedness of his face. The patch over his eye.

That was a reaction to which he had grown accustomed.

He was startled as well. It wasn't Thelma. She couldn't be the same age now as she was twenty years ago. Perfect face on flawless skin. The flair of an actress from the period of French cinema known as *La Nouvelle Vague*, combined with the contemporary beauty of the French actress Emmanuelle Béart. Same thing he had seen when he first looked at Thelma's face. The first time he had seen her was at Montego Bay. The last time was in Charlotte.

A whore who had moved around like a gypsy. Like she was running from her past.

He spoke to her in French, *"You are . . . very beautiful."*

"Thank you."

"What is your name?"

"My name is Özlem."

A Turkish name.

He said, *"You're French."*

"Why do you ask?"

"You remind me of someone. Do you have a sister?"

"Yes. I mean no. I had a sister."

"Is her name Thelma?"

"I had a sister named Nathalie-Marie Masreliez."

"I'm sorry. You reminded me of . . . I'm sorry to have bothered you."

"Who are you?"

"I am . . . nobody. Just a fool mesmerized by a beautiful woman."

She laughed. That jovial smile made her the duplicate of the whore from Yerres.

He told her, "Enjoy La Boca."

He hurried back, his handmade double-stitched Turpin shoes moving over cobblestone, the crisp air chilling his tailor-made clothing as he found his place next to The Beast.

The Beast asked, "What was that all about?"

"Mistaken identity on my part."

"Who did you think she was?"

"A French whore."

"That's vague."

"The one from North Carolina."

"From Charlotte?"

"Yeah. Bitch that ambushed me with that kid."

"She'd be the same age now that she was then? Impossible."

He adjusted his eye patch. "Anything is possible. When a man comes back from the dead, anything is possible."

"All the diseases. She's probably dead. And that kid, that whore's son is probably dead too. If not, he's somewhere locked up. Or an addict. But I'm betting on dead twice over."

"You're optimistic."

The Beast nodded. "Do you remember everything that happened in North Carolina?"

"Not everything."

The Beast touched his shoulder. "Watch out for the dog shit."

"Why don't they clean up behind their dogs?"

"They tried to pass a fucking law. Fuckers rebelled."

"I understand the women marching for abortions, the protests against Brazil, the protests against the paper plant in Uruguay, understand blocking the bridge and the port, the farmers demanding a better deal. Hell, they're even protesting a part of Avenida Pueyrredón becoming a two-way street, but who in hell rebels against cleaning up dog shit?"

They passed a man painted in silver and standing like a statue, tip bucket at his feet.

Medianoche said, "Is it time?"

"Close enough. Fuckers better be the fuck on time."

The Beast nodded at Señorita Raven. She reached inside her pocket, took out an iPod. Put the earphones on, clipped it to her waist. Señor

Rodríguez reached inside his back pocket and took out a paperback novel. Ray Bradbury. *Now and Forever.* Carried it in his left hand.

Colorful banners hung over a crowded cobblestone boulevard, CENTRO CULTURAL DE LOS ARTISTAS, a narrow bumpy road packed with tables for two or four, soft-back folding chairs with beer logos, and colorful umbrellas over each setup, the road about as wide as two European cars. Bright blues. Brighter reds. Brightest yellows. The tables were as vibrant as the buildings. *Porteño* couples danced the tango on raised platforms, performed in front of every café. Wooden seats filled the roads in the area where the Argentineans said the tango was invented.

La Rueda de Caminito. Mustard-colored café. Pictures of tango dancers over the doorframe. Outside seating. Three-piece band. Spanish guitars. Keyboardist. An Argentinean playing the German instrument called the *bandoneón.* A live tango show. Every table filled with tourists eating beef, pastas, cold cuts, and spinach.

They took separate tables. Medianoche and The Beast at one table.

The drop would take place here.

Señor Rodríguez and Señorita Raven sat at another table for four, not too close, their helmets in chairs. The music was loud enough to steal the clinking of forks on plates, loud enough to hide the sound of wooden chairs being moved on the cobbled sidewalk, loud enough to hide conversation. People smiled and took pictures; some took video as the dancers danced the tango, applauded the spectacular and jaw-dropping moves. Medianoche sat with a hand over his chin and mouth, hid the movement of his mouth, in case anybody on deck was skilled at reading lips. The Beast did the same.

Medianoche said, "Looks like something is on your mind."

"I came here as a young man. Before hyperinflation damn near killed the country."

"You came here a while ago."

"When Buenos Aires was still Buenos Aires. When every night in every barrio, there was dancing in the streets, not some fucking place that had McDonald's and Burger King on every block. Then I got that dishonorable discharge for a bullshit sexual misconduct charge. That blemish left me unemployable. Then I left my wife and kids."

"They left you."

"Same difference. They loved my money and hated my military ways. Ungrateful bitch and the kids she turned against me. After all I had done for her. Hateful bitch. Nothing more torturous than a love-less marriage. That is hell on earth. For everybody."

The Beast's mood had brought Medianoche back.

He looked around La Boca. Always aware of his surroundings. Habits of a soldier.

There was another mild aching in his eye socket, a pain brought on by the weather. The overcast weather made his deadened nerves struggle to live again.

In North Carolina, he had awakened in Presbyterian Hospital. Head in bandages. Tubes in his arm. Dryness in his throat. Forty-three days had gone by. A month and a half in a coma.

They told him that it was a miracle he was alive. Doctors had never seen anything like it. As if he had simply refused to die. He didn't give a shit about miracles. Wanted to know what had happened. They told him that he had been left for dead with a .22 bullet in his head. Wallet and money gone. Said he had been robbed. The rest he couldn't remember. Chalk it up to part of his brain having a goddamn hole in it. The memory from that day had been blown away. Police wanted answers. He told the cops to get the fuck out of his room.

End of story.

A miracle. Doctors and nurses came and stared at him. Brought in students; young snotty-nosed fucks who barely had pubic hair were taking notes. They all stared at the miracle.

Over and over telling him that he should've been dead.

But he wasn't dead.

He had made a call to The Beast. The Beast had come to rescue him, had flown in from Istanbul and arranged for him to leave the hospital without notice. Barely out of his coma, his partner in crime came for him.

That was loyalty. That was what was missing in the world.

Loyalty.

He had been driven to a safe house one hundred miles away from

Charlotte, taken to Columbia, South Carolina, recuperated on the soil where Union general William Tecumseh Sherman had shot his load and wreaked havoc on the State House during the Civil War. The Beast had looked out for him. Arranged a private doctor. Made sure he had what he needed. His nurse was a pretty girl who wore a short dress and a tight top that read DIAMONDS ARE PRETTY AND SO ARE PEARLS. BUT THERE'S NOTHING LIKE A CAROLINA GIRL. She was from Cape Verde, her heritage Portuguese and Creole. She was at his side, paid to give him whatever he asked for. His healer. She had taught him Portuguese. He taught her the art of sex. Soon he was sitting in a rocking chair, jaw tight, frowning out his window, seeing the world through one fucking eye.

The Beast had come to his rescue, then flown to Russia, to China, to Peru, then come back to South Carolina to check on him. Had come back to him with an offer.

The Beast had said, *"I'm putting together a group."*

Medianoche nodded. *"How many?"*

"Six. What do you think?"

"Four is manageable."

The Beast nodded. *"You game?"*

"Code name?"

The Beast smiled. *"Since it's four, The Four Horsemen of the Apocalypse."*

Medianoche hummed. *"Like the movie."*

"What movie?"

"The Glenn Ford movie. Came out in the sixties."

"Never saw that one."

"Rudolph Valentino was in a movie with the same name back in the twenties."

"The Italian who pretended he was Spanish and took the tango to America."

"My old man liked Valentino movies. Big Valentino fan. I liked the one with Glenn Ford."

"Was talking about the four horsemen in the Bible. Chapter six. Book of Revelation."

Medianoche nodded. Shook hands with The Beast. Gentlemen's contract. Deal signed.

Just like that, The Four Horsemen of the Apocalypse were born.

Memories dissipated.

Medianoche adjusted his eye patch, focused on the mission.

Señorita Raven was staring at him. Her face tight.

Again he looked around. Searched for an enemy underneath gray skies. Again he saw the Turkish woman who spoke in French, saw Özlem walking inside the colorful Caminito Havana with her friends.

Medianoche and his mercenaries sat and ordered food, passed up the Spanish, Italian, and *Porteño* dishes for grilled chicken and French fries, watched the tango show. The men in black pants, white shirts, and black vests. The women in dresses so tight, they told the truth about what was or wasn't underneath.

The tango dancers came over to the tables, hats in hand, those hats turned upside down accepting tips, taking photos for pesos. Dancers went to Señorita Raven, spoke with her, their faces amazed when she spoke. No doubt surprised that an Indian girl was fluent in their version of Spanish. The man smiled at her. Smiled at the assassin who had wavy black hair and shrapnel in her skin. Smiled at her like she was the most beautiful girl in La Boca. He held her hands and motioned toward the stage. People applauded and encouraged her to go to the raised platform. Señorita Raven glanced toward their table. The Beast nodded. It was okay.

Medianoche grunted. "Watch that arrogant bitch get up there and fall flat on her face."

"She'll be good for a laugh or two."

"The tango is for a woman who knows how to follow a man. Not for her. She'll collapse like the banks in Reykjavik. Her dance will be as useless as Iceland's currency."

Señorita Raven was helped up on the three-foot-high platform, a small stage that was probably nine feet by six. The dancer asked her something. She nodded and smiled. She was actually pretty when she smiled, despite the disfigurement.

Medianoche watched her, saw how she became feminine, adjusted into tango position. Her upper body was straight and tall. Knees bent and over her toes, weight back on her heels. Looked as if she was about to sneak up on someone without being seen. Her partner put his hand on the middle of her lower back. Señorita Raven adjusted her left hand, made her hand flat with the fingers straight. Then she placed her left hand around the man's right shoulder, her thumb against the lower part of his shoulder, her hand parallel to the floor. Medianoche nodded. The bitch had that much right.

The dancer's left palm and the palm of Señorita Raven's right hand connected at eye level. Again Medianoche nodded. Any beginner's class would teach her that much. Señorita Raven adjusted, stood a little to the man's right side, where the woman was supposed to dance, always to a man's right side. Like a good woman. The music played and the house singer came out, an octogenarian dressed in a gray suit and fedora, Carlos Gardel brought to life once again. The band played. The old man performed a wonderful ballad. "Mi Buenos Aires Querido." Medianoche waited to see Señorita Raven choke. Waited for her to make a fool of herself. But the man led her, and she followed. She moved with fluidity, maintained eye contact.

Tango.

The dance of passion. A dance where the man pursued the woman. Not a dance where the woman tried to outdance the man.

Not a competition.

A dance where a woman remained modest, moved with sensuality, every move saying that she hadn't decided if she wanted to surrender herself. Every move saying *convince me*.

The octogenarian sang, his baritone voice ancient and mesmerizing.

The dancer held Señorita Raven, his pursuit subtle, intensions known but not obvious, their movements slow and deliberate. Their passion escalated, intensified with the music. Señorita Raven was lifted, and she kicked her feet in a fast motion. There was applause. Medianoche looked around. Everyone was watching. Other tango dancers applauded. It wasn't a flashy dance. Señorita Raven moved her body in a sexy way, a subtle way, like the Spanish girls, perfect posture, went into the air and kicked her feet on her final turn, she amazed the crowd. The dance ended with Señorita Raven on one knee, her partner holding her across the small of her back, her back arched as her black hair fell away from her face, a dramatic and romantic finale that said she had been seduced, that he could have his way with her, that he could do whatever he fucking wanted to do.

There was a loud applause, cameras flashed as Señorita Raven was led back to her seat. When the dance was over, the man always walked the woman back to her chair. He returned her to where he had found her. A gentleman's dance. After the sensuality, the man remained the perfect gentleman.

Medianoche saw Señorita Raven staring at him. *Cabeceo.* Unbroken eye contact, not hostile but sensual, like they were at the *milongas*, where not a word was spoken when someone was courting for a dance. Or saying that they would be willing to dance with you.

Señorita held her eye contact.

Medianoche looked away.

Rejection.

The Beast looked at his watch. Then he looked at his other soldiers.

Medianoche said, "She likes attention."

"Her skills are excellent, but she is young and difficult."

"The soldier is trained in combat, but she's not pretty enough to win Best in Show."

"She might be full of shrap, but she can tango like an Argentine dancer."

"A dancer is only as good as the partner they dance with."

"You should dance with her before you kill her; that's if you end up putting her down."

"Can barely stand the sight of her. She reminds me of my last ex-wife."

"Maybe she'll be the next one."

"I'd kill myself first. I wouldn't fuck her if she was the last bitch on earth. Not even with your dick."

The Beast laughed. Medianoche didn't.

Medianoche saw her again. The woman who reminded him of Thelma.

She headed toward the section where the buses and taxis stopped.

Señorita Raven had eyes that took him back to Montserrat, to a woman he had loved.

And the French woman reminded him of a woman he hated.

The Beast nodded. "It's time."

A swarm of kids came up, homeless kids, *villa* kids, hustling for change, asking to draw a one-minute picture for pesos. Begging kids were everywhere. If they could crawl, they could beg. If they had hands, they could steal. A teenager went to Señor Rodríguez. Brazilian punk with long hair, dyed blond, twisted into a Rastafarian style. Clothes six sizes too big. Influenced by Americans who had been influenced by their own prison culture. He had the same paperback book Señor Rodríguez had placed on the table. The ruffian wore an iPod Touch too. Same as Señorita Raven's. He smiled, broke into some juvenile rap, something about dropping it while it was hot, then asked Señorita Raven if she liked Spanish music. Medianoche couldn't hear but read the ruffian's lips. Señorita Raven nodded. He took his earphone and gave it to her so she could listen.

He said, "We should exchange iPods. My Spanish to your American hip-hop."

Señorita Raven and the boy traded iPods. Then the boy traded books with Señor Rodríguez. Same book. Only the book Rodríguez held was filled with money. The payment for information that was on the iPod. The bait to bring them closer to Scamz.

Whatever the fuck that was.

Then the Rasta Brazilian walked away.

The Beast nodded at Medianoche. Medianoche nodded at Señorita Raven.

Medianoche stood up, left pesos on the table for the uneaten food.

Señorita Raven came to Medianoche, slipped the iPod Touch inside his pocket.

Her finger touched his hand. Her energy once again mixing with his.

She looked him in the eyes and said, "Sir, now what, sir?"

The Beast stepped up, handed Señorita Raven the package with the long-bladed knives.

"Señorita Raven. Señor Rodríguez. Follow the Brazilian punk back to his nest."

Señorita Raven nodded.

The Beast said, "Have them ready for questioning. Medianoche and I have to attend a short meeting."

Señorita Raven and Señor Rodríguez trailed the Brazilian, helmets in hand.

Medianoche and The Beast headed in the opposite direction. Near La Bombonera there was a BMW. M5. Black on black. Next to that BMW were two black motorcycles. Iron horses. The señorita and the señor. The BMW was the Beast's machine. Medianoche was driving. The Beast owned the car. Never drove. Would rather walk or take public transportation.

They got inside the car. Medianoche started the engine.

Frank Sinatra was on CD. Picked up where he left off. *September of My Years.*

Medianoche restarted the song. Took his nine millimeter out of his holster, placed it in his lap. The Beast did the same. Medianoche headed through the city, took Avenida Almirante Brown, passed miles of graffiti, public housing, cantinas, *farmacias, locutorios,* warehouses, Shell Gas stations, lave-rap, *maxikiosko, bicicletas,* cut over to Calle Defensa, rode down the narrow cobblestone road lined with antique shops until it ended at Casa Rosada, the presidential palace, but not where the president slept. Plaza de Mayo was across the street. A protest was in progress. People dressed up like rats, cockroaches, and flies. Activists from Greenpeace. Big banners protesting landfills and the government not complying with the zero-garbage law.

The city had at least a thousand monuments and all were covered in pigeon shit and marked with graffiti. They were back in the heart of downtown and the financial district, had taken the road from La Boca to the edges of Puerto Madero, had taken a fifteen-minute ride from poverty back toward prosperity. Frank Sinatra was crooning "Last Night When We Were Young."

They drove more than twice the posted speed limit, zigzagged from lane to lane, didn't leave much distance between cars, rode bumper to bumper and door handle to door handle, hit curves like they were in the final lap of the Indy 500.

Medianoche drove like the rest of the drivers.

He was driving the man who had saved him.

He was loyal.

The woman he had married on the island of Montserrat didn't understand loyalty.

Not even when the contract read "until death do we part."

That had been the agreement.

One day, one way or the other, it would have to be honored.

Capítulo 15

el diablo y los malvados

Medianoche sped down Libertador toward Recoleta. To his right, hidden beyond trees and the train tracks in Retiro, were the slums of Villa 31. On his left, in plain sight, were the French Embassy, Four Seasons Hotel, Patio Bullrich.

Paradise and Hell no more than a mile apart.

Medianoche's cellular rang. It was Señor Rodríguez.

Medianoche answered, "Speak, soldier."

"Sir, we took out five hostiles. Stun and flash. There is a lot of equipment. Satellite phones. Computers. They were hackers. They brought knives to a gunfight, sir."

"Señorita Raven?"

"A bit ambitious. Don't think we had to take all of them out. But she did."

"How many left?"

"Four. The one who made contact and three more. Everything is under control."

"Text me the address. You have two hours. Have them ready when we return."

Medianoche hung up.

The Beast said, "Problem?"

"Nothing those young fucks can't handle. We can run this errand first."

The Beast's phone vibrated. It was his servant, Draco Calamite

Ganymedes. Medianoche didn't listen in. Wasn't his business. The conversation was between God and servant.

There were dozens of *paseaperros* out walking dozens of dogs at a time, all sizes, all pedigrees of shit droppers. Every bus stop filled with people waiting in impatient silence. Medianoche was always amazed by how the Argentineans waited in line at bus stops, how everyone went single file to get on board, but underground boarding the subte, it was sheer madness.

Medianoche turned around at the Buenos Aires Zoo, satisfied they hadn't been followed from La Boca into the edge of Palermo, then drove around the roundabout and its Spanish Monument, Monumento de los Españoles, doubled back toward Recoleta, passed embassy row and Audi's Rond Point Restaurant, parked in underground parking at Recoleta Plaza. The fair in the plaza and on the streets was busy, tourists all over, live performances, miles of local artists and tents, art, crafts, everything for sale, even with clouds in the skies and a chill in the air.

Medianoche followed The Beast as he headed underneath the RE-QUIESCANT IN PACE engraved at the crown of the Greek Doric-style entry to the Recoleta Cemetery, a tourist attraction, thirteen acres that was like a city made of narrow streets and lined with trees, more than six thousand vaults, some larger than an average-sized condo or apartment.

A city of the dead.

Instead of homes and apartments, tombs and mausoleums stood side by side, domes higher than the twelve-foot concrete walls, elaborate and ostentatious, some pristine and surrounded by statues, most with broken glass and cobwebs, their marble and stone dingy and unkempt. Both the remembered and the forgotten dead slept inside the sprawling necropolis.

Medianoche walked with his hands behind his back, like an older Italian, as they mixed with the curious, passed by dozens of feral cats that lived on the grounds, saw a dozen more cats lounging in the aisles and eating hamburger meat, as they walked by the final resting places of politicians, poets, soldiers, explorers, priests, and the plain old filthy rich of Argentina.

They made their way to the section on the Calle Vicente Lopez side of the cemetery.

The Beast said, "I'll be in front of Brigadier General Juan Manuel de Rosas."

Medianoche nodded.

Row 114. Black marble front for Familia Duarte. Where Eva Perón was entombed with her husband, Presidente Juan Domingo Perón. Not what tourists expected. In a cemetery where some had final resting places the size of cathedrals, Eva Perón's tomb was tucked down a narrow row, a row barely big enough for two people to stand side by side, not off to itself but sandwiched between other tombs, on a row filled with resting places for the long-ago dead. That alley was crammed, filled with a long line of tourists snapping photos. Leaving flowers. Kneeling. Crying. Some were disappointed by the simple site. They had expected grandiosity. Thousands of miles traveled and thousands of dollars spent just to take a picture and frown.

Thousands walked that narrow aisle every day, no matter what the weather was like, and today was no exception. This was where Medianoche could see the client and make a decision to green light or walk away.

Medianoche saw her. Smoky skin. Dark hair underneath a dark scarf. A beautiful woman who looked like Isabel Sarli in the movie *El trueno entre las hojas*. Eyebrows dark, arched and thick. Not in need in the breast department. Large earrings. She stood at the end of the row, waited closer to the wall that separated the cemetery from Village Recoleta. The woman saw him. She was nervous. He nodded, then motioned to his right.

She nodded in return.

He exited the row, walked over one aisle. The woman did the same, met him halfway.

She was dressed in skinny jeans like most Argentine women wore, the style of Buenos Aires, jeans that molded to her curves from her hips to her ankles. She wore high heels that had jewels on the heel that sparkled underneath a dull sky. She had on a dark blouse made of silk, all of that topped with a ten-thousand-dollar fur coat and expensive sunglasses. She hid behind those glasses like the movie stars hid themselves in Hollywood. She carried an expensive leather duffel bag.

She stopped in front of him. He saw her watch. Cartier.

He nodded. "Eva Perón died of cancer in 1952, was only thirty-three years old."

She swallowed. Lips moved but no words came out of her mouth.

Medianoche frowned. "Talk. Or end up inside one of these tombs."

In broken English she stammered, "It was . . . really an insult . . . that that allowed . . . that *puta* Madonna to play Eva Perón in that horrible movie. It was . . . disgraceful to our nation."

Close enough. Now they could begin.

She stammered, "My English is no good. When I am nervous I forget my English."

"You were supposed to dress casual. And be discreet."

"This is my causal. Jeans. I bought nice jeans to wear. I am not wearing a dress."

He said, "You're in a cemetery in a fur coat and holding a Louis Vuitton duffel bag."

"Being here . . . in this sacred place . . . this is disrespectful to all Argentineans."

"Paying for death at a cemetery seems appropriate."

"I did not think of it that way."

"Did you bring what you were supposed to bring?"

She nodded. "*Sí.* Yes. I bring the money in the bag like you ask."

"You were supposed to use a simple bag."

"The bag . . . this is my sample bag."

"Simple. Simple. Not sample."

"See-emp-pale?" She paused. "No. The word . . . I do not know that word."

He said, "Go to Brigadier General Juan Manuel de Rosas."

"*Dónde es*— I mean where—"

"Walk out, turn left, first right, walk to the other side. Two rows before the wall. Number seventeen. There will be a man. He will take you where you can talk in private."

She left in a hurry, holding her fur coat as her heels sparkled.

Medianoche picked up the bag, headed toward the front of the cemetery.

Forty minutes later, the woman who looked like Isabel Sarli hurried out of the cemetery, more nervous now than she was before. After the deal was done, they always became nervous. She hurried down Calle Junín, moved around *paseaperros*, artists, and sidewalk vendors, hurried by tattered women holding dirty babies as they begged for pesos, rushed toward the restaurants in front of the Sahara, hugging her fur coat, her heels catching attention until she vanished.

Five minutes after that, The Beast walked out behind her.

Red lipstick was on his pants, around his zipper.

Medianoche asked, "Where did you take her?"

"There is a mini castle inside the cemetery."

Then Medianoche saw her for the third time. The woman who looked like Thelma.

She walked through the plaza facing the cemetery, still with her crowd of French tourists. Cafés and hotels were thirty yards away. The woman who spoke French stopped closer to the large ombú tree, a massive tree that had roots wider than a house, branches that extended for forty or fifty yards and had an umbrella-like canopy over a bricked roundabout lined with benches. Medianoche held the bag of money and walked by the young French woman and her friends as they stood in front of green wooden benches and took photographs. He passed by the woman who engaged that negative memory, moved through the crowd of sidewalk tango dancers, clowns playing accordions, kissing couples, beggars with dirty babies on their hips, and beautiful women offering free hugs. That memory faded as he entered underground parking.

Medianoche asked The Beast, "When does she want this done?"

"Tonight. You can handle it."

"Before the job for Caprica Ortiz?"

"We'll work that one in a few days. This is a simple job."

"Simple woman."

"And has more money than God."

"How does an idiot get rich?"

"Married well."

"Guess she's good in bed."

"She gives a good blow job, if nothing else. I almost asked her to marry me back there."

Medianoche nodded. "What about Señor Rodríguez and Señorita Raven?"

"You should sample Señorita Raven."

"Not even with your dick."

"Indian women are the best lovers on the planet. Not Brazilian women. Not African. Not Spanish. Not Italian. Not Asian. Not American. Not European. The best of the best is Indian. Bollywood. Bangladesh. Calcutta. Those beautiful women are the best of the best."

"Is that right?"

"Few years ago. Atheneum Hotel. Her name was Nina. Long black hair. Took her to eat at Fishbone's, then to Greektown Casino, spent some time playing slots, then strolled back to my presidential suite. She saw the sunken tub and took off her clothes. I didn't say a word. It was the sunken tub that closed the deal. I made love to her in the sunken tub, jets streaming. Then we did the same on the two sofas in the suite, and when the sun took away the mystery and the moods brought on by darkness, I paid her what she asked for a night of wicked sex."

"Mystery and moods brought on by darkness?"

"Was trying to be poetic."

"Just say you fucked her, paid her, and sent her home."

"That's not poetic."

"Mystery and mood and darkness. Geesh."

Medianoche laughed. The Beast laughed too.

The Beast pulled up his sleeve and looked at his watch. A silver Montblanc with a big round face. "Señor Rodríguez and Señorita Raven have been torturing the hackers for close to two hours."

"The prisoners should be singing a sweet Spanish song by now."

"Singing a song we want to hear."

Medianoche drove while The Beast opened the duffel, counted the piles of money, British pounds and U.S. dollars.

The Beast said, "We should've left the business five years ago. Before the U.S. crumbled and entered its second Depression and dragged the whole fucking world with them."

Medianoche nodded.

The Beast smiled. "When we get the second half of Hopkins's package, we can retire."

"Señor Rodríguez and Señorita Raven?"

"Expendable."

"When?"

"After they have served their purpose."

They shook hands.

Gentlemen's agreement.

Just like on that wretched day in South Carolina.

Capítulo 16

tortura

Warehouse area on the edge of La Boca.

Broken-down ships docked in the filthy bay, some leaning to their sides. One hundred yards away, droves of buses and taxis collected and dropped off tourists anxious to buy souvenirs at marked-up prices. Most of the tourists arrived in taxis, the way the hotels recommended.

But for some reason, the holders of the package had set up an operation here, where their activity would go unnoticed.

Medianoche drove through gloom and the rising stench wafting from the filthy waters beyond Avenida Don Pedro de Mendoza and the ugly sign for Barrio Bonito. Beyond where the tourist zone ended and beyond the Coca-Cola signs over La Esquina Café in Puerto Viejo. Beyond Astilleros Mestrina, its truck delivery door faded and ten shades of chipping and worn blue. The entire area fit the same description of neglect.

Medianoche eased down the cobbled road toward the warehouses. Señor Rodríguez waited out front. The only tourist that would stray this far from the safety and security of Caminito was a tourist who was about to lose his camera, his wallet, maybe his life.

Medianoche parked. Graffiti marked every wall, vulgarities and threats sprayed in juvenile handwriting. He went to the trunk of the car. Took out blue booties and surgeon gloves.

Señor Rodríguez said, "Sir, my car battery died about ten minutes ago, sir."

Medianoche asked, "Where did you get a car battery?"

"Sir, took it off one of the hackers' cars, sir."

The Beast said, "There is a spare inside the trunk."

Medianoche handed a pair of booties to The Beast. Same for the gloves.

Señor Rodríguez came to the trunk and took out the spare car battery.

When they had pulled booties over their handmade Italian shoes, they stepped inside the warehouse, pulling on the surgical gloves. What Medianoche inhaled at first reeked like a spoiled slumgullion. Faint screams came from above, one level up. Two hours of pain had lessened the volume. The walls of the warehouse were blackened from a fire that had happened a long time ago, its disgusting odor still in the concrete. Bodies were in the debris and on the stairs. Young men and young women. There were only two left. The ones who ran this operation.

Medianoche had already pulled out his gun, so had The Beast. They followed Señor Rodríguez. Puddles of water were at the bottom of the stairs; that puddle of stench grew as a stream of water ran down the stairs, stairs that were as broken as the North American dream.

The temperature was right above freezing. The brick walls kept in cold and refused heat.

Medianoche heard coughing, gurgling. Heard muffled screams.

Medianoche led the way and The Beast followed. They made their way up the shattered stairs. Walked into a concrete room that, relative to that trash and stench they had seen when they entered, was surprisingly clean. Señorita Raven was covered in plastic; garbage bags cut apart and pulled over her head, another around her waist, like a plastic dress that hung to the ground. She held a filthy water hose in one hand. In front of Señorita Raven, tied to a chair that had been turned on its back, was a middle-aged man, his head covered in a dirty towel. That towel was as dirty as the river, had been taped to the man's head with only small holes cut in the ratty material, holes for his mouth and nose. Very small holes.

The man's clothing had been cut away.

Señorita Raven let short bursts of water run onto that towel. The subject was struggling, panicking, unable to scream or too much water would get inside his mouth and nose. When the water wasn't running, the dampness from the towel continued, and with every inhalation he sucked in more water. The power of water was amazing. Damage to the lungs. Extreme pain. Brain damage. Eventually death. It had been going on for the past two hours. Water torture. Like in the Spanish Inquisition. Like under the Bush administration.

Other side of the room, there was a woman. About thirty years old. Overweight. Short. Spanish. Naked in a cold and damp room. Her breasts sagged. Her vagina was bushy.

She was positioned where she could see Señorita Raven's rendition.

The woman saw Señor Rodríguez walk in with the car battery and tried to scream, the gag inside her mouth muffling her hysteria as she fought in vain and struggled against her bindings. That woman was tied to a rusty, dented metal door. Clamps were on her nipples and inner thighs. Those clamps were hooked up to a dead battery. She had been left alone for ten minutes. That was how long ago the first battery had died. Ten minutes to feel relief from close to two hours of living in the basement of Hell. Now there was a brand-new battery.

Señor Rodríguez said, "What were you saying, Señorita Raven?"

"I was talking about wanting to get out later."

"Okay."

"I need to get out. Want to head down to Puerto Madero and lease a bike and ride on the dirt trail. Or take the train to Anochorena. Everybody is down there playing volleyball and Frisbee and flying kites. Soccer fields. Tennis courts. But it might rain. So I might run my daily 10K, do PTs, shower, grab a bite at Monaco, then spend all night on Facebook. With the rest of the bottom-feeders and losers. Like I do almost every night."

"You spend a lot of time on Facebook."

Two people experienced torture, set free muffled screams as she rambled.

Medianoche grimaced and said nothing. Wasn't his show. Not yet.

They wanted the prisoners to see them, wonder who they were before they spoke.

The Beast said, "Soldiers. What you're doing is cruel. That is absolutely cruel."

Señorita Raven stopped talking. Then she put the water hose down and moved away.

The Beast said, "Have you no empathy? These are human beings. My God."

Señor Raven disconnected the battery cables but didn't move the battery.

Medianoche stood in front of the terrified woman. He removed one of the clips and saw desperate hope in the woman's eye. Saw the diminution of her pain. Her bruised flesh held a magnificent rich and brilliant incarnadine color. He made an apologetic face. Then smiled at her.

He said, "I will make these evil people stop. Just tell me everything you know."

He thought of his voice as romantic, but not seductive. Charming. All he needed was sappy music to partner with his melodramatic acting, something to hoke up the dark moment.

Behind him, The Beast stood over the drowning man, and in a kind voice said the same. He pulled the towel away from the man, let him breathe. The man hadn't had fresh air in almost two hours. The Beast moved the towel but didn't turn off the running water. That simple sound of trickling water kept terror in the prisoner's eyes, held the desperation in his voice.

The Beast gave instructions, told Señor Rodríguez and Señorita Raven to leave the room, to collect all of the hardware on site and begin loading the equipment inside his car.

The Beast asked questions. Medianoche asked the same questions, as if an echo.

Both hostages told of the same thing. DMAs. Dead Money Accounts. Offshore accounts. Accounts in Zurich, others that spread from Andorra to Singapore. Money tucked away in the Caribbean. Hidden in Liechtenstein. Money that thrived under the veil of bank secrecy. Tax evasion money. Drug money. Stolen money.

Both mentioned the name Hopkins.

The Beast asked who was in charge of this operation.

Medianoche asked the same.

Both prisoners said the same name. Scamz. Both trembled when they mentioned that name.

He was one person. But he was in charge of many. In the UK. In North America. Now in South America. One of the satellite phones they had found inside the warehouse was a direct link to wherever he was on the planet.

They said he had died ten years ago and come back to life. Said Scamz was so evil that the Devil had set him free to keep him from taking over Hell.

Medianoche asked what Scamz was after.

The package was what he needed.

The package that now belonged to The Four Horsemen.

The Beast asked, "How do I find the person that you call Scamz?"

Medianoche asked, "Scamz, tell me how to get in contact with him!"

Both prisoners answered. The same answer. The same screams.

They repeated that along with the computer, there was a phone, a satellite phone.

The Beast asked what information was on the computer.

Medianoche asked the same.

On the computer there was information about Scamz.

And someone named Arizona.

And new files on someone named Gideon.

The Beast said, "Code name: Gideon."

Medianoche shook his head. Had never heard of Gideon.

The woman begged Medianoche, "Will you let me go? I have a son and a daughter. . . ."

On the filthy and broken concrete ground below her there was a puddle of piss. And shit. The stench of fear. And the woman wanted to get home in time to feed her children.

Medianoche whispered, "I will not kill you. I will not harm you. I will not touch you."

The Beast told the same to the man he questioned.

Medianoche said, "Just a few more questions."

The Beast spoke next, knowing they would alternate talking and questioning, and said, "A few more questions, and I will be done."

Medianoche said, "Scamz."

The Beast said, "Arizona."

"Gideon."

"What other names are you leaving out?"

"Who else is involved?"

"Who else besides the names you have given?"

"Are you sure the one called Scamz is the leader of that group?"

"Are they mercs?"

"Tell me all you know."

Thirty minutes went by.

The Beast had the satellite phone brought to him. He pushed in the numbers.

A female voice answered. "¿Sí?"

"Quiero hablar con Scamz, por favor."

There was a pause. Then the female voice became tight and asked, "Who in the hell is this?"

"Is this the one they call Arizona?"

There was another pause. "Who are you?"

"Put Scamz on. I have taken control of this operation."

"Where are the employees?"

"Chatting with Jesus or Beelzebub. Depends on how they lived their lives."

A moment later. "Sí. Someone wants Señor Scamz. This is Señor Scamz."

"Wonderful to hear your voice."

"I believe you have me at a disadvantage."

"I have half of the prize. I have one of the packages."

"And I guess that makes me the man who has the other half of what you want."

"You're British."

"You're American."

"I have your equipment. This operation has been shut down."

Scamz said, "My people?"

"Unfortunate accidents. All but two. The leaders."

"I take it you are the gentlemen who met with my associates from Uruguay."

"We were paid to meet with them. Paid by Hopkins. Now there is no Hopkins."

Scamz paused. "The Four Horsemen of the Apocalypse."

"*Sí*. I'm flattered you have heard of us."

"Soon you will hear about me."

The Beast smiled. "Soon."

"Yes, soon."

"Guess there is no room for compromise."

"Too much blood has been spilled."

The Beast nodded. "Agreed."

"What you have is no good without what I have."

"Same goes for you. But I think you've invested more. You have more to lose. For me, it's all gain. I heard Hopkins took you for a lot of money. You need this to make a profit."

The phones disconnected.

Two important devices were inside the equipment they had confiscated, both tracking devices. Both the size of a small cell phone. One had an amber light. The other red.

The woman who was being held told what the devices did.

The one with the amber light tracked one of the packages, the one The Four Horsemen had. That amber light meant that it was within range, could be pinpointed, given time.

The one with the red light tracked the other package. The one that Scamz and his organization had was out of range. Wasn't inside Argentina. Not yet.

The drowning man said the same.

The Beast made sure the booties were secure over his shoes, then stood up.

Medianoche did the same, went to the drowning man.

The man to whom he had made no promises.

The Beast went to the woman who had been tormented by electricity.

A broken woman to whom he had made no promises.

Medianoche pulled out his gun. The Beast did the same.

Four gunshots. Two more than necessary.

Then Medianoche followed The Beast down the concrete stairs. Dead bodies all over. No big deal. Lots of squatters in the area. Paseo Colón and Brasil streets had three-story buildings occupied by at least three hundred squatters. Violent evictions where squatters battled with the federal police and the border guard. There had been enough drug raids where the police had seized *paco* cocaine, the low-cost paste cocaine consumed by the low-income sectors. Or the ephedrine trafficking network, this might be seen as an extension of their killing spree. This bloodbath would get added to some list at some point.

The Beast looked around. "Is one of the bodies missing?"

Medianoche looked. "You think one of them got up and walked out of here?"

"There was a body there. On the stairs. I stepped over the body."

"Knowing Señorita Raven, she kicked it off the landing just to watch it fall."

Medianoche stood next to The Beast.

The Beast was fixed on that spot where he said a body had been.

Something wasn't adding up.

He didn't have to be Edmund Hlawka to see the numbers weren't adding up.

Medianoche said, "Rodríguez said they had taken out five hostiles. And four were left."

"Two were still breathing when we got here."

They walked, counted the dead.

Five and four. Nine. Only eight bodies.

Medianoche pulled out his gun, on full alert.

The Beast had already done the same.

Medianoche pointed. "Blood trail. Hard to see in this darkness."

"No footprints in the blood. We came that way. One of us would've stepped in the trail."

"They had to have moved after we came."

"When all of us were up top, one of the dead got up and walked away."

Medianoche asked, "You see the directional pattern of the blood, right?"

"Elongated. Tail the opposite direction from where we were."

"The pattern of escape."

The Beast said, "Drops are close. Some overlapping drops."

"Somebody staggered out of here. Wounded and barely able to walk."

"If one of them made it out of here, they won't make it far."

"A dying kid staggering out of here, not the ideal situation."

The Beast nodded, then walked to the others. He put bullets in the remaining bodies. Each shot a kill shot. His frown showing his displeasure.

Medianoche followed The Beast and did the same, each shot a kill shot.

Medianoche said, "If Señorita Raven wasn't so busy yakking about the goddamn Internet and Facebook . . . She's a distraction. This proves my point. She no doubt distracted Rodríguez."

"If you want something done right . . ."

"Could pop her, strip her down, leave her body with this crew. You could drive your car and I'd take her motorcycle. We could be done with her and gone in two minutes or less."

The Beast paused, thinking. He shook his head. "Now is not the time."

"She's 51-50."

"She's good at what she does."

"With 10-56A tendencies."

"She's good."

"Good but not irreplaceable."

The Beast put his gun away, pulled out the devices.

One blinked amber. Something was close. Medianoche knew that was the part of the package they had. One blinked red. Something was out of range. The second part.

The Beast said, "We need her to decipher whatever is on those computers."

"Unfortunately, Rodríguez is not as computer savvy."

The Beast marched on, headed out of the building.

Medianoche stayed behind.

He reloaded his weapon, double-checked the area, tried to track the blood trail. He ended up at a door that led out toward the colorful buildings in Caminito, those buildings just beyond the corner café, the last safe tourist spot in the area. But there were side streets that led deeper into the barrio. Deeper into the heart of La Boca, where living was substandard and reminded him of Jamaica, downtown Kingston, another war zone populated by the poor and undereducated.

He took a breath, the inside of the warehouse reeking like piss.

He stared toward Caminito, in the direction of the busloads of naïve tourists.

No police. No sirens.

No one screaming they had seen a bloodied, half-dead kid staggering their way.

Someone had risen from the dead. Like he had done in North Carolina.

Medianoche turned around. The dead remained limp and scattered at his feet.

He counted the bodies in the piss-smelling, charred room. The number hadn't changed.

This was their mausoleum, their Cementerio de la Boca.

Medianoche put away his weapon, walked to the smutty wall.

And with his gloved finger he scribbled three words: *Requiescant in pace.*

Chapter 17

shadow of doubt

Puerto Rico.

A red Ferrari 612 Scaglietti was about to pull out of the darkened parking lot at Rumba Bar. A three-hundred-thousand-dollar chick magnet that could do zero to sixty in a little over four seconds.

Two black motorcycles slowed down.

Hawks was on one. I was on the other. Both of us were out riding on a balmy night. We paused and checked out the swank ride. Hawks nodded. I did the same. She was a car person, loved fancy cars that cost more than a house. I sped up, kept going for about thirty yards, paused at the next intersection. Hawks revved her engine, pulled into the parking lot, and stopped next to the Ferrari. She wore a black helmet, matching jacket. Tight jeans and biker boots that had high heels. She gave the driver of the Ferrari a hearty thumbs-up.

The driver in the Ferrari smiled at her. She motioned for him to roll down his window.

She flipped up her face mask and asked, "*Qué tal?*"

"*Nada. Como está?*"

"*Bien. Todo bien.* Do you speak English?"

"Yeah. I speak English."

"Cool. Because my Spanish is horrible. That is one beautiful car. *Que lindo coche.*"

"*Que culo lindo que tienes. Me preguntaba si me podías montar como a esa moto.*"

"Whoa, slow your roll. I have no idea what you just said."

"I said you are one beautiful woman, from what I can see."

She motioned toward the club. "How is the music in there?"

"Great. Latin band playing salsa."

"Yeah?"

"You look good on that crotch rocket. Your ass up in the air like that."

She paused, tilted her head, pointed at him. "You look familiar."

She asked him his name. He told her. She asked if he was a hockey player.

He said he was.

She told him she was a big fan, asked if she could have his autograph.

The hockey man told her it was a hot night, said she should take her leather jacket and helmet off so he could see if her face was as pretty as the parts of her he could see.

She asked him for his autograph again.

He asked her if she had ever fucked a hockey player.

She laughed and asked him if it was the liquor or if he was always that rude to women.

He asked her, again, if she had ever fucked a hockey player.

She pulled a small circular object out of her jacket. It was a throwback to the old days. When people used to conceal guns. The hockey player probably thought he was looking at a circular cell phone. Or a compact for a woman's makeup. It was a palm pistol from the 1800s, made in France. An assassin's pistol. Made to be hidden in plain sight.

She raised the circular pistol and put a bullet between his eyes.

Then she put the assassin's pistol back inside her pocket.

The pop from that palm-sized gun had been covered by the music in the air.

Face shield up, Hawks eased out of the lot, zoomed by me, not breaking the speed limit.

Hawks said, "He was an asshole."

"I heard."

"That fucker won't be abusing any more women."

"Slow down."

"These earpieces are clear. Sounds like you're inside my helmet."

I followed Hawks, caught up with her, then we coasted side by side.

Before we had made this run, the satellite phone from Scamz had rung a dozen times.

They had an emergency in South America. Their emergency wasn't my problem.

Two hours later.

We walked out of El Centro Médico de Rio Piedras less than two minutes after we had slipped inside. We hopped on the CBRs we'd parked near the emergency room, sped away.

We'd left four bodyguards and one Colombian drug lord in need of burial.

We dumped Hawks's motorcycle a few blocks away. Hawks parked it and climbed on my CBR, the heat between her legs warming my back as we took to the darkened streets. We dumped my motorcycle a few blocks away from the resort, left it on a side street by Starbucks, made our way back to the La Concha Resort. We showered, changed, and headed back downstairs to a lobby that looked like the W on steroids; colorful lights, open space decorated with white leather and rattan furniture, customers crowded at a circular bar, international men in linen and women in minimalist dresses. A salsa band played. Everyone danced. We'd squeezed in some shopping earlier. We were in an area that was the cousin to Rodeo Drive. I dressed the way *he* dressed. Dressed like Scamz. Expensive suit and Italian shoes.

I'd bought a Rolex. Spent twenty thousand on a watch.

I'd bought Hawks a few gold bracelets and a minidress. The dress had one sleeve that was wide and had hints of retro to the design, the other side of the dress was sleeveless. The dress fit like a coat of paint, showed how slim her waist was, and gave the kind of cleavage that made a man dream of being breast-fed three times a day. The dress hugged the curve of her taut ass and showed miles of legs to die for. Her thighs were powerful without losing her femininity. Her calves were perfect. She was two yards of fabric from being naked. That dress showed what Hawks kept hidden in jeans and T-shirts. I'd taken her out of her cowboy boots and turned her into a fashionista. To go with her dress was a new pair of high heels, swank heels that were twelve centimeters high and had the signature red sole. It took her an hour to do her hair. She wanted it down, and she wanted it curled like she was going to the Oscars.

When she was done, I was in awe.

Hawks looked like she was ready for the cover of *Vogue*.

I looked at her and said, "Fuck."

She said, "Is that a noun or a verb?"

"Which do you want it to be?"

"A verb later."

As we walked out the door, the satellite phone rang. It had rung a half dozen times.

The Lebanese was on my mind, along with a cast of others. Scamz. Arizona.

Catherine and the DNA issues, X.Y.Z.

But Hawks was sexy enough to make me forget my name.

After three drinks and a handful of salsa dances and enough soft kisses to make my blood flow in a dangerous direction, Hawks was ready to strip down to her birthday suit. But I wouldn't let her go. We sat outside by the pool. They had a sexy lounge area, little cabanas not too far away from the throbbing music and the crowd in tight dresses and linen suits.

It looked like it was mating season in Puerto Rico.

We shared slow kisses. The dance of spirited tongues. Tongue chasing tongue. Then slow tasting. Tasting was more intimate than anything else. Slow kisses caused a fire to grow. And spread. Moans that started off soft became desperate. Gradual loss of control. The heat that gripped us in its sweet claws. Then the moans came from a place deep inside.

We were normal. With every ragged breath we became more normal.

Not killers. Each kiss pulled us away from that gritty world. Made us squares. Made us red-hot lovers. Teenagers on prom night. Made me want all the normal things I'd never have.

I kissed Hawks and felt her up. Sucked on her ear. Rubbed between her legs.

She moaned and laughed a sweet laugh. "Oh, my God, Gideon."

"What's the problem, Hawks?"

"You're getting me so hot."

I kissed her, then sucked her neck and rubbed her breasts. The sounds of the party were in the air. Other couples were in poolside cabanas and sitting on recliners.

Her hand went inside my linen pants. Hawks scooted down, took me inside her mouth, suckled me. I ran my fingers though her hair. Let her have her way. Closed my eyes and breathed in the salty ocean. The sounds of the waves crashing into the shore.

Every problem vanished.

When Hawks was done, I pulled her to me, kissed her again.

Hawks led me back to the suite, lights dimmed, windows open to the ocean, made me sit in the white leather chair while she danced like a señorita and sashayed toward me, sexy and classy, playful and giggling, taking off her jewelry, undressing and moving her body with the same confidence and rhythm Charlize Theron had in that J'adore Dior commercial.

Hawks leaned in, rubbed her breasts against my face, made my tongue chase her nipples. She did that over and over until I grabbed her waist and pulled her to me.

The satellite phone rang again.

Hawks paused, but I told her to not stop. I was more concerned with the other phone.

Hawks took to her knees, laughed and smiled and made naughty and playful noises as she took me inside her mouth. Then she made me feel so good I had to close my eyes.

She said, "My face is going to hurt tomorrow."

I touched her hair. "Why?"

"Blow jobs make a face hurt."

"Didn't know that."

"Glad you didn't. Really glad you didn't."

"Irrumatio makes a face hurt."

"Especially when a woman is sucking on an exorbitant chunk of meat."

"Exorbitant."

"What you have exceeds the customary limits in intensity, quality, amount, and size. You are one blessed man. A nice-looking, exorbitant mesomorph with a devil of a sin stick."

"You're tipsy."

"No, I'm drunk. And I'd advise you to take advantage of this moment. You might get a chance to do some things to me that many perverts have asked to do, and all have been denied."

I put Hawks against the wall, near the window, the ocean roaring seven stories down.

That satellite phone intruded once again.

I stayed behind her, dipped to get a good angle, had her breasts flat against the wall, my thrusting deep and steady. Hawks took her right foot, wrapped it back around me, then did the same with her left. I held her up. She craned her neck, reached for my face, kissed me. We lost the connection and I turned her around. Pushed her back against the wall and she hurried me back inside her as fast she could. I went in with power. Made her gasp. I put my hands under her ass, lifted her up, and she wrapped her legs around me again.

I was on fire.

Hawks was blazing.

I pulled her knees up, put her legs on my shoulders. Hawks wrapped her arms around my neck and held on, all she could do was hold on while I bounced her up and down as hard as I could. Skin slapped against skin. It felt good. Damn good. Didn't care about a phone or two million dollars or South America or Scamz or Arizona or Catherine. I just cared about this orgasm that had a grip on me, a stubborn orgasm had put its claws in me, had filled me with fire.

I moved Hawks into different positions, pleased her from different angles, desperate angles, skin slapping hard, each time like a brand-new massage.

She held my neck tight and buried her head in my shoulder, sucked my neck, bit my neck to muffle her moans. Hawks lost her breath and took what I gave, then exhaled hard and loud, made sounds like she was in pain. I moaned and carried her like that. Walked her to the bed. Put her down. The ball of fire inside me had taken control. It led me, made me wild, dragged me toward urgency, moved me hard and fast. Hawks's nails sank into my back.

The satellite phone rang.

I picked Hawks up, flipped her upside down, put her legs around my neck, held her by her waist, brought her dampness to my tongue, gripped her while her moans rose and her hair dropped and covered my toes. One by one, her high heels dropped from her feet. She masturbated me, took me deep inside her mouth, did that while I put my tongue inside her as deep as I could.

The satellite phone rang again.

And rang.

And rang.

Chapter 18

fear and anger

I stood in the window. The roar of the Atlantic matched my restlessness.

I was naked except for the Rolex. Beautiful woman in my bed. Expensive watch on my arm. Standing in the lap of luxury. Wondered if this was what it felt like to be Scamz.

The satellite phone rang a dozen more times. I had wrapped the sat phone inside a pillow and stuck it inside the hotel safe. Was tempted to throw it out the window, send it to the ocean. I took a deep breath. Hawks's sweat, perfume, and sex had dried on my flesh.

The shell-shaped roof of the La Perla restaurant was seven floors down. I spied like a sentinel, in my right hand the phone the Lebanese had delivered. My left palm was on the windowpane as I grimaced out at the Atlantic. A tsunami raged inside me as the Atlantic Ocean crashed into the dirty sand, whitecaps abusing the shore like repetitive thoughts.

A different phone. A different threat. Two-million-dollar blackmail.

Someone had me in another game of chess. I knew how to play chess. Pawns moved forward. Bishops moved diagonal, forward, and backward. Knights moved in an L-shape. The King moved one space at a time. The Queen moved any direction she wanted.

I couldn't move because I didn't know what piece I had, but I knew I was up against a metaphorical Queen. I guess that made me the King on this chessboard. The Queen had power, and when the King is captured, the game is over.

Somebody else had to die. Somebody had to be on the bad end of my fury.

I was tired of being fucked with. It had left me exhausted beyond repair.

I heard a noise and grabbed a gun in a motion so fast the world became a blur, aimed the loaded gun at the heart of the sound. It was Hawks. She was in the bed. She had fallen asleep with her high heels on. Her shoe had dropped off her foot and landed with a soft thud.

I put the Kimber back down, swallowed that anxiety.

Two hits. Three glasses of wine. Dancing for two hours. Sex like warrior gods.

Hawks should be unconscious until the other side of sunrise. Might sleep until noon.

There was a faint hum from inside the safe. The satellite phone wouldn't leave me alone.

I was temporarily free from my current obligation. But many others enslaved me.

I turned the radio up a touch. Romantic Spanish songs drowned out the buzz.

I needed time to myself. I needed to be alone so I could think.

I took out my iPhone, went into Safari and logged into GOTOMYPC .COM, entered an IP address of a computer inside a home in Powder Springs, Georgia. After I took control of that computer, I was able to tap into the surveillance system. I saw Alvin White was parked two houses away. He was dependable. Any time of day or night, he had my back.

My headache eased up a little. Not much. Just a little. I wondered if the house had been spied on before my enemy had made contact in Florida. If they had, I'd be able to tell.

I inspected three days' worth of footage on fast-forward, saw Catherine and the boys moving around the house. Steven was studying, then playing Wii Fit with Robert while Catherine read a novel. Nothing stood out. Cameras outside the house showed anyone who came toward the cul-de-sac, cameras in the back showed anybody who came to the back and sides of the house. Motion sensors were around the house, but none had been triggered at night. That meant no one was trying to sneak up to the house.

I went to the camera inside the kitchen. The FedEx box was still on the counter.

I went to the camera outside the house and found footage of a black car cruising the cul-de-sac, slowing in front of the house. Houses were on half-acre lots. There wasn't any reason for a car to stop in front of that house, not even if they were going across the street. It was a five-year-old Benz. Series 320. Soft-top. A man got out. Average height and build. He checked his watch. Walked the sidewalk. There wasn't any reason for him to park in that cul-de-sac and look around. He peeped at the house.

My heart raced.

Inside the house, on another camera, I spied on Catherine. She checked on the boys before she walked down the hallway, then down the stairs. She went toward the front door. Part of me wanted to scream for her to get the boys and get down into the basement. But what I was looking at had already happened.

Catherine was at the front door; the strange man who had been standing by the car went to the porch. Catherine hurried down the hallway. I thought she was about to call the police. She stopped at the alarm panel. Hit buttons and deactivated the alarm. Went to the front door and let him inside. He stood by the front door while she went back to the panel. She turned the alarm back on. Then she went to the man she had let inside, led him toward the living room. The lights were dim. It was hard to see his face. She poured him a drink. Used a wineglass. Poured herself the same. They were talking. Smiling and laughing. Then kissing. Catherine was in his arms, being felt up like a teenaged girl on prom night.

Childhood memories flashed. Red-light district memories.

She unzipped the man's pants. Her smile was clear as her face moved into his lap.

Memories thundered inside my head. I'd seen her do that many times. As a child. When she worked in piss-smelling brothels. Had seen her do the same to many men. Italian men. French men. Canadian men. Had seen her do things with women. Had seen things no child should ever see. I watched her with a maddening disdain. Memories were unearthed. Nothing had changed. I lowered the iPhone, headache rising again, a silent scream thickening every vein in my body. I raised the phone and what I saw, it felt like the sun was inside my head, burning my brain. I fast-forwarded. Almost two hours later, he tiptoed out of the bedroom. He was alone. The man eased out into the hallway like a criminal after a crime. The way I'd left many scenes.

My heart thumped.

Catherine came out of her bedroom. Barefoot. Now she had on a satin housecoat that hit the top of her thighs, opened enough to show she was naked underneath. Her hair was pulled back, no longer perfect like it had been two hours ago, that time based on the digital readout. More smiles. Short conversation. Then she went to the panel, turned off the alarm, kissed him again at the door.

I looked for the exchange of money; there was none, not out in the open.

Whoever that motherfucker was, he kept his head down, hurried to his Mercedes, and drove away. He had left the way men exited brothels. Head down. In a rush. Not wanting to be seen. If that had been a setup, a sting operation, she'd be taken away to the Powder Spring jail while the boys were taken by social services. They would end up in foster care.

I saw her soft reflection in the patio's window, saw her behind me.

Hawks was awake, watching me like the bird from which she had taken her name.

She sat up. Her dramatic mane fell, covered her breasts and thighs. She rested on white sheets, moonlight lighting up the contemporary room, an erotic painting come to life.

She yawned. "Everything okay?"

"Was checking on Catherine and the boys again. Just the cameras."

"They're okay?"

"I think so. So far."

"Was hoping that blow job put you to sleep. That was my best to date. I should be patting myself on my back. You should be in fetal position sucking your thumb."

"I'm tired. But I'm wide-awake. Thoughts are like caffeine."

"I'm going to keep having sex to keep your mind here. I will do whatever it takes. You're all mine in Puerto Rico. Now, if you want to talk to me about what's bothering you, want to figure out how to fix it, I'm here for that too. I don't care if it has to do with Catherine and the DNA. Or with the fuckers who are trying to milk you. Or if it has to do with South America. But whatever it is, you need to make me a part of it."

"Okay, Hawks. You're right. We had this planned, then the unexpected happened."

I turned the iPhone off. Put it next to the Motorola. Problems lined up like tin men.

Hawks reached for her fallen high heel, slipped it back on her foot, slid her other foot from underneath the white sheets, showed me both of her shoes, shoes she had worn while we had sex, a French number, open-toe stilettos with a rhinestone brooch as an accent piece.

She stuffed a white pillow between her long legs, her hips moving against that softness.

Her eyes were wide open. A fire was burning. Restlessness was in her eyes.

Hawks extended her hand, palm up, her finger making a slow come-here motion. I went to her. She moved the pillow, pulled the covers back. Hawks opened her legs. I eased down on top of her. Licked her nipples. Her nipples were lovely. Hard. Round. Thick. I touched between her legs, felt how wet she was, slipped inside her, made her moan.

I stroked her in slow motion. Made it build. Then slow strokes became deep and intense. Hawks turned me over, took my erection in her hand, put it between her breasts, put her hands on her breasts, moved up and down, moaned while I moaned, then guided it inside her mouth, sucked me in slow motion, stroked me in slow motion, sucked me harder, drove me crazy.

It felt good. But it disturbed me.

I'd just witnessed Catherine on surveillance doing the same.

And the undesired memories of our wretched relationship became too strong.

I was a young man again, a teenager, Catherine's mouth between my legs.

I held Hawk's head, wanted her to stop, at least until the horrific images went away.

Again a noise made me want to reach for the Kimber. It was an abrupt ringing. The phone the Lebanese had left behind had come to life. Another enemy was calling.

Someone else was trying to enslave me. I didn't like being a fucking slave. To my emotions or to any man, I didn't like being a fucking slave.

Hawks groaned, frowned, stopped pleasing me, and whispered, "It's them."

I nodded. "It's them. Whoever tracked me to Starbucks in Florida."

"Those jerks have bad timing. Real bad timing."

"Hawks. Need to get that."

She took a frustrated breath, staggered to the desk, and handed me the phone.

She said, "Can you trace the call?"

I said, "Will know in a few minutes."

"I'll handle that if you want. Get me a name and an address. Will take off these high heels, put on my cowboy boots, get on the next plane, and fix that for you."

Then I'd owe Hawks again. That was my thought. I'd remain indebted.

I answered but didn't say anything.

"Gideon." The same electronic voice. "Long time, no talk to."

I said, "Cut to the chase."

"Okay, let's get to the endgame. Three days. You will have three days to transfer the money."

"Where is this money being transferred?"

"You'll be contacted."

"You haven't shown me anything worth buying."

"Fair enough. I will transfer you a sample of what I have."

"You could've done that hours ago."

"First thing tomorrow. In the meantime, start preparing the money transfer."

They hung up.

Hawks asked, "That was them?"

I nodded. Then pulled her back. Had Hawks straddle me. Wanted to finish what we had started. Two seconds later, my iPhone rang. Hawks cursed again, then leaned over and handed it to me. She didn't get off me that time. She put her face in my neck and moved up and down.

I checked the caller ID. It was Arizona.

Hawks rolled against me, made me moan, made me hesitate, then I answered.

Arizona said, "They were in Memphis."

"Not Atlanta."

"Memphis."

"You sure? Want to make sure they're not heading toward my family."

"Not in the ATL area."

"Could they be bouncing their signal?"

"Doesn't look that way."

"Is that a yes or a no?"

"They are in Memphis."

Whatever magic Arizona had done with the SIM card had enabled her to piggyback the phone I had. When this phone rang, she was alerted, and she heard every word that was exchanged.

I swallowed before I asked, "You don't have an exact location?"

"Not exact. Triangulating off cell towers."

Hawks moved, her breathing staccato, rocked like she was about to come again.

I asked Arizona, "You know where they are, don't you?"

"They could be bouncing the signal off a few satellites."

"You know where and who, but you know if you tell me, I'll head in that direction."

"The IDs you gave me for Nicolas Jacoby, both were fakes. Great work, and both were fakes. Not a Nicolas Jacoby with those ID numbers in Florida or Denver. Whoever you're after, you had a link to him or her or them in your hands at Starbucks, and they walked away."

"What about the Lebanese?"

"I picked up information on over two hundred credit cards, lifted data from forty laptops, just as many BlackBerrys and cell phones. Add in the information snatched from the computers from the cars in the parking lot. I'll need a little more time."

"More time. This is simple shit for you. Have your database sort the data, female names, age between eighteen and thirty. That's simple shit. Why is it taking so long?"

"Give to get. You scratch my itch, then I scratch yours. You raise me on your list of priorities and I'll reciprocate. Don't blow me off and expect me to break my neck helping you."

Hawks held me, bit her bottom lip, and tried to swallow her rising moans.

Arizona said, "Are you okay?"

Hawks's moan slid inside one ear while Arizona's voice penetrated the other.

I said, "I need that problem off my plate. I need that problem off my mind."

"My team has been calling you for hours. Guess you only answer when it benefits you."

"Where is Scamz?"

"Buenos Aires. He had a satellite operation in La Boca. Lost communication."

"So you're telling me that you're positive the package is still in Buenos Aires."

"He's called you. Over and over he's called you."

"Well, you have me on the line now. What was the emergency?"

"Is the satellite phone not working?"

"It's working. But I'm not. That phone is not my electronic leash."

"One day. Can you give us one more day?"

"My schedule hasn't changed."

"The Four Horsemen. We have a serious problem. Be ready to make your flight."

"My schedule won't change."

Arizona said, "The sooner you can leave, the better. This is a major event. The package has been in one spot longer than anticipated. Other parties are interested and are organizing. I just got word that a group of assassins that call themselves The Seven Jamaicans are—"

"This Nicolas Jacoby thing. The Lebanese he was talking to. Detroit. I need that resolved. That's a major thing on this side of the table. Like you said, give to get."

"I need this South American issue taken care of. I need this taken care of now. Each second that it is delayed will make it more complicated. Too many parties are interested. Only God knows who else we will have to deal with in another day. Please. I need you now."

"You said I've never said no to you."

"You haven't."

I wrestled with Hawks and her fire. "After my next obligation."

She paused. "What can I do to get some consideration?"

"What are you saying?"

"My words were clear."

"He put you up to that?"

"No one owns me. You know that."

"Nothing. There is nothing you can do. My agreement is cast in stone."

"Okay. Understood."

"I need that Nicolas Jacoby information. I need that location in Memphis."

"Expect the same consideration. Expect the goddamn same. Expect *after*."

She said unkind things in Tagalog.

I said some unkind things to her in French.

Two seconds later, I hung up the phone.

Arizona's end had disconnected a second before.

Hawks stopped moving. "Everything okay?"

I held Hawks down on the bed, Arizona's voice meandering inside my head as I filled Hawks's vagina up with my frustration. Had to give to get, and I gave Hawks more then she wanted to handle, gave her enough to make her stop asking questions, stroked her hard and fast, did that until she came. And when she came I didn't stop. Kept going until Hawks pushed me away.

But I wasn't going away. I wasn't going to be pushed away.

I held her, made Hawks my prisoner.

An arrogant con woman had told me that I didn't know how to make love, said I knew how to fuck, and the better a man fucked, the more a woman would be convinced he was making love to her. The same went for a woman fucking a man. I'd learned that from Arizona.

I slipped out and Hawks moaned, rushed me back inside, held my ass and pulled me deep. Her breathing was thick, as hot as it was between her legs. Her fingernails went into my skin, marked me. I went deeper. The heat set fire to my angst-filled thoughts.

We moved together, moved until everything became urgent, labored, breath thickened as sweat rose. I jerked and groaned, fought with the fire, a battle I was losing one pant at a time. Hawks pushed me, had me sit back, rest on my elbows while she hurried on top of me, moving in her own urgent and labored rhythm. She moved like she was no longer in charge of her body, as if that fire inside her was pulling her. Hawks moved her hair away, caught her breath, then turned around until she was riding reverse cowgirl, moved that way awhile, then turned again, faced me, moved her ass up and down and smiled at my need to come.

We changed positions again, me on top, my weight between her open legs.

Hawks closed her eyes, made ugly faces as I made ugly faces and looked down on her.

Hawks pulled sheets, grabbed the covers, moved her taut ass with the frustration I gave her. My energy went deep. Her hips rose and met my thrusts until I went inside her hard, made her scoot away, went inside her hard again, made her scoot until she slipped off the bed headfirst. She fell and I grabbed her, held her as I kept stroking her, let her head slide until it touched the floor. I readjusted, gripped her thighs, stood up over her, had her upside down, our legs crisscrossed like open scissors, gripped her waist and leg, pulled her up into me over and over, stroked her as her hands found the floor, stroked her as she moaned and pushed back into me, stroked as she talked to God and turned around, moved into her as she cursed.

Once again, Hawks's pretty shoes fell off her feet one at a time.

"Gideon . . . damn . . . what has gotten into . . . into . . . damn . . ."

Her hands walked up the wall, her back to me, breathing hard as her hands made it up as high as my waist. Hawks held the wall with her back arched, her head back, hair trapped in sweat as she moaned and panted. She used the wall as leverage. My strokes were a sweet repetition that lasted until Hawks couldn't hold her weight up any longer.

I pounded her with aggravation as her hands walked back down the wall to the carpet.

I followed her, grabbed pillows from the bed and shoved them under her knees.

Her hands reached for the bed and she pulled her upper body across the mattress.

I was still behind her, went wherever she went. Her knees were on the pillows, upper body across the mattress. I grabbed a handful of her long hair, pulled it hard as I took her from behind, between the bed and the wall, used that wall as leverage, my heels pressed against the drywall as I went inside her, invaded her wetness with power, anger, a steady intensity.

Teeth clenched, I fucked her like I was trying to fuck a baby into her womb.

Chapter 19

End of the World

I took Hawks away from San Juan. We left the trendy part of Puerto Rico and went to Hacienda Juanita. Mile marker 23.5 in Maricao. Not a mega hotel, but a local *parador*, a family-owned hotel that had less than two dozen rooms. I showed Hawks the real Puerto Rico. No high-rises. No stores that brought to mind Beverly Hills or Champs-Élysées. No signs announcing that the rest of the world was entering a great recession.

She thought I had taken her back in time.

I asked Hawks, "Where are you working after Puerto Rico?"

"England. Someplace called Islington."

"Nice part of the UK."

"Another one at Lake Chargoggagoggmanchauggagoggchaubunagungamaug. That's up north in the States. Had to be drunk to name a damn lake something no one can pronounce."

"How many points is that word worth in Scrabble?"

"Probably two thousand. Chargoggagoggmanchauggagoggchaubunagungamaug."

Kimbers in our gear, we hiked over trails, ate ripe bananas that we picked from banana trees, walked through coffee plants, stood in a part of the island that had green mountains and beaches with golden sand. We ate at shacks that looked like they should fall under a good breeze, then we went back to the Olas y Arenas and had a beer and plantains.

Hawks said, "Something I want to ask. The thing that has my thoughts like caffeine."

"Okay." I'd felt this moment coming since last night. "Ask whatever you need to ask."

"And I'm trying to ask you as a friend, as a coworker, not as a . . . whiny woman."

"Okay. Friend and coworker, what's on your mind?"

A long moment went by before Hawks asked, "Is she special in some way?"

"Who?"

"The mysterious woman you're working for."

I paused. "She's not special."

"The tone of the conversation . . . the argument about you going to South America." Hawks paused. "Are you sleeping with her? Or have you been intimate with her?"

"I have. Hadn't heard from her in over a year. She's pregnant."

"Pregnant."

"Not mine."

"Wasn't going to ask, but okay."

"And the job is for her and the guy she's with now. They might be married. Not sure."

"He used her to pull you in."

"Nothing slips past Hawks."

"What is her name? Or are you not allowed to say?"

"Arizona."

Hawks asked, "Did you buy her shoes?"

"That a professional question?"

"I'm asking you as a woman. Tried to turn that switch off. Hard to do that with you."

"Nope. No shoes. Bought her some jazz CDs once, but she gave those back."

"Ever bring her down here to Puerto Rico?"

"Never took her anywhere."

"Never?"

"Never. Only slept with her twice. Both times were after jobs I had done for her."

"Guess that was a helluva way for her to throw you a tip."

"Hawks."

"I know. Very childish remark. Petty. But it was in my mind, so I let it roll down over my tongue. Just asking. I was a late bloomer in that department. Haven't been with many men, but I have been with the same men many times. Feels like I'm on the wrong side of the curve."

"You're great. All that matters is that you're great at everything you do."

"I do my best. Hard keeping up with a man like you. You're making me up my game big-time. You're very creative. And uninhibited. You are one nasty man. Like a damn porn star."

"Well, I grew up in whorehouses all over the world. Lost my virginity in a whorehouse."

"We really don't have to talk about that."

"You know my past."

"So South America is for her and her partner."

"All business between me and her. All business."

She whispered, "I don't care about her. A woman is just a woman. I have no illusions when it comes to you and me. I like you, I care about you, but I know who you are. I know what you are, so far as the type of man you are. But on a side note, for your information, there might be a lot of women out there, but none are better than me. I can pick up a 40-cal Beretta with hollow points, run it dry while being shot at, and reload without missing a beat."

"I know you can."

"Don't forget that you've seen me in action more than once."

"Sure have."

"The shit we did here, that was child's play, Hitman 101. I can rock an AK-47, M16, combat shotgun, 50 cal, M9, LAW rocket, and a few others that I don't need to mention. I can pop an Altoid and give a no-hands blow job that will make you cry for your momma and I can keep up with you in bed. What you give, I give it back. Sex with you is fun. You get nasty. I take that nasty and take it to a higher level. I'll never let you outdo me. I'm like that. And I make the best sweet potato pie this side of the Appalachians. Another woman means nothing to me.

You want her, get her and life goes on. There's always somebody next, if not somebody new."

"Hawks."

"What?"

"You can make sweet potato pie?"

"A damn good one."

"You've been holding out."

"A woman can't give a man everything at once."

"Guess not."

"My concern is the tone of the conversation. It was emotional. Tried not to listen, but I heard her. Your conversation, in my opinion, considering how long I've been in this business and know how it rolls, was unprofessional. My concern is simple and professional. I don't want you to slip. Doing a job for somebody and you have some sort of an emotional attachment, not a good thing."

"You're right. I can lose perspective."

"All that to say, if you need anything, let me know. I'm in the same business. I'm your coworker. We work well together. Always have. And there are excellent fringe benefits."

I reached for her hand, expected her to pull away. She didn't.

She gave me a sideways smile. "You sure it's not your baby she's carrying?"

"If it is, it would be the longest human gestation period in history."

Hawks relaxed against me.

We'd been here a few hours and had already left a trail of blood across the Commonwealth of Puerto Rico, the island some of the locals call Borinquen.

Warmth ran through my body. Warmth that told me I was still alive.

Thoughts dragged me across barbed wire, noosed me back to Fin del Mundo.

I said, "Hawks."

"Yeah."

"End of the World."

"What about the end of the world?"

"It's at the bottom of South America. Where the Atlantic and Pacific meet."

"This has something to do with Arizona?"

"Not directly." I took a moment. "She used to see this man. That was how I met her. Worked for him. Guy named Scamz. I had gone to this part of Argentina that used to be a prison town, Argentina's Guantanamo Bay until Perón shut it down. Was on a job for Scamz. The first man I knew to wear that name."

"The first man. So there have been others?"

"He has a son. His son has taken up his name."

"So the first Scamz guy, you and him were . . . cool."

"Never liked him. Worked for him because of the money. My greed got the best of me."

"Confusing, but okay."

"He had issued death warrants on two Ecuadorians. International con men. Ruthless men. Latin killers. A father and a son. Men in the same business he was in. The business of swindling. Men who had fled to the end of South America. To Ushuaia."

"Where is that?"

"World's most southern city."

"Uh-huh."

"I'd followed them for ten days. Ten long days and nights. Watched through binoculars as they walked past Moustacchio, waited patiently and planned as they ate at Chez Manu. It was in July. Wintertime."

"In July?"

"Seasons are reversed on the other side of the equator. If the sun came out, it was out for no more than four hours a day. Was cold at night, but not intolerable. Windy and rainy."

"Okay."

"Thought they were about to cross the border and slip into Chile, would've lost them if they had, but I found out they were about to flee the country for China. Took out their guards and got to them before they boarded Orient Cruise Lines, a plastic surgeon waiting for them at the end of that journey. It was beautiful down there. I had kidnapped my contracts and put them on a boat, taken them farther south, where there was nothing but ice and snow."

"Icebergs have always fascinated me. Always wanted to go to Alaska and see one."

"Yeah. They are some of the most beautiful things on the planet. And the deadliest."

"So you had caught the targets down at the bottom of South America."

"Yeah. I had done like I had been ordered, stripped the men of all ID and dumped both in the inhospitable, subpolar oceanic climate."

"That's nasty. And mean."

"My client was a revanchist."

"About territory and status."

"Yeah."

"I know quite a few ten-dollar words. We should play Scrabble."

"We can do that."

"So the targets."

"They were seasoned grifters my client had wanted to die in one of the most horrible ways he could imagine. He wanted them to freeze to death."

"There are horrible ways to die, and that is way up on the list. Slow-motion death."

"Yeah."

"You do it?"

"I had dumped them naked, left them beaten and weak, was going to let Mother Nature be the one to deliver the final blow."

"That's as horrible as hanging a man from a cross and watching him die."

"I know."

"You couldn't do it, could you?"

"Tried. But part of me, despite what I did, wasn't into watching men suffer."

"That's not your style."

"I was still new to the business back then. Was doing my best to make a living. Doing my best to impress. Doing my best to be good at something. I had killed before, but tracking two men, outsmarting their Brazilian and Peruvian hired guns, that was the one job that made me feel like a professional. Like I was a secret agent. That part of the job had given me a rush."

"What did you do?"

"I took out my gun. Gave those ruthless men mercy one bullet at a time."

"Damn."

"Took out the father first."

"That's the way life was supposed to be. A father should die before the son."

"Then I killed the son. I can still see the whiteness and ice reflecting sunlight while red seas of blood froze around their bodies. That stuck with me for a long time. Fucked me up."

"Damn."

"Yeah. Took it a while to go away. Then I chose not to think about it at all."

"We all do a job or two that messes us up."

"That we do." I took a breath. "The older man I put down, that was Scamz's father."

"Your client's father?"

"Scamz's sixty-year-old father. The man who made him a con. And one of Scamz's brothers."

"A father and a son. Scamz had you put down his daddy and a sibling."

"Yeah."

She paused. "They have no character. You're working for people who have no character. They are bottom-feeders. Don't go back to South America. Not for people like that."

"I don't have a choice."

"There is always a choice."

"I have a debt I have to pay. This job is about a debt I have to pay."

"Money debt? Like the mafia debt?"

"That bottom-feeder saved my life once. He did. That conniving fuck came out of the shadows and rescued me. Hard for me to admit it, but he did. Won't get into it, but he did. I want that off my plate more than anything. South America is what he needs in return. The idea that someone I . . . that he is responsible for saving me . . . part of me would rather . . . still be dead."

"Well, for what it's worth, I don't want you dead. You're too much fun."

"Maybe I should get it over with."

"What does that mean?"

"Maybe I should leave here and go to South America."

She said, "You told me you promised the boys a few things."

"I did."

"Be a man of your word. Don't be like my daddy. Make promises and not show up. Children hate to be left waiting. Just do what you promised. A man ain't a man if he can't keep his word."

"Daddy issues."

"Momma issues. Daddy issues. We all have at least one of 'em."

We went silent.

I said, "Scamz paid me to kill his father. I killed mine to save the whore that raised me."

Hawks's fingers came up and touched my lips. She had heard enough.

She said, "I could use a stiff drink right now."

"What's your poison?"

"Some top-shelf eighty-proof brown liquor."

"Yeah. Me too."

"Think they have a Scrabble board around here anywhere?"

"Doubt it."

"Should've packed mine. I have the deluxe edition."

Arizona was on her mind.

I could tell.

She said, "I bet you're a regular John Mayer. Gal pals all over."

"Not even close."

"Whatever."

Hawks was a killer, an official international assassin, but she was still a woman.

We headed back to the room.

We didn't talk about killing.

Hawks gave me what she thought I needed. I did the same for her.

But I knew she wanted more than I'd be able to give.

Still, I did the best a man could do when he had another woman on his mind.

Capítulo 20

Siete Jamaicanos

The Seven Jamaicans, a hit squad out of Kingston, arrived in Buenos Aires.

The Seven Jamaicans was a group made up of ten men. At times the number had been as many as twenty, but today there were ten. Half of them were dark-skinned, hair cut short. Men who worked in the murder, kidnapping, and drug trade. Men who dressed like executives, not stereotypes. They had flown up to Atlanta from Jamaica, then came into Ezeiza Ministro Pistarini International Airport. Flight 101 was due in at seven forty-five a.m. but arrived at six fifty.

The ten men breezed through customs, walked through the sparkling, overpriced shopping area designed to suck money out of the tourists' pockets before they made it to baggage claim, then stepped past the rental car and *remis* stands with no problem.

The leader, a man who was six foot five, reached into his pocket and took out a tracking device. His face always owned a little moue. The sensor he had been given flashed yellow. The package was within a few miles. The trip was not wasted. Half of the package that had been brought over from Uruguay remained here. The information they had obtained was good.

As the leader stood in the crowd, underneath dismal skies, a Latin man passed by him.

They never made eye contact as their hands touched, palms open.

The leader's empty hand now had two sets of keys.

Keys to two nondescript vans and a safe house in San Nicolas.

The word was that The Four Horsemen had stolen the prize for an American.

Today they would make The Four Horsemen look like The Three Stooges.

The Seven Jamaicans took their backpacks and exited the airport, walked to the parking structure across the street. Two vans loaded with powerful weapons waited for them.

They exited EZE airport, passed by Shell and YBF stations on autopista Ricchieri, and came up on the tollbooths that stood in the shadow of low-income apartments. Lines of cars queued up at a dozen booths. A van that was a few cars in front of them was taking forever to get through. A lane over, their second van was held up at the tollbooth as well.

The Seven Jamaicans opened up the containers inside their vans.

Weapons were inside. Weapons, ammunition, and hand grenades.

They had studied The Four Horsemen's techniques. They would bomb them the way they had bombed others.

The girl inside the tollbooth exited in a hurry, sprinting in her flat shoes.

All around The Seven Jamaicans, people were fleeing from their cars.

The Seven Jamaicans looked around, tried to see what had happened.

They expected to see the police.

There were no police.

None that could be seen.

No helicopters overhead.

Then.

The Jamaicans in the first van saw her first.

A woman in a black suit, long black coat, black hat, and a paisley tie smiled at them as she appeared off to their right, the side with the high-rise, low-income properties. The woman raised a semiautomatic grenade launcher. The assassins stared at the handheld rocket launcher, a launcher that could hit a target one hundred yards away. Nobody within ten yards could survive the explosion and fire. The Jamaicans looked down at the explosives in their van.

They screamed, yelled for the driver to move, to get them away.

The van rammed the vehicle in front of them. Then rammed the vehicle behind them.

Next to them, the members of The Seven Jamaicans in the second van were doing the same.

The first van had a better view of the woman, saw the grenade being launched.

The side of the van was hit. Followed by the explosion. Then there was a secondary explosion. The grenades they had inside added to the bang.

Those Jamaicans, deader than Elvis, Che, and Hendrix.

The Jamaicans in the second van screamed. Their driver rammed cars, tried to get their van free. The woman had lowered her launcher, smiled an evil smile, then pointed to her left.

The Jamaicans saw three armed men. All dressed in black. Different color ties.

The Four Horsemen.

Ten minutes after getting out of the airport, and The Four Horsemen knew.

The Horsemen opened fire on the second van with M16A2 semi-automatic rifles.

A beautiful horror at sunrise.

The Jamaicans screamed. They were trapped inside a van. Blocked in by other vehicles.

In war, vehicles were always the easy targets. Stationary vehicles were coffins.

Three of the Jamaicans escaped the second van, stumbled out, falling to the blacktop, guns in hand, shooting wildly. A second grenade was launched, hit the van, and exploded. Shock waves sent people to the ground. Innocent bystanders were peppered with shrapnel.

That bang was followed by more M16 gunfire that eliminated the three Jamaicans who had stumbled and fled out of the second van only to be knocked off their feet by the explosion.

It was like Iraq. It was like Fallujah. It was like the Falklands War.

Once again Medianoche led The Beast, Señor Rodríguez, and Señorita Raven.

Medianoche knew they could've handled this in a subtler manner.

The Italians. The Jews. The Israelis. The Russians. The French. Central Americans. They could all have trackers on this package and the other.

They could fuck with the Scamz organization, but Argentina was off limits.

They were sending a message to anyone else who thought about coming to Buenos Aires in search of the package they had. Enter at your own risk. And die with your first breath.

Chapter 21

lethal magnetism

Confitería La Rambla in Recoleta.

Blond wooden walls decorated with neon signs by Coca-Cola, Corona, Quilmes, Michelob, and Johnny Walker. Two televisions up high. Sixteen-inch tiles in shades of brown.

Medianoche was a block away from the disco techno music escaping the black-glass edifice called Club Black. Where Sodom met Gomorrah. Men in black suits waited on every corner, approached every tourist or single man without shame, offered a chance to buy overpriced drinks and lease the bodies of beautiful Spanish and Brazilian women.

Two couples left La Rambla within ten minutes of each other. One couple had been upstairs. Now the upstairs eating area was empty. Medianoche had checked. The café was small, a dozen tables downstairs, half as many upstairs.

Now five people were left inside La Rambla, not counting the young waiter.

Medianoche watched the five Italians imbibing coffee. They were gangsters, not thugs.

Gangsters were politicians and world leaders, men in suits, men with charm and grace.

James Cagney. Glenn Ford. Humphrey Bogart. Sterling Hayden. John Garfield. Robert Mitchum. Kirk Douglas. Tyrone Power. Orson Welles. Dick Powell. George Macready.

Men in suits. Crisp dark suits. Suits as dark as their .38s.

Medianoche regarded his watch, a Series 800 Movado, steel adorned with a full diamond bezel, seven sparkling diamond hour markers on a white mother-of-pearl dial.

His Beretta rested in his lap. He waited for her to appear, like she had done before.

He looked across the small café. Glanced at a table of well-dressed Italians. All Gucci and Montblanc. Every stitch of clothing tailored, their shoes handmade.

This job was about the woman at the cemetery. The client who had come to Recoleta Cemetery dressed in a dramatic fur coat and high heels that sparkled. The woman who had reminded him of Isabel Sarli. A woman who had paid cash for her vendetta, her revenge.

Just like Caprica Ortiz had done. That job still on hold.

The job for Caprica, it had weight, had meaning.

This job was a nothing job. Just a fucker who wanted another fucker dead.

A war without meaning.

He thought about Hopkins, Scamz, the package, and what the end result would be.

Soon they would have the second part of the package. No more shit jobs like this.

Medianoche looked around. A dozen tables. All empty except for one other.

When the waiter came, Medianoche ordered; *"Café con leche y tres medialunas."*

Son las dos y veinte de la mañana. Two twenty a.m.

The Italians talked, their conversation passionate, yet quiet and reserved.

"The U.S. should withdraw from most efforts to solve international problems."

"I do not trust the United States to act responsibly so far as the world is concerned."

They were a bunch of post-fascist-Berlusconi People of the Freedom conservative fucks criticizing the goddamn U.S. while in their own country the right wing had marched in. What the fascist fucks said rang out as being harsh, but they weren't in the top ten when it came to the most anti-U.S. countries. Still, it was kinder than what the U.S. said about others. And it pissed Medianoche off. Always would, no matter where he nested.

Medianoche peered into the night, saw the bitch. The diva.

She came from the direction of Callao, another main street that led to Libertador.

He saw how she let her presence be known, how she had stood across in front of the *lavandería* and allowed herself to be seen. She crossed the one-lane street and came inside the café, hands at her side. She always looked like Madhuri Shankar Dixit with shrapnel in her once-beautiful face. Thick eyebrows. Black, wavy hair slicked back on the sides, the top sticking up like a mohawk, a juvenile hairstyle that cried for attention.

She walked inside the café and the Italians stopped talking. Medianoche knew why. They saw her marked face. Saw what shrapnel had done. They thought the Indian woman could be a female suicide bomber and tensed like they were in Baghdad.

Señorita Raven unbuttoned her coat. No explosive vest. Just curves and breasts.

The men went back to their conversations.

Señorita took cautious steps, moved by Coca-Cola adverts and displays for desserts and *facturas*, nodded at the waiter, came to the back of the café where he waited, his back to the wall, underneath a Johnny Walker sign. She stopped in front of his table.

Medianoche's gun remained in his lap, business end pointed at Señorita Raven.

Señorita Raven said, "*¿Qué tal?*"

"English only."

"*¿Por qué?*"

"Because no one in the café speaks any goddamn English."

She nodded. He smelled her floral fragrance.

She wore a double strand of pearls on her left ankle. Wore shrapnel marks and war wounds like they were jewelry from Tiffany's. Good-looking. Smart enough. Professional. Sexual. Tonight, with her cleavage, suddenly sensual. Her cleavage was strong and her breasts kissed and stood high, that magic enhanced by the bra she wore.

Medianoche stared at her. Waited for her to talk. Or shoot. Her call.

She said, "You see how those Italians looked at me? Fucking Pope lovers. Following an out-of-touch old man who tells the world to not use condoms. That's why the ecologists and communists are over there in Paris throwing condoms at Notre Dame Cathedral. I hope they are throwing used condoms. Easy for a fucker who ain't fucking to tell fuckers who are fucking to stop fucking, which is fucked up. And those old fucks across the room. Did you see that racism? Imperialistic coffee-drinking fuckers looked at me like . . . geesh . . . like I was a goddamn terrorist."

"A mouth like yours."

"What about it?"

"Language." He shook his head. "Not like a lady."

"I was imitating The Beast. Fucking fuck this and fucking fuck that. When he gets mad, all he says is fuck this and fucking fuck that. Sounds like an immigrant thug. Cracks me up."

Medianoche wasn't amused. "Amaravati Panchali Ganeshes."

"Told you, I don't use that name."

"Not using it won't change who you are."

She said, "I've been all over the city today. I've seen five brown-skinned people. Light brown skin. Not many dark people. And not many people with blond hair, for that matter. Only a handful. But definitely not many darkies. Which was why it was so easy to find the Jamaicans at EZE. They definitely stood out."

He said nothing. Her conversation made no sense. He wasn't into riddles. Talking to a woman was like being in a foreign country where he didn't speak the language.

Medianoche asked, "What's the point of this rambling conversation, soldier?"

"Mind if I sit?"

"I do mind. State your business and keep it moving."

She nodded. "Who else is coming after the package? How many teams?"

"No idea."

"We can't keep everybody out. We can't catch everybody getting off the boats and we can't monitor every flight at every airport."

Señorita Raven kept her eyes on his gun, he saw that. The shrapnel gave strangeness to her beauty. Underneath the dim lights, for a brief second, she had looked like a work of art.

She said, "The way you stare at me . . . frigorific."

He didn't move as she stared, felt her taking in his roughness, her eyes never blinking as she stood and read his injuries, studied every line on the road map that lived on his face.

Señorita Raven took a small breath, maintained eye contact. "Was just saying there weren't many brown- or black-skinned people. It's like being in a Woody Allen sci-fi movie. Hey, did you know that if you counted up all of the illegal aliens from south of the border, the U.S. has more Mexicans, more Spanish-speaking people than Argentina?"

He stared. "You've been drinking."

"Long day. Was up at the crack of dawn shooting down tangos and blowing up vans. Then I had to wash my hair and get a manicure and pedicure. Did some shopping. Took a long bath. Played some music. Had a glass of wine. Maybe two. Nothing I can't handle."

He sipped his coffee. "Used to be more than fifty African nations in this area."

"Fifty African nations? Really? How long ago?"

"Nineteenth century. First half."

"Sounds like this should've been another Africa. What happened to the Africans?"

"You're not African, you're a goddamn Indian. What does it matter to a Punjabi who grew up in a loony bin in East Saint Louis? I'd understand if you were interested in the Slumdog Millionaires. Why the goddamn Africans? Nobody on the planet cares about Africans."

"You are so fucking insensitive."

"You want liberal, get off the battlefield and move to commie-homo-loving Hollywood."

"Very insensitive."

"Insensitive is a Jackson building a slavery theme park in Africa. Going to a slave port, building an amusement park in Nigeria along the site of a famous slave port, that is insensitive."

"Okay. I'll have to roll with that one. With reservation."

"You have walked in uninvited and invaded my table. You want that politically correct hypocritical bullshit, do an about-face and march your 51-50 ass where they soft-shoe the truth."

"I guess you've put me in my place. Something about Africans bother you?"

"Why Africans? Indians and Africans don't have the best relationship on the planet. Sounds suspicious when a damn cow worshipper is standing over me asking about bushmeat eaters. Is that insensitive too? They eat chimpanzee, gorilla, antelope, and rodent. Is that insensitive? You're standing over me breathing up all the good air and yakking about Africans."

"Sir, didn't mean to upset you, sir. But on a side note, I find it amazing how a man of your intelligence can offend so many people in one sentence. You're a regular Bill Maher."

Medianoche looked in her face, beyond the damage from war, into her eyes.

She returned his stare. Then she looked away.

She said, "Anyway. The slave thing. The fifty tribes."

He watched her hands, knew she was strapped, wondered what her angle was.

She maintained eye contact. "Fifty tribes. That meant that most of them were enemies. Or didn't like each other. But they worked together because they had a common enemy. Common enemies make enemies become friends."

Medianoche finally spoke, "The enemy of my enemy is my friend. Is that where you're going with this?"

Señorita Raven paused. As if she were trying to get to some point.

He asked, "Who is your enemy?"

"Mine is poverty."

"Mine is time."

"Same enemy everyone hopes to have in the end."

He nodded.

She asked, "How much time do we have on the Rabbit's Foot?"

"Rabbit's Foot?"

"The package. Since I don't know what it is, I call it the Rabbit's Foot. Anyway. I mean, we're all loaded up and on call, but no one seems to be as worried about it as they should be."

"Why are you so worried about someone else's money?"

"Who is guarding it? And where is it hidden? And if this is a team, why are at least two of us being kept in the dark on a package of such monumental importance?"

"Need-to-know basis. You know how that goes, right?"

"I need to know."

"Why?"

"Because I don't know."

"You will be given the information you need. When you need that information."

"Okay, so Hopkins was to pay us for delivery. Hopkins was blown the fuck up. We didn't get the rest of our payday. So the package is with the team. Well, we have the Rabbit's Foot. I overheard you say a few Russians were killed trying to get the package. And we took out two teams of ganja-smoking plantain-lovers this morning and shut down that route into the city until high noon. We own it. So it's our money now, right? It's The Four Horsemen's money. And I am one of The Four goddamn Horsemen. We're a team and I'm concerned with team business."

"Stay on your side of the line. Take orders."

"Who the fuck are you to tell me what I should be concerned with?"

There was no trust at their table. The gun in his lap confirmed that.

Medianoche said, "This conversation is treasonous. Give me one reason not to put a hole in your left breast."

"Because it looks better than my right breast. Firmer. More succulent. Beautiful nipple."

He didn't reply.

She looked at his gun, then looked at him and said, "I'm not wearing my corny tie."

"And?"

"I'm wearing a very pretty dress. Bought it at the Abasto Plaza Hotel Tango Shop. I was at El Ateneo most of the day, reading books and eating, then I got in a mood and went shopping."

"What's your point?"

"See the shoes? Comme il Faut."

"Tango shoes."

"Great tango shoes. The Manolo Blahniks of tango shoes. You can tell by the heel, if you know shoes. Women's shoes. Anyway. Tango dress. High heels. I'm not working."

"But you have a weapon inside your coat pocket."

"A throwaway .22. Nothing special. Not like the Beretta you have pointed at me."

"Why carry a throwaway tonight if you're not working on a reason to throw it away?"

"Single woman with a body like mine, dressed like this, walking these mean streets alone. People are crazy down here. Stabbing each other. Shooting each other. *For free.* Three boys got on a bus, tried to rob the driver, then cut off one of his fingers. That was in the big-money Palermo barrio. For no reason. That's ridiculous. It's not like Detroit, New York, or L.A., but still."

He nodded. "What's in the left coat pocket?"

"Tango gloves. They match the dress. Sexy. They come up to my elbows."

"Why the dress and high heels?"

"Was bored. Didn't want to go to Bar 6 or Moma Rocha or Bartok. Bar scene isn't my thing. Too much competition. Too many beauty queens and shallow men. Wasn't in the mood for any electronic music. Had hit La Preciosa, Crobar, El Cocobongo, Pacha, Live, and Amerika too many times. Did I mention that I saw The Beast's servant guy at Amerika? He's a regular there. Wouldn't be surprised to see The Beast there. Anyway. Wanted to get out of that condo and do something classy. First I thought about going to Biblioteca Café, then I said, nah.

Tango. I was thinking about El Beso again, but changed my mind, started thinking about La Catedral."

"Never heard of La Catedral."

"Underground tango spot on Sarmiento."

One of the Italians looked his way, saw a woman standing at a table. Not being offered a seat. Medianoche wasn't being a gentleman. He was being as low-class as his enemy.

Medianoche motioned at the empty seat in front of him.

He said, "Lose the coat. Keep those pretty hands on the table."

"Or what?"

"Or die where you stand."

Capítulo 22

asesinos

Señorita Raven took off her coat.

He knew her measurements. Knew them from her file. Five nine with nice breasts standing over a small waist that led to sweet hips; hips that stood guard over a distracting backside. Athletic, but still soft and feminine around the edges. Her formfitting tango dress was long and sleeveless. He knew her measurements, but in that outfit her figure was surprising, her cleavage equally disarming. Her dress was sultry, a revealing slit over the left leg that commenced a little more than a foot from her slim waist. Back out, arms exposed, Señorita Raven put her hands on the table, palms down, polished fingernails up.

She had a body that could cause an accident. Car accident or premature ejaculation. Either way, there would be a mess that needed to be cleaned up. He tried to imagine her without the shrapnel that tainted her beauty. Wondered what that arrogant diva had looked like then.

He looked at her wrist. Saw her watch. Ono Moda. Stainless steel with the classic signature dot of Movado. His brand. He clenched his teeth but didn't say anything. He wanted to, but not all thoughts had to become words.

Then she turned her palms up.

The healed slashes from her attempted suicide on display.

More scars. Lines. Like she used to cut herself. Used pain to hide pain.

She asked, "How well do you know The Beast?"

"Don't initiate a conversation you will regret."

"You've been working with him for years, huh? Decades, huh?"

Medianoche didn't answer. He found everything about Señorita Raven distracting. Her lips. The swell of her breasts. The way her backside shifted in her wooden seat.

Medianoche shifted, adjusted his eye patch.

She said, "He has so much information on all of us. Just curious. He recruited me."

"Where did he find you?"

"After I was kicked out. He came to me. Had no money. Was about to be . . . homeless. When Uncle Sam has used you, chewed you up and spat you out, nothing left to do but join the other down-and-out soldiers living congregated and sleeping on cardboard on Skid Row. Was about to consider being a stripper, robbing a bank, or making money on my back. But I guess with . . . this on my face . . . the only option would've been to put on a mask and rob a bank. Or get a job at Mickey D's on State Street in East Saint Louis and sling drugs from the drive-through window. Lot of people sling drugs out of fast-food spots. That was another option."

"Be grateful."

"I am. But was wondering, since we're a team, why does he get to sit on the package?"

"Stand down."

"What if he ran off with it, double-crossed all of us?"

"Stand down or get the fuck out of this café."

"What if he took the package he had and left?"

"It's no good without the other part, you know that."

"What if he negotiated with the people who have the other half?"

"We don't negotiate with terrorists."

She was as unstable as nitroglycerin.

She said, "Mind if I order a Quilmes?"

He moved the barrel of his weapon away from her direction. It was hidden under the table when the waiter came over, took her order, then left. From afar it would've looked like they were on a date. But he knew the men thought she was a working girl. Local coffee shops were a good place to find women in search of men. Café Orleans, Café

Exedra, many others had been great places to pick up some freelancing hookers. It was that time of the night.

She said, "I heard he was a pederast."

"Stand down."

"And that servant . . . heard he was military . . . discharged for his . . . sexual activities . . ."

"Soldier . . . stick to your own business."

"If that's his thing, that's his thing. I mean he is the man in charge. Just asking. Nothing surprises me. Not passing judgment. In ancient cultures, probably even before your time, kings and emperors used to have men *and* women at their disposal. Concubines and catamites. And wives. I love Greek mythology. Zeus was seduced by his cupbearer. A god that was on the down low. Nothing is new under the sun. In Rome it was cool for Roman men to get down with slaves, as long as the Roman man was the man doing the poking. Like they do in prison. Same thing. He who pokes is the king. He who gets poked is the maytag. They could butt-fuck the men slaves, but if they butt-fucked a regular nonslave man, they were put to death. And, oh, a man who liked to get down like that and was on the receiving end of the butt-fucking was called a pathicus or cinaedus. Means he was on bottom. Means he was the bitch. Means he was weak."

"Your mouth will be the end of you."

"Intelligence is always intimidating to those who aren't."

"Nothing intelligent about being vulgar."

"Was trying to keep the conversation on your level."

"That mouth will definitely get you put in an early grave."

"Not with the things I can do with my mouth."

Medianoche stared at her.

She smiled.

The waiter was back within the minute, a minute Medianoche had spent ignoring his target and staring at Señorita Raven. Nothing was said when the waiter returned with a bottled Quilmes for Señorita Raven. Nothing was said as the waiter opened the top and poured a taste of the beer into a glass. The waiter nodded, bowed a little, smiled, then left.

Señorita Raven picked up the beer, ignored the glass, sipped from the bottle.

Medianoche shook his head.

Señorita Raven sighed, put the bottle down, picked up the glass.

She asked, "Better?"

"This isn't East Saint Louis."

She nodded.

Medianoche asked, "No more bullshit. No jibber jabber. Why are you following me?"

She shrugged. "Wanted to watch you from a distance."

"Revenge?"

"For what?"

"Our moment on the elevator. When I had to put your young ass in your place."

"Water under the bridge."

"So you say. Women never let things go."

"I've been around men like you all my life. If I wanted revenge for every man that pissed me off, there would be no one left for us to pro-create with."

"You sure about that?"

"You saved my life. I'm sure. I owe you one big-time."

"The truth in exchange for the payment on saving your ass."

"Fire away."

"On whose orders are you playing Dick Tracy?"

"No one's."

"Whose orders, soldier. You're not that fucking dumb. Neither am I."

"Just wanted to watch you. Study you. Become a better Horseman. I say that on my mother's grave. On my sister's grave. I say that on all the graves of the women before me."

"And keep an eye on the package."

"That too."

"Well, you can see I don't have it."

"But you know where it is."

He remembered her up on that roof. How she had come from

above him, the direction the Uruguayan had fled, where the helicopter was flying in for package pickup. She stared into his eye as if she were reading his mind.

He said, "Explain to me why you were close to the roof. Explain to me why you were heading in the direction the Uruguayan was fleeing to catch that chopper."

She shrugged. "Got lucky. Didn't know how high you had chased him."

"Really?"

"Really."

He stared at her. Her face was as unmovable as the monuments in the city. The shrapnel was her graffiti.

She said, "I was wondering if you were about to snatch the package and catch that chopper yourself. Afterward, that is. You broke away from everybody. Like you were John fucking Wayne. Yeah. I wondered if you were about to pull a double cross. You shot at that chopper really fast, hit that spotlight like it was a signal to abort the mission."

"Never question my loyalty."

"Then never question mine."

Medianoche glared, watched her hold his long stare.

He said, "You seem to know a lot about the package we're after."

"Only what I've been told, sir."

"Which is what, exactly?"

"It was somebody's big payday."

"You're very concerned with other people's money."

"Told you, was almost homeless. Almost pimped myself out. Don't ever want to be that depressed again. Anyway. Poor people always think about what they don't have."

"The kind of money that would make you want to keep an eye on me."

"Maybe."

"Or The Beast."

"Not at all, sir. The Beast does nothing for me."

"What does that mean, soldier?"

"Nothing. He needs a new hairstyle. One color. Either black or white. That patch thing looks silly. Like something out of a cartoon. I'd never tell him that. He's a fucking lunatic."

Medianoche didn't argue.

She said, "I think we got off on a bad foot. I have a difficult history, you know that."

He nodded.

"And I said some stupid and immature things about . . . your injuries. You almost died and that should not be made fun of. No more than . . . than what I went through should be taken lightly. I was knocked unconscious. Thought I was dead. Woke up and didn't recognize my own face."

He didn't nod.

"Well, sir, maybe we could share a *mate* and reconcile our differences."

"*Mates* are for friends."

"I was willing to make an exception."

"Finish your beer, drop twenty-five pesos, and move on."

She sipped her beer, put the bottle to the side, sat back, her posture mimicking his.

She said, "Just wanted to thank you for saving my life."

Medianoche looked at her wrists, the cuts on her arm. "Anything else?"

"No, sir. Just . . . well, any pointers? Critique on my performance?"

"Learn some respect, learn to shut the fuck up, you might live to see twenty-five."

"I'm twenty-six, sir."

"Then live to see twenty-seven."

Medianoche regarded the Italians speaking in Spanish, evaluated the room, then looked at his watch, compared it to the time on the wall before looking at Señorita Raven again.

He looked in her eyes. The alcohol she'd had earlier made her glow.

She'd distracted him enough.

Medianoche stood up, adjusted his suit coat.

He said, "Excuse me for a moment."

"Sir, no problem, sir."

Medianoche went toward the kitchen.

He put his gloves on, then removed the gun from its holster.

Capítulo 23

el hombre muerde el perro

Medianoche's uncompromising death-stare was on the waiter.

The waiter was about thirty years old. His eyes were locked on the weapon. Medianoche motioned for the waiter to come closer, and he did as he was instructed, his legs barely able to hold him up. Medianoche took the waiter's wallet, looked inside, saw photos of him with a woman and two children.

Medianoche asked, "*Esposa. Hija. Hijo.*"

The waiter nodded. "*Sí, mi esposa y mis hijos.*"

It was his wife and children, a girl and a boy.

The woman's belly was full and round. He asked, "*¿Embarazada?*"

He had asked if the woman in the picture was pregnant.

"*Sí. Mi esposa está embarazada. Cinco meses.*"

The waiter told him that his wife was pregnant, five months.

Medianoche took the man's identification, the information that had his home address, stuffed it inside his suit pocket, then wiped the wallet off and handed it back to the waiter.

The waiter trembled. "*Por favor . . . Señor . . . por favor . . . es mi foto . . . mi familia . . .*"

Medianoche ignored the man's pleas, reached inside his pocket and took out a bottle.

The waiter was holding a tray, cups of coffee.

Medianoche opened the bottle, poured liquid inside each cup.

The waiter nodded, sweat sprouting on his brow.

This was South America. The land of drug runners. The land of assassinations.

Same as North America. Same as Europe. West Indies. Germany. Russia.

The waiter understood the ways of the world.

Medianoche went back to his seat, gun holstered, sat with his legs crossed.

He sipped his cappuccino and surveyed his target's reflection in the window.

"*¿Puedo hablar?*" Señorita Raven said, then in English. "Can I talk? *Con permiso?*"

Medianoche shook his head.

His ears were on the Spanish insults directed at his country of birth.

Then he glanced at Señorita Raven.

She continued, "What do you think of me?"

"You're nothing more than an impetuous child."

"I have been accused of being a little too ambitious. My strength is my weakness."

Medianoche looked at her eyes, then looked away.

She asked, "What do you think about me trying to connect with Blackwater?"

Medianoche ignored her; he monitored the Italians.

Señorita Raven said, "Guess you're not a fan of Blackwater."

"Blackwater shipped hundreds of firearms to Iraq without the necessary permits. Automatic weapons that ended up on the country's black market."

"Hearsay."

"Weapons used against the country that manufactured them. My country. Your country."

"That happens in every war, sir. Eventually the Native Americans upgraded from bows and arrows to six-shooters and rifles. Guess where Tonto and Geronimo got their weapons?"

"From traitors."

"My point is this; selling arms ain't nothing new. Every team has a traitor."

"Not this team. Understand?"

She nodded. "I understand. My statement was about the history of war."

"Do as instructed." Medianoche nodded. "A soldier follows orders."

"I thought you were more of a leader."

"One leader at a time. And that position is taken."

"You seem more like The Beast's lapdog. Not like his servant. Hope that doesn't offend you. You seem like his yes-man. You're like a machine that does what it's programmed to do."

"Quit while you're ahead."

Medianoche glanced at the Italian men.

The fresh cups of coffee had been served. The Italians sipped.

One of the Italians coughed. Picked up a paper towel. Wiped his mouth.

Another man coughed.

Then the last two coughed.

The chatting ending when Death grabbed one man. Before the other men could respond, Death strangled each of the men, choked one after the other. Each stumbled, reached to pull out his weapon, wobbled and fell to the floor, dropped to the Spanish tile fighting to stay among the living, legs moving, kicking, knocking over the table, spilling poisoned coffee.

Then the room went quiet; the only noise heard were the few noises from outside.

Medianoche moved to the windows, closed the curtains, hit the light switch.

He came back, looked down, and saw foam present on the lips of each fallen Italian.

Señorita Raven said, "You're working."

"Shut up."

Medianoche looked at his watch. Five past three a.m.

Medianoche nodded at the waiter. The man swallowed, body tense, his face the picture of horror. Señorita Raven stood, a small smile of amazement on her lips.

Medianoche stared at the dead men.

Twenty years ago, he would've bolted into the room with a gun in each hand and unloaded on his target and on everyone in sight, then vanished into the night.

The waiter begged, for his wife, for his children.

Medianoche asked the waiter if he would be able to remember him when he was gone. The waiter lowered his head, shook his head. Medianoche told the waiter that if he remembered him, then he would be remembered in return. The waiter shook his lowered head, a tsunami of terror in his splintered voice as he said he could not remember what he did not see.

Medianoche slipped into his long black coat, checked his watch, saw the time, then eased on his fedora, adjusted its brim. He patted the pocket that housed the waiter's identification and photo, his pregnant *esposa* and smiling *hijos*, then nodded.

The waiter nodded in return, fear and a deadly understanding on his face.

Medianoche's Italian shoes clacked on the Spanish tile as he strolled out the door. The night was cold, damp, that ache in his eye springing to life. Once again that North Carolina memory. A memory that ran like a subroutine trapped in an infinite loop. Like a computer deadlocked.

Señorita Raven said, "Sir, are you okay, sir?"

She was standing in front of him. Close enough for him to smell her perfume and the beer on her breath. Close enough to kiss. He didn't know how long she had been there.

He extended his arm, moved her out of his way.

Medianoche tilted the brim of his fedora downward, shadowed his face, walked past the Melia Recoleta Plaza Boutique Hotel, kept moving toward Callao, turned right on that wide street, headed toward the heart of Recoleta. Taxis, cars, buses, and pedestrians clogging the streets like it was high noon. Señorita Raven was no longer behind him. He dodged dog shit with every step.

He took out his cellular. Dialed.

The Beast answered, *"Buenas noches."*

"It's done. That little job is done."

"Good."

"Your location?"

"San Isidro."

"Thought you would be out at your ranch."

"Didn't want to get too far away. The package is in a *villa* near here. It gets moved again at the crack of dawn. Scamz and his crew, they don't have a lot of time. I'm monitoring flights, buses, and boats from Uruguay."

"Impossible to catch everything."

"That goes without saying. The next few hours will be with all of us on red alert."

"Any direct communications with Scamz?"

"They've gone silent."

"As expected."

"That said, how was your evening? Problems with the Italian contract?"

He was about to bring up Señorita Raven. Said, "Nothing I couldn't handle."

"Collateral damage?"

"Three. Had to put down three extra. Question?"

"Yes, soldier."

"Did you send backup?"

"Backup? When have you ever needed backup?"

"I thought I saw Señorita Raven in the area."

"She's not on my dime. She's on her own time."

"Everything is good with the package?"

"Everything is fine."

"The other half?"

"They will be here soon. If they are not already here."

"Sure about that?"

"They have no other options. We have the cheese, and they are the rats. They were in North America when we had that last conversation. But they could be here now."

"Should I come down there? Should we pick up the package?"

"No."

"We have better firepower."

"All is fine. I'm keeping the package moving. From hellhole to hellhole."

"Cheap labor."

"People will put their lives on the line for a few pesos."

"Your loyal servant?"

"Draco did good this morning. He was a major asset. Draco is working overtime. He's in contact with the package, coordinating the efforts, making sure the hooligans keep moving it."

"Draco can handle it if those Scamz fucks appear?"

"He was a marine. He had a problem and he handled it with style and grace."

"When was this problem?"

"Someone tracked our package. Someone from the Scamz organization."

"Scamz has a crew down here."

"A scout. That was late afternoon. But that scout is with the Jamaicans now."

"The Gideon guy, Draco took him out?"

"No, not him. Not sure if he's here."

"Scamz. That organization. What do they have on us?"

"Nothing that will do them any good. Don't worry. We're good. Will keep you posted."

Medianoche nodded. He said, *"Buenas noches."*

"Buenas noches."

He closed his phone, kept his stride strong and steady.

Soon he heard hurried footsteps. Señorita Raven was behind him.

Capítulo 24

malos recuerdos

After La Rambla.

Medianoche had walked ten blocks with that nonstop clicking following him. He was at Cordoba, another street filled with bars, the promise of sex, another area filled with madness. A moment later the clicking heels of tango shoes were beside him. She moved at his hurried pace.

Medianoche crossed Cordoba. The clicking of high heels remained at his side.

"Mind slowing down, sir?"

"What the hell do you want now?"

"Did that have something to do with the package?"

"Classified information."

"Well, then I think I should tell you something else."

"What, soldier?"

"It's about the waiter, sir."

He asked, "What about the goddamn waiter?"

"I killed him."

He stopped walking. Faced her. She had the throwaway .22 in her hand.

He growled, "I gave him a pass."

"Well, I revoked that pass." She dropped her .22 inside her purse and straightened her coat. "First, your ass could've told me you were about to kill a room filled with asshole racist U.S.-hating Italians. I would've left. You let me sit there while you were killing up the entire restaurant. I thought you were just drinking coffee and maybe looking for hookers or something."

"Why in the hell did you kill the man?"

"How many women have this shit in their faces? How many have almost been blown up? You think the waiter didn't see . . . this shit? I saw how he looked at me. He might've forgotten you, which I doubt very seriously, but I know for a fact that he never would forget my face. No one ever does. I have a face marked up by fucking frags. Who forgets seeing that shit? I act like I don't know that, but I do. I see my reflection every day. Even the days I get dressed without looking in the mirror, I see my reflection. I can tell by the way people look at me. Like I'm some goddamn freak. Like I'm some kind of sideshow. So yeah, I took him out. I killed him. So the fuck what? Stop acting like a one-eyed prick."

Medianoche took a deep breath, cold air fogging his breath.

What was done was done.

Taxis passed, water splashing underneath filthy tires. Buses passed, buses that looked twenty years old. People walked by, bundled up and attacking the cold, in search of a good time.

Señorita Raven said, "There was a cook hiding in the kitchen. Handled him too."

Medianoche growled, a monster about to break its chains.

Medianoche walked. Señorita Raven walked with him and did her best to keep up.

She asked, "Do you tango as well as The Beast says you can tango?"

He felt her hand on his elbow, her touch gentle, ladylike. She slipped her arm though his. He stopped, moved her arm from his, frowned at her. The beauty marked by shrapnel.

"*Quiero bailar.*" She smiled. "*Por favor?*"

He felt his breathing thicken.

She brought her face close to his as if it were the start of their dance.

In her eyes he saw a chance to return to Montserrat.

He grabbed her, held her shoulders and pushed her inside the recessed opening to Notorious, pushed her up against the business's dark glass door as taxis whizzed by, cars passed, and people walked on the opposite side of the street. He shoved her, made her back hit the door hard enough to knock the wind out of her body. He expected to hear her scream. Was ready for her to fight. She licked her lips and smiled. He grimaced at her. He was losing control. Losing goddamn control.

She whispered, "I can feel you."

He yanked away from Señorita Raven, grabbed his fallen hat, put it on, and stumbled away, hurried up the avenue, pulled his coat over his erection. He hailed a Radio Taxi, climbed inside as fast as he could, left Señorita Raven standing on the filthy concrete.

He opened and closed his hand, made a fist over and over. Disturbed. She traumatized him. He took out his cellular. Dialed a number he hadn't dialed in years. Area code 664.

The phone rang.

He knew Gracelyn was still there. She'd never leave her homeland. She had survived Hurricane Hugo in the ninth month of '89. Then in the fourth month of '96, she had survived the eruption of the Soufrière Hills Volcano that had devastated her birth land, destroyed her birth home in Plymouth. Lava and rocks had buried their capital city underneath forty feet of volcanic destruction, roads to the homes in the hillside wiped away, air polluted, rivers and golf courses erased and replaced by volcanic rubbish, two-thirds of her island uninhabitable. That was the Caribbean's own version of a modern-day Pompeii. That had been their Katrina. Her home had been destroyed, but her love for Montserrat remained unconditional. Nothing could deter her love.

She answered on the third ring. Her voice heavy with both sleep and panic.

"Hello."

He would recognize her voice in a crowd of thousands.

He heard her voice and at that moment he saw her as she was when he first met her, smiling, a black wrap around her hair, plain black sandals on her feet, wearing jeans that were cuffed up above her calves and a white T-shirt that had the image of Olaudah Equiano on the front.

That was the conversation starter, him asking her about the image on the T-shirt.

Her voice, soft with an almost Irish accent. West Indies meets Ireland.

The most beautiful voice he'd ever heard. The sweetest song ever written.

She had told him that Olaudah Equiano was kidnapped as a child and enslaved, beaten until he answered to the name Gustavus Vassa, a slave who had been taken from Benin, taken to the West African coast, to Barbados, to the English colony of Virginia, to London, sold at Deptford, then taken to Montserrat. In Montserrat he bought his own freedom for forty British pounds.

Olaudah was her hero.

She repeated, "Hello."

He was back in Montserrat with his third wife. A dark-haired virgin at the age of twenty-four. An unspoiled beauty, a woman who loved deeply. He had been the first man she had allowed to touch her in that way.

"Hello? Is anyone there?"

He smiled, opened his mouth, almost said something.

The military had been about love for country, but loyalty stood high above love. That was not Gracelyn. An uncomplicated woman from an island that had no stoplights, no clubs, no town.

He had told her who he was. Had told her the things he had done.

She had looked at him with eyes filled with fear. Said she could not continue lying down with a man who had murdered people. Olaudah Equiano had survived the horrors of slavery, had suffered and reclaimed his freedom. She said she could suffer and survive the heartbreak brought on by a man. She was deeper than the carnal aspect of the human comedy.

He had been run away, not by guns or bombs, but by the soft tears of a stubborn woman. A woman who cried as if she had been raped. The anguish. He remembered her goddamn pain.

"Hello. Who is this? Are you okay?"

Middle-of-the-night call, and she had answered with care and concern in her voice.

He managed, "Gracelyn . . . how are you?"

"I am fine. Who is this?"

The woman he loved didn't recognize his voice.

He'd become a stranger to her. He no longer existed.

The knife twisted as it went deep.

He closed his flip phone. Closed it hard.

Capítulo 25

crueles e inusuales

Medianoche exited the elevator, stepped back inside his condo.

His Tres Marías were waiting.

They all wore beautiful, long dresses, thigh-high slits up the sides. Tulip-hem crocheted dresses, accented with spot beads and fringe. The first María wore a red dress. The second María's dress was black. The third María was dressed in blue. The scent of gentle perfumes, three scents that mixed into one.

The first María hurried to Medianoche, smiling. "*Yo quiero bailar.*"

She said that she wanted to dance.

The second and third Marías did the same. "*Nosotros también queremos bailar.*"

Medianoche growled, went inside the bathroom, stared in the mirror, saw Gracelyn staring back, her image like smoke. He opened the medicine cabinet. Took out a small container. Unscrewed the top. Stared at the white powder. Tonight there was no hesitation. He put cocaine in the web of his hand. Snorted. Closed his eyes for a moment. Waited on that rush. Waited on the euphoric effect. Blood vessels constricted. Body temperature rose. Heartbeat accelerated. Fatigue was replaced by boundless energy. He reached inside the cabinet again. Took out the other small box. Ocular prosthesis. Opened the box. Stared at his faux eye. He removed his eye patch. Inserted the convex shell made of cryolite glass.

The prosthesis fit over his orbital implant and underneath his eyelid.

Ocular prosthesis in place, he left the bathroom.

The girl's mouths dropped open. Three Spanish gasps. No words.

Dancing started at two a.m. and went on until nine in the morning. It was still early.

He nodded at his Tres Marías. "Yeah, fuck it, let's drink and dance until the sun comes up on this town. Fuck Montserrat. Fuck Gracelyn. Let's go make some new goddamn memories."

They looked confused, frightened. His words had been filled with anger.

He calmed his voice, said, "*Yo quiero bailar.*"

One excited woman put on her coat and took his right arm. The other put on her coat and took his left arm. The third María danced and hurried in front of them, opened the door.

Señorita Raven was waiting.

He stared at her. She nodded as if she liked what she saw.

Medianoche pulled his arm away from the arms of his Marías. He moved by Señorita Raven. Marched to Señor Rodríguez's door. Knocked. He answered right away. Dressed in slacks and a gray sweater. A book in one hand. *El Arte de la Guerra.* His weapon in the other.

He looked surprised to see Medianoche with a faux eye. He said, "Sir, yes, sir."

"Take these beautiful women dancing. They want to tango. Show them a good time."

"Sir, yes, sir."

"Then bring them back to your room. If you're shy, relax. They'll take it from there."

"Sir, yes, sir."

Medianoche directed the women inside Señor Rodríguez's condo apartment. Then he turned around, marched past Señorita Raven, and went inside his condo.

He left the door open. His pace slowed as he went and sat on his bed, the mattress sighing under his weight.

Seconds went by.

The door to his living quarters closed.

First silence.

He wasn't alone. He smelled her perfume. Same sweetness he'd inhaled before.

Her clothes rustled. Then he heard the sound of tango shoes against the wooden floor.

She said, "Mind if I have a glass of wine, sir? I see some on your counter."

He didn't answer.

"How's about this, if you don't want me to have a glass of your wine, say something and I'll about-face and go to Soho. Otherwise, I will take your silence as an okay to proceed."

His heart raced. He centered his breathing. Waited.

She said, "Thank you."

He heard her in his kitchen. Touching his wineglasses. Pouring his wine.

"You have nice pictures on your wall. Wow. You have one of an African."

Minutes went by. Minutes filled with the loudness of her silence.

She said, "You stare at me. You always stare at me. And not like I'm a freak. I see the way you look at me. You look me in my eyes. You look at me the way men used to look at me. I used to hate when men looked at me that way. But now, I miss that. My injuries. My sacrifice. It makes people uncomfortable. People glance at me and turn away. Like the waiter did. Like the Italian men did. I pretend I don't care. They want to ask but are afraid to talk to me. And parents look at me like I will terrify their child. You . . . you look at me like I'm a woman. Like you can see who I am without the . . . without this mess. I need that from a real man, a man like you."

Then the sound of tango shoes walked across the wooden floor in his living room. The footsteps stopped. Music came on. "Tango Diablo." A song from the show "Tango Porteño." Tango. The dance of the poor. The dance that began in brothels. Africans had brought the dance, or brought the rhythmic dances that were the predecessors to the tango.

The footsteps came toward his bedroom.

Señorita Raven stopped in his doorframe, glass of wine in her hand, most of it gone.

Medianoche stared at Señorita Raven for a moment, her cleavage, the swell of her breasts, the shape of her legs. Carnal thoughts took hold. He licked his lips, then looked away.

She finished the wine, her heels clacking as she walked to the kitchen, and put the glass down, heels clacking as she paused in the living room. He thought she was leaving. Moments later, her shoes clacked as she came back and stood in the doorframe of his bedroom.

He looked at her again. Her breasts. Soft. Natural. The kind that made men betray orders and country. The kind that made men betray the families they had left back home. The kind that caused the savage part of a man to rise like the assault rates in the military. Her cleavage revealed just enough to frustrate and create fantasies. She raised her lowered head, her eyes focused, looked at him. Her coat was off. Some flesh revealed. Her long tango gloves were on. She had put them on after she took her wineglass back to the kitchen.

She smiled at him. A soft smile.

He put his gun to the side. He held eye contact as he stood.

Medianoche maintained eye contact as he pulled off his overcoat and let it fall behind him. Held eye contact as he first adjusted his suit coat, then adjusted his tie. Made himself into a well-dressed gentleman. Kept that eye contact as Señorita Raven walked backward toward the living room. He followed, his pace matching hers, never losing eye contact.

He held her hand. Adjusted into tango position as she did the same. Just like she had done in La Boca. Her upper body straight and tall. Knees bent and over her toes, weight back on her heels. He put his hand on her lower back and pulled her into a brutal embrace. Señorita Raven placed her left hand around his right shoulder.

They danced.

He gave in to the tango, allowed the dance to take over, moved around the living room, his moves more complicated than the dancer's in La Boca, more dramatic. He tested Señorita Raven's ability to follow, tested her ability to resign and let a man lead, found her skills and submissiveness surprising. Her moves were like the perfect partner, moving, moving, their dance taking them toward the kitchen, turning,

turning, back into the living room. "A Don Pedro Santillán." "Amor en Budapest." "Pregonera." "Yunta de oro." "Loca." Songs played. The moves intensified. The foreplay was over. He gave her momentum and she took to the air, kicked her feet like wings and did a wonderful *boleo*, hooked her legs around Medianoche's body in the move called the *gancho*, put her body on his thigh, both of her feet off the ground. The career assassin. The arrogant woman who killed and tortured. Medianoche's condo became his brothel.

In between songs, that was when the dancers were allowed to speak.

Señorita Raven said, "If a man dances two consecutive songs with a woman, he plans to take her to bed. And if she allows him to, she is willing to go to bed with that man that night."

Medianoche inhaled the wine on her breath, held his serious expression, and nodded.

She whispered, "This will be our fifth dance."

Then he pulled her up to him, held her close.

Her eyes. He couldn't escape her eyes. Couldn't escape her goddamn eyes.

Couldn't escape the pain and rejection he'd felt after that phone call to Montserrat.

The same as it had been the day he was kicked off the island by her tears.

He lifted Señorita Raven like she had the weight of a newborn baby, lifted her high, her legs opening, resting on both sides of his neck, the heat of her vagina in his tarnished face. They stumbled toward the wall, that wall stopping Señorita Raven from falling to the floor. He held her up, felt one of her hands on his head, heard the other grabbing at the white wall, slapping the wall until she found her balance, her hands sliding, knocking glass-framed pictures off the wall. Photos crashed. Glass broke. He inhaled her, put his mouth on her lace underwear. Was surprised she had on underwear. His lips and tongue pressed against damp lace. Her weight pressed down on his mouth. Her dress covered him as she ground against his nose, his chin, moved on the hardness of his chin, moved on his chin as she held him and moaned.

Her labored breathing gave way to operatic sounds, a repetitive E-sharp.

The music played and Señorita Raven moaned.

He felt her shivering. She moved against his chin, his nose. She was juicy. The scent of her orgasm on his scarred and battle-worn flesh. She shifted on his face, lost her balance, started to fall, but he held her body, took control of her weight as she slid down his muscular frame. A smooth tango. Held her as she arched her back and moaned. He brought her down from his face, eased her down to the floor, her body shaking, her hand trying to hold on to him.

For a moment she was limp in his arms, back arched, head back, hair hanging, as lifeless as the dead. Barely breathing. Her hand moved in slow motion, touched his pants.

He was as erect as an araucaria tree.

Her hand rubbed him as her breath caught in her throat. The sound of amazement.

"Pequeña" ended. "La Yumba" began.

He carried her into the bedroom, dropped her down on the bed, yanked away her panties, made her sit on him facing away, entered her with her dress pulled up and his pants pulled down. He squeezed her breasts. They felt like heaven in his hand.

"La Yumba" ended. "La Mariposa" played and gave way to "Zum."

Medianoche put her on her knees, took her that way.

"Grisel" and "De floreo" and "A Don Agustin Bardi" played.

Medianoche battled with her, let her adjust her tango dress and sit on him, let her close her eyes and ride the memories swirling around inside his body.

He turned her over hard. Took her with authority, controlled her the way a man was supposed to control a woman. Once again, her labored breathing changed into operatic sounds. E-sharp after E-sharp after E-sharp. The arrogant assassin wrapped her legs around his back, announced her orgasm. He pounded her, pounded and stared into her eyes. That combination of beauty desecrated by the horrors of the world. A work of art. Walter Pater said that it was the addition of strangeness to beauty that created the romantic character in art. He stared until he couldn't see the marks left behind by war. He closed his eyes. Gave art his power. Uncontrolled power. Each thrust created another E-sharp.

First his labored breathing, his deep grunts mixing with E-sharps, then the inevitable.

He announced his orgasm with an elongated grunt, roared and pulled away from her, fought her as she moaned she was coming and pulled at him. He struggled to break away. He refused to deposit memories inside her, was barely out of her as she gripped him and moved her hips and moaned that she was coming coming coming, as he held too many memories to control.

Memories flooded like an unforgettable day in December of 1963.

Medianoche caught his breath, then sat up on the bed, the mattress giving under his weight as his Italian shoes slapped down on the wooden floor in a hard one-two cadence. The room smelled of a new perfume. One more powerful than the sweet aromas the beautiful Tres Marías had left behind. A sweetness that mixed with the scent of Argentine cigarettes and Cuban cigars. Señorita Raven's perfume. He looked at the mess they had made.

Señorita Raven whispered, "*Una vez más.*"

"*No más.*"

Medianoche turned his head away. He felt the bed shift as Señorita Raven found her balance and pulled herself to her feet. He heard the rich material of her soiled dress moving across her bare flesh as she yanked it down, her tango shoes clacking as she searched the floor for her torn panties, and then her shoes click-clacking as she flipped on the light and stood in front of the closet-door mirror. He saw her. She frowned at her stained dress. Her heels clicked on wood as she moved by the bed.

Medianoche looked at his soiled suit, saw the aftermath of lack of willpower.

"You turned my expensive dress into a milky Lewinsky. I'd be too embarrassed to take this to 5àSec. Damn. They will know what this is. I guess I'll add this to our secrets, sir."

"What secrets?"

"You froze on the roof. Like a DVD on pause. You lied to the team, told The Beast you threw that man off the roof. You froze again tonight. For a good half minute."

He pulled his lips in.

She said, "I won't tell. I'm not a snitch. People from East Saint Louis don't snitch."

A minute passed. A silent minute that was louder than being under enemy fire.

He said, "You trying to hold me over a fire, soldier?"

"I have your back. Understand, as long as you have my back, I have your back."

"As long as I have your back."

"We have to look out for each other."

He frowned, her words sounding like blackmail on more levels than one.

Medianoche marched to his closet, opened a small safe, and took out a stack of banknotes. *Veinte pesos*. *Cien pesos*. Pictures of Argentine heroes and BANCO CENTRAL DE LA ARGENTINA printed on every bill. He took a stack of money and extended it to Señorita Raven.

She frowned at the money. "Is that for the dress or for the sex?"

"It's so we don't have a misunderstanding about what you think you saw or what we did."

"I was offering to have your back."

"I don't need a dumb, ignorant, vulgar, and arrogant woman watching my back."

"You're nothing but an old broken-down GI Joe that has lost his kung fu grip."

"A woman like you is made to be on her back. That's all you're good for."

"You are really messed up, you know that? I might have a few mental issues, I may have made some bad choices when I was stressed, but you are as fucked up as they come."

"You showed me what you were good for."

"Fuck you, you one-eyed piece of shit."

"Take the goddamn money." He barked, "*Largáte, puta.*"

Señorita Raven regarded the money, then him. He let the bills go as she took the pesos from his hands. Six, maybe seven thousand pesos.

She said, "This all you think I'm worth?"

"Better than the going rate. Consider the difference a tip."

Her hand raised high. She threw the money in his face.

Medianoche didn't flinch. His hands became fists, his eyes on her neck.

She said, "You fucking piece of shit."

Tango shoes rushed across the wooden floor, stepped on broken glass.

The door opened.

She said, "I broke into the main files. I wasn't going to be part of a fucking group of low-IQ losers without having a leg up, and that ain't no sex joke. I know more about what happened in North Carolina than you do. I know more about this Hopkins shit than you do. Fucking follower. You're nothing but a one-eyed loser that fucks whores because he doesn't know how to hold down a conversation and get laid by a real woman. You fucking piece-of-shit loser."

"Get out of my apartment. Take your lies and get out of my apartment."

"Don't you want to know what else I know?"

"Asking me about the package. Throwing yourself at me. You think I'm stupid?"

"The files, what I read, what I know."

"How did you know the Uruguayan man was going to run up and not down?"

"The Beast is not your friend."

"Why did you come out above me when the other Horsemen were down below?"

"I was the best thing you had going. To think I actually had a crush on your old ass."

"How did you know? Explain yourself."

"Racist, abusive, misogynistic fuck. Use that good eye and watch your back, old man."

"You weren't surprised to see that chopper. You fired, but you didn't hit the bird."

"You're on your own, you delusional, one-eyed, broken-down GI Joe."

"How did you know which way the Uruguayan would run?"

"That's all you need to know."

He barked, "Explain yourself."

"I know what I saw. I'm the one with two eyes, you broken-down, one-eyed prick."

Tango shoes clacked at an angry pace. His door slammed.

Medianoche scowled at the mess they'd made.

He heard Señorita Raven's door open. Then her door slammed.

He picked up his gun. Expected her to come back with her .22.

She had gotten inside his head. He was ready to put her down. Like he should've put Gracelyn down. He knew what he had to do. At some point he would put Gracelyn down.

That would be the only way to stop that program, to end that memory leak.

But for now, Señorita Raven. The dampness of her sex on his genitals, her perfume on his suit.

He waited in the darkness, watched it become a new morning.

Long after sunrise. He stood up. Angry. Was time to pay Señorita Raven a visit.

He heard the elevator open. Heard the Tres Marías and Rodríguez. The chortles of new lovers. Castellano chatter. All of them talking and laughing.

Señor Rodríguez's door opened. Then his door closed. Talking and laughter faded.

Medianoche sat in the dining room with the window open. Cool air came inside. He heard a moan that sounded like a beautiful flute. Another that sounded as seductive as a violin. Then another that was as musical as an *arpa de dos órdenes*. Then came the sound of a man, a melodic Spanish guitar.

Random moans, like foreplay, as if they were tuning up.

Then they found their rhythm.

Song after song, he heard the musical moans of his Tres Marías being sullied.

He nodded.

The Tres Marías had moved on without hesitation. They had failed the loyalty test.

He went to the front room. Broken glass. Fallen pictures.

His chest rose and fell.

He looked down at his soiled clothing. He felt no relief. Only anger. Unadulterated anger. For being weak.

He picked up his Beretta.

He wanted to put a bullet inside Señorita Raven's thoughts and memories.

His breathing thickened with anger.

He picked up his phone. Called The Beast. There was no answer. He was calling to request permission to kill Señorita Raven.

The air in his lungs was fire. More anger than he could control.

He stood and walked across his wooden floor. He checked his weapon. Made sure it was loaded to the teeth. He went into the hall, stood back, about to kick open Señorita Raven's door, knowing he was strong enough to kick the door flat-footed and cause that door to fly off its hinges.

Then Señorita Raven's door opened.

She knew he would come. She was waiting. She was ready.

There was nothing but darkness inside her apartment. Had to be a trap.

The fire in his lungs didn't care. He'd leave her in a shallow grave. In the conservation park in Puerto Madero.

Medianoche stepped to the open door, his gun leading the way.

Saw her across the room. Waiting, not hiding.

She stood there. Anger heating her face. Unadulterated anger. She held a gun in her hand. Not the .22. A nine. She had upgraded her firepower.

Her gun was in her right hand, being held steady by her left.

Medianoche wasn't afraid.

From next door came the sound of a headboard slapping against the wall, a maddening violence that blended with the moans from one of the Tres Marías being fucked to high heaven.

Medianoche stepped inside Señorita Raven's apartment.

Gun trained on his body, Señorita Raven was naked, her young breasts standing firm.

No bulletproof vest. An open target. An easy target.

She said, "You want to know why I tried to kill myself? I'll tell you. I was so broke, so down and out, I gave an asshole a blow job for a hundred dollars. That messed up my head more than the war ever did. That took me to a new low, put me in the gutter with Norway rats. And now you fuck me and throw money in my face like I'm one of those sluts working at Newport."

"Lower your weapon."

"Lower yours. Lower yours and I'll lower mine."

He lowered his gun, knowing she would do the same. Like she had done on the roof.

Then he would shoot her, leave hot blood spurting on white walls and wooden floor.

This time was different.

While the desperate sounds of unrelenting sex covered his auditory senses, while a headboard banged the wall like the Devil was fighting to get free, it happened.

With tears in her eyes, the psychotic bitch fired twice.

Chapter 26

petit carême, au revoir

The report of .22s killed the silence in the open field.

Underneath overcast skies, sweat ran down my face and trickled down my back as I stood in red clay earth, the reverberation of death and violence a deadly song.

One of the .22s was in the hands of a gunman with short blond hair. He had a strong build. The other gunman had strong legs, was as dark as the night, his roots in southern Africa.

Hawks wasn't with me. We had parted ways, her next assignment across the pond.

Another gunman appeared, this one huge, hands the size of baseball gloves, fists like bricks. He raised his shotgun and pulled the trigger, its blast shattering its target. That destruction paused us all. The shotgun blast was an exclamation point. A powerful blast that would leave a man's guts on the ground as his soul rose to be judged by the king of judges.

The sound of violence faded as the scent of cordite mixed with the humid winds.

I was back in North America. The southern portion of the United States. Georgia. Standing in an open field a few miles beyond Woodstock. At an abandoned horse farm that was a long way from civilization as we knew it. A place surrounded by trees, an area where no one could hear anyone scream. The closest house was more than a mile away. Our gunfire would be unnoticed.

I looked to my left, my attention on the blond-haired German boy and his dark-skinned African brother. Steven and Robert, both dressed in jeans with jackets over their soccer jerseys. They were in elementary school. They were the boys I took care of with my blood money.

Steven motioned toward the battered wooden fence; most of the bottles and cans were knocked down or shattered. Without smiling he said, "*Dieses mal ist es mir besser gelungen.*"

The boy with the blond hair and the solid build had a fading German accent.

"*Ja, das stimmt.*" I cleared my throat. "Now say it in English."

"I did pretty good this time."

"You're getting to be pretty good."

"I held the gun the way you taught me and did much better."

"Yeah, you did pretty good this time. Much better."

Robert said, "Are we done shooting?"

His accent was more British, each word articulated and clear. That clarity was a reason for the other kids to tease him. The way he played soccer was a reason for them to admire him.

I nodded. "We have to get back. Alvin has to meet with Catherine."

Robert frowned. He was intense. No one scared me, but he rattled me. Because of the guilt.

I wondered if his mother would approve. But the dead couldn't approve of anything.

Robert said, "They always had guns. I remember them well."

"Who?"

"The devils on horseback. They did bad things to people. They did bad things to my mother. I still see them in my dreams. I see what they did to my mother."

I rubbed his head. Wanted to fix his problems. Didn't know how.

A soccer ball was near Steven's feet. He kicked the ball and ran toward the car, left his gun where he was supposed to leave it. Robert chased Steven and called for the ball.

Then I looked to my right, looked at a man who was big enough to block the sun.

I said, "Time to clean up."

"Yup."

That big man was Alvin White. He was the size of a mountain and built like a superhero, Captain Steroids. He was a former heavyweight boxer who was known in some fighting circles as Shotgun. They called him Shotgun because when he hit a man, it sounded like a powerful shotgun blast. He was willing to do whatever he had to do to make money and feed his family.

He said, "You should go ahead and look at that DNA stuff."

I nodded. "Time to get you to your appointment, Shotgun."

"Ain't nobody called me Shotgun in a while."

"Time to get you to Catherine. She'll be waiting on you."

This was my last obligation. Promises I had made to the boys. Yesterday I had taken the boys bowling at Midtown Bowl in Atlanta, then we drove to Skate Towne in College Park, skated for four hours, then ate at the Cumberland Mall because the boys wanted Chick-fil-A. After that we had gone shopping at Old Navy on Cobb Parkway, updated their wardrobes before we ended the evening by catching a movie next door at the AMC.

Catherine had had yesterday to herself. And based on the surveillance, she'd been busy. Busy up until I brought the boys home in time to get a late dinner and go to bed.

Steven got my attention and pointed up the road. "Somebody's coming."

Robert turned nervous, fear in his eyes as if he were back in his nightmares. Not all devils came on horseback. Some came on iron horses manufactured in Detroit.

Two GMC trucks pulled up and slowed about fifty yards away.

I thought about that shootout in Miami.

I yelled, told the boys to get behind the car.

With my right hand I reached inside my jacket and pulled a fresh clip from my pocket and reloaded. Alvin knew I had some problems that only bullets could fix and did the same, reloaded his shotgun, fast, like he was the new and improved Rifleman. He stood strong, a warrior ready.

One was a Ford F-150, the other a larger F-350. Rebel flags on their front license plates. The good ol' boys parked. Two men, two women, three teenagers, and around six children and two toddlers eased out of the vehicles. The men and the teenagers had lumps in their jaws. Chewing tobacco. Wore Braves baseball caps turned backward. The women each had a baby on one hip, and on the other hip they carried six-packs of beer. They wore their hair pulled back in ponytails, tight jeans and worn Levi's jackets. Both women had cigarettes dangling from their lips.

They all had weapons. The kids had rifles. Carried them like they were professionals.

My mind went back to Miami Gardens Drive. To the Lebanese woman in Starbucks.

I said, "We better go."

Alvin said, "You see their license plates?"

"Was too busy keeping my eyes on their guns."

"Both of them start with the number 14 and end with the number 88."

"Know what 14-88 means?"

"White supremacists."

"Yeah. The number 14 represents the fourteen words written by David Lane."

"Any idea what those fourteen words might be?"

"'We must secure the existence of our people and a future for white children.'"

"The 88 part?"

"Eighth letter in the alphabet. The letter *H*. Double *H*."

"Double *H*?"

"As in 'Heil Hitler.'"

Alvin grunted. "For real?"

I nodded. "A lot of them name their kids that way."

"What way?"

"First and middle name both start with an *H*. Double *H*. Heil Hitler."

"Hidden right in front of our faces. Will have to pay more attention to that from now on."

I said, "Let's get you and the boys out of here."

Alvin shook his head. "The way I see it, if I leave right now, it will look like I'm running."

"Could look that way."

"I don't run from nobody who walks in the same dirt I walk in."

"Neither do I."

"The boys have to learn not to run from people like them."

"Yes, they do."

"Especially Robert. He's African. If he's going to live in the United States, he'll get fed that racism every day. Too many of them down here. Always leave when you're ready to go, not when they want you to leave. A man has to learn to stand his ground, or get buried in the ground he's standing on."

I nodded.

I went back the fence, put up two dozen targets. I handed the boys their guns, told them to stay near the car. I kept a gun at my side and my eyes on the rebels. Alvin took a sawed-off shotgun out of the trunk of his taxi. He had enough weapons to start a small war.

He blew away targets, reloaded fast, blew away more targets, reloaded, did the same.

I stood behind him, firing shots at the ground around his feet.

Combat training. It was a loud, powerful, terrifying performance.

It let the enemy know we weren't a pack of deer hunters.

Alvin fanned out, moved left and fired, reloaded as I fired at his feet, then he moved right and fired. He did that over and over, his gunshots as rapid as a lightweight boxer's blows.

When it was done, when the gunshots faded, Alvin scowled at the rebel flags.

The members of the 14-88 club looked our way, their eyes focused on him.

Alvin wiped sweat from his brow, reloaded his shotgun, and held his ground, stood in dust, inhaled pollen. He had initiated call. Now he waited on response.

My gun was loaded. I'd become his wingman.

The men in that racist group nodded their heads.

One simple nod.

Alvin did the same.

One simple nod.

Respect. Or fear. Didn't matter. Alvin could leave on his own terms.

Alvin said, "Government keeps talking about terrorists overseas, but I'm more worried about the rednecks in my backyard than Bin Laden. Rednecks been terrorizing black people for hundreds of years, so terrorism ain't new to us. Slavery. Lynchings. Church bombings. Getting water hoses and dogs put on us. Terrorism ain't nothing new to the black man. Not at all."

Powder Springs, Georgia.

An area where the Cherokee Indians used to rule before being forced onto the Trail of Tears. An area that had many trees and hiking trails. That was where I had found a three-level house for Catherine and Steven. Now, because of my misdeeds and bad luck, Robert had joined the crew. I'd gone from being a loner, only worried about taking care of myself, to practicing selflessness and being overwhelmed, taking care of three people besides myself.

Catherine came to the front door when we pulled up in front of the house. We were riding with the windows up and AC on high, the cold air taking the edge off the unbearable heat. It was overcast, but the heat was wrapped around everything in the South.

Apprehension danced inside my gut. Like it always did before I did a contract.

My next one was in Buenos Aires. For Arizona. That thought had my head in a vise grip sponsored by regret while a noose of resentment tightened around my neck.

I despised her as much as I used to desire her. Was close to hating her.

And when I hated someone, that wasn't a good thing, not for them.

I waved at Catherine. She smiled and waved back.

Before she was Catherine, she was a whore named Thelma.

I have no idea who she was before that. I only knew that Thelma wasn't a French name. She had come to North America and changed her name in order to fit in. Same thing she had done for the boys. Steven used to be Sven. Robert's name was new as well.

Just like Gideon wasn't my birth name.

We were children of whores. We were whores and killers pretending to be squares.

Catherine wore jeans and a pink-collared blouse. She was French, born in the land of fashion, and she was an excellent dresser. Only she did it on a budget. Everything fashionable and inexpensive, more than likely from discount stores like T.J. Maxx or Ross.

I felt some uneasiness. Some anger. Some fear.

That surveillance video played inside my head. The man who had hurried inside the house I had given them fucked her, and then hurried away like a john. We had lived that life all of my youth. She'd said that she no longer worked in lingerie, said she no longer serviced men and women by the hour. The woman who reared me owned a natural beauty and a graceful charm that made her a cynosure, but she wasn't the center of attention. She looked like a homemaker, a conservative PTA mom who took care of her boys and minded her own business.

Catherine called to Alvin, "Where is your study notebook?"

"In the trunk of the car. Let me run back and get it."

"Did you do your homework? Did you write sentences like I asked?"

"Yes, ma'am. Well, I finished up most of it."

"Most is not all. You must take this seriously. Don't waste my time."

"I know, ma'am. I know."

"Come prepared."

Catherine called Robert and Steven, only called once. She never had to call them twice.

She never shouted, her voice soft and firm, a serious mother.

She said, "Come wash up and eat. Baked salmon and vegetables."

The boys booed.

I smiled a jealous smile. When I was a child, our relationship had been ugly.

It had been abusive.

The boys stopped kicking the soccer ball, ran to Catherine and gave her kisses.

Catherine hugged the boys, gave them equal love. She smiled and rubbed the boys' heads. Boys who had been friends in London, now brothers in the United States.

Alvin opened his trunk, rushed to get out his materials for school.

I stood close to Catherine and said, "Let's open the FedEx and look at that DNA."

She held on to her smile, but her eyes changed, the joy lessened.

She said, "Now?"

"After you finish with Alvin. After he leaves. Just me and you. We settle this."

She nodded. "This is why I kept it. I knew you would want to. I knew you would."

Catherine went inside, small box in her hand, laughing with her *fútbol*-loving sons.

Her laughter wasn't strong, a pretty laugh filled with nervousness and worry.

I thought about what I had seen on camera, her and that man.

I looked at the boys.

Robert's mother was brutally murdered. Like I was told mine had been.

That was our bond.

The other boy, Steven, was possibly kidnapped.

Like I might've been when I was a baby.

Thelma. Not Catherine. Thelma.

I had no idea who she really was.

I was afraid to face my own horrors. I wanted a window, not a mirror.

I remembered what she had done to me when I was almost a man.

Remembered too much.

There was no optimism in my heart.

Only cynicism.

And the deadly hate.

Chapter 27

last regret before reality

Alvin's lesson lasted close to two hours.

Every minute had passed like an hour of acidic angst.

I'd been on the iPhone, again reviewing footage. I saw Catherine's latest secrets.

I had tried, but the things I'd seen in my life, they couldn't be forgotten.

The things I had done, they couldn't be undone.

It felt like I was back inside a brothel. I took a deep breath and smelled the past, perverts' sweat on come-stained sheets and mattresses, the leftover stench from my childhood.

The stench had returned and wouldn't go away. Maybe it had never left.

I was in the basement when I heard the big man come down thirteen carpeted steps that ended on a tiled floor. The subterranean area had been finished after my ordeal in Antigua. Alvin and I had done all of the work. We had added a bathroom. Built a room for Catherine's treadmill and EFX machines. There was a room for the boys that had a thirty-two-inch flat-screen television and Wii equipment. And there was a room no one could see. I opened a section of drywall that appeared unmovable, unhitched and slid that drywall to the side. I took a key and opened two dead bolts that were on a steel door that exposed a hidden room, one impenetrable to gunfire, big enough for ten people to sit in and wait for trouble to pass. I hit a switch, and twelve recessed lights came on, made the room bright as day. Four guns were in that room, all nines.

Alvin asked, "Where you off to next?"

A new anger rose. I took a breath, then answered, "Argentina."

"That in Spain?"

"South America. Straight south. South like going to Hell."

"Hot down there, huh?"

"Cold. Short days. Seasons are reversed. Our summer is their winter."

"Bet some pretty women down there. Would love to see winter in the summertime."

I rubbed my eyes and said, "But you're not ready."

"I'm ready. You see how I can handle myself. I'm ready." He pulled up his shirtsleeve. "Look at these guns. Been working out. Sculpted, lean, hard muscles. Been on that P90X program like you told me to get on. Got into the best shape of my life in record time. Been eating right, on that creatine and whey protein. Look at my abs. That's an evil six-pack. Mean, ripped muscles like you, like I'm an MMA fighter. Been working out with some MMA guys over in Buckhead. Getting in some judo and grappling. That and boxing over at Crunch on Cobb Parkway. Been studying Krav Maga too. Fists and elbows and knees. Real fighting. Doing the kind of fighting you and that Hawks woman you told me about were trained to do. Street shit. I didn't look this good when I was in my best shape when I was in the ring. I'm faster. I'm lighter."

"Are you bulletproof?"

"As bulletproof as you are."

"What would you do if you were in a situation and you had to read?"

That shut him down.

I said, "What if your life, or somebody else's life, depended on you being able to read a sign?"

He nodded. I'd hit his sore spot with words that were as strong as a knockout punch.

I shook my head. I'd stated my position. And it wouldn't change.

Alvin opened the hidden doors, inspected the safe room. He was good with his hands. He could walk into a forest with a knife and build a house. My friend could build or fix anything.

I took a deep breath, licked my lips. "Where's Catherine?"

"She's waiting on you. Think she's nervous. She had a hard time concentrating."

"No reason to be nervous, not if you've been telling the truth."

"She's a good woman. No matter what, she's good to those boys."

Now he didn't want me to open the FedEx. I smiled. She had said something to Alvin, used her charm, pulled him to her side. He had reversed his course over the past two hours.

I asked, "What did she say to you?"

"She's a good mother. You can look at them boys and tell she's a good woman."

"Don't get blinded by her beauty. Don't ever get blinded by a woman's beauty. If somebody had told me that before I went to North Hollywood, my world would be better."

"What happened in North Hollywood?"

"The beginning of a long line of bad decisions."

He nodded. After that, I didn't press it. He'd been put in a difficult position.

We talked. Had a serious conversation. A scary conversation.

He thought he knew me. But he didn't. He had no fucking idea who I was.

No fucking idea of my life and the things I'd done.

When that talk was done, we shook hands. We had an understanding.

My confidant said his good-byes to the boys and headed home to his family.

It was time for me to climb thirteen carpeted stairs and deal with mine.

Chapter 28

the lady from Yerres

My demons roared.

It was time to face the life-changing issues I had avoided for too long.

I'd centered my breathing, the smell from old whorehouses blown out of my nostrils.

The house smelled like salmon and vegetables, had the scent of vanilla plug-in air fresheners, looked like a home that Beaver and Wally Cleaver would approve of.

Steven and Robert raced out the back door, down the stairs into the backyard.

Catherine called after the boys, "You can play one hour. Do you hear me?"

My mind remained restless. On Arizona. On a man I owed a favor. On South America.

And on the motherfuckers who were blackmailing me for two million dollars.

My iPhone rang. It was Hawks. I didn't answer. Seconds later she sent a text. CALL ME. It wasn't tagged with an emergency code. So she could take a number and get in the queue.

The television was on local news. Thieves had burgled two Kennesaw eateries, stolen sixteen flat-screen televisions. Rapper Soulja Boy Tell 'Em was attacked in his home and robbed of five large and jewelry. Unemployment was at its highest in sixteen years. Two of the women in *The Real Housewives of Atlanta* had been evicted from their homes.

Then one of the stories put a spear in the center of my chest.

The next story was about a Riverdale mother who moved out of her marital bed so her husband could sexually assault their daughter. A mother who got her own daughter intoxicated on vodka and forced her kid to sleep with her father, a father who fucked his own child.

Everywhere I looked, fucking pedophiles.

I sat at the dining room table. The FedEx box in front of me.

X.Y.Z.

I touched the box. Had a déjà vu moment.

Catherine walked into the room. She lingered in the doorframe for a moment.

We made eye contact.

Her eyes broke away from mine, went to the box.

Our elephant.

She went to the cabinet, took out two Starbucks cups. She took out Earl Grey bags, put one inside each cup. The teapot on the stove whistled, and she filled the cups with hot water, then put one in front of me. She handed me a spoon. Honey was on the table. I added honey to my tea. Then she picked up the honey and did the same. And as I stirred my tea, she stirred hers. She didn't sit down. She stood by the stove and sipped, her fingers opening and closing, her expression that of weariness.

Catherine asked, "Are you sure this time?"

I nodded. "Are you ready?"

"I am ready."

She sat at the circular dining room table, nervous, sweat beading on the tip of her nose. Her brown eyes became vulnerable. She held herself, rubbed her hands up and down her arms.

She said, "Remember this."

"What?"

"I am the one who told you to keep that . . . that package. I told you to keep it. You were going to throw it away, destroy it, and I am the one who told you not to throw it away."

"I know."

"Because I knew this day would come."

"I know."

"I am the one who fed you, who made sure you had clothes on your back."

"And you put a knife or a gun in my hand, sent me to kill."

"Bad people. They were all bad people."

"Some people deserve to die. You told me that. Some people deserve to die."

She pulled her lips in, closed her eyes for a moment, then once again looked at me.

She nodded. "That is what I told you."

"You said my father told you that. And that was a lie. Everything has been a lie."

All of my phones rang at once. The phone from the Lebanese. The satellite phone from Scamz. My iPhone. The house phone rang too. All phones went unanswered.

We sat still until all the ringing and buzzing stopped.

Catherine wrung her hands. "Before you open it . . ."

"I'm listening."

"See me as who I am now. Don't see me as you saw me . . . when you were younger."

"When you came into my room. And abused me."

"That was not me. That was someone else, someone young and foolish."

I rubbed my temples. Wiped my eyes.

Then I opened the FedEx box, ripped open the edges, pulled out the envelopes.

Catherine sat across from me, tears falling down her face.

Catherine was X. Steven was Y. I was Z.

I opened Z first. Then I opened X. Left Y sitting to the side.

I read Z. Then evaluated X. Read the words from DNA Solutions.

Lightning flashed behind my eyes.

I held the truth, a reality she couldn't change, couldn't manipulate with lies.

It hurt. It angered me.

My right hand turned into a fist. I said, "How do you do it?"

She took deep breaths, let them out in short, nervous bursts.

"How do you lie so convincingly? Is that part of your job?"

I didn't think I would be angry. I had told myself that I wouldn't be angry.

It was a deadly struggle.

I said, "You're. My. Mother."

She swallowed, moved her hair. She couldn't look at me.

I closed my eyes, tried not to explode. A thousand flashbacks from my childhood. Sex. Drugs. Violence. Johns. Whores. Guns. Knives. Death. And incest. Half the time we had no food. Scapegraces eating cold chicken given to us by some goddamn stranger. Eating greasy-ass handout chicken. Eating scraps from someone else's red-and-white bucket. Being homeless all across the United States and up into Canada.

She said, "I gave you what you wanted. What you *needed*. You needed me to not be your mother, and I gave you Margaret. I took the memory of my dead friend, a friend who was murdered, and I made her your mother. I gave you your freedom from me. All you had to do was walk away. All you had to do was leave and forget about me. But . . . you wouldn't let me go. Yes, I am your mother. The woman who birthed you. But I am not the one who did horrible things to you. That was Thelma. And Thelma is gone. Thelma is . . . dead. She is dead."

"Why would you do that?"

"All of my life . . . I have been . . . I have told men what they want to hear."

"Like a whore."

"I gave you what you wanted. I gave you what you wanted."

I knew twenty-two ways to end a life. I imagined doing all of them to her.

The perfect end to a Shakespearian tragedy. No, not Shakespeare. Sophocles. *Oedipus the King*. The Greek tragedy about the fucked-up royal family. A man who killed his father. And slept with his mother.

I stood up, broken, and moved toward the woman who had mind-fucked me all my life.

I heard the boys. Heard Steven and Robert laughing, arguing, playing. That sound of their merriment saved her. I put my back against the wall, held my head in my hands.

The boys. Steven and Robert. They didn't ask to be born into this madness.

This was bigger than Catherine and me. Bigger than any fool in this room.

Catherine was scared shitless. She didn't run. She sat with her arms folded, bounced her legs, lips tight, eyes closed, remembering all the lies, swallowing them over and over like she was swallowing hot semen.

What she had done to my body and my head, it was irreversible and irreparable.

She said, "I have asked God for forgiveness. I have fallen to my knees and bowed my head in supplication, begged for forgiveness. If God can forgive me, why can't you?"

"Because I'm not God."

"Why do you act like one? Why did you bring me to North America and lord over me?"

A man could always forgive. Forgiving wasn't the problem. Forgetting was the problem.

She said, "I admit my faults. I made bad choices. I didn't do a good job rearing you."

"You didn't rear me. You used me to kill. Whores, con men, and thieves reared me."

"But I did what I had to do to protect you. I could've left you on the steps of a church the day you were born. I could've abandoned you on the steps of a home. Or left you in the garbage. Many frightened girls leave their newborn babies in trash cans. But I kept you and reared you. I had nothing, was in a strange country with no money, and did what I could. Yes, I was a horrible mother. But I did what I had to do to protect you."

I swallowed pain that went down like razor blades. I walked toward her, moved past her angst, went into the kitchen, and poured myself a glass of water. Needed cold water, not hot tea. I looked out at the boys, then poured a second glass of water, went back into the dining room, put that glass of water down in front of Catherine, next to her cup of tea.

She sipped her water and put the glass back down on the table.

I asked, "Who was the man you had over?"

The new conversation stunned her, caused her jaw to drop, left no room for lies.

She asked, "How did you . . ."

"Are you still a sex worker?"

She shook her head. "Don't believe you asked me that."

"The man you brought here in the middle of the night, what do you know about him?"

"How did you know about him?"

"Knowing is my business."

"You're spying on me?"

I repeated, "What do you know about him?"

"He's my friend." She took another breath. "We go to movies."

"You're a liar. I don't know you. You've lied about so much."

"I am not a sex worker. You know I am not a sex worker."

"Where do you and your friend go to the movies?"

"In Austell. The theater around the corner."

"When do you go to the movies?"

"During the day. When the boys are at school."

"Where did you meet him?"

"Borders."

"Which Borders?"

"In Austell. On East-West Connector."

"You met him at a bookstore."

"Is Alvin spying on me?"

I paused, almost snapped and told her the truth. I backed away, didn't play my hand.

My eyes went to that FedEx package. To the DNA results. Fuel to my anger.

I said, "You sucked that man's dick in the living room and the boys were upstairs, a few feet away. I know how I grew up. I know how they grew up. They've seen things that children shouldn't see, things a child shouldn't see his mother do. I saw your life, know Steven saw you working as a whore in London and wherever you were before you ran to London. I know Robert . . . his mother . . . he has probably seen the same. I want that shit to end. I brought you here because I want that shit to end."

She was rattled, embarrassed, confused, and angry.

"Robert and Steven. Did they see me with him?"

"If you are back to whoring . . . don't conduct your business . . . in the goddamn living room."

"Stop accusing me of being a sex worker. That life is over. I swear to God."

"They didn't see. The boys didn't see."

"Then . . . how would you know what I do inside my own home? How would you know what I do when you are not here? When you are hundreds of miles away, how do you know?"

Silence.

"I'm a woman, Jean-Claude."

"I know you are, Catherine."

"All of my friends, I left them behind. I have the boys. Only the boys. I love them. But I get lonely. I need . . . adult conversation and interaction. I need . . . I am a woman."

"Okay."

"I've done so many bad things in my life, but I am still a human being."

"Are you?"

"I had not been with a man . . . since London. And not like this. Never dated. Wasn't sure I knew how. Wasn't sure if I could. The first men who touched me, they were relatives that molested me. When you are a girl and that is all you know, that is how you learn to relate to men. Many men have touched me, out of need, out of anger, but never out of love. This is the first time I've been with a man who . . . he only knows me as Catherine. That was who he was with. He was with Catherine. Not with the girl from Yerres. Not with the woman you remember when you were a boy. Not with the woman you beat with your fists and put in the hospital, then came to Amsterdam and London to find with all of that hate in your heart. He was with the woman I am now. He was with Catherine. There was no money exchanged. He took me skating during the day. We went roller-skating at a rink in Marietta. Once we walked on the Silver Comet Trail. Once we walked the Chattahoochee Trail. Another time we went to the cinema. We held hands at the cinema. That was new for me. It was like . . . a fantasy. Something I never had the chance to do as a young girl. A man's touch that wasn't about violence or sex. Or about me needing money. That's what regular people do. They meet. Talk. Decide if they like each other enough to date. They date. Then they decide whether they want it to be more."

I raised my hand. Had heard enough.

She asked, "How did you know about him coming inside my home?"

"What does he know about you?"

"I can't hide my accent. I told him I was from Paris. I created a life for myself. A new, respectable life. Said I was married twice in Europe. Once to a German, once to an African. Marriages that I don't want to talk about. I told him what I have told everyone else. He respects that. He knows I love books, that I love movies, that l love languages. He thinks I'm funny. He laughs at my jokes. He tells me that I am beautiful. He admires me for being a single mother raising two energetic boys."

"World-class liar. That's what you are. A world-class liar."

She shook her head, lowered her face into her palms.

I stared at the DNA results, two-thirds of X.Y.Z. resolved.

It took a moment before Catherine raised her head, her body language weak.

There was one more test result between us. One more variable in the equation.

The answer to Y. The answer to Steven.

The boy with the blond hair. The boy who spoke German as if it were his first language.

I opened the DNA and read his truth. Read what Catherine already knew.

I read it over and over. What I read didn't change. Another truth stared back at me.

I looked at Catherine.

"Jean-Claude . . ."

It took me a moment to find my voice. "Steven told me he shot a man."

"Steven told you that."

I stared, waited for her to talk.

She said, "A man who . . . was beating me."

"That had to be déjà vu."

"It was."

"You get all of us to kill for you. All of us."

She didn't say anything.

I rubbed the back of my neck. "Where were you that time?"

"Begleitagenturen."

"The kid killed a man in Germany."

"A customer who attacked me."

"Like when we were in Montreal. Or was it like in North Carolina."

She sad nothing.

I moved my hands from my neck, rubbed my temples and my forehead.

She wiped her eyes.

I said, "Stop crying."

"God. I can't cry? You tell me to not cry like you own my anguish. You give orders, do this, do that, not do this, not do that . . . like . . . like . . . like that horrible man."

"What horrible man?"

She said, "My father."

"Those tears are no longer currency."

Tears fell as her nose filled with snot. I went to the kitchen, grabbed a few napkins and handed them to her. She thanked me, then blew her nose over and over.

"You make me feel like a prisoner."

"What were you when you were whoring on Berwick Street? Did

you have a house, a decent roof over your head? Did you have a car? You lived in the gutter. You have lived in the gutter all of your life. I pulled you out of that gutter. Now you're in a dream house. Living a middle-class life. And you know how all of your bills get paid? I do things to make this possible. You don't have to work. All you have to do is live a decent life and take care of those boys. Stop crying. And give me a break with that prisoner bullshit. If anyone is a prisoner, if anyone in this room is a prisoner, it sure as hell isn't you."

"What am I doing here?" She spoke in a strong whisper, one filled with anguish and anger. "You pay for my life here, yes, and I appreciate that. But there is no freedom. You tell me I am still that bad person, that young girl who was so terrified of the world, that young girl who was abused, that young woman who sold herself to people . . . to strangers . . . and did that to feed herself . . . took strangers to bed to feed and clothe you as well. Over and over I sold myself for you. Now . . . somehow you watch my every move and you talk as if you have the power to sanction every aspect of my life, even my tears."

"Stop crying."

She nodded, struggled, but the tears continued.

"Until I know who your friend is, until I'm comfortable with him, keep him away from here. If he comes back, I'll go see him. And when I do, he'll never be seen again. Understand?"

"I do what other single mothers do. I do what a lonely woman who needs the company of a man does. I do it so the children do not see. It is not out in the open. That is what we do."

"You get his information. His address, his driver's license number, bank statements, you get everything you can, and you pass that information on to me. He has to be checked out."

She coughed, struggled to breathe, her face as red as fire.

She said, "I care about him."

"Get his information."

"He trusts me."

"Then getting it should be easy."

"I am not a thief."

"You are a liar. And a liar is the cousin of a thief."

She sobbed.

I said, "Do what you do best. Tell him what he wants to hear. Then rob him."

I took heavy steps toward the kitchen, looked out the bay window at the trees.

I wasn't close to the truth. Was only scratching the surface.

I watched the boys play outside, struggled with myself, stubborn tears in my eyes.

I didn't want to be angry. Wanted to be over it. Wanted to move on. But I was stuck.

A few seconds passed and I saw her reflection in the window.

Thelma stood behind me. Not Catherine. Thelma. Saw the angry French woman. The woman I knew still existed. Saw the woman that had sent me to go kill her enemies. Saw my first handler. She had picked up a knife from the table. Her brows were drawn down, upper lip raised. She had tightness under her eyes, the look of violence, the look of a killer.

She whispered, "Why do you push me?"

"Put the blade down."

"Why do you insist on badgering me and resurrecting that other person?"

"Put it down now."

I saw it in her reflection. She wanted to stab me in my back over and over.

She growled out, "Why are you trying to destroy me?"

"Steven is my brother."

My words stopped her movements but didn't slow her rage.

I repeated, "Steven is my brother. The DNA says he's my brother."

"He's my son."

"He's my brother."

"You're envious. Covetous of the love I give him. Your hatred eats you alive. He loves me and that makes you resentful. I don't know why it does, but it does. You hate what we have."

"You're delusional."

"You are so . . . so . . . so resentful of our happiness that you have to take it out on me."

"When I come back from South America, I should take the boys with me."

"Take them?"

"The boys should come with me. You don't deserve them."

"Don't taunt me."

"I don't taunt. I'm not in the taunting business."

"I'll kill you before I let you steal my son and Nusaybah's son from me."

"I'll do what I have to do to protect Steven and Robert."

"You won't take them."

"I will take Steven. He's my goddamn brother. And I will take Robert."

"Robert's mother . . . she is dead because of you. Don't ever forget that. My best friend is in a graveyard in London because of you. She was slaughtered like an animal because of you."

I turned and faced her.

Her lips trembled. "You are not God."

"But you are a pedophile."

"I did something horrible . . . when I was drunk . . . once . . . only once."

"You are a pedophile."

She gripped the knife like she was ready to run the sharp blade through my gut.

"You're not God."

I said, "But you can be God. Do it. Destroy what you created."

She pulled her lips in, gritted her teeth. "You came out of me."

"I am what you and an evil man created."

"I suffered a horrible labor, gave birth to you, natural childbirth in a small, filthy hostel."

"Do it. Be God. You said some people deserve to die. You were the one playing God."

"Two days in labor. And I went through that pain alone."

"Undo what you have done."

The blade touched my shirt, the tip pushed inside my gut.

Phones rang.

I spoke over the cacophony. "Do it."

Her eyes met mine. Pain stared at pain. She tensed, veins appeared in her neck.

Phones stopped ringing.

She firmed her grip and frowned like she was ready to destroy the monster she had created. But she backed away, lowered her head, her brown hair falling free. She put the knife in my hand, handle first. I put the knife on the table, blade first. Then I went back to the window. Blood dripped where she had pushed the knife. She had broken my skin.

She whispered, "Don't take them . . . Steven and Robert . . . don't take them from me."

That FedEx box had been opened. What I knew couldn't be erased.

I asked, "Why did you have me? Why did you have a baby?"

She said, "Please don't take my sons away from me."

"Why did you bring me into a world as fucked up as yours?"

"Why didn't I have an abortion?"

"Why didn't you have a fucking abortion?"

"Is that what you wish I had done?"

It took a while to recover my voice. "What is your friend's name?"

"Jeremy Bentham."

I paused. "Get his information."

There were footsteps on the carpeted stairs. Two sets racing up from the basement.

Catherine called out. "Take your shoes off."

The running stopped. The boys did what she commanded. That bought her some time.

She straightened her clothing. Did her best to become Catherine.

Her new name was the name I had picked out for her when we were homeless in Montreal. It was the name of the street we had walked when we were homeless.

I'd never seen her birth certificate. Had never seen mine.

I asked, "Who were you before you came to North America?"

"When I was in Yerres."

"Who were you in Yerres?"

"Before Thelma . . . there was a frightened little girl named Nathalie-Marie Masreliez."

"Nathalie-Marie Masreliez."

"Yes."

I said, "I've never heard you use that name before."

"It is a name I have not uttered since . . . since . . ."

"Since Yerres."

The boys hurried into the kitchen, ran by laughing and arguing, their conversation swift as they bolted to the refrigerator in search of snacks and juice. They were too busy talking about who was the best soccer player on Wii, oblivious to the angst that filled the air.

Then they took their snacks and took to the stairs, went toward their rooms.

Again, it was the killer and the liar.

She said, "I never know what to expect from you. Never know which version of you will show up at my door. The smiling you. Or this version of you. You're passive-aggressive."

"I can just be aggressive, if that's what you prefer."

"Always passive-aggressive."

"Being passive gets me nothing but new lies to replace old lies."

"You're sick. One moment you act like you love us. Like you might have a small spot in your heart, a little love for me, despite our horrible past. And the next you hate me."

"Maybe I just hate myself for allowing myself to care about a woman like you."

Eyes filled with tears, she looked away from me.

I said, "Your friend has been here at least three times in the last week."

"How did you know?"

"He was here today. Came an hour after we left. Was here for an hour."

"If you were not here . . . how did you know?"

"Don't ever lie to me again."

She raised her voice, "*How do you know what I do when you are not here?*"

Catherine trembled, hunched over, and wrung her hands. Blood drained from her face. She made a wounded sound. Then she exploded. She threw her cup at the wall, sent hot tea and honey everywhere. She pulled her hair. Her eyes went to the knife. She knocked her chair over and hurried out of the kitchen. Her feet hurried up the stairs. Her bedroom door closed. The boys called out to her. She didn't answer. I stood and walked to the sink, poured out my unfinished tea, then cleaned up the mess she had made, before I headed toward the front door.

The boys were on the stairs.

Robert's face owned no readable expression.

But Steven, the boy who had almost killed me once before, frowned.

He frowned like he was Cain ready to bring his weapon down on Abel.

Chapter 29

pain

When a man scratched a scab, an old wound reopened.

I left Powder Springs, drove the back roads toward Hartsfield airport. It would be at least a twenty-mile ride. Twenty miles of thinking. I thought it would just be me and my thoughts, but my iPhone rang. It was Hawks. She had called me a half dozen times. Would call until I answered.

So I answered.

She said, "Got off the plane at Gatwick and checked my messages. The Islington order was canceled."

"That's the way it works."

"All of the funds were transferred. If they reconsider, they have to pay again."

"Nice. That's the best kind of job. One you get paid for and don't have to do."

She paused. "Gideon."

"Hawks."

"Want me to meet you for that South America thing?"

"Go see Buckingham Palace. Go to Notting Hill Gate and walk Portobello Road."

"I'm on Expedia. I can leave here and get to Buenos Aires by eleven tomorrow morning."

"Why don't you go see *Zorro the Musical* or *Star Wars the Musical* or—"

"Because I don't want to go see a stupid musical. Plus I hate musicals. Either sing or act. Don't do both. That is the dumbest mess in the world. Singing what you're saying."

Her persistence put another vise grip around my head. She meant well. But it was irritating. Hawks had my ears, but someone else had my eyes. I passed by dozens of billboards and city buses, adverts to the number-one news station in Atlanta, the number-one news anchor, the Jewel of the South, smiling down on me at every turn. A devil with an angelic smile.

Hawks said, "You okay?"

"We opened the FedEx box."

"What happened?"

"Anybody but her. Anybody but her." I took a breath. "We have the same DNA."

"She's your sister?"

"Worse. One level up."

"Are you shitting me? She's your mother? The things she did to you . . ."

"And the kid . . . Steven . . ."

"Was that little boy kidnapped like you thought?"

"Steven wasn't kidnapped."

"He's . . . her kid?"

"He is my brother. The DNA says he is my brother."

Hawks paused. "He looks nothing like her. Who is his father?"

"Could be any man who had a dick and a dollar."

"I mean, is he safe with her? Both of those boys, are they safe with her?"

I took a few hard breaths. "No more talk about Catherine. Never mention her again."

There was another pause.

"Gideon. Last thing about that and then I'm done."

"Okay. What?"

"You were always telling me about Berwick Street. I caught a taxi and went over there. Had to see it. Walked around that area. Good Lord. All the prostitutes and the porn. The boys lived in that filthy environment? I saw the signs for models. Took me a minute to realize what a model was. And the smells. Chinatown was around the corner, so it was like Chinese food mixed with filth and an orgy. It looked like an area filled with pimps and sex slaves."

I paused. "Why would you do that? Why would you go there?"

It took her a moment to respond to my tone. "I'm not your enemy. I'm the only person in your life who's not tied to you by money or a past you want to forget. I'm your friend."

"I have to go."

"Let me come help. I can meet you in Buenos Aires."

"No."

"Your head's in a bad place. People are blackmailing you for a ton of money and that call about South America, the people you're supposed to be working for, not good people, not at all. All I can say is that you're a mess. The whole time we were in Puerto Rico—"

I disconnected the call. Cut her off midsentence.

Another billboard for local news and the Jewel of the South whizzed by.

A lot of thinking could be done on a twenty-mile journey. By the time I was on Thornton Road, my iPhone hummed. Area code 809. Arizona sent footage from a swift and brutal battle in Buenos Aires. Whatever information she had about my other problem was being withheld.

Had to give to get.

I didn't play the video right away. Other issues controlled my mind.

I pulled over near a Jeep dealership in Lithia Springs, just on the other side of I-20, paused long enough to send a text. JEREMY BENTHAM. SMYRNA, GEORGIA. I tagged that text with ASAP. For a moment, I blinked and I was back in London. Maybe Hawks being in London made me think about those days in London. When I was holed up in a hotel room in Bloomsbury.

Anger in my heart was as strong now as it was then. Lies revealed. Old pains resurrected. I sent a second text. NATHALIE-MARIE MASRE- LIEZ. YERRES, FRANCE. FIND OUT WHO SHE IS. Then I cursed. The truth didn't always set a man free. Sometimes it was better to be ignorant.

Too late. The red pill had been swallowed. Now I had to keep it moving.

I mixed with the madness on Thornton Road, sped toward the airport. Dumped the car. Got my electronic ticket and made it through security without a problem. Took the train to terminal E, came up the escalator facing a tribute to Reverend Dr. Martin Luther King Jr.

I sat at the gate with my back against the wall, looking at everyone.

I connected to GOTOMYPC.COM, looked in on Powder Springs.

The boys were in the den, watching television, while Catherine hurried around the house. She picked up picture frames, books, rushed from room to room inspecting anything she thought might have a camera inside. I backed up the footage. She was tearing the house apart. The time stamp told me she had started as soon as I had pulled away. She had raced inside her bedroom. I couldn't see what she did in her bedroom, but when she came out, one hand was on her waist, the other pulling her hair, trying to figure out a puzzle. She was on a mission.

I sat down in first class. Sat next to a clean-shaven Russian who had salt-and-pepper hair and a handsome face that looked like an older George Clooney from some angles and Cary Grant from other angles. A chisel-chinned man who fancied double-breasted suits. A man who had on white shoes. He put his ticket down on his armrest, the name Archibald Leach printed out across the slip of paper. He wasn't Archibald Leach.

That chisel-chinned man's birth name was Konstantin Pentkovski. He was one of the men who had trained me in this business. He was looking at a video on his iPhone. It looked like a ferocious John Woo movie. Explosions. Men being gunned down. Heads exploding.

But it wasn't a movie.

It was footage from The Four Horsemen of the Apocalypse.

That bloodbath pulled my attention.

A big man boarded the plane. A man so large he had to bend over so his head didn't bump the top of the cabin. Black suit, white shirt, red tie. Shoes polished to a spit shine. His calloused hands didn't match his clothes. He had one piece of carry-on and an old winter coat with him. He sat in first class, across the aisle from Konstantin and his white shoes. The big man looked nervous, uncomfortable. My mind moved from Powder Springs toward South America. The doors to the plane closed. Then something happened. There were several audio dings. Alerts. The lead flight attendant went to the front. The doors to the plane were opened. Security stepped on the plane and handed the flight attendant a slip of paper. Security was always a bad sign. Three names were called. Archibald Alec Leach. That was Konstantin. They called James Sawyer. That was the big man in first class. Then they called John Michael Kane. That was me.

I knew that Konstantin and me could handle whatever happened.

The big guy was new to this business. The big guy was Alvin White.

Chapter 30

trapped

Airport security surrounded us like prison guards.

Led by a silent team of guns and badges, we were taken to another part of the airport. Nobody said anything. A stack of dead bodies was on my mind, starting in North Carolina and ending with Hopkins. I'd only talk if they asked questions, and depending on the question, might not talk then. We were put in the backseats of three different security cars and driven across the tarmac with lights flashing. It was about a two-mile ride to an isolated section that had a fleet of private planes. There we were taken out of the cars and led by the officers. We weren't in handcuffs. We grabbed our bags, and the officers walked in front of us until we made it to the roll-up stairs. We were escorted to a different plane. It was a Gulfstream G550. An ultra-long-range business jet that had four living areas, three temperature zones, and Rolls-Royce engines.

Four flight attendants greeted us. A slender Ethiopian with long wavy hair, beautiful skin, and keen features. A modelesque Russian. A gorgeous Arabian princess with an hourglass figure and a French accent that sounded like soft jazz on Sunday morning. And a Brazilian with heavenly curves that set a new standard for beauty. Professional women wrapped in class and dressed in red uniforms dabbed with soft perfumes.

Three hired guns and four attendants took up cabin space on a luxury plane big enough to hold eighteen, three times that if they were partying like they were at the Hard Rock. This plane had been arranged by Scamz. Konstantin told me that he had sent Scamz my request for a private plane to Buenos Aires. We'd been pulled out of a flying Motel 6 and put inside a flying Four Seasons.

Then I realized I had made a mistake. The plane wasn't a G550.

We were inside a G650. A Gulfstream that wasn't officially on the market yet. A plane that could fly at supersonic speeds and could cover 7,000 nautical miles on one tank of gas. I'd flown a Cessna. But this was like being snatched out of a Pinto and thrown inside a Lamborghini. Full kitchen. Bar. Satellite phones. Wireless Internet. Entertainment center. One hundred thousand pounds of plane that cost fifty-eight million. The kind of plane the super-rich had, the kind that could land at any airport, large or small. Which meant it could slip onto a small island or into a large country. A good way to avoid air traffic and land in Argentina undetected.

Konstantin stopped and went to the cockpit. Met the pilot. Looked the plane over.

I looked out the window.

We had our bags with us, but they were loading metal containers on the aircraft. High-speed private planes were used for the same reason high-speed boats were used in Miami. To move illegal cargo the shipper didn't want in reach of the long arm of the law.

Konstantin came and looked out a window, saw what I saw.

I said, "This is one hell of an upgrade."

Konstantin nodded. "I'm not impressed. And you shouldn't be either. Our flight time has just been cut in half, more or less. They are rushing us there. Not a good sign."

The Brazilian flight attendant asked if we needed anything right away. Said there was a catalog of movies and music. Then she told us we could spread out and have our own sections of the plane if we needed privacy.

We sat down in the section the farthest from the cockpit. The leather furniture felt like warm butter. I took to a massive recliner. Alvin White took to the largest sofa I'd seen in a while.

Konstantin stood near me. "*Ty skazal chto on ne umeet chitat?*"
You said he can't read.

I responded in Russian, "*Net, no on horosh s pistoletom.*"

No, but he's good with a gun.

Konstantin nodded. "*On ubijza?*"

He's killed before?

I looked at Alvin, then back at Konstantin. "*Pomog mne. Prikonchil dvooh dlya menya.*"

Helped me out. Took out two men on my behalf.

Konstantin took in Alvin before he spoke again. "*On zdorovyj my-zhik. Oni ego pristrelyat v pervuyu ochered' esli delo do etogo doidiot.*"

He's a big guy. Would be the first thing they tried to shoot, if it came to that.

Again I nodded. "*Ny my ego pristroim.*"

We'll find a way to use him.

Konstantin said, "*I esli ja s nim ne polazhy, ja ego sam prikonchyu.*"

And if I have a problem with him, I will put him down.

Russian gangsters were ruthless. No compassion. They would do a blackout, kill the whole family, women, children; would put a bullet in everyone and the dog.

That was the cloth Konstantin was cut from.

He took to another recliner and faced Alvin. Konstantin was finished with me. For now. I knew to stay out of the next conversation before it started. I picked up a newspaper they had on board. *La Nación.* Pretended to read an article. "*El rapero Lil Wayne hace música para tontos.*"

Konstantin looked at the big man. "So you're the guy Gideon wants to take a chance on."

"Yes, sir."

"You're as big as Nikolai Valuev."

"Almost. He got me by a couple of inches on height. Not on reach, though."

"What's your name?"

"Alvin White."

"Your other name."

"Shotgun."

"Alvin White is your real name?"

"Yes, sir."

"Never use it. Don't ever say it again. The one on your passport, that is who you are."

"James Sawyer."

"If that's what it says on your papers, that's who you are."

"Yes, sir."

"Nothing in your pockets with your real name on it? No family pictures? No credit cards?"

"Nothing but the passport Gideon arranged for me to have. That and a few dollars."

"You're big enough to hurt more than a few people. But have you killed anybody?"

"Yes, sir. I have."

"Would you hesitate to do it again?"

"No, sir. I wouldn't."

"Answer me this, Shotgun. Ever killed a woman?"

Shotgun paused. "No, sir."

"Can you?"

He paused again. "Sir . . ."

"Because a woman will kill you. If you see a woman and can't do the same thing you say you can do to a man, we'll send you to an airport and get you back to Georgia the minute we land in South America. You go back home and pretend you never met me and you erase Gideon from your memory, because if you cause me a problem, that problem won't last for long."

"I understand."

"I'll tell you I'm not too happy having to meet you this way. Not under these circumstances. You haven't been vetted. You think on that, big man. You think on that. I'm going to show you some footage. A woman is in this group. She's the perfect example of what I mean. Ruthless and professional. She moves and kills just as good as the next man."

"Okay, sir."

"You're nervous."

"Yes, sir."

"Why?"

"First time on an airplane."

There was a pause.

Konstantin asked, "How do you travel?"

"Car. Greyhound sometimes, if we have the money."

Konstantin smiled, his grin thin.

Shotgun smiled a little too.

Then Shotgun said, "Mind if I sit by the window for a minute or two? Would like to look out and see what the world looks like from way up in the clouds."

"It's nighttime."

"That don't matter. I have to look at something to stop looking at those pretty women."

"They are a distraction."

"Yes, sir. A couple of them keep looking at me and smiling."

"Go look out the window, Shotgun. I need to speak with my son, Gideon."

"Anybody ever tell you that you sound like Al Pacino?"

Konstantin nodded. He'd heard that a thousand times before.

Shotgun moved to the end of the sofas and looked out at the world.

First time in a plane and Shotgun was in a Gulfstream 650, flying somewhere between Mach .85 and Mach .90. The monitors told us that we were flying at 700 miles per hour. The speed of sound was 770. We were covering one mile every five seconds. We were flying above fifty thousand feet. Above air traffic. Above bad weather. Right below satellites and a hint of God's frigid breath. I had never flown this high or this fast and wanted to look out the window too, but I faced Konstantin. I faced the man who had been a father to me.

Konstantin said, "*On ne durak. Y nego umnoe lizco. Kogda v kostyume, ja-by podumal chto on bankir, eslib on nebyl takim muskulistym. Nado chto-by on byl bystree. On-to umnyj, no on dolzhen byt' bystree.*"

He doesn't look dim-witted. He has a smart face. In the suit, I'd think he was a banker, if he wasn't so muscular. He needs to be quick. He looks smart, but he needs to be quick.

"*On bystryi.*"

He's quick.

"Pistolet ili ruzhjo?"

Handgun or shotgun?

"I to i drugoe. No pistolet emy bolshe podhodit."

Both. But the shotgun suits him better.

He said, "Thieves in law."

I said, "*Vory v zakone.*"

We had our own rules. We had our own law.

Konstantin was battling prostate cancer. It didn't show, not to the average eye, not to someone who had just met him. But I had known him for almost a decade. After I had made that trip to the End of the World and Beginning of Everything, I had been sent to Konstantin.

I said, "How's the cancer? The chemo?"

He waved like it was nothing. "I'm still aboveground."

"I didn't want you in on this."

"Well, I didn't want you in on this."

I left it at that.

He said, "Hawks called when I was at the airport. Said you hung up on her."

"Keep her out of this."

"Said she wants to help. I told her it wasn't my call. She's stubborn. You know that."

Konstantin picked up a remote, aimed it at the big flat-screen. The television came on. CNN played in high-definition. Hopkins' death and financial problems the lead story. A six-billion-dollar fraud. Hopkins was dead, and people were panicking. He had owned major shares in restaurants in the Lesser Antilles, gyms, had investments in banks, parking lots, high-rises, newspapers, had offices in Nashville, Dallas, London, Japan, and Buenos Aires. He had been accused of money laundering for notorious Mexican drug cartels, for triads, for a dozen underworld organizations. News showed photos of Hopkins shaking hands with politicians who had been bamboozled. Thieving politicians bamboozled by a con man. Irony and justice. There were many others on that list. Close to forty thousand clients in more than one hundred countries. Plenty of greedy bastards. The list of people who wanted him in the ground was as long as the miles being covered on this flight. The list of people who had died was just as long.

Hopkins was in the same league as Madoff and Stanford.

That had to be the money people were slaughtering each other to get their hands on. That was what Scamz and Arizona had been up to for the past year.

And that missing part of the package was the key. One of the keys.

The Russian and Ethiopian flight attendants brought us champagne. Then they brought us hot towels to clean our hands. The Arabian princess came close; her ethnic features and the complexion of her skin reminded me of the Lebanese girl from Starbucks in Florida, my other unsolved problem. A threat that could have Catherine and the boys in jeopardy. The Arabian princess saw my expression and looked nervous. She had come with a cart filled with food. Black lumpfish caviar on toast. Caviar from Petrossian Boutique in Paris. Russian cuisine and Fabergé eggs. Cups of borscht. Tea from London. Fresh luxury chocolates from Paris, small, rich chocolate squares flown in from the store named Christian Constant.

I had taken Hawks to Puerto Rico, flown down in back-row seats in coach.

The Russian flight attendant spoke in her native tongue, told Konstantin that there was something special for him. Konstantin nodded. She picked up a remote and pointed it at a sensor in the wall. Music came on. Songs by Mixail Krug, Vladimir Vysotsky, and Bulat Okudzhava. It was the musical genre called Russian chanson. *Blatnaya pesnya*. Criminal songs that praised the execution of traitors. It was the Russians' equivalent of gangsta rap.

Konstantin smiled.

He sipped vodka straight up and as a chaser. First he sampled the rye bread, then the herring dish. The Russian flight attendant brought Konstantin a gift. It was a bottle of Sovetskoye Shampanskoy. The number-one Russian champagne. An ass-kissing gift from Scamz.

There was real silverware. I picked up a knife that had a wooden handle and a blade sharp enough to kill. I wrapped that blade in a napkin, tucked it inside my suit coat.

I stared at the Arab woman.

She had an uneasy smile that told me she was surprised that I wasn't overwhelmed by her beauty. But she was smiling at a man who had been all over the world.

She went to Alvin, tended to his needs, his broad smile good for her ego.

She glanced back at me.

I turned away, unaffected.

I rubbed my eyes. Massaged my temples. Took a few deep breaths.

I thought about Catherine and the boys. Wanted to go back there and fix that, not speed toward more problems. And I wanted to fix that other problem, the one that would cost me two million dollars. I couldn't guarantee that Catherine and the boys would be safe unless I did.

My mind ached, felt as if it was being whipsawed.

Konstantin said, "Eat. Don't offend our host, even if the *kozyol* isn't here."

With reluctance, I joined in. I became more concerned with offending Konstantin and his Russian ways than the shyster who had furnished the feast of the three kings. I ate caviar and sipped sparkling water. It felt like I was sitting on top of the world.

This was what it felt like to be him.

I whispered, "I get it."

The flight attendant let us know that Scamz would call for a video-teleconference when our meal was finished.

I'd heard his voice and now, once again, I would have to look into his face. He'd had a leash around my neck and he'd been tugging on it for three fucking days.

Like father, like son. Ruthless father and coldhearted son.

If I never saw his face, if I never saw Arizona's face again, my world would be better.

While we waited for the king to call his knights, we hooked up

Konstantin's iPhone to the sixty-inch flat-screen. We played the grainy footage from The Four Horsemen of the Apocalypse.

Moving toward a storm, we sipped champagne, ate caviar, and watched death.

We studied how they moved like a boxer studied his opponents.

The way they worked as a team was both beautiful and terrifying.

The equipment they had was top of the line.

Stress lines grew in Konstantin's forehead. Alvin bit his bottom lip and rocked a little.

I rubbed hand over hand, massaged damp palms until those palms turned dry.

We all fell silent.

Konstantin had another drink.

I took a coffee.

Shotgun had the same.

We talked awhile.

Then the flight attendants all came back, stood in front of us, smiling.

They let down their hair.

We pulled away from our conversation about The Four Horsemen.

We sat back and got ready to watch another show. The flight attendants changed the music, danced, and stripped down to their Victoria's Secret. Each took turns dancing erotic dances that represented their countries. They became friendly. Real friendly.

The Russian chatted up Konstantin.

The Brazilian and the Ethiopian paid attention to Shotgun.

The beautiful Arab girl came to me, determined to make me smile.

Her French accent took me back to Montreal, to days when I was a happy little boy sitting on a stoop, reading a comic book, a sunny day, Catherine sitting at my side, smoking a cigarette.

The Arabian princess told me, "You are very handsome. Like the son of a king."

She was determined to make me smile.

We conversed in French. Her soft touch and softer words were like gin and Viagra.

An hour later, the phone buzzed. The women dressed and turned the monitor on.

It was Scamz.

It was the man who had stolen his father's name and now wanted to claim his throne.

Arizona's baby's daddy.

Chapter 31

love, hate

Five hours later.

The Gulfstream entered airspace over South America's east coast. Dark skies. Cold rain. The kind of cold rain that made corpses shiver in their graves.

Summertime was over. Winter had begun.

We landed in the darkness at Jorge Newbery AeroPark. The airfield that faced the brown waters of Río de Plata and was fifteen minutes from downtown Buenos Aires. It was the same airstrip the president used. Our Gulfstream was parked next to President Cristina Fernández de Kirchner's version of Air Force One. An older man waited on us. He stamped our bogus passports without asking any questions, entered the information into the computers. The cargo that had been loaded was removed, taken to a small truck, and whisked away uninspected. Alvin followed Konstantin and me as we walked behind a security guard. We loaded up in a van and were taken to Jazz Voyeur, located on floor −1, the basement level of the Melia Boutique Hotel. It was three hours before the lower section opened for breakfast. We entered through a back door, unseen by the night staff.

The basement restaurant was a five-star room. Flourescent and recessed lighting shone on every white tablecloth inside a room big enough to hold a hundred patrons. Low ceiling, polished wooden floors, and exposed brick walls, each wall lined with poster-sized black-and-white photos of jazz musicians. Jimmy Heath on sax. Joe Henderson on sax. Paolo Fresu. David S. Ware. Lester Bowie.

George Coleman. Chet Baker. Dozens of photos decorated the four walls.

A black baby grand piano marked the center of the room, and a man in a black suit was playing what sounded like Beethoven, one of the lost songs. It was our Latin benefactor, his black suit a tailor-made British cut. He played almost as well as his father used to play. Almost.

He said, "Gentlemen."

"Scamz."

"Gideon."

Konstantin nodded.

Alvin remained silent. He looked around, holding in his amazement, his first time seeing a brand-new world.

Scamz continued playing like he was at rehearsal for the Metropolitan Opera. He had on a suit that looked like it had been designed by Alexander Amosu, a designer who made two-piece suits that went for more than one hundred thousand dollars.

Sierra was at a table. Her hair was pulled back. If my mind hadn't been filled with other thoughts, her beauty might have been disturbing. Her brother was at the same table. Both had wineglasses in front of them; a half-empty bottle of Villavicencio mineral water was on the table.

The brother took note of Konstantin and me, but when he saw Alvin, intimidation flashed in his eyes. Sierra looked at us, then looked away, not even a head motion as hello.

Scamz said, "Have a seat. Five minutes."

I said, "This is supposed to be urgent."

"Five minutes. We are waiting on the part of the package we have to arrive."

"Who else is in this hotel?"

"No one. I rented the building."

"Every room?"

"Every room has been rented."

"That's about sixty or seventy rooms."

He nodded.

I nodded. "I need a gun."

"Why?"

"Because I don't have one. And get the same for my friends. That video you sent us, if that's who is after you, you should have quadruple security posted at every entrance. You should have men on the rooftops and on every block for three blocks out. Don't bring me down into a fucking death trap. And kill the Liberace routine; lay off the keys and get me a fucking gun."

He stopped playing. His fingers froze on the keys. He didn't look up.

He said, "Sierra. Get the man what he requested."

Sierra nodded at her muscular brother. Her brother reached underneath their table and took out a box. Several boxes were next to him, all stacked next to the wall. He had been guarding the hardware. He opened the smallest of the boxes. I went and looked down at the contents. Five nine millimeters were inside. New guns. And more than a few clips. I took out two of the nines, handed them to Konstantin. He nodded. I took two more, handed those two to Alvin. I kept one for myself. Then I took out extra clips, passed those to my friends.

I turned to Scamz and said, "Something is missing."

"Missing?"

"You get me something heavier than these pop guns?"

Scamz nodded.

Arizona's brother brought out another box. He put it down and ripped open the flaps. I looked inside. Three shotguns. Two had short barrels. I nodded at Alvin. He came over and looked at the hardware, inspected it like he was a pro. Straps were in the box. Alvin took off his coat and took out one of the straps, attached it to both ends of one of the sawed-off shotguns. He looped the strap over his broad shoulder, then put his jacket back on. It was concealed the same way Clyde Barrow used to carry his Browning A-5. Alvin moved with it, tested to see how fast he could draw it. It was impressive. Like watching Chuck Connors in *The Rifleman*.

Alvin nodded at me.

Scamz picked up where he had left off, went back to playing the piano like he was at Royal Festival Hall. He looked cool. But he was nervous. Playing that piano was his tell. He was thinking, considering, plotting, and trying to deal with his insurmountable level of stress.

Loaded gun in hand, I felt better, like a baby who had been given a pacifier.

I looked at Sierra and said, "Suppressors for the nines?"

Another box was produced. Suppressors were distributed while Beethoven played.

There was more food. A buffet of exotic fruits. Melons. Mangos. Grapes. Kiwi. And plates filled with *facturas*; bite-sized pies and cookies, croissants and *medialunas*.

There were two exits. I checked both, always looked for the exits.

One was a wooden stairway that had sharp turns and ended one level up at the rear of another restaurant and bar area. The second was the glass elevator at the opposite end of the room. I didn't like being in a basement. A basement was a death trap.

Konstantin sat at the table near me. Shotgun came back to the table and sat next to Konstantin. I looked into Alvin's eyes, read his mind, then I nodded.

With a shotgun under his coat, a nine in his gigantic hand, Alvin went for more food.

I guess he was Shotgun now. Had to stop thinking of him as Alvin.

I went for water, poured some in a wineglass. Konstantin did the same.

Scamz was making me wait. Like I had made him wait. Establishing who was the boss. Arizona was probably doing the same. Mind games. Boardroom psychology at its best.

I didn't belong to any organization. Never would. I was my own boss. I was my own man. Had been my own man since I was a teenager. Would be until I took my final breath.

I preferred to work alone. But this didn't look like that kind of job.

On the plane, hours ago, that conference call, that was on my mind now.

Scamz had had workers on the hunt for the last few days, trying to pick up a signal, had them moving twenty-four hours a day, moving around the capital city and deeper into the outlying areas. One had picked up a signal at Retiro. Retiro was like Grand Central Station meets a mile-long sidewalk swap meet. Bus stations, train stations, and a subte line damn near on top of each other. Then the signal had moved with the pace of one of the departing trains.

His worker had raced to a car and taken to the streets, drove as the train moved. He made it to the Belgrano stop ahead of the train but didn't have time to get out of the car and run to the train. He sped past rugby, soccer, and polo fields, ran red lights and followed the train past the Mercado and Rivadavia stations. He was hoping that whoever was transporting the package left the train and made the job easier.

The signal was strong for forty-five minutes, until the driver sped by the San Isidro station. Then the signal faded. They had left the train.

The worker sped back, parked, and searched the area. Jogged around Belgrano, an area lined with two-story buildings, shops on the first floor and apartments rising over the stores. He moved on and paused at a five-way intersection that fed into a traffic circle, Pico monument and a flagpole in the center of the circle, where Belgrano, 9 de Julio, and Acassuso kissed like lovers at a swingers' club. From there, there were four ways the signal could have moved.

The worker took 9 de Julio until it ended at Avenida del Libertador, both streets no more than two lanes wide and intersecting in front of La Catedral de San Isidro. First he went inside the church. The package hadn't gone in that direction. He ran out of the church. Across the narrow street was the start of a park that was filled with vendors. The signal had gone down the concrete walkway, crossed the street, and went into a crowded plaza that had restaurants and more shops. The signal moved to the right. Toward the entrance to another train. Tren de la Costa. The city trains cost one peso twenty centavos. The coastal train, seven pesos. The coastal train ended at Parque de la Costa and Tigre.

The worker had hurried and hopped on that train.

That was the last time Scamz had heard from that worker.

From where I sat, I had a clear view of both the stairs and the elevator.

I saw the mechanisms on the elevator move. That elevator should've been on STOP so there would be only one way in and out. I held my weapon and watched the empty glass carriage ascend. A minute later it descended, no longer vacant.

I saw the lone passenger appear inch by inch.

Low-heeled shoes. Fashionable pants. Swollen belly.

It was Arizona.

Her brown hair was pulled back from her face. She was dressed in all black, a loose blouse over her pregnancy swell. She had a black purse over one shoulder and was carrying the same black briefcase she'd had when I met her at the Starbucks in Aventura, Florida.

I'd gone to Powder Springs, and a lot of emotional damage had erupted since then.

Emotional damage that had been caused by a woman who was just like Arizona.

Catherine was nothing more than a con.

Arizona's heels clicked across the wooden floor as she walked into the room.

She saw us and nodded.

Konstantin nodded in return. I offered no reply. Neither did Shotgun.

Then she said, "Gideon."

"Arizona. Anything changed?"

She said, "We have a signal."

"Are they tracking you at the same time?"

"They stole the computers, took the dedicated trackers from La Boca."

"So they have a signal too."

"We can only hope so."

"You told me they compromised one of the satellite operations."

"La Boca. They destroyed the small site we had used to track the package when it was in Uruguay. They killed seven *Porteños*. Slaughtered them. Same as they did the Uruguayans."

"They killed everyone."

"Slaughtered. Like they were animals."

"I stand corrected."

"One escaped. He is in critical condition at Alemán. He was stabbed and shot. He saw them. Said there were two younger ones. A man and a woman. She had marks on her face."

"Tribal markings?"

"Not sure. She was with a Latin man. Then two older men came. Said they spoke English."

"British or American?"

"He thought they had American accents. Their leaders."

Konstantin paused. "The list of things Gideon requested, where are they?"

"Still working on a few items."

"You've had three days."

"So has Gideon. If he had been here, maybe the La Boca operation . . . never mind."

"You want us to walk away? You show us respect, or we walk. This is your operation, not ours. If people died, that is blood on your hands, not ours. Remember whose problem this is. And remember who we are."

She smiled. It was a bitter smile.

She said, "Apologies. Guess this load I'm carrying is having an effect on my disposition."

Konstantin returned a cruel Russian smile.

He was unaffected by the swell underneath her blouse. Unaffected by her beauty.

I asked, "That other matter, do you have that information?"

Arizona's eyes came to me. "Not at the moment."

"Did you reverse-engineer that information and find out what I needed to know?"

"I did what I could do with what you gave me to work with."

"Well, can I get the information? I can put someone on it while I'm here."

"Sorry. Not at the moment."

Her obstinate expression told me she had me in checkmate.

My glare told her to not confuse being in check with checkmate.

She gave me the face of Queen Scamz. I offered her Gideon.

Arizona put the briefcase down in a chair two tables over, put her purse in a different chair. She sat on the piano bench next to Scamz and joined in the Beethoven melody. She was better than the new Scamz. Much better. Played effortlessly.

The music was intense, beautiful, a duet that sounded like controlled madness.

She glanced my way and I saw what I wanted to forget.

I saw the Parker Meridien in New York.

I saw the Carolina Inn in North Carolina.

I saw us together.

I saw a million reasons I needed to stand up and walk out of this country.

Chapter 32

like father

Three identical Peugeots and two local delivery trucks were out front.

The vehicles were parked on the one-way street in front of the hotel, spaced between the hotel and El Sanjuanino Café. A *farmacia*, newspaper stand, blocks of high-rises, and a mall for the rich were in that direction; embassies, cafés, dry cleaners, and more apartments occupied the two-lane, one-way street behind us. Five-star hotels sparkled and added prestige to the area.

Cold winds blew frigid rain and dampened everything.

Every corner, every window, was a potential ambush.

I told Konstantin, "I don't like this."

He nodded. "Same here."

"This is a mission for a thousand or a mission for one."

Shotgun was right there, listening, nodding, his hand on his loaded weapon.

We went out first, walked the strip, checked the windows in the apartments, spied the roofs. If they were out there, they were stealth, had blended in with the rain and wind.

They weren't here. Because if they were, we'd all be dead.

All the vehicles were less than two years old, and none had GPS. That didn't surprise me. Argentina was about five years behind when it came to high-tech luxury devices.

Scamz said, "Hopefully, these vehicles will suffice."

"Since you don't have a Challenger Battle Tank, I guess they will have to do."

"I was hoping something less conspicuous would work in our favor."

I nodded. "Considering what we're up against, based on what I've seen, a Humvee with a 240 Gulf machine gun mounted on the rear and another mounted on the passenger-side door, that would've been more appropriate. I don't give a shit about conspicuous."

Before we loaded up, Arizona's muscular brother did a sweep of the vehicles.

We stood underneath the red awning of the Melia Boutique Hotel, freezing air fogging our breath as we carried lead-spitting heaters underneath our clothes. We looked like businessmen in suits and overcoats. I preferred jeans and Timberlands, and a matching Kevlar vest.

I told Scamz, "You're a little paranoid."

"Hopkins should have been paranoid. A lot of men like you are out there."

I nodded. "Lot of men like me. And people like you know them all."

"That wasn't meant as an insult."

"It wasn't taken as one. A fact is a fact. You steal money from wherever you can steal it, and when all goes south, when someone steals from you, that is when you dip into your stolen funds and finance your own revenge. That's when my phone rings. That's the cycle of the business of revenge. You come to people like me for a reason."

"You're here begrudgingly."

"I'm here, that's all that matters."

He glanced at Arizona, then he nodded.

I didn't know what that meant. I didn't care.

Shotgun looked around, then up at the European architecture.

I said, "You okay?"

"Winter in summertime. These some beautiful buildings. Like in the movies."

I nodded. "Not too late for you to go back home to your family."

"How far am I from home?"

"Over five thousand miles."

"I didn't come this far to go back home. That's a lot of gas to burn up and turn around."

I nodded. "I could always send you to a hotel. You could go look around."

He shook his head. "Didn't come here to see the sights. Came here to work."

Konstantin and Shotgun went together.

Scamz and Arizona's siblings stayed together.

I took one of the Peugeots. I wanted to ride and let The Four Horsemen track me. I needed the package to make that happen. That meant I had to face Arizona. All business.

Arizona said, "The package is with me."

"Give it to Scamz. Let pretty boy ride with me. We'll be the sitting ducks."

She paused, then shook her head. "The MacGuffin remains with me."

"You don't trust Scamz with it? Then give it to your brother. You and your man can—"

She cursed in Tagalog, said other things just as harsh, then snapped, "This thing you do with me . . . the irritating thing . . . please . . . don't do it now. Not now."

I paused when I knew I didn't have time to hesitate. Not with the package being tracked.

I didn't need a pregnant woman slowing me down. I didn't want the smell of her perfume and old feelings creating an anchor. Or resentment. And I didn't want Konstantin and Alvin to be the first line of defense. If anyone was shot at first, I wanted it to be me and somebody else from her team. But we didn't have time to argue. Not when Arizona was already getting inside the car. I didn't want her to become my burden, and I didn't want her unborn kid on my mind. The pregnant grifter kept her purse on one shoulder and held the briefcase like it held the codes to activate a nuclear bomb.

I despised her.

We took to the streets. All of us were together at first. Then Konstantin and Alvin broke away. They had their assignment.

We rode the area for a while, then Scamz and his crew vanished from the rearview. They had to track the other package.

It was just Arizona and me.

Veins popping in my arms, lips tight, eyes checking traffic behind me and traffic in front of me, I drove Avenida Alcorta at a high speed, the same fast and furious tempo all the locals drove in the rain. That video of The Four Horsemen played in my mind. I changed over to Bullrich and Justo, Belgrano, ended up at 9 de Julio, cut over to Rivadavia and rode the avenue that ran aboveground on top of the A line of the subte, the oldest line, which had wooden cars that looked at least a century old.

Arizona asked, "Why are you taking these streets?"

"I don't want those madmen to know if we are aboveground or down below, not right away. Thousands of cars, hundreds on every block, so if they are gunning for what you have, if they want it bad enough to kill everybody in sight, we have to be on the lookout for them. They will have to figure out what we're riding in. We'll have to do the same for them."

"What if they don't take the bait?"

"I'm just a guy with a debt and a gun. The rest is your problem."

I kept to the big streets, the long avenues, lots of traffic, droves of people. We had ridden the almost seventy-block length of Corrientes, had started this leg of the drive at Avenida Federico Lacroze up in the Chacarita barrio, rode it from that barrio's cemetery down through the Jewish barrio named Balvanera, went back toward the former boxing arena named Luna Park, and ended up in Puerto Madero, the most expensive Latin neighborhood in South America.

Nothing was happening. My anxiety was in the red. Calmness was always the prelude to madness. I got back in traffic, drove Justo. It was like driving from Harlem down through Times Square then heading up Park Avenue. Bodegas and shops every step of the way.

I told Arizona, "Keep your eye on that BMW. Two lanes over."

"I'm watching. It's changing lanes a lot."

"It's been behind us since we crossed Gascón."

The BMW was there for about another mile. Then it was gone.

Arizona asked, "Think that was them?"

"Look for another vehicle following us now. And cops. Be on the lookout for cops. Down here, the only thing more corrupt than a criminal is a cop."

Arizona took her gun, held it on her belly, made sure her weapon was loaded.

She said, "There are two motorcycles back there. They're matching our pace."

I adjusted my gun. Arizona did the same with her weapon.

The motorcycles she was worried about sped by, both drivers glancing at cars as they changed lanes, searching before they cut in front and turned. Then the motorcycles were gone.

I said, "A woman was on one of those motorcycles."

"What gave it away? Her nice ass?"

I wanted to curse her. But I didn't. The BMW and those motorcycles had me on alert.

Arizona said, "They're out there. They want this package. Without what I have, there will be no access to the funds. They want the money as bad as Hopkins did."

I asked, "How does it feel to have fifteen mil?"

"Having it feels a lot better than losing it."

I moved though the epicenter of the financial district. More restaurants than I could ever eat at in three lifetimes. Flower- and newsstands on every corner. Passed ten women for every man. The lingering scent of coffee and grilled beef filled the damp air.

I didn't see the BMW. Didn't see the motorcycles we had seen before.

As far as I knew, they were following us like we were on Twitter.

I paused in Puerto Madero, near the Prefectura Argentina Edificio Guardacostas. It was the building that housed Argentina's coast guards. Lot of security. Lots of guns. I cruised the area, kept my driving in a small radius, parked in front of the bricked businesses near Farmacity. The drugstore faced where Corrientes ended. I saw the Obelisco in the distance.

Arizona called her brother and Scamz, checked in and tried to find out if they had pinpointed the signal for the other package. The signal had gone from green to amber. That meant the other half of the package was mobile, being relocated to another area.

They would be able to tell if the blip was in Puerto Madero, sitting somewhere around the row of bricked businesses that housed five-star restaurants, an area that used to be a warehouse district, now the area of the new rich. The warehouses ran up Justo for miles toward Costanera Sur Ecological Reserve. Corrientes ended here. Like it was the End of the World.

There was a steady stream of buses and taxis. The bus lines were across the street, dozens upon dozens of buses loading up, lines more than fifty long at most stops this time of day. Across the street, four train tracks led to Instituto Tecnológico Buenos Aires.

Two armed guards were on the sidewalk near us, tan uniforms and orange reflective vests. Rain drummed the car as I looked around. I wanted to find The Four Horsemen. Didn't like being hunted. I'd been hunted too long, all over the world. A man could only escape so many traps. I was made to be the hunter, not the prey.

I said, "We need to stash the package. Set them up. Let me get Konstantin and Shotgun in position. When they go for it, we corner them, take them out from behind."

"In broad daylight."

"It's overcast. Dark enough. The rain helps make everything obscure."

"I'm not comfortable with that."

"If we ride around until we're out of gas, we're fucked. The moment we pull into a Shell or YPF, they could block us in and gun us down. I suggest we use the package as bait."

Arizona said, "No. I don't want to do that. I don't want to use the package as bait."

"These guys are good at using explosives."

"They won't use explosives, not on the package, not if they want it intact."

"Then let's hope they want it intact."

To my right, I saw the armed guards on the sidewalk.

I saw their unmistakable expressions.

Death charged toward us.

I saw their panic, their mouths open wide as their body language became defensive.

Gunfire peppered the businesses behind them as they reached for their guns.

They tried to draw their weapons, but they were caught off guard.

One head exploded like a melon that had been dropped from twelve stories high, abrupt redness and brain matter covering the glass of the pharmacy and the sidewalk he had been patrolling. Before the second guard could fire a shot, his head had opened up too.

A shadowy figure raced up from behind. Dark clothing, dark coat, dark fedora. A patch over his eye. I saw the patch. And when he raised his head, I saw part of his face.

For a moment . . . everything moved in slow motion, so slowly I could see every separate raindrop, could've counted each one before it touched the ground.

I was sucked into a nightmare.

A ghost charged at me. I saw the man I had killed when I was seven years old.

Then came the silenced gunfire, muffled explosions that spat out hot lead.

Six shots that came so fast they would've sounded like one gunshot.

The surreal moment exploded, and reality rampaged back at twice the normal pace. Rain fell like rocks, beat the car a hundred times a second, echoed like rapid fire from a submachine gun. With the rain falling, with the cacophony of sounds, no one noticed the muffled noise.

If I'd been in any other vehicle, I'd have been sleeping with the fish.

The car's windows were bulletproof, one inch thick. But that didn't stop me from flinching when the bullets struck the glass at eye level, didn't stop Arizona from doing the same.

Then another merc dressed in black appeared, a sledgehammer in his hand. That sledgehammer came down hard. The window took the impact and didn't give.

All of this happened as people stood in the rain. They probably thought they were witnessing a botched assassination. Or a wicked battle between Colombian drug dealers.

Arizona tried to duck down, bullets bouncing off the window at her head.

My foot pressed the accelerator to the floor. Tires spun on wet pavement as the rear end fishtailed and bumped the ghost that had caused me to freeze in time.

It had bumped him. He was solid. He was real.

Bullets bounced off glass as I got the fuck out of that war zone.

The first man I killed.

I'd seen his ghost.

Capítulo 33

antiguos fantasmas

Estación Retiro.

The French-style station building was one of the largest transportation hubs in Argentina. Subte Line C, omnibuses, city buses, taxis, and trains. People moved in every direction. Tourists and *Porteños* with babies, backpacks, and tons of luggage. High-rises were a block away on Libertador, the Sheraton Hotel and the British Clock Tower in the distance.

Medianoche had hurried to his car, followed the Peugeot to that rambunctious area.

A fucking bulletproof car. Medianoche wasn't surprised. Bulletproof cars had become commonplace when the economy had hit rock bottom and the have-nots started robbing the wealthy, yanking them out of their Benzes and BMWs and demanding a quick ransom. Express kidnappings were a profitable epidemic. The doors and windows of that car were solid enough to stop a sledgehammer's blows and shake off AK-47 blasts.

A lot of money was on the line.

Many people had expired in pursuit of these the two packages.

Dented by gunfire and a blow from a sledgehammer, the Peugeot had fled down Avenida Alicia Moreau de Justo, then fishtailed and cut up San Martín. That block-long street was one-way traffic divided by a concrete island, dead-ending at the train station, forcing a left or right turn.

Traffic was impossible. Horns blew as rain fell hard on the unmoving vehicles, the rain trying to wash away the smell of *pollo*, empanadas, *huevos fritos*, carbon monoxide, and dog shit.

Medianoche abandoned his car, kept his gun down low as he ran up the line of cars, his run parallel to the markets and sidewalks two lanes away. He sprinted past slow-moving people and stomped through puddles, water splashing like he was in the fields of Africa. He slowed his run twelve vehicles later and crept up on the Peugeot. A car that was trapped because three cars in front of it were blocked by city buses. It was easy to spot with damaged glass and bullet wounds in its impenetrable frame. Both doors were ajar. He peeped inside, business end of his gun leading the way.

The car was empty. Abandoned on the left side of the street.

Police had shut down the area. The avenue was blocked. It was one of many disruptive protests sponsored by the *piqueteros*. Protestors marched up Ramos Mejía toward Libertador and Avenida Alem, droves moving toward San Martín Plaza, most of them banging pots and pans, creating a loud racket.

Medianoche cursed.

The children and grandchildren of immigrants protested another corruption. People who had worked in silver and tin mines were marching side by side with bankers and clergy from the Catholic Church. Fucking plate-banging protestors who had no regard for rain, at least thirty thousand carrying damp banners and wet signs, thousands using black garbage bags and clear plastic as raincoats, their inexpensive shoes and blue-collar clothes soaking wet, the winter storm magnifying their determination to change the cold ways of their brutal world one protest at a time.

They blocked traffic, banged pots and pans, and chanted.

Medianoche wiped rain from his face, searched for his targets.

Women had united underneath dark skies. They were shutting the city down. Would march until they reached Plaza de Mayo. Refused to let buses out of the terminal. Cars and taxis were at a standstill. Women protested gender violence. Gigantic banners screamed that more than a thousand women a month had to dial 911 because they were abused and beaten by partners, former lovers, and boyfriends. The crowd was as wide as the avenue, and at least a mile long.

That was why the Peugeot was abandoned at Madero and Mejia.

Medianoche turned back to the car to look inside, wanted to see what had been left behind. As soon as he turned, the car burst into flames. He jumped back from the flames.

That had been done by a remote.

They were near. Wherever they were, they could see him.

He moved past the fire, hurried through the rain, and searched for the targets. Across the concrete island were businesses that stretched toward Avenida San Martín. Buses had pulled into the gridlock. Medianoche spied toward the British Clock Tower. That area was fenced off. There was no quick way to get inside. Then he evaluated the area toward the strip of mom-and-pop businesses, but his instinct said the enemy hadn't gone that way.

He looked straight ahead. Beyond the protesters was another wall of people trying to get to trains, subtes, and buses. There were a half dozen entrances to train stations, and each entrance stretched at least a quarter mile. He looked to the right, toward the station for the omnibuses. He looked to his left. Foot traffic hurried across twelve lanes, battled the weather and headed beyond the soldiers who stood in front of the monument at Plaza San Martín. Droves of people moved toward the park at the top of the hill.

A dozen directions to flee.

Medianoche looked at the sensor. The signal was bright green.

They were still here. They were close. Might be as close as the Peugeot that was burning a few feet behind him. People passed as rain fell on garbage-bag raincoats and umbrellas held high.

Medianoche noticed a young man was staring at him as protestors passed.

Gideon.

Midnight. He heard the name Midnight shouted among the din.

Gideon stared at him. A vague face separated by a thousand human shields.

People passed. More umbrellas up high. More garbage-bag raincoats.

Medianoche took a step as he blinked.

Then Gideon was gone.

He had vanished like a vampire, as if he never was.

Medianoche looked to the left, to the right, tensed, wondered if he had frozen up again.

He searched the crowd again. Rain and gray skies made the pandemonium a blur.

Señorita Raven and Señor Rodríguez negotiated the horn-blowing traffic, pulled over and took to the sidewalk, parked their motorcycles and looked into the crowd, then came to his side.

His soldiers were soaking wet. They'd been riding in the rain for hours.

It had taken them hours to finally locate the fuckers with the package.

Medianoche stood, one gun resting in the small of his back, two more inside holsters underneath his coat. He wanted to howl like a wolf. But he frowned and adjusted his eye patch.

Señorita Raven looked at him, said nothing. Medianoche saw her thoughts on her face, saw her being professional. Her taste lived inside his mouth. Her smell permeated his flesh.

Medianoche stood behind Señorita Raven.

Last night. After the tango. Clothes stained by sex. Her scent on his genitals. He had gone to her apartment. He was ready to kill her. She had fired at him twice. Put two bullet holes in the wall near his head. He hadn't flinched. Wasn't afraid. Had stared at her. Dared her.

Then he had left.

There was a pecking order. Called The Beast until he made contact. The Beast was out handling part of the Caprica Ortiz contract. He had put two of the men who had been responsible for the thirty thousand missing in the ground. Medianoche cut to the chase, asked permission to put Señorita Raven down. He told The Beast that she had crossed the line. She had shot at him. Twice. He'd had enough. The Beast listened.

But his request was denied.

The Beast had told him, "Friends close. Enemies closer."

"Sir, yes, sir."

"We have bigger problems. My servant is monitoring the sensor."

"There a problem?"

"Draco informed me that the sensor went from red to amber."

"How long ago?"

"Within the last hour."

"Red to amber. They are in the area."

"You sound surprised. They had no choice."

"City or province?"

"Not sure. So we need Raven. Get ready. All of you. We have work to do."

Medianoche said, "Friends close."

"Enemies closer. When this is done, we can dispose of all enemies."

"Well, it's about to be World War III over here."

"Not yet."

"I'm warning you the way they warned America about Bin Laden before nine-eleven."

"Not yet, not yet."

Her presence was hard to deal with, made him feel like he was naked with clips on his nipples and nut sac, a car battery supplying the juice that exacerbated his torture.

After hanging up the phone, he had gone back to Señorita Raven's apartment. Went back and faced the woman who had shot at him twice. The woman who thought she knew his secrets. He stepped back into her den of rage and dejection. She was still naked, gun in hand.

She fired at him again. The bullet hit the wall. She was in the middle of a meltdown.

He didn't know if her problems were chemical or behavioral.

Or if the horrors of war had given her demons she'd never be able to escape.

But he knew they ran deeper than giving a man a blow job for a C-note.

No matter what, she was his enemy.

Friends close. Enemies closer.

He knew what he wanted to do. But he was a soldier. And a soldier followed orders.

Even when the orders made no sense.

He told her, "You're right. I did freeze."

"Get out."

"And a soldier should have another soldier's back."

"Get out, you one-eyed, fucked-up, broken-down piece of misogynistic shit."

He walked toward her loaded gun, took slow steps until the barrel was close enough to touch his skin. Then, with a finger, he eased the barrel to the side.

She scowled. "Get away from me."

He touched her breasts.

She swallowed. "Get your hands off me."

He lowered his head, sucked her nipple.

She sighed. "Stop . . . stop doing that . . . you one-eyed . . . you one-eyed . . ."

She melted down to the wooden floor, legs opening.

He said, "You're crazy."

"And crazy gets your dick hard."

He took her on her living room floor. Holding his gun in his hand, he had entered her hard. She had held onto her gun, wrapped her left arm and legs around him.

"What's the matter? Can't get it up?"

"I can get it up."

"Doesn't feel like it."

"Arrogant bitch."

"One shot and that old gun's no good."

"I can get it up, dammit."

"Get off me."

"Shut up."

"Get off me."

He sucked her breasts and moved in slow motion. He was erect, but not as hard as he could get. It took longer. Another sign of aging. The tingling swelled and his erection strengthened. Again he was twenty years younger. Then he picked up the pace.

She was the enemy.

Every time he stroked her too deep, too hard, her gun discharged. Bullets hit the ceiling. Bullets hit the walls. He stroked her. Her gun exploded. She moaned. She fired until it was empty. After that, she dropped her spent weapon on the wooden floor, the barrel aiming at her head as she grabbed his hips. She thrust upward and he felt her returning the animosity.

It was as close to World War III as the world had ever been.

It wasn't pretty. It was a brutal fight. Biting. Grabbing. Strangling. Pushing. Pulling. Slapping. Scratching. Grunts and curses. Sliding across wooden floors. Knocking over books. Knocking over end tables. She growled at him and gyrated her Punjabi hips like she was a belly dancer in heat. Rough, loud sex. Crazed and nasty sex. Crazy women were always the best fucks. They always fucked a man in a way that made them unforgettable.

He knew he had made another mistake. But that mistake had felt damn good.

And it was a mistake he might do again, if she lived that long.

She moaned that she was coming.

He came with her. Fucked her until her orgasm was finished.

When it was done, he was panting.

She was panting too. Panting as if she were recovering from anaphylactic shock.

He stood up, pulled his pants up, picked up his gun.

She was sprawled out. Her gun empty. Marked like territory.

At that moment she would've been an easy kill.

But he had orders.

He told her to get cleaned up. To get dressed. Told her that The Four Horsemen had work to do.

The bird had landed, and it was time to go hunting.

She had responded, "The other part of the package is here?"

"Clean yourself up, soldier. Get dressed. Get in uniform."

"Yes, sir."

He went to her window and pulled back her thin curtains. It had started raining.

Then he frowned at the fresh bullet holes decorating her ceiling and walls.

Each shot like a lethal orgasm.

He'd never been inside her living quarters.

She had IKEA-style furniture mixed with furniture from Walmart. There were hundreds of black-and-white pictures on her virgin-white walls. Señorita Raven before the shrapnel. Before the military. When she was prettier than Madhuri Shankar Dixit.

Her apartment was a shrine to the physical beauty she used to possess.

He had been inside her, as close as enemies could get. That was a few hours ago.

Now it was time to soldier up, and deal death to their rivals.

Señor Rodríguez said, "We only have one tracker."

Medianoche nodded. It would have to be enough.

Señor Rodríguez changed clips in his nine. "The stations take up a city block. At least three sections to the buildings. The one ahead, that one over there, and the section down at Padre Mujica, where the omnibuses are. At least three. What if they get a taxi? Or a bus?"

Medianoche said, "Nothing is moving except the trains. Every bus and taxi is blocked."

Señorita Raven said, "The subte. They could be heading for the subte. Or the trains."

Medianoche said, "We follow. We find. We improvise."

Just then, police blew whistles, officers ran toward the protest, ready to shoot to kill.

A group of hooligans had shown up and disrupted the demonstration. A police officer was attacked. Medianoche and his team kept moving. Not their problem.

They pushed by women with photos of other abused women taped to their chests. Images of a young black woman with a swollen face caught his eye. The black woman's damaged face was taped to the front of a young Spanish girl's plastic raincoat. The name RIHANNA was written across the bottom with a black magic marker.

Inside the main terminal, there were thousands of people with backpacks and bags. Hundreds with umbrellas.

Subte C. Gate 3 heading to Suarez. Gate 4 heading to Tigre. Trains loading and unloading on the concrete platform. Vendors in the crowd screaming they have café for sale. Medianoche moved past a blind man selling magnifying glasses for five pesos and pushed his way through a long, snaking line at one of the *boleterías*.

Medianoche was more concerned with the *policía* than with the civilians. More concerned with surveillance cameras high above. Cameras pointed down from almost every angle.

Not the ideal scenario. But war wasn't about the scenario being ideal.

War was about adapting to terrain and circumstance.

Medianoche struggled through the crowd and took the entrance closest to Avenida Libertador and Plaza San Martín, moved through exiting foot traffic, felt like a fish swimming upstream as he moved by lines of people with suitcases, some with makeshift cardboard luggage, some using plastic bags to carry their belongings.

Sensor in hand, Medianoche walked the line, looking into the crowd.

Señorita Raven said, "I should check the next terminal."

Medianoche said. "Affirmative. Stay on air. Rodríguez?"

"Nothing, sir. I'm in front of the escalator for the subte."

"What about the trains?"

"Platform is crowded, but the trains aren't boarding and they don't leave for another ten minutes. Going downstairs to check the subte, then double back to the trains. How is the signal?"

"Signal is still good. Raven, double back and go with Rodríguez."

"I can handle it, sir. We can sweep, meet in the middle."

Medianoche said, "Affirmative."

The signal was as green as new money in the United States of America.

And getting greener as he headed across damp, dirty red tile toward the *boletería*.

Rodríguez came back on. "Downstairs. Bottom of escalator. I see the package. It's a briefcase, same as the one we took from the Uruguayans. The tango holding it is—"

Señor Rodríguez grunted, his words cut short.

"Señor Rodríguez?"

No response.

Medianoche hurried through the multitude, took to the escalator. Only two escalators. One going up, one going down, descending into a cavernous section that had graffiti etched in the walls. He rushed into a stench and staleness he didn't have time to process.

At the bottom, he paused at a kiosk that was illuminated with a green Beledent sign.

"Señor Rodríguez, where are you?"

No answer.

"Señorita Raven?"

She responded, "Almost back inside the station."

"Rodríguez?"

No answer.

Señorita Raven could hear him. It wasn't being underground that was causing interference. He went to the right. A crowd was exiting the subte, rushing his way, hurrying to the single escalator. Another train pulled away. Package could be gone. Rodríguez could be with the targets. Train disappeared. Signal remained green. Package hadn't left. Rodríguez had to be here. Had gone silent. He looked around. Bar Tolo had a few customers. No sign of Señor Rodríguez. Saw armed policemen, casual stances, smoking cigarettes. At least a hundred more people were in line at another *boletería*. Looked toward the lottery agency. No sign of Señor Rodríguez.

Medianoche called him again. No response. Newspaper stand. No Rodríguez.

Nuestras Café. No sign of his Spanish soldier.

Anger mixed with anxiety.

Medianoche saw another exit. Plaza San Martín. The signal remained strong. He was rushing that way.

Then.

"Sir, I'm downstairs."

Medianoche stopped. "Señorita Raven."

"I'm at the bottom of the escalator. I turned left."

"Find him?"

"No sign."

Medianoche moved past a dozen armed policemen. He turned around. At the base of the escalator, straight ahead, was another entrance, stairs that went straight, extended beyond a photo shop that had Kodak banners in its window. Again, droves of people stormed toward him, again he found himself swimming up the goddamn stream of never-fucking-ending pedestrians.

At the end, where it took another sharp left, he saw Señorita Raven.

"Sir. Sir. Sir."

The voice was in his earpiece. It was Señor Rodríguez.

"I . . . I found the package. Main level. They're already on the train. Train going to—"

His words stopped.

Medianoche asked, "Which train is the package on?"

Heavy breathing. People talking in Spanish. Background sounds. A commotion.

Medianoche led the way, hurried back to the main level, the stairs ending in the middle of a swarming crowd at the Tomonado kiosk. The gates for the train were to the right.

The trains were boarding. Track 3 and track 4. Trains to Tigre and Suarez.

Medianoche called Señor Rodríguez again. Señorita Raven did the same.

No response.

Medianoche went to the gate. Stopped at a turnstile. Too much security. Needed a fucking ticket. He pointed and Señorita Raven nodded, hurried through the mob of commuters. The line at the electronic ticket booth was long. Señorita Raven went to the front of the queue, cut the line, and went next, pissed everybody off.

She could handle the situation. With a smile, curse, or with deadly force.

Medianoche moved back and forth, his attention now on tracks 3 and 4.

He looked at the tracker. Still green. Still bright green. Package was close enough to touch. Rodríguez had said they were on the train. Not *at* the train. *On* the train.

The only trains were at tracks 3 and 4.

Medianoche tried again. "Which train are you on Señor Rodríguez?"

Nothing.

Señorita Raven returned, handed him a ticket.

The signal was green.

But the trains were too close to each other to tell where the package was.

Nothing from Rodríguez in more than two minutes. Two minutes was a devil's eternity.

Señorita Raven, "We have to make a move."

"My thoughts exactly."

"Sir, yes, sir. What are our options?"

"Would rather we took the same train, worked from opposite ends to the middle. Not possible at this point. You take Tigre. I'll take Suarez. Walk the train from end to end."

"Will be hard to do anything subtle if we come in contact with the tangos."

"Like you did in Iraq, follow your gut."

"I'll attack the enemy like they are the Taliban."

Gate 3 was for Suarez. Gate 4 for Tigre. Both trains were northbound.

He hit the turnstile, went with the crowd swarming to the left.

Señorita Raven hit the adjacent turnstile, moved with the masses rushing toward the right.

Capítulo 34

muerto es muerto

Morning commuters were lined up on the platform in single file. More vendors moved back and forth through the crowd, carrying a half dozen colorful Thermoses and yelling they had café for sale. Four-decade-old trains. Worn rubber skid-proof floors. Windows scarred, vulgar words etched in some of the glass. The air was damp, thick, and stale. Most windows had been opened for ventilation.

There were five cars to each train. Each car was about twenty-five or thirty meters long. Three doors to each car, doors at opposite ends and in the middle.

That meant there were three ways to escape each goddamn car.

Fifteen exit points on each train.

The worn blue-and-white train to Suarez pulled away as soon as Medianoche entered the lead car. He flexed his fingers inside his gloved hand. Half the seats faced forward, half backward. A single seat facing the aisle was next to each door. The train was leaving the yard, and as far as he knew, he was being moved away from the other members of his team. Being moved away from the package. Soon, two dozen tracks funneled down to a single pathway cutting its way out of the city of Buenos Aires. Medianoche put his right hand deep inside his coat pocket, his fingers gripping a smaller backup gun. A .22 that didn't have a silencer.

There was no security on the train. No police officers. No security cameras.

Hustlers squeezed by, moved back and forth, announcing the product they were selling for a few pesos, yelling like they were Latin auctioneers. Train was packed. Everyone held overhead rails and backs of seats to maintain balance as the rocking threw passengers into each other. A Castellano rapper blasted his music, began rapping for donations.

Medianoche yelled, "Rodríguez. Which train did you board?"

No response, only the echo from the falling rain mixing with Castellano chatter.

Medianoche yelled, "I'm on the train heading toward Suarez."

Nothing but the irritating voice of that damn Castellano rapper.

He said, "Señorita Raven?"

"I'm here, Medianoche. I mean . . . I'm still here, sir."

"Where are you?"

"Tigre train." Señorita Raven's voice was in his ear. "My train is still at the station."

"No sign of Rodríguez over there?"

"Halfway through the train. Hard to squeeze by all these people. Sardines in a can."

"Get to the end of the train. If he isn't there, if you don't see the package, abort mission."

At the start of the second car, Medianoche saw Señor Rodríguez, seated in a hard plastic seat that faced out toward the aisle. People stood around him, heavy coats and soaked shoes squeaking on the train's floor, oblivious to the soldier as he held his gut, his head leaning back against the wall. The carriage whined and pitched along the tracks, the floor soaked from umbrellas leaving water trails.

The water at his feet as pink as a beautiful rose.

On one side of Rodríguez was a young couple, tongues moving inside each other's mouths, kissing like they were alone. On his other side was a man in a Brazilian jacket, hair in braids and cheap golden rings on every finger and his thumbs.

None was the enemy. He had to be sure before he took another step.

As soon as Medianoche leaned forward, Señor Rodríguez spoke in a pained whisper. "Saw the package . . . briefcase . . . same as the one we got . . . from Uruguayans . . . two tangos . . . man . . . woman . . . saw them run . . . getting on train . . . was right behind them . . . then . . . this big guy . . . big fucking guy . . . didn't think . . . didn't know he was with the two tangos . . . fucker hit me . . . rabbit punched me on my chin . . . fucker's fist was like a brick . . . he walked away . . . got back off the train before it left . . . was dazed . . . then this other guy . . . awwww fuck . . . guy with package . . . shit . . . he came out of nowhere . . . blade in my chest . . . handle broke off . . . fuck . . . took my earpiece . . . and my gun . . . sorry . . . so damn sorry . . . the package . . . it went . . . it went . . ."

"Took your earpiece?"

Medianoche paused.

Then came the rugged voice of an angry stranger.

"Yeah. I borrowed his earpiece."

Medianoche stood up, looked through the crowd. Someone squeezed by, shouting out loud, selling Claro SIM cards for five pesos. He wanted to elbow that fucker in his face. Then the lady with the baby squeezed by again, her dirty hand outstretched.

Medianoche asked. "Who is this?"

"They call me Gideon."

"Gideon."

"Is this . . . the man wearing the eye patch?"

"Yes."

"The other one . . . she called you Medianoche."

"They call me Medianoche."

"Medianoche. That means Midnight."

Medianoche paused. "What are you?"

"What do you mean?"

"You don't sound British. Or Latin. Or double *E* double *U*."

"I look forward to . . . to seeing you . . . again."

"Have we met?"

"Once."

Medianoche said, "I doubt that."

"Why?"

"Because you're still living. If we'd met before, we wouldn't be having this conversation."

Gideon said, "I thought the same thing."

Medianoche leaned closer to Rodríguez. Blood was dripping into his dark clothes.

His hands pressed down on the place the blade had been shoved, like he was trying to hold his life inside his body. Medianoche looked into his eyes, told the wounded soldier to hold on.

The knife had been pushed through the Kevlar. That took power. That took rage.

Medianoche told the soldier that back at this apartment, Tres Marías waited for him. So he'd better hold on. His three *amigovias* would want to go out and dance the tango very soon.

Señor Rodríguez nodded, smiled a little, struggled to breathe, then managed to say, "Kill the sonofabitch, sir. I'll be here when you get back, sir. Sorry I messed up, sir."

Señor Rodríguez nodded a painful nod that said he would be okay.

Medianoche pushed people aside, passed by crying babies, men who were coughing like they had the flu, women blowing their noses. He made his way past disgruntled faces and headed down the aisle of the crowded train.

Medianoche put his hand inside his pocket. Kept his gun inside his hand, finger on trigger. He moved by people, past train hustlers and pickpockets and mothers with children.

Medianoche saw the expressions on the faces of the passengers change, like a storm warning. The baggy-pants-wearing rapper stopped rapping. With the abrupt silence, the crowd tensed, horror sprouted in eyes, some ducked while others moved away from what looked like a South American assassination in the making.

They were all terrified, fixated on something behind him.

Medianoche pulled out his gun and prepared to turn, all done in one smooth move.

As he turned, the handle of a gun came down across the back of his head. His gun exploded, shot a round into the ceiling. People screamed. Dazed, Medianoche felt the business end of a gun pushing into the back of his neck, the metal digging an inch deep into his skin. He found his balance, heard tense breathing. The man who had gutted Rodríguez was behind him.

Gideon said, "Hand me your gun or die where you stand."

Capítulo 35

tren de la muerte

Death stood behind Medianoche.

People yelled like they were trapped inside a burning building, rushed away from them as if the flames from their conflict were burning their skin.

"*Now.*" Gideon's voice was firm and deadly. "Hand me the gun now."

Medianoche dropped the gun, didn't hand his weapon to his enemy.

More yells came from the terrified commuters.

A blow struck the side of his head. A stunning blow that ended with the business end of a nine millimeter in his face, halting Medianoche's retaliation. Gideon swooped up the dropped gun, tossed it out the open window of the moving train, checked behind him, then backed up a step. Gideon stood strong, brows drawn down, raised upper lip, tightness under his eyes.

The unadulterated look of violence. Same expression Medianoche possessed.

Gideon said, "Now give me the gun."

"Just did."

"Don't fuck with me. Your second gun. Your backup."

"Oh, that gun."

"Hand it over. Use two fingers. Grip it by the barrel. No fast movements."

Medianoche tightened his jaw, defiant, no man's prisoner. At a disadvantage.

Gideon repeated himself, his voice hard, eyes focused, his last warning.

Medianoche eased his second gun out of his coat, business end first. Gideon took the weapon and tossed it out the window of the train as it rambled through the rail yard. Medianoche stared at the rugged young man as the rugged young man stared at him.

Spanish panic rose, commuters trying to figure out what was going on, asking each other if the battle was over drugs, over a woman, knowing that people killed over things much smaller.

Gideon said, "It's you. It's fucking you."

Medianoche ignored the assassin's words, kept his attention on the killer's eyes, and took in the position of the gun and his enemy's body language, looking for an opening.

Gideon took a breath, shook his head in disbelief. "You were shot in North Carolina."

Again, North Carolina.

Medianoche snapped, "Who are you?"

"I'm asking myself *what* the fuck you are."

Medianoche saw an opening, started to move in.

Gideon reacted, snapped out like a venomous snake.

Medianoche was struck in the face, hit on the chin by Gideon's left fist, a strong blow that staggered him, sent him back four steps. Lights flashed in front of his eyes, and he found his footing. Medianoche shook it off, stood erect, adjusted his eye patch, and growled.

Gideon stood in front of him, both hands on a gun aimed at the center of Medianoche's forehead. Medianoche glimpsed the crowd, looked to see who was with Gideon. All he saw was a crowd that didn't speak English, but their wide eyes said they understood body language.

Mouth bloodied, Medianoche repeated his question, "Who the fuck are you?"

Gideon growled, "I'm the kid who shot you."

He growled, "Bullshit."

"You were trying to kill . . . my mother."

"What was the mother's goddamn name?"

"Thelma."

Medianoche didn't reply. Done talking. He was ready to slaughter the man standing in front of him, and that death would have nothing to do with the mission, nothing to do with Hopkins or Scamz or the wounded soldier who was in the train behind Gideon.

"Sir . . ."

Señorita Raven's voice was in his ear, back in range, monitoring the conversation. She could hear everything.

Gideon kept his gun raised, its barrel pointed at Medianoche's head. Gideon reached to Medianoche's face, grabbed Medianoche's ear so hard it felt like it was being ripped from his face, and snatched the earpiece out.

Medianoche frowned. Communication broken.

Medianoche held his ground as he tried to remember the face of the kid who had shot him. The memory and the reality, they refused to amalgamate. The man in front of him meant nothing. But it wasn't over. What he had glimpsed behind Gideon told him it wasn't over.

He saw Señor Rodríguez. A soldier who had made it to his feet and stumbled through the crowded car. A wounded soldier who was one car behind Gideon, people parting as the wounded man grabbed railings, his face drenched in sweat, features in a severe knot, expressing intense pain as his blood drained from his dark clothing and left a river of red on the filthy floor.

Medianoche had to keep Gideon talking while his soldier fought with pain, while his soldier struggled to take out his weapon, the crowd around them panicking in Castellano chatter.

Medianoche said, "Well, Gideon. You seem to know a lot about me. Wouldn't doubt if you have information on the rest of my soldiers. Wouldn't doubt that at all."

"This is not a fucking joke."

"You claim that you're the whore's kid. You're claiming to be that snot-nosed kid."

Gideon's face remained tense. "Do you know who I am?"

Señor Rodríguez made it to the opening separating the cars. His bloodied hands were unsteady as he used all of his energy to pull his rain- and blood-soaked coat back, exposing the handle of his backup gun.

Medianoche said, "Gideon. You said your name was Gideon."

"Do you know who I . . . do you know who the kid was that . . . shot you?"

"We can get off the train and talk. Let's do that. Leave the train and chat."

"Did you know that it was your son who shot you?"

"What are you talking about now?"

"I'm your son. Might be. That is what I've been told all of my life."

Medianoche smiled a little. Smiled because, in his periphery, he spied Señor Rodríguez as the wounded soldier leaned against the wall, a crowd of frantic people around him, his hand trembling. Medianoche saw his severely wounded soldier move his bloodied hand from his injury, saw him move his hand from his loosened and severed guts and fight to take out his nine.

Medianoche swallowed. "Who told you that bullshit?"

Gideon said, "Thelma told me that."

Medianoche saw Señor Rodríguez as he battled with pain, as he swallowed and struggled to breathe, then saw his soldier exert all the energy he had in his body to raise the barrel of his weapon. Bloodied hands on his tool of death, it was a struggle Señor Rodríguez lost. But he kept trying. That soldier was not a loser.

Medianoche gave Gideon no clues.

Medianoche asked, "Where's the package?"

Gideon snapped, "Fuck the goddamn package."

Medianoche waited for his brave soldier to make his play as the overconfident assassin in front of him unknowingly breathed his final breath.

Gideon said, "You were with Thelma in Montego Bay. Nine months before I was born."

"Do you have any idea how many men screwed Thelma in Mo Bay? She had men at her door with Jamaican dollars or American dollars or British pounds. Some might've had food stamps. What, are you going down the list? You understand how a brothel works? Guy before me took his dick out, my turn came up, I put my dick in, and when I left, the guy after me put his dick in. Has it taken you twenty years to get to my name? Well, you can keep on searching."

Medianoche saw Señor Rodríguez take two more steps, leaving more blood on the floor. He moved closer as if he knew he was in no condition to hit from beyond point-blank range.

Medianoche kept Gideon's attention.

Medianoche yelled, "Where is Thelma? Is that whore here? Does that whore have something to do with this mission?"

"She . . . Thelma died in Europe. She died in London."

"Too fucking bad. Would've loved to help her see the end."

"She's dead. Thelma is dead."

"You've got some mental issues."

"Makes the job easier to digest."

"And let me tell you this. Let me tell you something from my heart, young man."

Gideon hesitated. He showed weakness and hesitated.

Gideon swallowed and said, "Go ahead."

"If you're the snot-nose fuck who left me for dead and cost me my fucking eye, if you are that trick baby grown up, you better *finish the fucking job* now because I'll come at you like the fucking Bible, the part that says *an eye for a fucking eye*, you fucked-up piece of shit. If this is the real fucking deal, if you're that kid that was with that pathetic whore, if you've come out of fucking nowhere, you'll wish you had stayed wherever the fuck you were. And if this is some bullshit the fuckers on that arrogant fuck Scamz's team have concocted, I will still *take you out* the same way, just for trying to fucking get inside my fucking head, you fucking fucked-up fuck."

His anger was at Gideon, but his words were orders for Señor Rodríguez. *Finish the fucking job.* Señor Rodríguez raised his gun, the train vibrating and whining as the weapon exploded.

The shot missed Gideon and hit a woman in her chest. She was dead before she fell.

There were screams on top of screams. Terror and hysterics spread through the train.

Medianoche sprung at Gideon and was greeted with a kick to the gut that took him to one knee. In pain, Medianoche looked up, saw Gideon spin, his gun searching for his target.

As Señor Rodríguez struggled to hold on, he fired again. He was too wounded to fire straight. His desperate shot hit another passenger, sent the passenger falling to the floor.

Gideon pulled off three rapid shots. One found Señor Rodríguez's chest, hit his bulletproof vest. The second shot found his neck. Before the blood could spurt, the third shot hit Señor Rodríguez's head, left blood and brain matter decorating the wall and people behind him.

Medianoche pulled his wet overcoat to the side, the material heavy, slowing him as he hoisted out his third gun. Gideon whipped back, shot him twice, both shots striking center mass. Medianoche fell, the velocity of the bullets hitting him like a baseball going one hundred miles per hour, taking him off his feet.

Gideon saw he wasn't down.

By the time Medianoche had his weapon and his balance, Gideon had escaped into the next car, fled through the crowd. And as the train slowed down, Medianoche caught a view of Gideon taking to the open window and leaping off the train into a wasteland of mud, bottles, and debris. In that section, the drop wasn't far. The train was only about three feet higher than the area that led to the platform. Medianoche shoved people out of his path, pushed them to the floor as he rushed to get to a window. He yanked the window up as far as it would go, a frigid hard wind pushing a freezing rain inside. The train was slowing down, but it was too late for him to jump. The terrain had changed, the train now twenty feet aboveground, iron rails and other objects appearing as the train slowed down. If he jumped now, he would jump into a vertical bar or a concrete pole, break his neck or his spine.

The train eased into the station; terrified passengers crowded against the door, ready to escape. Low-class apartments with clothes hanging on patios had passed by on the journey; the same for clay tennis courts and a disco called The Roxy. Now there were only two tracks. Medianoche saw where he was as the largest mosque in South America and two gigantic markets, Jumbo and Easy, came into view. He was near

Jumbo Palermo Commercial Center. Avenida Bullrich and Cerviño. The racetracks of Palermo Hipódromo were not far away.

Medianoche looked at the dead woman. Her mouth was open. Her eyes were open. She was looking up in the air. Dead. Then he looked at her screaming, crying, traumatized, mourning *hijos* and *hijas*. In combat, he had seen that sight more times than he could count.

The consequences of war never changed.

War fathered many orphans. Gave birth to many widows and widowers.

He paused. In war, they never left the dead or wounded. The Taliban always removed the bodies of the wounded and the dead. So did al-Qaeda. So did the United States.

But he didn't have a choice.

The terrified man who had been shot in the leg stared like he would remember him.

Medianoche shot the man the way he wanted to shoot Gideon.

Once in the eye.

Lights out. Memory removed.

Medianoche stepped over the body of his dead soldier, then left the train with the panicked crowd. He bolted toward the back of the train, jumped down into the tracks, raced back in the direction Gideon had leapt out of the window. Ran through wind and rain, ran over uneven tracks, his gun in his hand, expecting to be fired on at any moment, ready to return fire. He had seen Gideon move like a cat and jump out the window of a moving train. That fucker had to be injured. He could be down in the mud, broken glass and bottles, cut to pieces from his fall. His leg could be broken. Or he could be unconscious. Ready to be taken away and questioned.

Ninety seconds and a quarter mile later, Medianoche was back at the area where Gideon had bailed. Medianoche moved across the ground, hot sweat mixing with the cold rain. He felt a throbbing in his knees, his breathing labored from the sprint down the uneven and littered railway.

Gideon was gone, the ground too wet to show any tracks.

Palermo Parks, that big complex of parks, wasn't too far. So were rose gardens and artificial lakes. Another hub of activity led toward Santa Fe and Plaza Italia.

Gideon had a hundred ways to flee.

Medianoche reached inside his pocket, pulled out the tracker.

It was amber. Not green. That son-of-a-whore Gideon was in the area. But the package wasn't near here, not near Palermo. The package hadn't been on the goddamn train.

His gut instinct told him that it had never left the station at Retiro.

Medianoche didn't give a fuck about a kid who had been yanked out of the cunt of a whore. Especially one who lied and claimed he had come from the juice in his nuts.

Fucking mind games from a young fucker who trembled like he had mental issues.

A fucker who had fucked up and killed a soldier.

A loyal soldier.

Gideon had killed a Horseman.

Nobody killed a Horseman and lived to talk about it.

Nobody.

Mouth bloodied, chest aching from the impact of the two bullets that failed to open his chest, head throbbing from being beaten by a young punk's gun, Medianoche bolted through the mud and debris, brain about to explode, a vicious hunter tracking his prey.

Chapter 36

crimes of the father

Once upon a time I killed an assassin named Midnight.

Years ago I killed Midnight to protect the pedophilic mother who made me a killer.

That was back when I was seven years old.

But Midnight wasn't dead. The man I'd been told was my father had risen from his grave.

My mother had been strangled, was dying right in front of my face. Picking up the gun. Pulling the trigger. The sensation that ran through my body when the gun discharged. Midnight's head jerking back. His body falling to the floor. The thud from his body dropping echoing between my ears. I was seven. But I was no longer seven. I was every sin I had committed all at once.

Shooting my father had made me a killer. Had given met the honorable feeling that came with exacting a righteous death. Had taught me that some people deserved to die.

Traumatic memories alternated, bombarded me like punches.

Oedipus the King.

Thirty minutes later I'd made it to the barrio called Belgrano, the boulevard crowded. I was alert as I moved through a chilling rain. I heard sirens in the distance. Trepidation motivated my wounded stride. Couldn't stop sweating. Body temperature was high enough to set my clothes on fire.

As the assassin called Hawks would say, I was STFO.

A vibration in my pocket caused my trigger finger to get excited and my heartbeat to speed up.

Cell phone. The Motorola. The blackmail phone.

That fucker really had bad timing. I didn't want to answer, but I did.

I snapped, "What do you want now?"

"Busy?"

"Always busy."

First a pause, then the electronic voice. "Is the money ready to be transferred?"

"One, it's not the fucking deadline."

"We're aware of that. Needed to make sure all was falling into place."

"And two, the information hasn't been received."

"It was sent."

"Well, it wasn't fucking received."

"It was fucking sent."

"What, are my fucking words not coming through? It wasn't received. So resend."

"I will resend, but there will be a fucking administrative cost for doing so."

"Administrative cost?"

"The price just went up to two and a half million. Keep being an asshole. The numbers will go up as the clock counts down on you. All I have to do is push one button. One button."

"One button."

"All I have to do is use one finger, push one button."

"One finger."

"That's all it will take. And your life will change forever."

"It changed when you made the first phone call."

"And it will take two point five to get it back to where you want it."

"After this is done, how will I know you won't send the information to worldwide law enforcement anyway? What guarantee do I get? You know who I am, and I have no idea who you are. So, if you ask me, this thing is a little off balance, tilted in your favor."

"Guess you'll have to trust me."

"I'll have to trust a thief."

"From the mouth of a man who murders."

"For thieves and politicians who don't have the balls to do it themselves."

"So you say."

"Would love to chitchat, but I'm on the clock and I have to run."

"Where you off to?"

"I've got work to do."

"Well, work hard, kill enough to have the money ready to be transferred."

I hung the phone up. Didn't have time to deal with that shit. And if this day didn't end in my favor, nothing on that end would matter, not at all. At least not for me.

My thoughts weren't on the Lebanese, not on the patsy at Starbucks in Miami, not on being blackmailed for two and a half million U.S. dollars. Not on Arizona being pregnant. Not on Scamz.

Every thought was on Midnight.

On the man they called Medianoche.

I put the Motorola away and took out the iPhone. Shook my head. There wasn't any time to call Catherine. Not when I knew I was on the run. Didn't know what I'd say. I wanted to know if she knew that Midnight was alive, if she'd known all along, if that lie was another one of her lies used to manipulate me. Too much on my mind. No time to pull up the cameras at the house. Not when bullets could fly in my direction at any moment.

I had to stay focused in order to stay alive, had to keep moving in case the city was looking for me, had to call and make sure Arizona had gotten away from the station at Retiro.

The Queen of Scamz answered on the first ring. "Gideon?"

"I made it out."

"I intercepted that call from your blackmailer. Heard the conversation."

"Were they still in Memphis?"

"They're still in Memphis. They went back to Arkansas and Mississippi but came back to Memphis."

"Whoever it is, they're on the move."

"Maybe they are in the same business you're in."

"Or the business you're in."

I battled with rage, disbelief, and guilt.

Staying on that train and waiting for Midnight had pulled innocent people into this deadly game of chess. A woman had been killed in front of her children. In front of strangers.

Arizona had entered the car on one train, moved through the crowd and hurried down a door and exited the train on the opposite side. She had mixed with the people who'd just arrived at Retiro, headed back toward the station, held her belly with one hand and the briefcase with the other. Konstantin had his eyes on her, was waiting for her, kept her moving until they made it back into the mouth of the protest. Alvin and Konstantin were already at Retiro when we arrived, had made it there about ten minutes before we had. That was our designated bailout point. But the protest changed everything. We would've dumped our car and hurried into theirs, but they had been blocked in by the demonstration. That altered our plans. We took the package to the train. It was Alvin's swift punch that staggered the assassin who had followed us onto the train. He had thrown a phantom blow like the one that had put Liston on the mat. And while the merc staggered, I'd gutted him and eased him back into a seat. Alvin had walked out the opposite side of the train too, a large man in a crowd of not-so-large people.

Konstantin and Shotgun had done what I'd told them, had gotten Arizona out of the area.

I'd told them to keep moving and not look back. Had them remain silent until I called.

If I lived long enough. At that moment I was being driven by some other force.

Arizona said, "I'm with Konstantin and Shotgun."

"No one came after you?"

"We've been on the move. Konstantin kept us moving."

"How long have you been where you are?"

"We just walked into this location. Where are you?"

"Avenida Federico Lacroze. Heading toward 3 de Febrero."

"You're close."

"Stay alert. Will meet you at the rendezvous."

I turned the phone off.

Left leg aching, clothing muddied, scratches on my face, I limped by a train platform, saw a crowd, looked up to make sure no Horsemen were on the platform looking for me. I had made it to the Colegiales stop on the city line. Looked around, hand on gun, evaluated the crowd.

I had to stop for a moment. Had to catch my breath. Had to shake off the pain in my leg.

I'd killed one of those psychotic bastards. The one they called Rodríguez was dead.

And I'd had a chance to kill the one they called Medianoche.

Should've left his brains decorating the walls of that train.

Didn't matter who he was. Or if he'd risen three days after I had killed him the first time.

I didn't know him. He was nothing to me. As Catherine . . . as Thelma was nothing to him.

I should've killed him again. Should've taken head shots, not body shots.

Had to focus. Had to stay alert. Had to stay alive under these dismal South American skies. I mixed with the crowd, caught the light up at Avenida Cabildo. I saw motorcyclists and moved out of sight. Two of the Horsemen had been on motorcycles. There was a fourth one. The Beast. I hadn't crossed paths with him yet. Had no idea what he looked like.

If he wasn't present, that told me who was babysitting their half of the package.

Or he had a sensor and was shadowing the package we had.

But I knew that it wasn't about the package anymore. Not for me.

Midnight. Medianoche. A ruthless mercenary.

His blood, my blood. Or so I had been told.

His face, scarred, battered, aged. And he'd returned from the dead.

I kept moving. Pain slowed me down but didn't stop me. There was sweat, mud, and rain inside my clothes and shoes. I'd rinsed my face well enough, but my clothes were as murky as my mind.

An entrance for the green line Olleros subte station was on every corner of the bustling intersection of the shop-filled street. There were signs for Esso, Standard Bank, and Claro standing sentry over the avenue in the middle-class section of the barrio. I had looked up again, afraid a sniper might be waiting on a roof, covered in camouflage, nothing exposed but the barrel of his rifle, the way I had taken more than a few people out in the past. Or standing in the next shadow. I'd never gone up against anything like The Four Horsemen. They weren't untrained rappers or vindictive politicians. They were merciless. They'd killed two officers in the dimness of the morning, had killed strangers on a train. Only a fool wouldn't be afraid. People moved like trails of ants. I hurried across the street, past Forrest Gump Bar Café, past businesses and apartments. On the corner at 3 de Febrero was a two-level Starbucks.

The sign at the coffee shop said it was closed, due to open soon, the fourth Starbucks in Buenos Aires. Windows were covered in newspapers. Guarding the door was Shotgun. He had one of the sawed-off shotguns in his hands, two nines tucked inside in the waist of his pants.

I said, "Shotgun."

"Look like you been through hell."

"In the middle of hell and standing in the heat."

He was out of his suit and had on jeans, Lugz, and a dark sweater. His clothes matched the casual dress of the neighborhood, were better for the frigid temperature outside. It was just as cold inside the building. No heat. Our breath fogged with the damp, chilling air. The coffee shop was two levels, but it wasn't large, not like the Starbucks in the U.S. Downstairs had enough seating for about ten people, upstairs probably had the same close quarters.

Shotgun dug into his back pocket and took out a small package, tossed it to me.

It was a blue-and-white package of BC Powder.

He said, "Looks like you need that."

"A man after my own heart."

I opened the BC Powder, downed it dry, hoped it took the express lanes to my pains.

Shotgun said, "Everybody was getting worried about you."

"They're worried about the package, not me."

"Well, I was getting worried about you, homie. So was the boss man. He didn't say he was, but the way he was pacing and talking in Russian, I knew his blood pressure was up."

"You did a good job back there. Real good."

"Told you I'd been working out. Best shape of my life."

"Real good job. He was about to draw down on us. And he didn't give a shit about Arizona being knocked up. He would've shot us dead right there and vanished in the crowd."

He nodded. "What happened after we got the pregnant woman from down there?"

"Got ugly. Shootout. Mass hysteria. People died."

"Bad guys are the ones that died, I hope."

I shook my head. Shotgun had called them bad guys. Like people did when they saw things in shades of black and white, in good and evil. We were all bad guys.

I said, "The other one . . . the one who was leading them . . . he got away."

"How?"

I licked my lips and said, "Temporarily."

He nodded.

I said, "They have on bulletproof vests. Might be bulletproof clothes. I shot him twice. Bullets bounced off him like he was Superman. So assume they are all wearing the same gear."

"I saw the killer woman. She had on all black and was soaking wet. She walked right by me and hurried to the other train. Her face . . . her face . . . it was pretty, but it wasn't pretty. She's an easy one to spot. She had a lot of marks on her face. Like she had . . . been in an explosion."

I took to the stairs.

My body ached, and I kept that pain hidden the best I could as I ran up one level. Shotgun knew I was hurting; he didn't know how bad. I didn't need to become the weak link. My bags were upstairs. Nothing inside the bags but clothes. No time to clean up. But I changed clothes. Put on jeans. My hands were numb from being damp in the winter air.

And being inside a building that didn't have heat wasn't helping the numbness in my fingers subside.

Konstantin and Arizona were upstairs.

No sign of Scamz. That meant he was with the other team.

I went to Konstantin.

He said, "Son, they need to remain mobile."

I nodded. "I need so say something."

"Speak."

"I think . . . I think Midnight is alive."

"Your father?"

It felt stupid to say that. I knew what I'd seen and I still wasn't sure.

I went over that day in my mind. Not in a coherent way. Not in a logical way. I had no time for logic. Flashes came and went. That day in North Carolina. It was a puzzle I didn't have time to solve. He was alive. If he saw me before I saw him, he would leave me suffering from lead poisoning. And now he used the name Medianoche. He was one of The Four Horsemen.

That was what I told Konstantin. I'd cut to the chase, said my old man wasn't dead. I told him that the man I'd been told was my father was my enemy. Had always been my enemy.

Konstantin put his hand on my shoulder. He did that to calm me down.

He said, "How sure are you?"

"I'm not sure about anything anymore. But I shot him twice."

"So he's wounded or dead."

"Neither."

"What happened?"

"Bullets bounced off his Italian suit. Kevlar. Saw the bullets fall. Saw him get up."

The Russian assassin paused.

I nodded.

He said, "That means he has a South American tailor and spares no expenses."

I nodded.

He asked, "You want to get off this job?"

"No. As far as I'm concerned, he's nothing to me. He just tried to kill me, and I returned the favor. He's nothing to me and I'm nothing to him. This is my debt. I'm not walking away from a promise. I'm seeing this through. But I wouldn't be hurt if you and Shotgun left at this point."

"You're favoring your right leg."

"Never been better."

"Talk to your employer. She's being difficult. I almost walked away. We've been here thirty minutes and that is thirty minutes too long. We need to move. Not a time to rest."

"So you're not leaving."

"You're stuck with me, kid."

Several laptops were up and running. Looked like a scaled-down version of Jack Bauer's Counter Terrorist Unit, here in Buenos Aires to safeguard the world from radical threats.

Arizona was in front of the laptops, two satellite phones at her side. The black briefcase that everyone on the opposing team was willing to kill for, her MacGuffin, was near her feet. Never left her side. She saw me and stopped typing, put her hand on her swollen stomach and stood up. For a moment I saw softness, a flash of worry that turned to relief in her eyes. In that moment I had flashes of us when we were at Chapel Hill and the Carolina Inn. I saw her naked, giving herself to me. Her swollen belly reminded me that those disturbing flashes had no value. That momentary flash of us as lovers deepened my anxiety and negative feelings.

I told Arizona, "We can't stay here."

"I know. I'm pulling up footage from the street cameras around the city. Want to find the BMW the Horsemen used, see if we can run the cameras backward."

"We don't have time for you to play with Google Earth."

"Linking into government satellites. Bouncing signal. Will only take a minute."

"We don't have another minute."

"The BMW that trailed us, trying to reverse-engineer and see where the car originated. Find their Batcave. And we have a screen up, can see what's outside and on the streets."

"Are you fucking deaf? You need to be mobile until we get a handle on this. They use flash and bang. They're military. Hiding behind a closed door and windows covered in paper means nothing. Not a damn thing. They could have infrared heat sensors aimed at us right now. They could pinpoint all of us and start shooting at us like we're sitting ducks."

"Back the fuck off. I'm trying to get some idea of where their base is."

I asked her where the rest of her team was, asked if that other half of the package had been located. I was ready to switch from being hunted to becoming the hunter.

Sierra and her brother were in one of the vehicles, moving around the city and the province, out driving around and doing their best to get a fix on the other package.

She said, "They're close. When they get a better fix, they will contact me."

"If they aren't killed. If they get spotted, they're dead."

My words sent a noticeable chill down Arizona's spine. She actually cared about someone other than herself. Her siblings were armed, but they needed skills that went beyond ramming people with cars. Toe to toe, they wouldn't be a match for a trained assassin, let alone mercenaries. They were grifters. They were knives going to a fight where grenades are used.

My eyes went to the briefcase Arizona guarded with her life. A piece of a puzzle she was risking to sacrifice her siblings and her unborn baby to protect. I needed that package. I wanted them to come after me. I wanted Midnight to come after me. I needed this headache to end.

I said, "I need everything you have on one of The Horsemen. Medianoche."

"We have nothing more than what I have already given you and the Russian."

I wiped sweat and leftover grit from my face, then went to the window, peeped out at the street.

Arizona stayed on task, breaking into government Web sites, directing satellites until the area outside came in as clear as a hi-def movie.

She zoomed on one laptop. On another she had a six-block radius. On another she had the footage she was looking for. The BMW that had trailed us. Arizona had my angst level up as she tried to find out where the BMW had come from.

Arizona told me, "You left me vulnerable."

"You were covered by my team."

"An old man and a giant who used to be a second-rate boxer."

"A seasoned assassin and an ambitious man you shouldn't take for granted."

"I'm paying you to cover me. I hired *you*. Not them."

"Keep your lies straight. Scamz hired me."

"Technicality."

"Talk to him if you have a problem with the way I work."

"I'm talking to you."

"After a year. You pop up with this bullshit."

"Gideon . . ."

"And they are working with me. You don't get to call the shots."

"I've never worked with either of them before."

"And they've never worked with you. First time for everything."

"You left me vulnerable. You stayed on the train and left me vulnerable."

I said, "Now would be a good time to decide how bad you and your team want this."

"You were flown down in a Gulfstream. Draw your own conclusions."

"You see what you're up against. You've seen the footage. They are hot on you. You could leave now. You could vanish and they would never be able to find you and your team."

"Why didn't you leave Retiro with us? You had time to get off the train with me."

"Had to make sure someone was . . . had to see if someone was still alive."

Arizona thought I was talking about the merc they had called Rodríguez.

I said, "Give me the goddamn package. You're wobbling and slow. I don't need your swollen feet slowing me down. This isn't like London. You and Scamz and your crew should—"

"*The package stays with me.*"

"You think we'll take your half, find a way to get the other half and vanish?"

"Nothing surprises me."

"Glad I know where we stand. You're right. Me and you together, that was no good."

"We were never together. Not the way you see it in your mind."

"Good. So keep it professional and I'll do the same."

"Gideon."

"Yes, Queen Scamz?"

She took a breath that told me she was irritated, stressed, and sleep deprived. "Gideon, at the risk of sounding redundant, the package stays with me. It will not leave my care."

I rubbed my temples, then said, "Okay, Queen Scamz, get what you have to get so we can get out of here."

"Stop calling me that."

"That's your handle. That's your goddamn handle."

"You're scared?"

"I'm half past scared and you should be a quarter to terrified. The longer we stay here, the more dangerous it is for my team."

She snapped, "Look. Let me finish what I'm—"

"Last time, shut it down."

"Well, Gideon, you'll want to see this before I shut it down."

I leaned in, my eyes on the computer screen.

Photos of me.

My blackmailer had sent the information, only the phone I had didn't vibrate.

Ten pages of information.

Information my old enemy in Detroit had bought.

What I saw was worth what he was asking for.

Capítulo 37

un soldado se murió hoy

The Four Horsemen had become three.

Rain fell, and lightning lit up the sky as Medianoche sat with his angry mercenaries.

He knew it would be like this.

In war, when a comrade had fallen, the adrenaline rush always washed over everything logical, the call for revenge a trumpet that blared loud enough to terrify the deaf.

Once again, all were dressed in black Italian suits. Black fedoras. Black overcoats.

They were at The Beast's apartment. Laying low. Too many dead bodies in the street.

Everything from Puerto Madero to Retiro to Palermo was dangerous, the Argentine police trying to make sense of the early-morning killing spree that had left no suspects.

Sensor in one hand, gun in the other, Medianoche stood next to The Beast.

Señor Rodríguez was dead. Someone's son. Someone's brother.

He was dead. Killed by Gideon.

The boy who claimed to be Medianoche's son. A lie Medianoche would never believe.

The Beast said, "Señor Rodríguez was twenty-four years old."

Señorita Raven vented, "His body was left on a train like he was a used Coke bottle. There was no dignity in his death. He died a hero.

He died protecting Medianoche. Señor Rodríguez deserved better than to be left on a fucking train heading to the ends of nowhere."

Medianoche glanced at Señorita Raven, saw a young soldier who was fuming, hyped, pacing back and forth, a loaded nine in each hand. She needed revenge on behalf of a fallen comrade. She'd seen her fellow soldiers lured into ambushes, walk into booby traps, had seen comrades blown to bits, lose limbs in explosions. She had almost been blown up herself, the explosion filling her face and body with shrapnel.

The Beast said, "How many were there?"

Señorita Raven took a breath. "Two were inside the vehicle we pursued. A man and a woman."

The Beast said, "Only two?"

Señorita Raven said, "One man and one woman."

Medianoche interrupted, "But there were at least three at Retiro. Two were inside the car that held the package. They definitely had the package. Rodríguez said there was a third."

The Beast nodded. "I should've been there. This wouldn't have happened if I had been there. We'd have the package and this would be over if I had been there."

Señorita Raven snapped, "And Señor Rodríguez would be alive."

"They had a special car." Medianoche gritted his teeth. "The protest slowed us down."

"I arrived to Retiro just as your train pulled away. Was stuck in the mob."

Señorita Raven shook her head. "It was the crowd, sir. Too many civilians in the line of fire. Was impossible to get a direct shot. Impossible to pick out tangos when you're surrounded by thirty or forty thousand protesting civilians waving signs in a downpour."

The Beast nodded again.

Medianoche said, "First blood. They have drawn first blood."

The Beast said, "We will draw last blood."

Señorita Raven said, "Buckets of blood. No matter who they are, no matter who Gideon is, buckets of blood. No matter whose son Gideon is, no matter who his mother is, no matter who his father might be, he has to pay for what happened to Rodríguez."

Medianoche took a deep breath. "Something you want to say, soldier?"

"No, sir. But maybe I should ask if there is something you want to say?"

"Maybe if you had stayed with Señor Rodríguez, then this could've been avoided."

"We went over the options, sir. We agreed as a team."

"Well, then, you know things can go wrong. If you ever doubt things can go wrong, look in a mirror. Look at your face and see how the best-laid plans can often go awry."

"You don't want to go there, Medianoche. You don't want to test me and go there."

The Beast said, "Señor Rodríguez is dead, soldiers. Nothing we can do to change that."

Medianoche walked away, went to the window.

The apartment was meticulous. Smelled like baked fish and vegetables. War memorabilia were everywhere, so much that the apartment looked like a museum. Two books were on the table. *Las Venas Abiertas de América Latina* and *La Noche de los Lápices*.

His body ached. Knees hurt. Pain in his chest from being popped twice. Head throbbed.

Age. That slow-moving end that seemed like an out-of-control freight train.

He wanted cocaine. He wanted a line of cocaine to clear his head.

Medianoche said, "Gideon . . . the assassin Scamz imported . . . he claimed to know me."

The Beast said, "Repeat that, Medianoche."

He did.

The Beast said, "Know you from where?"

Medianoche added, "North Carolina."

"How?"

"The kid that shot me. He claimed to be that kid."

The Beast said, "Impossible. That's bullshit if ever I smelled it."

"I know. He claimed it was my nut that fertilized that whore-bitch's egg."

"Wait. Let me understand. He claimed to be your goddamn son?"

"Nothing to it. He was running some mind game."

"How old did the Gideon guy look?"

"He looked young but sounded older. Looked like a merc."

"Nationality?"

"No idea."

The Beast hummed. "Scamz is British. We know that for a fact."

"Then Gideon could be British. He did mention London."

Medianoche turned, faced Señorita Raven.

Enemies close.

Medianoche said, "Gideon had Señor Rodríguez's headset. Señorita Raven was on comm. She can verify. I'm sure she'll be more than happy to add to what I heard. I think that's what she was getting at. No secrets here. Just didn't see the point of repeating a lie."

The Beast rubbed his chin. "Señorita Raven. Comments?"

She looked at The Beast and nodded. "The tango said he was the kid that had shot Medianoche, sir. Called Medianoche 'Midnight' and said that was the name he had known him by when the incident occurred. From what I heard, Gideon sounded like he knew a lot about what happened in North Carolina. That was the reason he had stayed behind when the others had escaped with the package. To confront Medianoche. Our soldier was already wounded and escape would have been easy. Gideon said he was somebody named Thelma's kid."

The Beast paused. "Thelma. He actually said that name?"

"Said he was Thelma's kid. And Thelma was dead. Said she died in London."

The Beast shook his head, as if what he was hearing was impossible.

Then he said, "The easiest thing of all is to deceive oneself, for what a man wishes, he generally believes to be true."

Medianoche said, "Demosthenes."

The Beast nodded. "Demosthenes."

Medianoche adjusted the patch over his missing eye, that North Carolina memory on fire, flashes of being shot, of that snot-nosed kid coming and going. He frowned at Señorita Raven.

Medianoche said, "Still, I find that very questionable. Very convenient."

She said, "What do you mean, sir?"

"Right after you reveal that you broke into my files, that you have inside information on my life, that you have read my personal files, after you've followed me all over the city, this so-called assassin named Gideon shows up and repeats word-for-word everything you said."

"What are you saying, sir?"

Medianoche barked, "Don't pretend to be ignorant. Your IQ is too high. What are you after? Maybe you are part of some subgroup, and this mission is a conflict of interest."

"I have no idea what you mean, sir."

"Sarcastic bitch. Explain why you were above me, why you broke rank, continued the chase, and came out of the building above me. Explain why you were up close to the package and the helicopter that came in to pick up the Uruguayan that had the package?"

The Beast said, "Medianoche, soldier, slow down. You're making no sense. Pull up a chair, take a breath, have a seat and explain what you're saying."

Medianoche did, told The Beast all that had happened, laid his suspicions on the table.

The Beast turned to Señorita Raven.

She blew it off and said, "It's simple. I was at the door right after you ran out, saw you going up. I took another set of stairs, came out over you, wanted to box the runner in."

"Why don't we pull up the blueprint of the building and you show me these invisible stairs. I might be a one-eyed fuck, but I'm not a no-eyed fool. Manipulative *puta*. You've been very concerned with the package. Too concerned about how much it's worth. Why is that?"

"*Hacéte coger*, you incompetent one-eyed fuck."

The Beast waved his hand, motioning to everyone to stand down.

Medianoche backed down, engaged in a brutal silence.

Señorita Raven bounced her guns against her thighs, her jaw tight.

She said, "I will not be quiet, sir. I'm not a snitch. A lot of things happened in Iraq and Afghanistan, things that were left between soldiers, things that never should have happened, and things that never should have gone unpunished. Medianoche came into my quarters *uninvited*. He entered with a firearm at his side. His body language and the way he intruded my quarters, he came as a hostile."

The Beast nodded his head. "What happened, soldier?"

"I demanded that he leave my quarters immediately."

"Then what?"

"He refused. And he raped me."

Medianoche snapped, *"Be very careful what you say."*

"Medianoche entered my quarters unannounced, without knocking, just walked in my door. I had just undressed. He caught me off guard. He was angry. I was naked, scared, fired two warning shots, told him to leave and he refused. He came to me and he raped me. I didn't want to shoot a soldier. Sir, understand, one of a female soldier's biggest fears is being raped by her own comrades. We remain silent too often when it happens. I refuse to be silent. We are supposed to be able to rely on each other, supposed to have each other's back. Just like in Iraq and Afghanistan, our male comrades are assaulting us women who are there trying to defend the country. Comrades are supposed to protect each other. Are supposed to look out for each other. Well, he came into my quarters, overpowered me, and raped me. I'm not a snitch, sir, but I am brave enough to report the assault."

The Beast looked at Medianoche. "Is that true?"

"Not true. That slag followed me to my apartment, drank wine, and we had sex."

Señorita Raven snapped, "I asked permission to enter. Your door was wide open, for whatever reason, and I asked for permission to enter."

"You've got balls. Bitch, you've got some balls."

"Glad one of us does."

"She came to my apartment and we had sex."

"I came to check on you. You had issues earlier in the evening. The job you had done in Recoleta. You left a witness. You exercised faulty judgment that would've compromised the entire group. I took up that issue with you on the streets, and you became violent. You fled in a taxi. When I returned to my quarters, I saw your door was wide open. That looked suspicious, especially with us guarding a very important package. As far as I knew, the package could've been under your care and you'd been attacked. I stepped inside your open door and called your name to make sure everything was okay. I called your name over and over before I entered. There was no answer. So I came inside the open door to make sure everything was okay. I announced I was inside. There was no response. I found you sitting on your bed staring at your wall. I checked in on a fellow Horseman, as a soldier should, and you forced yourself on me."

"Nice spin."

"And Medianoche had white powder on the tip of his nose. He behaved like he was *bajo la influencia de la cocaína*. I can only assume that influenced his behavior toward me."

"Real nice spin."

"Then you insulted me after you forced yourself on me . . . you misogynistic prick. Why would I ever touch you again after the way you treated me after that two minutes of nothing?"

"I went to her apartment."

"My door was closed. You entered my quarters without permission."

"Your door wasn't locked."

She growled, "But it was closed. My goddamn door was closed."

"And we had sex again."

"You entered my apartment with a gun in your hand. I asked you to leave. You refused. I fired warning shots. Sir, he fought with me. My gun went off as we struggled. You can look at my walls. I was being held down, had to fire from the floor as he held me down. You can verify the trajectory angles. I haven't changed anything. Sir, if you would like, I can show you the damage. My furniture was knocked over in the fight. My quarters are now as they were when it happened. I haven't changed a thing. I haven't moved a thing. He's been staring at me since I joined The Four Horsemen. Staring and leering. And he attacked me on the elevator. Attacked me in front of everyone. Then he came inside my quarters and raped me. Sonofabitch."

Medianoche snapped, "You wanted it, you slag. You were rubbing on my goddamn dick. You wanted it."

"Just like a rapist. Always thinks a woman wants it. When I say no, I mean no. No does not mean yes. How many women have you raped? How many women have you done that to?"

The Beast snapped, "Enough."

Then he sat like he was the emperor of Rome. In control. All powerful.

The Beast asked Señorita Raven, "What did you do after the alleged assault?"

"He got off me, ordered me to clean myself up, and walked out like . . . like . . . like I was nothing. It was time to report for duty. I reported for duty like a soldier is supposed to do. I put that to the side and reported for duty. We have a mission, I had orders, and I reported for duty."

Her bottom lip trembled. She wiped tears from her eyes.

She said, "And now, because we were following the command of a coked-up, broken-down, one-eyed rapist, Señor Rodríguez is no longer with us. He's dead out there. Like trash."

"That was brilliant." Medianoche clapped his hands. "A regular Meryl Streep."

She snapped, "*Rapist*. Put that in your goddamn files, Medianoche. *Rapist*."

"I saved your life, you fuckup. I saved your goddamn life."

"Is that what made you think you could treat me any fucking way?"

She cursed him over and over, tears falling, the look of a rabid dog.

She snapped, "Señor Rodríguez deserved better. And I deserved better. This is not Afghanistan, and I'm not your fucking wife. You don't have the right to rape me."

If he didn't know the truth, he would believe her.

The Beast said, "No crying."

"Sorry, sir. I know."

"No crying in baseball. No crying in war."

Medianoche growled. He should've killed her when they were on that roof. She was as bipolar as Iranian president Mahmoud Ahma-dinejad. She had no business chasing behind men and studying war. This one was smart enough to be a doctor or a lawyer. A fucking waste of intelligence. And beauty. Now she was nothing. And as crazy and suicidal as they came.

The Beast said, "We will discuss this later."

She nodded. "I'm fine, sir. But I do want that incident on record."

"We don't exist. We have no records."

"Well, I want that noted in the records we don't have."

"I want both of you to take a few breaths. Take some time. Think. Rethink what happened. Let's see how we can repair this damage. We have too much at stake."

"I have no problem being a good soldier. I've never had a problem. I don't hesitate or freeze up. I'm not slow. I'm not disrespectful. I don't attack my comrades."

Medianoche shook his head side to side.

Señorita Raven said, "Rodríguez was left on a train. Like he was trash. If I am KIA, is that what happens to me? I get left like I'm dog meat? Like I'm nothing? Hell, the Taliban don't leave their dead be-hind. They're scum, but when they die in war, they die with dignity."

Medianoche regarded The Beast. His eyes said to stand down.

The Beast said, "A soldier is dead. We want revenge. That's why we have so much tension. It is no one's fault. War has casualties. Good men die. The situation was not ideal for retrieving the soldier's remains. Not without risking a battle with the police. The train was crowded, but no one will admit they saw anything. We have to move on, stay focused. We still have a mission to accomplish. The enemy would love for us to turn on each other. We're stronger. We're better. We're smarter. That's all that matters at this moment."

Medianoche nodded. Señorita Raven did the same.

The Beast said, "We have to remain bonded. Not as friends. As soldiers."

The Beast's servant, Draco, walked into the room. He was dressed in his black tuxedo and white gloves. He held a silver tray with a tea-kettle. He also carried a wood-veneered *mate* cup, a hollow gourd, and a metal straw, a silver *bombilla* that was used as both a filter and a straw. The Beast added several spoonfuls of herbs into the hollow gourd. Then he added a shot of top-shelf whiskey before adding hot water. A few moments passed. Tense moments.

The Beast said, "For Señor Rodríguez."

The Beast took a small drink of his *mate*, then passed it to Medianoche. Medianoche put the *bombilla* to his lips, sipped the bitter *mate*, and passed the hollow gourd to Señorita Raven. She did the same, took the *bombilla* in her mouth, sipped the bitter herbal tea, passed the *mate* cup back to The Beast, then stared at Medianoche.

She had been on communications when he had battled Gideon.

He knew she had heard everything.

She had seen him freeze.

She had stalked him, she had lied, seduced him, and called him a rapist.

He stared at her, but that enraged liar refused to look him in his eye.

The Beast passed the *mate* around again.

Medianoche reeled in his urge to kill, reeled it in slowly.

The Beast asked Señorita Raven, "How did you get into the files?"

She cleared her throat. "Where there is Wi-Fi, there is a way, sir."

The Beast nodded. "You're a brilliant young woman."

"Thank you, sir."

"Truly an asset to this organization."

"Thank you, sir."

Rain thickened. More thunder. Winds blew. There was snow in the mountains, would be skiing only a few hours away. But Medianoche was on fire, and Buenos Aires felt like hell.

Draco brought gear, dragged in four heavy duffel bags.

Medianoche grabbed one. Señorita Raven did the same.

The Beast grabbed the third duffel bag.

Medianoche clenched his teeth when Draco grabbed the fourth.

Draco was more than a servant. He was another man who had been discharged from the military. He had killed more than a few times. And now he was a substitute for a hero.

That fourth bag was meant for a fallen soldier.

Not for a goddamn gunsel. Not for a Log Cabin Republican.

But The Beast had issued his orders. Orders were to be followed, not questioned.

Medianoche said, "Gideon is mine. You can injure him, but the final blow is mine."

Señorita Raven said, "Then you'd better have your *son* in your crosshairs first. A good soldier died defending you. He was my friend. The only real friend I had of the opposite sex."

"Gideon is not my son."

"Then you won't have to cry when I'm done. His death will be slow and deliberate."

"Gideon is mine. Get in the way, there might be a problem."

"Then you'd better adjust your eye patch and watch out for friendly fire."

The Beast said, "Enough."

Medianoche let it go. For now.

Their vehicles had already been loaded; Medianoche had supervised that task.

Nine millimeters. Shotguns. M16s with grenade launchers attached.

Medianoche was ready to lead The Four Horsemen toward war.

Chapter 38

dystopia

This section of the *autopista* barely rose over the roofline of what Buenos Aires called the *villas*. Yards away, some section of the *villas* rose higher than the *autopista*.

Favela in Brazil. *Callampa* in Chile. *Pueblo jóven* in Peru. *Katchi abadi* in Pakistan. Shantytown in Kenya. Bidonville in Algeria. Township in South Africa. *Barong-barong* in the Philippines. *Jhuggi* in India. Ghettos in the United States. And the *villas* of Buenos Aires.

They were all the same.

Slums.

Synonyms for poverty. Synonyms for neglect.

The slums were a place that the storm did no favors. And neither did the government.

We'd been here for fifteen seconds. And tonight, that felt like fifteen hours.

A sloppy, cold rain was coming down in solid sheets of despair. That meant it was flooding down below. And what was floating in the rivers created by the downpour, the stench wafted up here, twenty yards off the ground. The slums didn't have a sewage system. And when it rained, human feces flooded the walkways and the rugged roads, created streets of liquid shit that cat-sized rodents surfed into the crowded, box-sized homes of the slum dwellers.

Sierra and her muscle-bound brother were standing in the downpour. They shared a big black umbrella. This was as close as they could get to the package. This spot on the *autopista* was where the signal was the strongest. They had been here the past thirty minutes. Had located the signal, then parked until we arrived. We had pulled up in two more cars, so now we had three cars parked back to back.

Arizona and Scamz stayed inside their automobile, windshield wipers working overtime.

They had the package. If trouble pulled up, they needed to be ready to escape.

Konstantin and Shotgun stood in the rain next to me, headlights from impatient and erratic lane-changing drivers passing us at more than one hundred kilometers per hour.

We were dressed in blacks and grays, Konstantin forgoing his traditional white shoes for black military boots, boots with no-slip bottoms, made for chasing, made for running, the latter more important. The same type of boots Shotgun and I had on now.

Two duffel bags were at my feet. It was the equipment I would need.

My team had night vision monoculars. While Shotgun and Konstantin looked down at the slums, I glanced back toward the lead car. Arizona looked at me through the window.

Memories remained.

I turned away, stayed focused on what I did best.

I turned to Konstantin. "I think you should get back in the car with Arizona and Scamz."

"Just in case The Four Horsemen arrive while we are all exposed."

"Yeah. Just in case they have to pull away under fire. I want to make sure they have some firepower with them."

"How is Scamz behind the wheel?"

"I have no idea. I know Sierra is a horrible driver. No idea about Scamz."

Konstantin frowned, then he nodded and headed toward Arizona's car.

He got in the backseat and closed the door.

I felt better. Not a lot better. But it took that concern off my mind.

My concern wasn't Arizona or Scamz or the package.

My concern was Konstantin. He had cancer, and I didn't want this weather making him ill.

He didn't need to be here, but he was. That Russian was a tough sonofabitch.

I put my monocular back up to my eye and spied down on seventy thousand people in less than two miles. The area was unofficial, not on any map for tourists. From there I could see it looked like some residences had three generations of a family inside one-room dwellings that were stacked on top of each other, walls and homes made of tin, warped wood, some with no windows and no heating, nothing built to code. Pirated electricity lines ran from telephone wires, jerry-rigged and dangerous. The barbed wire along the freeway that was meant to keep the immigrants fenced in was used to hang laundry on. Miles of cheap clothing were getting a frigid bath, laundry that had been left out in the rain, as if the heavens had become the best washing machine in the world. DIRECTV dishes hung from a lot of the dilapidated dwellings. Those had to be stolen dishes. No one down there had that kind of disposable income.

I thought I saw some men with guns, but they were street scavengers moving around. Dead dogs. Dead cats. Rusted cars. Mountains of trash. The area was a dumping ground. Even in the cold rain, the smells were strong enough to numb the senses.

The adjacent train yards had old, rusted eighteen-wheeler containers stacked five high in some places, creating a wall around the slums to keep the poor from claiming more land and spreading poverty a mile closer to a different class of people. They were walled in like they were subhuman, primitive, inferior. This section of Argentina was their shame, where the military had tried social cleansing back in the late seventies. It had doubled in size since my last visit.

Shotgun said, "They living like they in a concentration camp."

"More like Hoovervilles. The way people lived during the Great Depression."

Shotgun nodded. "You sure what we're looking for is down there?"

"Looks that way. Unless it's a setup, looks like it's down there."

"You looking for it right now?"

"Nope. Still looking for snipers. Anyone patrolling with a gun."

"I didn't see anyone with guns either."

"The rain has most people inside. Few people out."

"God is on our side."

"There is no god down there. At least not one that works for the people."

Thirty seconds had gone by. My heart thumped inside my chest.

There was a shack with a hand-painted sign that said it was the community center. That area was busy. Saw men sitting in windows playing cards. Saw young girls with babies on their hips. Saw kids drinking a colorful soda made of sugar, drinks that filled empty bellies and rotted teeth. A young boy peered out of the front entry of a habitat made of tin and cardboard.

The package was down there somewhere.

Shotgun said, "No other way in?"

"No time to look for an alternative."

I took out the sensor, looked at the LED. It was green. A steady green.

The package that Arizona wanted was definitely within striking distance.

I didn't want to be here. I wanted to be back in Puerto Rico. Wanted to be with Hawks.

I wanted a lot of things.

A minute had passed. It was time for the rest of the team to take their part of the package and get out of here before it was too late.

I told Shotgun, "Stay with the package. Keep moving. Stick to the *autopista*. Drive fast."

"You're going down there all by yourself?"

"It's a job for one. Or a job for a million."

"Or a job for a fool."

I said, "Stay with the team. Keep the package moving."

Shotgun sprinted back to the cars.

Konstantin, Arizona, and Scamz were in the first car. Sierra and her brother were in the second car.

The cars pulled away, but I wasn't left alone.

I thought Shotgun would get inside the third car and drive off with them. But he didn't.

Shotgun ran back, his coat soaked and heavy with the weapons he carried underneath, that hardheaded mountain wiping rain away from his face, a face that held an intense expression.

He said, "I'm not letting you go down there by yourself."

He didn't understand and I didn't want to say what was bothering me. Catherine. Midnight. I was the offspring of two people I despised. Two people who should have died long before I was born. And now I was working for a man I despised as well, working for a woman I used to love and wanted to hate. He would never understand how tortured I felt, would never be able to comprehend my numbness. A numbness that came and went on waves of anger.

I waited for a break in traffic, then we grabbed our gear and bolted toward the center of the *autopista*. Passing cars slung water at us while I opened my duffel bag. I took out a hook and other equipment, and I put on my assassin's gloves. Shotgun did the same, then he secured the hook to the metal railing as rain came down cold and steady. With the hook attached to the railing, I climbed over and began my descent. I had to hurry and lower myself down into the slums, and hoped to enter this spot unseen. I came out on top of an unsteady structure. Shotgun lowered the duffel bags. Then he came down, his weight so severe I thought the cord would snap.

We walked to the edge of the structure, used more rope and lowered the bags down, then we dropped down into what looked like mud but smelled like disease. Dozens of rats and ten times as many cockroaches scattered when we touched the murky ground.

We opened the bag, put on two gun holsters each, and checked the duffel bags for the other supplies. That was when I looked at the front of the shack to see where I'd landed.

AQUÍ SE CONSTRUYE
CENTRO DE SALUD FUNDACIÓN
MÚSICA ESPERANZA, BSAS

Shotgun looked at words that made no sense to him, asked, "What kind of place is that?"

"Health Center. They are building a health center."

Graffiti marked every piece of concrete, was on every flat surface, as far as I could see.

We heard movement. Shotgun moved his coat and pulled out one of his double-barreled weapons. I held my nine in my right hand, used my left hand to steady my weapon, took fast steps, and moved in search of a target. We heard the noise again, fanned out, and checked the back side of the building. There were four people. They had almost been gunned down. It was three boys and one girl. All dressed in dirty clothing, all had filthy faces. They were underneath the *autopista*, the section that separated two sides of the *villas*. The girl was in jeans and tennis shoes, brown hair pulled in a ponytail, ragged coat on, down on her haunches giving head to a boy who was smoking his drug of choice from a glass pipe. Another boy was standing to the side, pissing on the ground, so high on *paco* he had no idea what planet he was on. The third boy saw us and came toward us, gun in his hand. A gun that had been manufactured in the U.S. and had probably made its way through Mexico and Central America before landing here.

He held his hand out, said he wanted five pesos or he would blow my brains out.

He barked, *"Usted tiene que pagar para venir aquí. Igual como usted paga para ir a Palermo. Me pagás. O me das paco. O te voy a disparar."*

The little fuck told me that I had to pay to come into the *villa*, just like I would have to pay to go to a club in Palermo. He told me to pay cash, give him drugs, or get shot.

I had a gun, my partner held a shotgun, and the young boy demanded five pesos like we were two foreign ships moving through his sacred waters. Five pesos was the price of coming into his *villa*. That was the price for him not to shoot me in my head and walk away. I had put men in the ground all over the world, and now a boy who had rotten teeth was extorting me.

A monster clawed its way from my heart to my gun hand.

Rage made my finger tighten on the trigger.

I imagined that case-hardened boy with a hole where his ignorance used to be.

Being with Shotgun kept me grounded.

I kept the monster inside of me on its chains, growling, barking.

That boy was lucky.

I'd let that monster go, I'd let the monster inside me free, but not right now.

I handed the boy a five-dollar bill, the equivalent of more than fifteen pesos.

The wind kicked up the stench from dank sewage, an amalgamation of overwhelming funk that dangled in the air like invisible smoke, like perfume smells at the entrance to Macy's.

I breathed though my mouth as I put supressors on my guns.

Shotgun did the same.

We had an audience. The young fuck who extorted me hadn't left.

The ruffian used the palm of his dirty hand to wipe his runny nose, looked at Shotgun, grabbed his crotch, and with a hard-core sneer said, "Suck my dick, Sha-keel O'Neal. Sha-keel O'Neal, suck my dick, you summer bitch."

Shotgun frowned.

The feral drug-addicted boy was as bold as a Somali pirate. And he was as dangerous as a member of the Triad demanding extortion money. He was bone-thin and laughed like he was the young runt destined to run the slums. He scratched his neck, frowned and scratched harder, pulled up his sleeve and scratched his arm hard enough to break the skin. Both places where he dug his filthy nails had circular red rashes. I noticed spots on his neck. The boy had some sort of bacterial illness.

I asked him how long he had been itching and scratching.

He said two years. Maybe longer.

I asked him why he didn't go to the clinic and get it checked out.

He said the clinics were too crowded. And the doctors were always on vacation or on strike, said they did nothing for the people. I nodded. He smiled and I saw his rotten teeth.

I told Shotgun, "Ignore the shit the kid says. But don't take your eyes off him."

"I'm about to snatch that gun out of his hand and slap a brand-new taste in his mouth."

The boy turned to me, asked me if I wanted to buy some time with the *chica*.

I told him no.

The boy laughed and looked at Shotgun again. "Suck my dick, Sha-keel O'Neal. Sha-keel O'Neal, suck my dick."

Shotgun checked his extra ammo as he asked me, "What's his problem?"

"Drugs."

"I can tell that. What's that boy on?"

"It's called *paco*. Low-grade and toxic."

"What's in it?"

"Shit's mixed with sulfuric acid, kerosene, rat poison, and crushed glass."

"No wonder he's so stupid."

"Yeah, damn. Get on that shit, you'll wish you were addicted to crack. This time next month, if he doesn't get help, that kid will have brain damage."

The boy who had just finished sullying the young girl came over, gun in one hand, the other hand extended like he was from the local collection agency. More extortion. Another gun-toting case-hardened pervert with a filthy face and a mouth filled with rotten teeth. I handed him a five-dollar bill. He turned and ran back to his amigos, holding a gun the way he should've been holding a schoolbook. I doubted if either of the boys was thirteen years old. Down here, in a world that had more children than adults, they thought they were men.

I told Shotgun, "We have to hurry."

"Lead the way."

As rain chilled us down to our bones, and our breath fogged in front of our faces, we crept into a South American hell that was hotter than any heat the Devil could bear.

If this were summertime, or if the rain weren't falling in sheets, the streets would be crowded. Everyone would be out on stoops. People would be grilling on the streets. If we moved quickly, we'd look like nothing more than shadows floating by dirty windows.

Walkways were congested with pushcarts full of bottles and paper.

That was the recyclable refuse of the *cartoneros*, the foragers who worked all night collecting recyclables and made four dollars for eight hours of labor. We squeezed by that fire hazard and struggled into a precarious situation, moved in the world of the undesirable, the stench of urine and bad diets strong as we sloshed across murky ground and trash, passed by dozens of passive dogs, crept down a narrow passageway that was barely shoulder-wide, came out in a section where people lived outside underneath tents, moved on, found a section that had ragged concrete, and moved deeper into the *villa*. Then we made our way through a section where the sewer line had overflowed and shit floated in the streets like tall ships heading out to sea.

Shotgun jumped like The Four Horsemen were on top of us.

But it was a different kind of vermin.

Rats swam by us like they were on the Olympic team for synchronized swimmers.

I asked, "You okay?"

"What they feeding these rats?"

The same pollution we walked through was the contamination that was tracked into homes. Rats, roaches, insects, bugs, ants, all of that was squatting in front of the squatters' homes, waiting to slip inside as soon as a door or window was opened. Smells burned the hair in my nostrils. We moved by people, normal people, people who saw us, then ignored us as we passed. Men smoking cigarettes and drinking beers, men playing cards. Young girls with babies. All around us, from every other window, Spanish music was loud. Every country played its own music. The loudest music was called *cumbia villera*. Songs with powerful music and vulgar lyrics, the kind that would make Snoop Dogg C-walk, hold his nut sac and pump his fist.

Every culture had thugs and pimps, every culture had its own version of gangsta rap. The music was loud, but not loud enough to muffle the thunder of a dozen rapid gunshots.

We stood, weapons drawn, waited to be fired upon by The Horsemen, anticipated their rabid charge, knowing that at this point in the game, we were outgunned. Heard shouts. Screams. Then more gunshots. Followed by more horrifying screams.

A group of hooligans sprinted through filthy water, firing wild shots behind them.

They were Bolivians screaming vulgarities in Spanish.

A group of Chilean thugs chased them, guns in hand, firing away.

They were like Crips and Bloods going at it in the streets of South Central Los Angeles.

We moved away from the tribal warfare.

Yards away we saw a body in the middle of the muddied road. People stood around him, but no one helped. He was dead. The end result of the two groups we'd just seen.

Shotgun asked, "What was that all about?"

"Lot of social problems down here. Lot of internal conflict."

"Thought you said the people on the other side of the walls were the enemy."

"Look at the bars on the windows and doors. Their neighbors are their enemies too."

We kept moving. The gear we had was heavy, our clothes weighted down by rain.

We had to hurry.

We clung to the shadows as cars passed by, headlights illuminating our surroundings. It reminded me of the photos of Berlin after the fall back in the early forties. We moved through a section of the slum that was so fucked up that the level of poverty was impossible to absorb.

We paused in front of a red door that led to a small business that sold pizza, sodas, and beer. I got down low, looked at the sensor. Heard a beep. Six seconds passed. Then I heard another beep. Five long seconds later, there was another beep.

We were getting close, heading the right way.

We spaced out, put a few feet between us, and headed toward the heart of the *villa*.

We passed a section that didn't have running water, saw people lined up with old pans, plastic cups, metal bowls, anything that could catch fresh rainwater.

There were more gunshots in the distance, beyond my range of hearing. Gunshots and fast-spinning tires moving frantically across the blacktop lanes and being forced off the *autopista*.

I couldn't hear Arizona's screams, couldn't hear Scamz's curses, couldn't hear Konstantin's panic, or Sierra's frantic breathing as her brother yelled to speed up and get them off the fucking *autopista*.

I didn't know what was going on outside of this world. All I knew as we walked through filth and past graffiti-filled walls, five minutes down here had to feel like five hours in Vietnam. My focus was here, with the other team. Rain came down harder. The smells had wrecked one sense, and the coarse, vulgar, and loud *cumbia villera* music kicked in and damn near numbed my other senses. I had to focus and was on battle sensory overload. The sounds were so loud, it would be impossible to hear someone behind us until it was too late.

Shotgun kicked at something, then drew his double-barreled weapon down on the problem.

Another rat had run across his boot.

He cursed, inhaled the numbing stench, then let out a nervous laugh.

Shotgun whispered, "Close?"

"Damn close."

We stopped. Took out our night goggles, looked around.

There was a five-story dilapidated structure set in the center of that block of misery. The door was covered with a frayed and wrinkled bright-yellow Daffy Duck poster. Six men were outside, all at ground level. They weren't The Four Horsemen plus two. But they all had guns. Big guns. Small guns. Revolvers. Nines. One held an AK-47.

I shoved the sensor into my back pocket, dug around the ground. Found an empty Quilmes bottle. Then I took off my coat. And my shirts. Freezing rain poured down on me as I reached to the ground and smeared mud and filth across my chest and shoulders.

With hand signals, I directed Shotgun, had him move to my right, get into position.

I stepped out of the darkness, staggering, chanting like I was at a soccer game, standing in the risers at La Bombonera, yelling and dancing like I had an invisible partner.

"*Yo te sigo a toda parte. Y cada vez te quiero más.*"

Six guns rose up at me, but lowered when they saw I had on no shirt. I looked like a member of *los descamisados*, the shirtless ones, what they called the poor people who had supported Perón. I chanted a chant for Boca Juniors, the team every *villa* rooted for.

"*Boca, mi buen amigo. Esta campaña volveremos a estar contigo.*"

The guards waved fists and chanted along like it was the national anthem.

"*Te alentaremos de corazón. Esta es tu hinchada y te quiere ver campeón. No me importa le que digan. Lo que digan los demás. Yo te sigo a toda parte. Y cada vez te quiero más.*"

I danced a drunken dance, cursed the rival soccer team, River Plate. "River, *hijos de puta*."

The guards applauded.

I stumbled, went down on one knee, empty bottle in my left hand.

They called me an idiot. Laughed and told each other that I was a drunken fool.

They relaxed, waved me away like I was a poor man begging on the streets of Recoleta.

Down on one knee, I dropped the bottle and pulled out my weapon.

Surprise brightened their eyes.

I dropped two. The one with the AK-47 was my first target. He suffered a quick head shot and so did the man standing to his left. Both toppled facedown into puddles, souls evicted from their bodies before they realized what was going on.

The others started to fall back, mouths opened to scream as they brought their guns up.

Four guns were coming up against my one.

Shotgun had moved through the rain and, while they had watched me dance my drunken dance, he had positioned himself behind them and to their left.

Shotgun took over, and three went down in what sounded like Thor's thunder.

A thunder that would wake up the *villa*.

He gave them an ugly death, left those men dead with gravel, shit, and mud in their guts.

I raced toward the building the men had guarded, a nine in my right hand. Shotgun's weapon was aimed up, moved from window to wall, searched for trouble as he watched my back.

My filthy body was cold, my adrenaline high.

The beeps accelerated. Its cadence stressed like my own heartbeat.

Filth covered my skin, and I was aware of my own mortality.

Gunshots came from upstairs, came out of the dwelling that was decorated with the bright yellow Daffy Duck poster. A boy came to the window, fired down at us and screamed for help, said to stop us from getting up there. Now we knew which dwelling the men were guarding.

The package was there behind a goddamn Looney Tunes character.

Before I made it to the bottom of the stairs, gunshots rang out from behind me.

Then more gunshots rang out from both sides.

Six assassins were charging at us from three directions, guns blazing.

I was focused and unaware that, while me and Shotgun found ourselves trapped in a shoot-out and had to fight for our lives, my friends were in the streets struggling to stay alive.

Capítulo 39

búsqueda implacable

Thirty aggravating minutes ago.

Medianoche shifted gears and came out of a fishtail, with Señorita Raven riding his bumper, her headlights flashing in his rearview mirror like the eyes of a monster.

He accelerated, sliced through the rain, sideswiped an ancient city bus, and ran a herd of motorcyclists off the road. Señorita Raven did the same, her charge causing a dozen motorcyclists to tangle and fall like tenpins.

The package was in front of them, fleeing at one hundred and thirty kilometers per hour.

The Beast leaned out of the passenger window, fired a series of shots.

Medianoche battled to get a better position.

Then The Beast came back inside the car, wiped rain from his face and from his salt-and-pepper mane. His angry Rocky Marciano expression deepened.

The Beast said, "Fucking rain and fucking traffic fucking up all of my fucking shots."

Medianoche chased his enemy across the rain-slicked streets of Buenos Aires.

The deadly war to get the spoils continued.

It had taken hours, but they had tracked the moving target, found them on the limited-access highway, and chased them from the *autopista* to the maze of surface streets, this part of the battle moving from

9 de Julio to Avenida Santa Fe to Avenida Callao, then back to the edges of Recoleta. Gunshots from The Beast had sent them off the wide-open *autopista* and running into an area that had more nooks and crannies than an English muffin, zipping up and down streets smaller than the women from Peru and tighter than virgin pussy.

Driving their second BMW, a quick and agile 328i, Señorita Raven's insane maneuvers had almost trapped the package, had forced them to accelerate, run the red light, crash into unaware and stubborn vehicles, then flee down Libertador, broken taillights broadcasting the car's injury.

Scamz and his team were in two Peugeots, just like the one they had traced to Retiro.

Two Peugeots and one package.

Medianoche asked, "Which car has the prize?"

The Beast held the sensor, its beeps rapid and consistent.

The Beast said, "Fucking prize could be inside either fucking one."

Señorita Raven said, "Fifty-fifty."

Her voice came through the car's speakers, crystal clear.

The Beast said, "Either or. Unless they fucking split, we won't be able to fucking tell."

"Sir, I can hit one with a grenade."

"No. You hit the wrong one, we're fucked because the package might explode and we'd lose a king's fortune."

"I understand, sir."

"Draco, how are you holding up over there?"

"No worries, sir."

Both BMWs had Bluetooth and hands-free systems built into the hardware. They used cell phones, kept the channel open. Medianoche hit the MUTE button, made it so the Bravo team couldn't listen in.

He barked, "Contemptible, insubordinate bitch actually said I raped her."

"Stay focused."

Medianoche said, "Gideon is inside one of those cars."

"You believe what he said?"

Medianoche swallowed. "Señorita Raven said that she had accessed other files."

"Did she?"

"Said that I didn't know what had happened in North Carolina."

The Beast nodded. "Focus on the mission at hand."

"Do you know what happened?"

"Stay focused."

"Is that an order?"

"That's an order."

Medianoche nodded.

The Beast said, "We'll continue this discussion at the appropriate time."

Medianoche hit the MUTE button again, communication reestablished.

The Beast said, "Señorita Raven, maintain position. Anticipate the unexpected."

They sped through the Paris of the South.

The enemies kept swerving, using narrow streets and open traffic to their advantage, zigging, zagging, and bumping across six lanes until they came to where Callao ended at Libertador. Both Peugeots made left turns, slid sideways and drifted across twelve lanes, made hard contact with fast-moving traffic and sped on, and tried to hide in the pandemonium.

Medianoche split lanes, sideswiped arrogant drivers who refused to get out of his way, the same thing that the fleeing cars were doing, the *calles* and *avenidas* lined with accidents.

The Four Horsemen chased Scamz and his people through the winter storm.

They were lions chasing gazelles through a forest, the gazelle knowing that if it made a bad move, if it slowed, slipped, or stumbled, the hunt was over.

The lion only had to remain in the race and stay patient.

Then they would have the second package.

Then he could get answers about North Carolina.

Recoleta became as surreal as a Salvador Dalí painting.

Buildings melted into the background.

They sped toward Palermo, made quick changes and bumped Fiats,

Fords, and Renaults out of the way. Medianoche cut off incoming traffic, almost misjudged oncoming velocity, and swerved back just in time to avoid a head-on collision. The car he'd almost hit lost control, went into a skid, and crossed into opposing traffic, hit a Volkswagen head-on.

Headlights and rain came at them at dangerous speeds. Winds picked up, and the skies lit up with what looked like a streak of lightning. Windshield wipers were on high, moved back and forth and left the blur of thousands of red taillights in his eyes, taillights that looked like the eyes of demons. There were wide eyes and expressions of horror on every face revealed by slivers of bright lights. High-rises, embassies, and swank French-style homes were nothing more than shadows as they sped by the dramatic lights in front of MALBA.

By the time they reached Club de Amigos, Medianoche was almost on the target's bumper. He wanted to ram their bumper, send them flying and flipping, crashing on the edges of the Japanese Gardens. But they changed lanes and kicked up rainwater as they sped toward the roundabout at Avenida Sarmiento, another goddamn roundabout that had never-ending traffic.

One of the fleeing Peugeots sideswiped an older Radio Taxi, a side impact that first shocked the driver, then forced the black-and-yellow taxi off the street and across the median. The taxi bounced around, out of control, until it struck a hundred-year-old tree dead-on.

Medianoche closed in on a target that fought to maintain control in the storm, jockeyed for position with Señorita Raven, that 51-50, 10-56A slag trying to beat him to the prize.

As she had done on the roof.

Medianoche kept the lead, refused to let Señorita Raven pass his bumper.

Four seconds behind the closest target.

Three seconds.

The closest target swerved, tapped its brakes, had to slow down to keep from spinning out. The gazelle had stumbled, desperation in its body language as it struggled to recover.

The lead Peugeot accelerated away from its partners in crime. They were approaching a large monument at the center of the roundabout at Avenida Sarmiento. That was where six lanes of traffic crossed another six lanes of traffic. Medianoche knew that meant he and The Beast could get slammed by traffic in the intersection, knew his team could get knocked out of the chase.

He refused to let those fuckers escape again.

Medianoche gunned it, moved between cars at top speed, the four wheels of his BMW struggling to maintain a strong grip on the damp pavement. He slammed the back corner of the Peugeot, did a strong PIT maneuver. The Peugeot began to spin out of control, turned like a top, and crashed hard into the base of the statue of General Justo José de Urquiza.

Traffic lost control trying to avoid the inevitable crash, spun out as horns blared; some drivers ended up turned around 180 degrees, others ended up spinning out closer to the planetarium. Traffic heading toward the zoo slid to a bumper-bending halt.

The gazelle was down, knew the lion was on its heels.

Medianoche braked, skidded to a halt.

Then the second Peugeot reappeared. It had never left. The driver had maneuvered the roundabout, had covered most of the three-hundred-and-sixty-degree circle and boomeranged back, accelerating toward their BMW like the monument of General Justo José de Urquiza was Jupiter, and its gravitational forces had slingshot them out of the elliptical orbit.

Medianoche cursed. The Beast cursed louder.

Before Medianoche could kick into drive and engage in a defensive maneuver, the bright headlights came at him like enemy fire. The Peugeot rammed into the back quarter of the BMW, sent him and The Beast jerking, cursing and spinning out of control, crashing into the curb and short wrought-iron fence that was around the three-story-tall monument.

Fiberglass, metal, and glass met at high velocity.

Señorita Raven had come out of her own orbit and crashed into the second Peugeot, had sent that car reeling. The result of that unforgiving impact and velocity whirled Señorita Raven's vehicle out of control.

Medianoche checked on The Beast, saw he was okay, already undo-ing his seat belt.

Medianoche shoved open his car door, stepped out into the frigid wind and rain at the same moment someone exited the back door of the first Peugeot. They came out of the Peugeot firing rapid shots. Medianoche ducked behind his door and drew his weapon, then stood and returned fire. He expected to see Gideon, wanted to see that sonof-awhore and get his shot. He wanted to do that before Señorita Raven stole his kill. It wasn't Gideon. They were being fired on by a man who, in the bad lighting and rainfall, looked like Cary Grant. He was quick with a gun and drew down on them, fired rapid shots as members of his team moved from wrecked cars.

Within seconds, The Four Horsemen had weapons drawn.

A muscular man with Asian features and long hair raised his weapon. He had exited the second Peugeot and joined the firefight. The Asian wasn't as good as Cary Grant.

The Beast let off two shots. Both head shots.

The muscular man's head jerked back, his body paused, then he crumpled.

The man who looked like Cary Grant continued to return fire, his shots directed toward Señorita Raven and Draco.

Then Draco went down. Wounded. Or dead. No way to tell in the rain.

Medianoche gritted his teeth. Hoped that gunsel wasn't dead. They needed firepower.

A Latin man faced them as well, using the car as his shield, his gun drawn.

The gunfire paused. A momentary cease-fire.

The Beast yelled, "Scamz. Is that you?"

"It is."

"Finally. You're a hard man to find."

"With whom do I have the pleasure of conversing?"

"The Beast."

"You are a persistent man."

"Money is a wonderful motivator."

"I concur."

Car headlights brightened up the scene; the Latin man nodded.

The Beast yelled, "You're outgunned. We have an M16 grenade launcher. It's over. Hand over the package, and I will let you and the remaining members of your team live."

"That's kind of you, considering the reputation that precedes you. The boy who survived in La Boca, he didn't have anything positive to say about your encounter. I believe that you extended my people in La Boca the same offer. I hope declining that offer doesn't offend you."

The driver of the second Peugeot got out, left the safety of the vehicle. It was a woman. Long hair and Asian features. She ran to the Asian man who had stepped out of her car and been killed. She was unarmed.

The door to the first wrecked Peugeot opened.

The sensor sang an anxious tune made of rapid beeps.

The package was inside that car. A few feet away from them.

Medianoche trained his gun on that car.

A woman got out of the first Peugeot, the one they had rammed into the monument. Asian features again. She was pregnant. They had a goddamn pregnant woman on their team.

Women entered war like it was a goddamn tea party.

She made it out of the car and held her belly like she was about to miscarry.

The complications of war never changed.

Medianoche kept his weapon trained on a goddamn pregnant woman that made him, for a quick moment, think about the Israeli army T-shirts that depicted pregnant women in a sniper's crosshairs, the message being that killing a pregnant woman was a two-for-one shot.

The Beast said, "Sorry I killed Gideon. But he left me no choice."

Medianoche said, "That wasn't Gideon."

"So, he's MIA."

"He could be in one of these fucking cars that are stopped behind us." Medianoche turned, positioned himself. "At least two more are on that goddamn team, and both are MIA. Rodríguez said that there was a big guy. The guy that you just put down doesn't fit the description. He was muscular, but he was short, not big."

The police were caught in the carnage of the other accidents that had spread from Libertador to Callao to the edges of the monument for General Urquiza. Sirens were in the distance, and a cacophony of blowing horns and screaming voices mixed to make this backed-up traffic looked like a parade of terror.

The pregnant woman held her belly and went to the other woman. She stood by the woman who was grieving over the body of the dead fool who had fired on them. The pregnant woman pulled on the arm of the grieving woman. The first woman pulled away from the pregnant woman, refused to leave the dead body of the Asian man in the freezing rain.

But then she did. She pulled away from the pregnant woman, stood and pulled out a weapon, a nine millimeter, and began firing. She walked toward them like she was Angelina Jolie.

Medianoche put a bullet in her shoulder, sent the gun flying and the woman falling. She took the bullet and went down without making a sound, not a scream, as the pavement rushed up to meet her. The pregnant woman fell to her knees, blocked the fallen woman's body with her own, waved her hands in frantic and desperate motions to show her empty palms. She called out in the rain for them to not shoot, her body language begging them not to gun them down.

The pregnant fool sacrificed her life and the life of her unborn child to save the stupid tight-eyed bitch who had fired on them. Sisters. They had to be idiots spit out of the same womb.

The dead man was either a lover or a relative.

Either way, that dumb fuck was leading them into the next life.

Scamz yelled, "Get her back to the car. Get her back to the car now."

The women held each other and moved back toward the car, the wind and rain soaking them as they hurried back toward the safety of a bulletproof automobile.

The Beast fired shots that landed at their feet, refused to let them get away.

The assassin who looked like Cary Grant returned fire, his shots good, despite the wind and rain. Whoever he was, he was a well-trained shot.

He'd die next. Kill the strongest, and the rest would piss their panties and surrender.

Señorita Raven screamed, "Where is that sonofabitch Gideon?"

The Beast said, "Soldiers, stand down. Follow my command. Do not take another shot until I give the order. Scamz? You heard. I have ordered my men to stand down."

The British accent replied, "I heard exactly what you wanted me to hear. Exactly what that means to your soldiers, well, that remains to be seen."

"Where is Gideon?"

No one answered.

Medianoche looked through the storm. There was no sign of Gideon. If that son of a dead whore was here, he should've shown his gun hand by now. Now wasn't the time to be coy.

Scamz said, "We will give you the package. We will bring you the package."

"Bring it to me."

"But first you have to let the women go."

"Such a fucking gentleman."

"The women leave first."

"No one leaves before I have the package in my goddamn possession. Time is not on your side. And it is not on mine. Ten seconds. Ten seconds or this will become a bloodbath. Look to my other soldiers. The girl. She is holding an M16 grenade launcher. Either we get the package, or no one gets what Hopkins died to get. You die or you get nothing. Your call."

The Beast made a motion, and Señorita Raven aimed her M16, launched a grenade as a warning shot, and a second later, there was an explosion across Avenida Sarmiento near the Planetario Galileo Galilei and its artificial lake, an eruption at Palermo Vivo that created more horror and car accidents.

Traffic halted, glued by fear.

Buenos Aires trembled like a child having a recurring nightmare.

The Beast said, "My soldiers are cold, angry, and restless. Five seconds."

The pregnant woman hurried, reached inside the car and took out a black briefcase. She moved her hair from her face, held the briefcase in front of her stomach, protected her baby.

He'd seen it before, killers and cons, terrorists and mercs, all wanted to be good mothers.

But war was war. War wasn't pretty. War was about winning.

Medianoche yelled, told his team to keep on eye on their gunman.

With each step the pregnant woman took, the sensor's beep quickened.

A beep every three seconds. Every two seconds. Then one long beep.

Then she was two feet away, a sliver of light across her tight eyes.

Medianoche said, "I should kill you right now."

She didn't say anything.

Medianoche said, "Drop it. Drop it or that pretty girl behind you gets one in the head."

Her jaw tightened. Anger. Hostility.

He barked, "Last warning."

She swallowed and dropped the briefcase to the pavement. A knife with a six-inch blade fell from behind the briefcase. A weapon she had tucked away. Same type of blade that had been shoved in Señor Rodríguez's chest. A blade she had wanted to put in one of their guts.

She was willing to take out one of them and die.

She trembled, but not out of fear. Medianoche saw a fire in her eyes that said she wanted to kill.

The Beast said, "You must be Arizona."

"Fuck you."

"I take that as a yes."

"Fuck you."

"You sure you want to play it like that?"

"Fuck you."

"Sorry about your boyfriend."

"He's my brother. You killed my brother."

"So you thought you would get close enough to get revenge."

"Fuck you."

"Try anything, you will be able to have a family reunion with your bro in the spirit world."

"Fuck you."

Medianoche looked into the cold brown eyes of the angered pregnant woman.

The tight-eyed bitch brandished her anger, didn't mask being pissed off.

Her face covered with frigid rain, her clothing soaked, she owned an evil expression.

Eyes dark, frowning, shivering, her teeth chattering, she extended the package.

The woman was a killer. Medianoche saw it in her face. She had killed before.

And she wanted to kill now.

The Beast shoved the sensor inside his coat pocket, needed a free hand but wasn't going to put down his weapon, and took the handle of the briefcase with his left hand.

With his gun hand, he knocked the pregnant woman to the asphalt. Pistol whipped her hard enough to make her wet hair stand on its ends as it flew away from her face.

Her team screamed, threatened to kill them all.

Scamz made threats as he stayed hidden behind a bulletproof car door.

Medianoche didn't flinch. He knew what was going to happen. Knew The Beast would knock the anger and attitude off her pretty face. She had brought a knife to a gunfight, then uttered six disrespectful curses too many. The Beast stepped up to the downed con woman, put the bottom of his shoe against her face, pushed grit and filth against her face, shifted his weight, snarled, and pressed her face like he wanted to shove it through the wet concrete, pressed down on the woman as she yelled out in pain, her legs kicking, her hands struggling to push his weight away. She fought to get that shoe off her face. Concrete dug deep into beautiful skin and marred vanity. Pregnant or not, to get the information he wanted, Medianoche knew The Beast would treat her to a rendition. Or pass her over to Señorita Raven, let that loon do what she did best. Maybe order a death by a thousand cuts and make Arizona regret the last few days of arrogance. When he needed to be, The Beast was a beast. A man who would win a war by any means necessary.

Medianoche held his position, kept his weapon trained on the enemy, searched for Gideon as The Beast stood over Arizona with his gun pointed at her head.

The Beast pressed harder, made her scream into the freezing rain, left deeper scars as he pushed like he wanted to crush her skull, then moved his foot from her bloodied face.

Bleeding, hair tangled, soaking wet, Arizona raised up on one elbow, spat at The Beast.

"Fuck you."

The Beast fired two shots.

Both shots barely missed her head. He had missed on purpose.

She held her stomach and pulled into a fetal position.

Now she was terrified. Now fear painted her face.

The Beast smiled. He had victory. They had both packages.

Arizona snapped, "*Andá a cagar*, sonofabitch."

Then he shot the pregnant woman in her leg. Made her roll and scream.

Her wounded sister tried to run to her, came in their direction stumbling.

A bullet from Señorita Raven took her down.

The Beast growled down at Arizona, said, "And fuck you too. Slant-eyed Asian bitch, fuck you too. Double-crossing, swindling bitch. You might've gotten lucky and blown Hopkins the fuck up, but that fucking shit does not fucking work where I am in charge, you fucking fuck. Your fucking deceptions end right the fuck here."

The men on her team stepped out like protective lions, Scamz and the man who looked liked the dead movie star fired on them. But Medianoche's and Señorita Raven's gunfire was too quick, accurate, and powerful, sent them scattering back behind bulletproof doors.

At that moment, Medianoche heard The Beast's cell phone ring.

A goddamn Frank Sinatra ringtone in the middle of a goddamn war.

Medianoche kept his eye on the downed women, saw the man with Cary Grant's face wasn't making any foolish moves, did those checks while The Beast stood over the downed pregnant woman and answered his goddamn phone in the freezing rain.

Whatever The Beast heard on the other end made him curse like thunder.

Medianoche knew that meant that there was a problem in the *villa*.

And Medianoche knew that problem was Gideon.

In the distance, on the other side of unmovable traffic, he heard sirens.

Medianoche hurried, opened the trunk of the BMW, and Señorita Raven did the same with the vehicle she had been driving. The Beast ran into traffic, approached a dull-colored commercial van, a Renault Traffic. The Beast put two shots into the window of the van, exterminated the driver, who refused to open the door, reached through the broken glass, and yanked the driver's body out into the streets.

Medianoche fired on the tangos as he carried his duffel bag. Señorita Raven did the same. When they made it to the van, The Beast covered them, fired on Scamz and his crew. The Beast continued firing, kept Scamz and his team at bay while he and Señorita Raven grabbed Draco and threw his lifeless body inside the commandeered Renault.

Medianoche regrouped and covered The Beast as he backed away, covered The Beast as he turned around and prepared to rush inside the Renault under fire. Medianoche remained focused on the gunmen, men who had spread apart, found difficult angles to track.

No one watched Arizona.

No one saw her fight her pain, grab a bumper, and battle to stand up.

By the time Medianoche saw her produce a second knife, it was too late.

It was a throwing knife, a blade he knew couldn't do any harm.

Not in a gunfight. Not in the rain. Not with the winds blowing. Not from a pregnant woman who had been beaten and shot and left on the ground, moving like a dying snail.

As she held her fat belly and struggled, wobbling, with one hand, it looked like she threw the blade and lost her balance, fell as the blade went tumbling, headlights causing it to gleam slivers of brightness as it went end over end. She had thrown the blade with awkwardness and desperation.

The Beast was at the door of the van, Draco's unmoving frame blocking the entrance from inside.

Medianoche tried to move, tried to block the blade as it spun through rain and headlights.

His gun hand missed the blade by inches and he stumbled, fell into the side of the van.

The blade hit The Beast hard, sunk into his back up to the handle.

First, The Beast grunted like he had been punched, then his eyes widened as the pain registered. The Beast screamed and lost his balance, fell backward out of the van, but his hand gripped the door, that powerful and pissed-off soldier refusing to go down on the battlefield.

Medianoche grabbed the wounded soldier, pushed him back inside the Renault.

Then Medianoche rushed behind the wheel. Time was not on their side.

The Beast, blade in his lower back, blood spilling, in severe pain, cursed and yelled, asked about Draco. Unable to move, he was more concerned with his soldier than himself.

Señorita Raven yelled, "Sir, let me see your wound."

"Answer me, dammit. How bad is Draco injured?"

"I can't detect a pulse, sir."

The Beast panted. "No pulse."

"You have a knife in your lower back, sir."

"Is he dead?"

"No pulse, sir."

"*Is he dead?*"

"He's gone."

"Who stabbed me? Who fucking stabbed me?"

"The pregnant woman."

"A fucking pregnant woman."

"She threw the knife like she was raised in the goddamn circus."

The Beast shifted in insult and injury, gritted his teeth, and suppressed his deepening agony as he snapped, "Kill those fuckers. Make sure they're all fucking dead."

He screamed, a wounded emperor demanding revenge for the death of a catamite.

Señorita Raven aimed her M16 at the con men, at the pregnant woman, at the man called Scamz. She fired rounds at the fleeing cons and killers, then sent two consecutive grenades, left a duo of beautiful explosions at the base of General Justo José de Urquiza, devastation that hit targets and left Peugeots exploding and creating wicked balls of fire, gruesome flames that heated a chilling night and rose up into the mouth of the winter rain and the brutal darkness. The explosions shook Palermo and lit up the area surrounding the planetarium, gave a wonderful luminance to artificial lakes like it was the glorious Fourth of July in the United States.

Chapter 40

village of death

The winds picked up.

They blew the scent of fresh killings across damp air that smelled like death.

Six more Peruvian gunmen had shown up.

Now six more Peruvian gunmen were dead.

They had left their posts in the rain. Men who had assumed only a fool would attack them in weather this bad, so they had taken a break, gone to have *cervezas* and smokes.

I'd put down four, and Shotgun had added two more to his tally.

The shoot-out had cost us three more minutes.

I had to move before more assassins came running.

Had to get up the stairs to the dwelling that had the yellow Daffy Duck poster on its door.

Freezing rain tried to numb my hands as I sloshed through mud that felt like quicksand. Looking for more shooters, I headed up to the second level of a structure made of ten different types of wood, wood from trees, wood from desks, every scrap of wood nailed at odd angles, the heads of some nails sticking out while other nail heads were broken off in a way that left sharp edges of metal sticking out like knives. Shotgun had grabbed the gear I had left behind, my duffel and top clothing, splashed through mud and over the newly deceased, followed me, guarded me, and made sure my heart didn't get lead poisoning or my brain didn't experience abrupt ventilation. The music remained deafening, the rain relentless, and the Spanish chatter had risen in volume.

When the gunshots had stopped, more immigrants came outside. The ones who were curious and bold enough to follow trouble.

Shotgun was too big to come up the stairs. But we couldn't separate. He maneuvered and squeezed, came up the twisty metal stairs anyway. The Latin people were short and sturdy, with the builds of laborers, tango dancers, and *fútbol* players. Some of the women were barely four feet tall. Not many of the locals reached six feet. None were as large as Shotgun.

The stairs were made for them, not for my friend.

But the giant kept coming, the stairs whining and vibrating under his weight, my weight adding to the stress, shaking the building like an intruder on a spiderweb.

It felt like the stairs were straining to stay connected to the building.

A chilling breeze rushed by my face and I smelled kerosene.

I made it to the door with the Daffy Duck poster on its front, then stepped to the side. Rusted security bars covered the windows. They had fired down on us from that window a few minutes ago. Now they had barricaded themselves inside. I leaned, frowned past the rusted bars, and spied through a window so dirty it was almost opaque.

What I saw beyond the puke green brick walls and clutter told me what I had suspected. It was a small kitchen used as a home-based cocaine den. A family business where the woman of the house cooked up the drugs while the guards stayed on lookout. The smell of kerosene and other chemicals was strong. That section of the building was as explosive as a meth lab.

As soon as I peeped, screams came from inside. At least two men and a woman.

There was also a small Peruvian boy who wore blue-and-yellow Boca Juniors soccer gear and held a goddamn AK-47, a weapon he aimed at the window, threatening to shoot if we didn't get away. The weapon he had was older. Looked like a SAR-1, a Romanian AK-47.

In broken English, the kid scowled and yelled, *"Say hello to my little friend."*

Then the pint-sized kid pulled the trigger and sprayed, sent bullets and broken glass flying in our direction. We had both jumped back, the brick walls inside the house making the shots ricochet. The woman and the man screamed for the kid to stop, and the shooting stopped as fast as it had started.

I took my gun, raised up, and aimed inside those cramped quarters, everything at point-blank range. The man ran toward the window, a long-bladed knife raised high, ready to chop my hand off. I pulled off two shots, both below the waist. The first shot caught his thigh. The second shot opened up his kneecap.

He went down, his momentum taking him into the broken window, glass stabbing his face. He collapsed, screaming that he'd never be able to play *fútbol* again.

I trained my weapon on the woman. Had no choice.

She was armed. No more than four foot two and holding a revolver half her height.

I fired once, hit the back wall near her.

The woman dropped her gun and ran back into a corner, hands over her head.

She unleashed a scream that must have sent a chill through every beating heart in the *villa*.

A fire erupted in the kitchen area. A fire that would kiss chemicals and cause an explosion. I yelled for her to stop the fire. Yelled for her to stop the fire now.

The downed man yelled for his son to shoot me.

My eyes went to the boy with the AK. The boy who thought he was Al Pacino in *Scarface*. His ancient weapon had jammed. The kid had no idea what to do now.

His eyes met mine.

He saw anger. Now he was afraid. But he refused to let that terrified expression stick to his skin. An older man was on a cell phone, in a corner, screaming that they were under attack by two Americans. Americans who had gunned down six guards like they were nothing.

They weren't calling the Argentine police. Or the Buenos Aires fire department.

They were calling The Beast. They were calling The Four Horsemen.

That meant they weren't here.

I had to get inside. I rammed the door a couple of times. It had been barricaded. I clenched my teeth, summoned all my strength, and yanked on the security bars covering the window. They gave a little. I yanked again. Again. Then I felt a hand on my shoulder.

Shotgun said, "Let me have a go at it."

We changed positions.

Shotgun yanked the bars, almost pulled the wall off the building.

Down below, I saw more men running our way with guns.

I let off a few rounds and they stopped where they were.

The wind and rain made them all hard targets to hit.

I let off a few more rounds, sprayed left to right, and they ran back into the shadows.

Shotgun grunted, yanked on the bars twice.

I grabbed a clip out of my back pocket and reloaded, trained my gun on the roofs, fired twice when I thought I saw movement, then repositioned and aimed at the ground.

Shotgun grunted and yanked again. Sounded like he had ripped the side off the building.

The metal bars came out of the concrete walls into his rough, blue-collar hands.

He threw the bars and at least forty pounds of attached concrete over the railing, threw it into the rain and let it all crash on top of the dead men we had left down below.

I was inside that window before the last of the debris rained to the ground.

I picked up the knife the wounded man had tried to attack me with, then snatched the jammed AK from the hooligan kid, threw both weapons behind me, back near the window. Then I kicked behind me the revolver the woman had held, added that to the pile and trained my gun on the man who was the head of the household.

The kid came at me. A kid who knew an adult would never hit a kid.

He was wrong.

My punch put him on his ass with his face bloodied, narrow nose probably broken.

The diminutive mother screamed and ran to her injured son, wiped his bloodied face like he was five years old. She yelled and pointed, told the man to give them what we wanted.

The sound of rain rat-tat-tatting against tin was unnerving, each tap like a gunshot.

The man went to the brick wall, took down a worn poster of Che Guevara.

Behind the poster was a wall safe big enough to be inside a bank. He opened the safe and moved drugs to the sides. Then he pulled out a black briefcase that was identical to the one Arizona had kept at her side, the one I had seen at her feet at the Starbucks in Aventura. Where all of this began. The sensor told me that I had what we had come for.

What many had died for.

The drug makers had sat on more money than they could ever fathom and had no idea.

He told me I wouldn't get away.

I said I know. Told him I knew The Four Horsemen were on the way.

But we would be gone.

And to give my regards to the one they called Medianoche.

The man shook his head no, and snapped, *"No van a venir. Ellos están aquí."*

He frowned, told me that they weren't coming.

They were here.

He had called The Beast as soon as he heard the gunshots.

The Four Horsemen were here and I would regret this moment.

I yelled out my panic, told Shotgun to start making his way down the stairs, told him to move as fast as he could because it was about to get ugly. Real ugly. I kept my eyes on the people in front of me while I picked up their weapons, threw them out the window, let them fall down into the mud. I made them all get down on the floor with their backs to me and their faces turned away. Otherwise I'd get shot or stabbed in the back as I tried to escape. Had to keep my eyes on them as I crawled out the window. On the one-foot-wide landing, the stairway wobbling underneath me, I saw that Shotgun had made it halfway down.

I didn't move. My weight and his weight might rip the stairs from the wall.

Had to wait for him to clear the winding and weakened stairs.

Heart racing, briefcase in hand, I listened. The rain. The storm.

Somewhere behind those clamors were the echoes of hooves.

Not horses, but frantic Horsemen charging through the slums, racing this way.

My breathing shortened from taking in so much damp and cold air. My heartbeat was fast. I looked out over the disarrayed shantytown, the beauty of the richest area in South America glittering in the distance. We had to get through the rain and mud to those bright lights.

The muzzle flashes came first.

The flashes were the harbingers of hard bullets in search of soft targets.

My feet struggled to move as fast as my racing heart.

Then came the explosions.

One hit the side of the building and shook me hard.

The stairwell started to give, fasteners popping out as metal whined, as the winding stairs came loose. It came detached from the fucking wall as gunshots peppered the building.

The world around me exploded and I fell like I was being thrown out of an airplane.

Chapter 41

battleground

Muzzle flashes. Bullets. Explosions.

Surrounded by a promised death, I hit the ground hard, the wind knocked out of my body, tangled up in the stairway, a prisoner struggling to breathe in air so thick it felt poisonous.

Shotgun held his ground and fired back, his shots fast and nonstop.

Shotgun yelled, "You hurt?"

I wiped mud from my face and mouth. "Don't think so."

"They're crazy, blowing up everything in their way."

"Yeah. They're crazy."

"Well, guess I'll have to get crazy too."

Shotgun had changed weapons. He had an M16. He let out a magazine and a half of rounds, shot like he was John Rambo. His shots were swift but controlled. He tried to make every round count, and he tried to throw more shots at them than they threw at us. It was like two fighters in the ring trying to outpunch each other, only these punches were deadly.

I wrestled my way out of the debris of the metal stairway; had landed in a sewage-tainted area littered with dead bodies, mud, and a dislocated window. The package was near me. Before I could pull it from the mud, the boy and his father had raced to their destroyed window.

The people who had stepped outside to watch ran away, fled through the muddy streets. Some ducked down narrow passageways while others hid in crevices.

Hundreds of innocent people, mothers with babies, fathers and their children, they all ran.

And we saw at least two shadows running up the center of the muddy road.

I saw two, but that didn't mean that there weren't more.

They brought their assault toward us, the weapons in their hands unmistakable.

The mud that slowed our retreat did them no special favors.

We fired shots that slowed their ravenous charge, like rapacious wolves hunting prey.

Then we did what the smartest men in the world would do.

We dumped most of our gear, lightened our load by one duffel bag. Couldn't chance dumping it all, no matter how much our gear weighed. Shotgun kept one of the duffels, hiked the strap over his left shoulder, kept a weapon in his right hand, and ran hard.

We slipped and slid for a moment. The mud-covered ground didn't let our pace match the energy we expended. We found our feet and ran hard but couldn't run fast.

Mud added what felt like fifty pounds to my pants.

I led the retreat, fearful, cold, and shirtless, muddied briefcase in one hand, a dirty gun in my waistband, another muddied gun in my hand. We bolted through acres of vertical, disorganized clusters of warped shacks and abandoned buildings, scrap-wood walls held up by cardboard, tattered bedsheets used as curtains.

Behind us was an explosion. Sounded like the bang from an M79 grenade. Wasn't sure.

What I knew was that the drug den we'd just left was going up in flames.

I heard that boy, his father, and his mother screaming that they were on fire.

They had no stairs to exit. They were trapped.

There was a second direct hit, definitely not an accident.

The Horsemen had rewarded them, the price of failure.

We fled into a decrepit section that ran between wrecked buildings, escaped the direct line of fire, cut through another section that was nothing more than a primitive congregation of shacks. We ran by people who looked like they were dying. Some had roofs that had leaks that let rivers run through their dwellings. Some had no roofs at all. The storm was killing them. They weren't on raised ground, and sewage had flooded their tents. They stood outside, huddled around their belongings, drowning on dry land. We ran past them.

The Four Horsemen had a sensor to the package in my hand. It would lead them to wherever we ran. We'd become mice in a maze of cockroaches and rats.

We came out on another muddy road and we slid, battled the terrain.

A flare went up into the night, vandalized the darkness we needed.

And showed our enemy was behind us.

We were sprayed with automatic weapon fire, bullets hitting concrete and tin, ricocheting and pinging, every shot trying to find its mark. We battled rain, mud, and gunfire. Then my heart triple-timed when I heard Shotgun let out a sound of deep agony. He went down but never let go of his weapon, kept shooting as he tried to scoot across mud and get to safety. I fired away to protect Shotgun. Fired until my clip was empty, reloaded, fired again, shots going off as a barrage of bullets kept coming at us as fast as the raindrops.

By then, Shotgun was back on his feet, blasting away, giving as good as we were getting.

The flare faded, and darkness returned.

Then everything around us started exploding.

The explosion was sudden and deafening, made my body tense while my heart galloped and my ears rang like church bells, its power stealing most of my senses.

Then came a second explosion.

They had a fucking grenade launcher. Mud, filth, parts of DIRECTV dishes, parts of bricks, tin, cockroaches, parts of exploded rats and dogs, all kind of debris and filth mixed with South American contamination and the freezing rain, it all fell from the sky.

It seemed like we were under attack by the Taliban.

I looked at Shotgun. Blood trickled down his face. A wound was open on his muddied cheek. If the explosion had sent shrapnel to any other part of his body, it was too hard to tell.

I yelled at Shotgun, "Can you move?"

"Just tell me which way."

"Claro. Have to get to the building with the Claro sign on top."

"I'm with you."

The natives panicked, some yelling from home to home, some screaming that the military had returned, that this was the government attacking, once again engaged in social cleansing.

They were closing in on us.

The gunshots that hit the ground behind us verified that fear.

I asked Shotgun, "You hit?"

He grunted out his pain. "Just keep shooting."

Shotgun kept blowing off rounds. Kept slugging it out.

One of those Horsemen had tracers, bullets that ignited and burned, lit up the night and told the other shooters what trajectory to follow, told them where to put their shots.

Two more explosions rocked the *villas*.

One explosion was twenty yards behind us, the other, twenty yards off to the left.

Each boom shocked our systems, added a streak of fear to Shotgun's face.

Another grenade overshot us, hit a cell tower that was in the center of the slums.

The tower rocked, vibrated, then leaned forward. It fell slowly at first, metal screeching like a wounded monster howling out in agony, then picked up speed and landed hard.

Debris mixed with the chill from the sky and rained down on the back of my head.

Pickup trucks roared our way, loaded with Latin hooligans, all with guns.

Then one of the trucks exploded. The other careened through a pile of trash, flipped, and landed upside down in a pool that was a mixture of waste and viruses. When the headlights had hit their eyes, our enemy thought the hooligans were on our team.

There was the screech of incoming, and another grenade hit the flipped truck.

Whoever was injured was dead.

We ran, the fire from those burning trucks brightening the night.

More people ran too. They ran through mud and stumbled across potholes, fell in lakes and made it back to their feet stumbling, screaming, and scattering in all directions. Others stood in doorways, terrified and curious as they watched the explosions like it was a John Woo movie.

A group of men standing at the edge of the roof of one of the dwellings started firing down at us. We were trapped. Snipers were in front of us. The Horsemen behind us.

Shotgun fired back toward the Horsemen while I shot up at the roof. We shot fast, shot often, had to get firing superiority in every direction. I focused on that rooftop, had to send up more shots than were coming down from those made-in-the-U.S.A. weapons.

One of the snipers dropped, tumbled, bumped over shabby construction, ragdolled from the fourth level of that building, and crashed headfirst on a section of broken concrete.

I kept firing and hoped more fell the same way.

The others ran in the other direction.

We had an opening, an opening we took without hesitation.

I asked Shotgun, "You okay?"

He grunted. "I'm okay."

I shoved the package into his arms. Then I pointed toward the bright lights.

I told him, "Run. I'm going to be right behind you. We're almost there."

"You hurt?"

"Run, Shotgun."

"You keeping up with me?"

"I'll be right behind you. Get to the spot, give that to Arizona."

"Where you gonna be?"

"Behind you, big man. I'm going to keep them off your ass."

Shotgun struggled and took off his heavy coat, dropped everything except for the package and took off. Moved like an injured football player. He ran toward railroad tracks that led to the designated end zone. Ran by the flags all over Villa Miseria. Chile. Bolivia. Paraguay. Brazil. Uruguay. Colombia. Peru. Shotgun ran through flags for every country and subculture like he was running out of South America until he got to Georgia.

I was right there with Shotgun until we ran beyond the last of the darkened structures that had no electricity; the explosions had killed sections of the pirated power. We passed the last of the tents on the edges of the settlements. We struggled to keep our footing as we hit a strip of uneven concrete and stumbled over loose ground, then splashed through infectious rivers, struggled to make it to the railroad tracks. It was wide open for at least two hundred yards.

That would be dangerous. If they sent up another flare, we'd be easy targets.

I told Shotgun to sprint while I covered him. I'd keep them busy.

He followed my orders and raced as hard as he could, his injured stride not losing any pace, his left arm pumping like a piston, a mountain of muscles on a desperate mission.

Behind us, the sections of the *villa* were trying to burn, only the rain refused to let it go up in flames like Detroit in 1967 and Los Angeles in 1992. But the *villas* did have a dangerous glow.

I fired shots toward the enemy.

Shotgun fled over two dozen train tracks, ran over them, pulling his knees up high, like a footballer in training camp running an agility drill over empty tires, and when he made it to the end of the tracks, his run cut to the left, where he ducked behind a wall of train cars, used them as shields as he made his way to the outskirts of the *villa* and vanished into the center of darkness.

I arrived at the wall.

I stopped running.

Rodents were all around me, terrified out of the empty containers by the explosions.

My breathing was labored. I was wounded. Could barely hear. Could hardly see.

I coughed over and over, struggled to catch my breath, then I nodded.

I had done what I had promised.

I'd retrieved the package.

My debt to that sonofabitch Scamz was paid in full.

Shotgun was safe.

Warmth covered me. A powerful adrenaline rush that replaced my blood with liquid fire.

I was finished running.

North America. Catherine. Steven. X.Y.Z.

Being blackmailed for two-point-five-million dollars.

It all rushed back inside my head, and I shoved it all away.

My mother had told me that my father was a military man. An army man. She had said that while he paid her to do what whores did, he bragged that he used to jump out of planes, took sniper training, and made Delta Force. She told me that they drank and got high and she did to him the kind of things a woman in her profession did, all for a price. Said he ran his strong hands through her pretty hair and held her close, treated her like a lady, told her his secrets. She had said that my father was strong, that he fought bulls with his bare hands.

The night I had killed that evil man, my mother had remained calm.

She had put sheets over his body. And we had left him dead on the floor of that whorehouse in Mecklenburg County.

I'd asked my mother, "Did I do a bad thing?"

She had shaken her head, then said, "Some people deserve to die."

That day lived inside me.

I trembled, shivered.

Rain had numbed my hands, but I held my guns and turned around. Covered in mud and sewage, marked by shrapnel, I moved through the area where the rats had claimed territory, limped back toward the glowing *villas* and The Four Horsemen.

Anger rose like a balloon filled with helium, the string unreachable, unable to rein back, and now anger had to fly until it couldn't fly anymore.

In agony, as freezing rain struggled to wash mud away from my body the way the River Jordan washed away sins, I jogged back toward the slums. I headed back toward Midnight.

The bastard child went in search of the vile father.

Capítulo 42

paseo por el infierno

Man was a desperate animal.

Medianoche ran through *asentamientos irregulars*, a shantytown that blazed with incredible noise and fury, like the Great Fire of London and the Chicago Fire united. A sea of flames licked the skies behind his charge and cast long shadows as destruction littered his every step. Inside dwellings, he imagined people had fallen to the floors, a Pavlovian response to hearing gunfire. Others fled into the weather like it was the end of days.

The Book of Revelation come to life.

Medianoche frowned at the wet sensor and jogged on treacherous terrain made of potholed, flooded roads, his breathing labored as he inhaled toxic fumes.

The sensor remained bright green.

The enemy was within one hundred yards, maybe as close as thirty.

Players had switched packages like teams switching fields at half-time, but the game wasn't over, was never over for a battle-hardened warrior.

Medianoche moved through the chilling rain with Señorita Raven's fury at his side, the shadows of Gideon and his oversized compadre the target of every obsessive shot from his 5.56.

The Four Horsemen down to two, but twice as deadly as four.

Medianoche's ragged breath fogged in front of his face as the temperature dropped.

His feet were numb from the water, his Italian shoes soaked in liquid refuse.

Señorita Raven ran like a furious psychopath and decimated the shantytown like a trooper from the 1st Cavalry Division instructed to burn a village on the Bong Son plain in central Vietnam after soldiers had been wounded and killed by the enemy.

Hombres, mujeres, chicas, chicos, hijas, hijos, abuelas, abuelos, tíos, tías, primos, everyone with common sense fled as vermin scattered, the noise and fury overpowering.

The beeps on the sensor told him the target was fleeing at a faster pace.

Medianoche yelled, "They're running. We didn't stop them."

"Give me the sensor."

"Why would I do that, soldier?"

"Because I'm faster than you. I can catch them."

"What, you expecting another chopper to drop in after you obtain the package?"

"You're breathing like you're hypoxic."

"I'm fine."

Medianoche picked up his pace, his breathing labored as he carried his SWAT-style rifle and XD45 pistols, his wet combat gear weighing him down as his steps sank into soft ground.

Medianoche slowed, his 5.56 sweeping the area. Señorita Raven did the same with her M16, being aggressive yet cautious. Medianoche expected one of the targets to stop, try to pick them off. Because that was what he would do. The rain had washed away all footprints, but they were on the right track. Gideon and his team had lightened their loads. Weapons and spent ammunition shells littered the flooded terrain. Shell casings had become bread crumbs from the tormented *villa* into the mouth of darkness. Señorita Raven tossed her M16 to the ground, lightened her load, and pulled out XD45 pistols, same as Medianoche had ready to bring into action.

The Beast was wounded, unable to stand on his own, unable to walk.

Señor Rodríguez had been KIA. And that unqualified piece of shit

Draco had been killed faster than the first line of men who had stepped off the boats at Normandy.

Medianoche was stuck working with the arrogant slag who had accused him of rape.

A woman who didn't have what it took to be a soldier, let alone a Horseman.

Medianoche asked, "Can you be trusted, soldier?"

"I'm a loyal soldier. My record speaks for itself."

"Does it?"

"We're on a mission. That package is my first priority."

"Is it?"

"I can run a five-minute mile."

"Maybe on a sunny day in Mendoza. Not in this weather and not on this terrain."

"Two things you learn how to do in East Saint Louis, run and fight. And no matter where I am, I'm good at both. In the gear I have on now, I can manage a mile in about six."

"You're soaking wet."

"Give me the sensor and pull up the rear. We have to get to them before they get reinforcements. And we have to do that now before this turns into our Iraq and Vietnam."

Winds blew frigid rain into Medianoche's face, each drop like being stabbed with ice.

She said, "At the moment, we have a common enemy. We are on the same team. You're hot-blooded and stubborn and full of yourself. But we are on the same team."

Medianoche growled as they ran through ramshackle strips of human agglomeration, cursed as they ran though ankle-high rivers of stench and litter, as they took aim at every cat or dog that ran by, chasing prey through a darkened labyrinth inside an inaccessible fortress.

He hated what he had to admit. Señorita Raven was right.

Tonight she was faster.

Tonight.

The leader didn't have to be the fastest. He only had to know how to lead.

And with The Beast off the front line, he was the leader.

He had to push his anger to the side.

And do what was best for the team.

Every war and battle became an end to itself. At some point, it would no longer be about the package. It would simply be about winning. And they were beyond that point.

Medianoche knew that The Four Horsemen, despite the casualties, had to win.

He stared at Señorita Raven like they were among the *milongueros* and *milongueras* in a *cabeceo*, held strong eye contact, maintained that eye contact as they faced each other.

He studied her, looked for deception in her angered eyes.

She said, "Whatever problems are between us, they are irrelevant."

Medianoche nodded. "Millions of dollars irrelevant."

"Maybe a billion dollars irrelevant."

He took a deep inhale, exhaled, then extended the sensor to Señorita Raven.

She held the edges of the sensor with her fingers, but he didn't let go.

He kept eye contact with her. Stared into a face marked by shrapnel. At eyes that reminded him of what he wanted to forget. She looked at him and held his stare.

Again, he felt like they were about to kill each other.

He let go of the sensor like he was letting go of the prize itself.

Señorita Raven battled the rising wind, sprinted toward the wall of containers and the railroad tracks. He charged for another quarter mile, sections of the shantytown crumbling behind them. Her pace, her agility, her determination to recover what was lost was as hot as the fires. Medianoche followed her trail, her sprint incredible. Tracker in one hand and XD45 in the other, she ran into the darkness, obscured by the falling rain.

Medianoche slowed down when the mud tried to pull him into the earth, but he didn't stop. He adjusted his eye patch, then wiped water from his eye.

From his only eye.

Another explosion came from behind him, an earth-shaking bang louder than the crude *cumbia* music that drowned out the escalating screams of the dead and dying.

He turned quickly, aimed his weapon at the glowing shantytown.

A settlement that looked like the back end of a battle from the Old Testament.

His weapon searched side to side, found no threat lurking behind him.

Only hell.

And when Medianoche turned back around, when he inhaled cold air and was about to continue the chase, he saw that he was no longer standing alone on the edge of stolen grounds.

He had company.

His company stood there, covered in contaminated sludge, highlighted by flames.

For a moment, as Medianoche stood in the winter rain, a downpour that created a web of murky floods that reminded him of the Baldwin Hills disaster in December of 1963, he thought he saw the familiar silhouette of his own father. He thought he saw his drunken, abusive father.

But it wasn't him.

The young man they called Gideon was in front of him.

The assassin who had put down Señor Rodríguez was a few feet away.

The sonofawhore who had cost him an eye was close enough to kill.

He looked like a wild animal. An enraged, wounded animal that had escaped its cage.

Medianoche raised both XD45s and prepared to fire.

Then sparks exploded behind his eyes.

North Carolina.

The sparks ignited memory, and Medianoche was yanked from the battlefield and thrown back in time to North Carolina.

Once again, daguerreotype memories played at ten frames per second, the edges still dull, the images still in black and white, each image blurry like a hand moving back and forth in front of his face in fast motion. A war went on inside his head, ground zero being where the bullet had penetrated his skull, that missing memory blazing, battling to reboot. A thousand sparks.

He was facing a beautiful French whore who used the name Thelma.

The French whore was angry. Shouting in his face, pointing behind him. Pointing outside. Someone was out there. Lurking in the dark. The whore was angered, cursing Medianoche in French, making threats in English. Said she knew his secrets. Said she would tell his secrets. Then he grabbed her arm and she slapped him, spat in his face.

Snatches of a heated conversation, cries of terror bombinated about his head.

Daguerreotype memories played at twenty frames per second.

He slapped her.

She screamed and attacked him. Came at him with a steak knife.

He overpowered her, took the knife, threw it across the room.

Then he choked her.

She had tried to kill him.

His odium no longer under control, he was going to return the favor with his bare hands.

Inside that memory, Medianoche looked through a window.

He looked outside and saw a man watching.

A man in a dark suit was waiting, standing like a pallbearer.

Medianoche saw The Beast. He was there.

The Beast was there in North Carolina.

Then the snot-nosed boy came out of nowhere.

Gun in hand, anger on his face, his little fingers pulling the trigger.

The gun exploded.

Then blackness. Darkness. Permanent midnight.

Medianoche howled.

He battled like a madman, broke through that memory like an out-of-control car speeding through darkened glass. He battled his way back to reality, came back to darkness and freezing rain, and pulled the trigger fingers on both guns, wanted to blast Gideon back to the hell he had come from. But it was too late. Gideon tackled him, hit him hard, took him off his feet as both guns exploded. Medianoche grunted, hit the ground hard and lost his weapons. He rolled in the mud and came up on his feet empty-handed.

Gideon rushed to pick up the guns. Medianoche bolted toward Gideon but slipped in the muck. By the time he got to his feet, both guns were in Gideon's hands.

Medianoche growled, "Shit shit shit shit shit."

Gideon snapped, "What the fuck was that? What just happened to you?"

Medianoche didn't answer. "A fucking *guacho*."

"What?"

"You're a fucking *guacho*. A goddamn mutt."

"Fuck you."

Medianoche smiled. "You fucking sonofawhore."

"What just happened? Looked like you were in a coma."

"You got lucky. That's all you need to know, *guacho*. You got lucky."

Gideon was trembling. The weather was getting the best of him.

Medianoche felt the same chill on his wet and heavy clothes.

He asked, "Where is the package you stole from us?"

"We got it. That's all that matters to me. I got what I came to get."

"Won't do you any good, Señor Guacho. Won't do you any goddamn good."

"I don't care. Not my problem."

"We'll track it down before it leaves the area. We'll have it back in our possession. Yours is a Pyrrhic victory. Whoever has it, my soldier is right behind them. And my soldier is both capable and ruthless, takes no prisoners. Your friends, we put a few of them down, took possession of the package they had."

"You're lying."

"Look behind me. You see those fires? That was only the continuation of what has been a frustrating day. We caught up with the Peugeots, and your friends were given the same wonderful treatment. The young man with the long hair, that incompetent fool is dead. That dumb sonofabitch Scamz is probably on the same express train to Hell. Both of the Asian girls are copilots on that journey. The pregnant woman was feisty, sneaky, good with a blade. But after I beat her ass, a few grenades changed that attitude of hers."

"The pregnant girl . . . where is she?"

Medianoche paused, detected some emotion.

He asked, "The pregnant bitch, was she carrying your kid? The tight-eyed gook they called Arizona? I tried to crush her goddamn skull into the concrete. Her pretty little face wasn't a pretty little face when I was through with her. She was just another tight-eyed gook with road rash down to her neck."

"Shut up."

"What's the problem, Señor Guacho?"

"Stop calling me that."

"Why, Señor Guacho? Something about being called what you are bother you?"

"Because I said so."

He wanted to keep Gideon angry. Wanted him off balance. Needed him emotional.

Powerful emotions highlighted Gideon's filthy face. "Where is Arizona?"

"Was I vague? Or are you deaf and stupid? That bitch was a two-for-one."

"You're lying."

"We captured those fuckers in Palermo no more than an hour ago. Your soldiers are dead. Casualties of a war they had no business fighting. Never step into a man's homeland and expect to defeat him in combat. General Lee learned that lesson when he went north and lost. And so did America in Vietnam and in Iraq. Your friends, they're dead. But our objective must remain clear. What you have and what we have, when combined, it's a lot of money. Your team with one half of the package, my team with the other half. So we're back at square one. The game is back at zero-zero."

Gideon said, "You went to Montego Bay nine months before I was born."

"You're back to that bullshit."

"I never left *that bullshit*."

"What do you want?"

"I don't know. I thought I knew, but I don't know."

"You put a bullet in my head in North Carolina. You put a bullet in my goddamn head and cost me an eye and part of my fucking memory. And as far as I'm concerned, you owe me."

"You were there, in Montego Bay, with Thelma."

"So were dozens of British and American and Chinese cruise ships filled with tourists."

"They're not important."

"It was a goddamn whorehouse. New customer every fucking hour. Men lined up to fuck her the way Argentineans line up to get *helado*. *She was a goddamn whore motherfucker*."

"No one else is important."

"Are you not listening to what I'm saying? I fucked Thelma and so did everyone else. She was just like the whores walking around Microcentro and Palermo and Recoleta and all over this damn city. I paid up front, fucked her until she screamed. I busted a nut and walked away. You want to know the price? You want to know what was on the menu? And they do have menus in Montego Bay. You pick a whore and you pick what services you want from the menu. And being the father of a child with a whore, well, that wasn't on the goddamn list. And if you are here because I busted a nut inside a lying whore, why in the world would I want you to be my fucking son? You might be that whore's kid, but you sure the fuck are not mine."

"Sure." Gideon nodded. "Now that we have that out of the way."

"Your sperm donor might be an astronaut, a lawyer, or a clown in the circus. But it's not me, you dumb fuck. I can't have kids. I got my nuts cut a long time ago. I had a vasectomy when I was eighteen. I have no idea why she picked me out of the lineup, but she picked the wrong one. Gideon, I don't know who the fuck you are, what game you're playing—"

"Fucking liar. All of you are fucking liars."

"You're a fucking mental case."

"She told me you were my father."

"I don't know what the fuck this has to do with the mission we're on, but whatever you're trying to pull, if this little fucking mind game is suppose to make me forget you have left two of my men dead and one of my men wounded, maybe dying in this shit-filled slum—"

"She said you were my father, but I don't give a fuck. You're a piece of shit. You're no soldier. You're nothing like the man I had in my mind. He was an honorable warrior. You're a thug in a bulletproof suit. You're nothing better than a money-hungry fucking thug."

"From the mouth of a fucking hoodlum."

Gunshots erupted.

There were a dozen gunshots off in the distance. From the direction of the train tracks.

The direction Señorita Raven had run.

The direction of the package.

Gideon turned for a moment, only a moment.

Medianoche charged at Gideon, ready to kill or ready to die.

He would do one or the other.

Medianoche tackled Gideon hard enough to send both guns flying from his hands and tumbling into the filth and darkness. They splashed into muddy lakes created by rain and runoff from sewage. Medianoche grunted, moved like he was twenty years younger, and took Gideon down on broken glass and plastic, tin and rusted metals. Mud splattered and debris was squashed underneath Gideon's shirtless body. Medianoche tried to knock the wind out of him.

Gideon cried out in pain, his howls reaching up into the dark skies.

Medianoche pulled back his fist and beat Gideon.

Gideon struggled to block as Medianoche threw blow after blow.

Medianoche wanted to knock an eye out of Gideon's face.

Gideon's left eye was swollen shut, his rugged face bruised by a barrage of punches.

Medianoche hammered Gideon, battered him.

Gideon struggled, wrestled with him, finally pushed him away and got free.

The fires highlighted his enemy.

Gideon struggled to his feet, moved like every part of his body was numb from the rain.

Medianoche went after Gideon again.

It felt like the rain had added a thousand pounds to his bulletproof clothing.

Medianoche hit Gideon hard enough to knock him out, a blow that twenty years ago would've left a man twice his size in a permanent coma. He struck him again in the chest, hit him with a blow hard enough to stop a heart from beating. Gideon didn't go down, stood like a wounded machine. Then Gideon came at him hard, threw elbows, threw head butts hard enough to break Medianoche's nose. Medianoche returned the fury, hit Gideon and made that sonofabitch slip in the mud. And while Gideon fought to get his footing, Medianoche threw a hard right hand, a blow to the face that made his enemy stagger, but his enemy refused to fall.

Medianoche kept pounding Gideon.

The weather had done half the work, had weakened his opponent.

Each blow sent Gideon staggering, slipping and sliding like an outclassed amateur boxer being knocked across the ring, being hit at will by a seasoned pro.

Gideon refused to fall. He stayed on his feet, remained upright, one eye shut.

He was a man halfway blind.

Medianoche swept him off his feet, sent him down into the broken glass and debris once again, the stench of sewage splattering up across his suit.

He grabbed Gideon's neck, choked him.

Medianoche barked, "You think I give a shit about the son of a goddamn whore?"

Medianoche put his weight into his gloved grip, strangled Gideon.

Then when Medianoche found he couldn't strangle the sonofawhore the way he wanted to, he pummeled the sonofawhore's face again. Medianoche's breathing was deep, ragged, labored from the running and fighting, his breathing shortened by the cold air that attacked his lungs.

But Gideon was suffering in the same winter storm, shirtless, exposed to the elements.

Medianoche yanked off his leather gloves, grabbed Gideon's neck with his bare hands, the rainwater coming down harder, drowning Gideon as he was being strangled.

When someone was choked in the movies, they died right away, died a quick death, as if strangling was as fast as putting a bullet in the enemy's heart.

Not in the real world.

It took forever to strangle a strong man. The fingers had to be strong enough to maintain the grip needed to cut off the flow of oxygen and create that hypoxic state to the brain, hands had to be strong enough to dig into muscle, strong enough to clench down and apply a deepening pressure, powerful enough to do all that while the enemy shifted and turned, battled to stay alive.

Strangling a man was the hardest way to kill a sonofawhore.

Strangling was the most personal way to kill a man.

And this was personal.

Medianoche choked Gideon until his hands ached, until his hands grew numb.

He choked that sonofawhore until he stopped struggling.

Until he was dead. It was time to bring the white tape and mark the dead body.

Medianoche pulled away, gritted his teeth as he struggled to catch his breath.

He opened and closed his fingers, the numbness up to his wrists.

He had done it.

Medianoche had killed the motherfucker that put a goddamn bullet in his head.

He had left Gideon dead, faceup, hands outstretched, on his back like he was on a cross. Medianoche struggled, slipped in the mud as he made it back to his feet.

Shit, mud, and debris covered his saturated clothing, added weight.

It was done.

Now he had to find his guns and go toward the package.

He didn't have a sensor. He had to go where he had seen gunfire.

He had to catch up with his soldier.

Then.

Gideon coughed. He moved. The sonofawhore was still breathing.

Medianoche staggered across slippery terrain, rain falling from above and fires behind him, his world blanketed by music and screams. He kicked trash away, searched until he found a sharp piece of metal in the mounds of refuse and debris. He'd killed men with shanks before.

Gideon had made it to his knees. Then pulled up on one foot.

As Gideon scowled, Medianoche evaluated the beaten man in front of him.

Gideon had one swollen eye. The half blind scowled at the half blind.

Medianoche hurried toward him with the shank, its point as sharp as a steak knife.

He would make Gideon all the way blind.

An eye for an eye. Plus another eye for claiming to be his goddamn kid.

For the rest of his days, Gideon would be able to see only darkness. That sonofawhore would spend the rest of his days seeing the blackness that came with meeting Midnight.

Gideon charged at Medianoche like a wounded bull, each step splashing sewage. Medianoche planted his feet, lowered his shoulders, twisted his hips, and swung the sharp metal like it was a right hook, swung it hard, a knockout punch that was aimed for his neck, for the jugular. But Gideon feigned high and went low, caught Medianoche off guard, grabbed his body and tried to pull his legs from under him. Medianoche's blow went across Gideon's back, took skin and blood before he lost the shank, trying to fight for his balance.

Gideon was quick. He was wounded but quick. Fighting like a wild animal.

Medianoche saw Gideon's hands were filled with mud and sewage. He tried to slap the filth into Medianoche's good eye. Medianoche moved his head, bobbed, weaved, turned his face away. The filth was smeared on his forehead and drained down over his eyes, compromised his vision.

Gideon wrestled him across sludge, grunted and pushed him hard. The loose ground gave, and some spots were like quicksand. Cold water and mud plowed up Medianoche's boots to his ankles. Medianoche went against Gideon, man against man, ego against ego, brute strength against brute strength, but Gideon found footing and leverage and raced Medianoche backward until he was slammed into an abandoned car.

Medianoche hit the car hard, spun, and threw punches, hooks and jabs, managed to get in a knee to the face, but that didn't stop Gideon. It looked like pain fueled him.

Gideon grappled, tried again to pull his feet from under his body.

Medianoche held on to the car, fought to keep his legs from being yanked out from under him, tried to throw blows with one hand while he held on to the rusty Ford Fairlane with the other. Medianoche maneuvered, got Gideon off him, wrestled and went for a choke hold, this one from the rear. But Gideon was slippery, skin covered in filth, hard to grip.

Medianoche countered the blows, broke away from Gideon, staggering, dazed.

Medianoche nodded, stood with his hands on his hips, tired. But determined.

He was a soldier. A warrior. No retreat, no surrender. Failure was not an option.

Gideon landed a roundhouse kick in his face. A kick Medianoche saw coming but was too exhausted to block. It was a swift kick that connected with his nose and sent him down into the mud. Then Gideon was behind him, holding Medianoche down. Medianoche struggled to get free as Gideon fought to get him into a sleeper hold. Medianoche threw an elbow, landed another solid blow to Gideon's face, and Gideon lost his grip.

Then Gideon began pummeling him with big jackhammer punches.

Each jackhammer blow felt like being pounded with six hundred pounds of fury.

Medianoche went blow for blow, answered every goddamn punch.

He saw Gideon was breathing heavy, too heavy to go the distance.

Gideon bull-charged him again, and Medianoche still traded blow after blow.

Until one landed on his chin. That blow snapped Medianoche's head back, stunned him.

Medianoche tried to recover, put his head down to avoid the rapid blows.

But he felt the pain come down as fast as the raindrops from the dark clouds above.

Countless blows to the back of his head led him to the edge of consciousness.

More blows were delivered to the side of his head, each blow on the same spot.

Then all right-handed blows, blows from a fist that came down like a hammer.

Blows that hammered the back of his neck like a metal baseball bat.

Medianoche was blinded by severe pain, choking on the blood in his mouth.

He tried to escape, crawled across the mud, hands numb, unable to feel.

But the rest of his body was a big ball of pain.

Gideon rode his back, held on, followed, delivered blow after blow.

He delivered big shots that left him sinking to the ground.

Left Medianoche unable to defend himself from the strikes of a madman.

Unable to defend himself against the son of a whore.

Medianoche collapsed, his pain incapacitating.

It was as if the world had been pulled from underneath his feet.

His back was against the world. Cold rain fell on his face like liquid ice.

He saw other shadows, mountainous silhouettes coming up behind Gideon.

It was a giant carrying an unconscious Señorita Raven over one shoulder.

A briefcase was in his left hand.

And a short-barreled shotgun was in his right hand.

The giant threw Señorita Raven on the ground, her limp body landing hard in the mud.

Then he aimed the barrel of his shotgun at the center of Medianoche's forehead.

Chapter 43

the road to ruin

I didn't remember much, not for most of the next hour.

I was in bad shape. Felt like I had gone ten rounds with Manny Pacquiao.

The fight had punished me. The exposure to the weather had devastated me.

I was in pain. I shivered like I was naked at the End of the World.

All I knew was that I was inside a stolen car. The agony I felt was worse than death. Shotgun put the car's heater on high and sped away, jumped in twelve lanes of traffic, had no idea where he was going. The big man helped me walk across railroad tracks and out near the Claro building, pretty much carried me when I moved too slow, and crammed me inside the backseat of a car he had hotwired, and sped away. The fires at the *villa* were going strong. The sirens were loud, the police and emergency crews entering from the opposite direction we had fled.

Raindrops the size of golf balls fell though the city lights. Shotgun passed *supermercados*, flower stands, and electronics shops while I struggled to stay conscious, afraid that giving in to the need to let my body drift toward being unconscious would send me into an irreversible coma. Tried to focus, read signs to stay alert. Saw a street marker for Avenida Dorrego. A billboard for the University of Palermo stared at me. Avenida Cerviño. Chilean-owned stores Jumbo and Easy. Centro Cultural Islámico Rey Fahd. Avenida Bullrich. Avenida Honduras. La Esquina Country Store. El Timón de Don Jesús restaurant.

We zipped through an area lined with crowded cafés, antique shops, and warehouses.

Shotgun still had the package. The briefcase was in the backseat with me, resting on the floor. He hadn't come in contact with Arizona or Scamz. He hadn't mentioned Konstantin.

That was bad news. Real bad news. I thought about what Medianoche had said.

They had caught them. Destroyed them like they had done the *villas*.

My hands sweated with hate.

Pain pulled at me, tugged me like a rope tied to a moving train.

Shotgun kept yelling, checking on me, his voice echoing and a thousand miles away. He drove like we were back in a deadly car chase. Each rotation of the tires made sounds that echoed like we were being gunned down. Streets were too bright, looked like grenades were exploding around us. Shotgun sped down crowded streets. He drove the same crazy way they did here. He knew how to drive like he was crazy. He was a taxi driver back home. I lost consciousness for a moment and dreamed, fell into a nightmare that we were on Avenida Rivadavia and Avenida Pueyrredón and had been rear-ended by Medianoche, had been forced toward the sidewalk, Shotgun unable to prevent running over pedestrians as he took out newspaper and flower stands. I jerked out of that nightmare, unsure if it had been real or not.

By the time I was able to pull myself up, the inside of the car was so hot, I was drenched in sweat. The stench that covered me was so strong, Shotgun had let down two windows.

I looked through my uninjured eye and saw he had turned onto a street in an Armenian neighborhood. We were on the edges of Palermo Hollywood, not far from movie and television studios, on a short block between Niceto Vega and Cabrera. I had Shotgun pull over in the middle of that section of Armenian culture. It hurt to move, but I had to get out of the car. Saw a school. Church named after San Gregorio Iluminador. Restaurant Armenia. Blue Sun tanning salon. The Armenian nightclub was busy, crowded, music thumping. We were in an area with businesses standing three levels high. Tree-lined street.

Roofs made for snipers. Fronts of buildings painted reds and greens and blues, but not over the top. Asociación Cultural Armenia. Unión General Armenia de Beneficencia. Saw a large sign declaring the area Centro Armenio. The street had the same name as the subculture that lived here.

Shotgun helped me get out of the car, held me like I was a helpless and decrepit old man.

While a crowd of Armenians watched, I stood on the curb and vomited a never-ending pool of anger and resentment. I wanted to go back and find Midnight. Wanted to finish this.

Shotgun held me up, didn't complain about me soiling his shoes and pants.

The Armenians thought I was drunk. No one cared about a drunk, shirtless man.

Shotgun said, "We need to get you some clothes and get you cleaned up."

I nodded. "I need antibiotics for these cuts."

"Where can we get some?"

"We have to find an open pharmacy. But not now. We have to find Arizona and Konstantin. We have to get to the next safe house they had lined up. See if they are there."

Then I vomited again.

When I was done, Shotgun helped me back in the car, put me in the front seat this time. He crossed Cabrera and as we sped into Soho, the area became like the village in New York meeting Melrose Boulevard in L.A. Ugly and crude graffiti became artistic and colorful markings outside rows of condo and shops. Trendy bars with long lines in the hippest area in the city.

Every ache I had was singing as Shotgun sped down Armenia, the stolen car bouncing on the cobblestone side streets. He drove until the graffiti became ugly and dangerous markings, cut in and out of traffic, passed by an Israeli school, and sped toward the Botanic Gardens.

He almost hit two city buses, a 152 and a 68, when he turned right and jumped into the madness on Santa Fe. By the time I saw the bright green sign for D line subte entrance at Scalabrini Ortiz, Shotgun had calmed down. Sweat ran down his face the same way the rain was falling, hard and steady. He was scared. By then I was sure we didn't have a shadow.

That package in the backseat, I knew how it could lead trouble to my front door.

Then we sped to the next safe house.

Barrio Norte was on the outskirts of Palermo. The safe house was on Avenida Salguero near Avenida Santa Fe in the area some called Villa Freud. Hundreds of boutiques stood side by side with acres of cafés and restaurants. Most were crowded. We were tucked in with hundreds of belle époque apartment buildings and modern high-rises.

If trouble showed up, it would take them a while to narrow down the building, even longer to narrow down the apartment. At least that's what I was hoping. But flying grenades wouldn't care. Part of me trembled from that race to get out of the *villa*. Part of me remained terrified.

But I'd never let that fear show. Only a dead man or a psychopath didn't own fear.

There was a small television on the table. I turned on the local news. It showed bombings and bodies that had been left at a roundabout on Alcorta near the Japanese Gardens. Dark footage shot in the rain. Bodies covered in sheets. I recognized what was left of the Peugeots. That added a new ache to my body, one that started at my heart and worked out.

Across the narrow street, a band played. Tuba. Trumpet. Sax. Guitar. Drums. Each note hit my nerves like a brick being dropped from six feet high, down to the center of my scalp.

Shotgun said, "How's your head?"

"Throbbing on both sides and down the middle."

"Why didn't you let me kill that man? All I had to do was pull the trigger."

He was talking about Medianoche.

I didn't answer. I'd stopped Shotgun from pulling the trigger. It wasn't his death to give.

Shotgun asked, "Who was he?"

"Nobody. He was nobody. Nothing to me."

He nodded. "What do we do now?"

"We wait to see who shows up. Hopefully, someone from our team will find us first."

"We ain't heard from them since they dropped us off on the highway."

I nodded. "I know."

"They didn't show at the Claro building." Shotgun paused. "Think they might be dead?"

Again I didn't answer.

I picked up a bucket of ice, frozen water I'd taken from the refrigerator and dropped into a small mop bucket. I limped across the wooden floor and stood off to the side of the window, kept a loaded gun near where I stood. After I took a deep breath, I stuck my hands into the bucket of ice and groaned with the pain. I'd washed my body the best I could, had left a pool of filth and grime in the shower, but I felt nasty. Filth had saturated my skin, sunk into my pores. Grit was underneath my fingernails. My body ached from being beaten. My hands were swollen from returning that beating. Hands and legs hurt so bad I was barely able to stand up in the shower. Could barely see out of my right eye, but the vision in my left was good enough to mark a target.

A trumpet blared and a sax joined in, followed by a tuba, guitar, and drums. Those noises and the pain told me this was real. This shit was real. Midnight wasn't dead.

Across the street was the Thelonious Club. Jazz screamed into the streets.

It would be like that until sunrise.

The club was in full swing. The rain had stopped and a crowd was out front, all dressed in winter coats and wearing scarves. A couple of people were smoking Achalay, a few others were puffing on cigarillos, Lucky Strike, and Philip Morris, but most of the crowd were sucking on Marlboro cancer sticks. The smell and smoke from the carcinogens drifted up to our cracked window, its stench no match for the stench I'd worn before. The sign out front said CAPACIDAD LIMITADA BONO CONTRIBU-CIÓN. Ten pesos. Less than three U.S. dollars to party until dawn.

There were dozens of men in baggy, wrinkled jeans. Women in tight, straight-legged jeans.

I studied them all. Any one of them could be a gun for hire.

My business didn't discriminate. Hired guns came in all shapes, sizes, and colors.

And ages. Anyone old enough to hold a gun could be a killer.

I said, "Konstantin would've called by now. They're not coming."

"I have that same bad feeling."

"They are in one of three places."

Shotgun said, "In the hospital. In jail. Or dead."

I nodded.

Shotgun grunted. "We have one of the briefcases, the one we just got."

"And The Four Horsemen have the other one."

"They caught up with our people on the highway."

"That's what Medianoche said."

Shotgun made a mournful sound. "What do we do now?"

Again I didn't answer.

As the trumpet blared and the band joined in, as at least four kinds of cigarette fumes rose through the damp air and made their way into our hideout, a black Peugeot pulled up out front.

The security gate opened and the Peugeot pulled into the narrow driveway that led to underground parking. Five minutes passed before there was an anxious knock on the front door.

We answered, guns in hand, fear in our hearts, fingers on the triggers.

I was up front. Would be the first to catch lead. The way it was supposed to be.

Shotgun was off to the side, weapon aimed chest high, center of mass.

The first face I saw was Konstantin's. His right ear was bloodied as more blood drained down the center of his face. His left arm was pulled tight to his body, his hand wrapped in ripped cloth that protected a bloody fist. His jaw was tight, teeth clenched. He was Russian. He was strong, even with cancer. Scamz was with him. He was battered, bleeding from the left side of his forehead, only one shoe on, a backpack over his shoulder. Both men were soaking wet and muddied. They looked like they had tunneled their way out of a death camp.

But the third survivor held my attention.

Her marred face, matted hair, swollen lips, bruised and broken skin, bleeding flesh wrapped in tattered clothing, all of that added up and made her look like a vagrant.

I didn't recognize her at first.

Then I saw her swollen belly.

A trail of red marked the floor like a pathway for the Grim Reaper to follow.

Arizona bled like she was dying.

Capítulo 44

hombres de guerra

Anosognosia.

It felt like Medianoche was experiencing anosognosia.

He tried to speak, and his words were slurred, like alphabet soup. Felt as if the right hemisphere of his brain had been damaged, as if he were battling cognitive-communication problems. A blanket had been thrown over his memory. Like when he had been shot in the face.

Then it went away.

The right hemisphere of his brain snapped awake.

But the pain from the fight kept him on his back, panting, struggling for air.

He rolled over on his left side, put his aching hands down in the soupy mud.

His hands went deeper into the runoff from the *villa*, vanished up to his wrists.

Outraged, battered, and bleeding, Medianoche rose to his feet one grunt at a time, a warrior wounded, but a warrior whose battle was far from over. One fight never won a battle, and one battle never ended a war. He stood in the freezing rain, wiping his muddied hands on his muddied clothing, his breathing ferocious, his language as foul and disgusting as the contaminated slime and filth that covered his Colombian-made uniform.

The *villas* burned behind him. Shelters made of plastic tarps and sticks like the slums near Mumbai collapsed as he stood. Slumdogs screamed and ran through the catastrophe.

His blood was his fuel. His blood anointed him with power to return to war.

He clenched his teeth, ready to run against an army of troops, ready to leap over walls.

He stood, the world slippery and unsteady beneath his feet, the taste of his own blood in his mouth, ready to kill as he searched for Gideon, ready to launch a demonic attack.

Señorita Raven coughed as she rose up from the same hungry mud, made it to her feet, and searched for her weapon, saw she had been disarmed. She stood ready to fight or attack.

Medianoche watched her, an incensed silhouette glowing in the flames.

She opened and closed her fingers in a way that told Medianoche her hands were numb. She took two steps, abrupt steps that splashed chilled refuse on his pants, then she bent over like she was dizzy, severely disoriented, as if she had been hit in the gut and the pain had returned with a vengeance, growled, then she wretched and spat out a mouthful of blood.

When she stood up, he saw her nose was bleeding. Half of her face was swollen.

Medianoche said, "You okay or do I need to carry you?"

"He shot me. Fucking shotgun blast took me off my feet. My uniform took most of it. Don't think there was any penetration."

That was her answer. She was hurting, but she wasn't dying.

Medianoche inspected the flaming battlefield. In the distance, people from the slums were still running, fleeing, their shadows looking like ghosts risen, spirits haunting a graveyard.

Gideon and the giant were gone.

Rain drained across Medianoche's face and felt like ice, rivered across his numbed and swollen flesh, flowed over his injured lips, and went inside his bloodied mouth.

He reached for his eye patch. It was gone. Had come off in the battle.

He wiped his mouth, ignored the discomfort, and said, "We still have half of the prize."

"Half gets us nothing. Half won't get us a fucking thing."

"Gets us nothing. Gets them nothing."

Señorita Raven coughed. "We should have it all."

"We have to get to them."

"We have to get to those fuckers."

Medianoche nodded. "We have to get that briefcase back."

"We have to get back to The Beast. Have to get back to the van."

"They could track him. They could've tracked him down."

Medianoche took a deep breath, an inhale that told him that his ribs and kidneys had been pounded by hate, a breath that told him he might piss blood later.

He began a slow, uneven jog. The jog changed into an aching run that held a stoic military cadence that ignored ten levels of pain and suffering, an aggravating ball of agony that coursed through every vein.

They hurdled over dead bodies and debris that polluted the fields where orphans played.

Ran through flames and a world filled with the poor and destitute.

Medianoche tasted his own blood, drank it like wine, became intoxicated with anger.

He ran back through the fires and destruction in the *villa*. Ran past settlements that collapsed like communism in Russia. Ran through enraged immigrants who looked like the evil dead. Señorita Raven struggled to maintain the pace but remained at his side, her every exhale powerful, intense, determined. As if the taste of her own blood fueled her insanity and anger.

Fury and insanity grew like a tumor.

Hurting head to toe, Medianoche raced back to a decrepit road near Avenida Gendarmería Nacional. He didn't slow his run until he was a few yards from their stolen van, a van that had one dead and one wounded soldier inside.

The van had been left on a bumpy and unpaved street on the edges of the slums. The muddy roads weren't good enough to drive, would've left them stuck and vulnerable.

They'd been forced to go in on foot.

The Beast was outside the van, leaning against the passenger-side door, grunting like he was suffering. Medainoche knew The Beast was still bleeding from his lower back.

The Beast had gottten out of the van with a weapon in one hand.

He guarded their half of the package as if his life depended on it.

The black briefcase was behind The Beast. He frowned and held up the sensor.

He cursed, then said, "The fucking package."

Once again it was time to reload and move before a lost battle became a lost war.

Chapter 45

walk softly, stranger

Arizona bled a river of pain.

Shotgun stepped up and took her from Scamz, handled her gingerly.

Scamz could barely stand, as if he had used all of his energy to get her this far.

Arizona held her swollen belly and gritted her teeth like she was dying a slow death. Dark smudges covered her face, looked like the blackness of asphalt and tar. Her lips were split and swollen. One eye was red and purple, puffed and closed.

Her elbows and knees were bloodied, skin ripped away. Almost every fingernail was broken and the tips of her fingers were scarred, bloodied, and swollen, as if she had clawed herself out of a pile of concrete.

But that wasn't the biggest concern.

A lake of redness grew between her legs, flowed down her inner thighs, mixed with the rain that saturated her clothing, dripped to the wooden floor, left a cherry river marking her path.

She was in bad shape. Needed to be medevaced to an emergency room.

My voice was strained when I said, "We need to get her to Alemán Hospital."

Scamz panted, "Put her in the bedroom . . . get her on the bed."

"We need to get her to the goddamn emergency room."

"If I don't do what bloody has to be done, they will find us, and an emergency room will do none of us any good, unless we're on the bottom floor where they lock away the dead. There are more than the bloody Four Horsemen after the bloody packages. Germans. Serbs. Albanians. So shut your mouth and put her on the bloody bed like I told you to do."

He took a step toward me, gave me a shove, and I grabbed that motherfucker. I wanted to pound his Latin face with my swollen fist and beat that British accent out of his pretty-boy face.

But Shotgun grabbed me, stepped between us.

I could've hit Shotgun in the mouth right then. But I knew better than to try.

I pointed at Scamz. "You're about to take a one-way trip to the End of the World."

Konstantin snapped, "Gideon, stop. Get your head on right, son."

I barked at Scamz, "I'll drop your ass off with your other fucking relatives. I will do the same thing I did for your old man, the *real* Scamz, you fake bitch, and leave your ass dead on ice with your fucking grand-dad and uncle. You ever come at me like that again, that's your ass."

Scamz reached into his backpack, pulled out a gun, held it at his side, finger on trigger.

I exploded, "Playing a goddamn piano and fucking the woman your daddy used to fuck and stealing his fucking name does not make you your fucking daddy, you bitch."

Scamz aimed it at me.

I growled, "I dare you. I fucking dare you."

Konstantin grimaced, swallowed his misery, and stepped into the line of fire.

He became a human shield.

Konstantin snapped, "*Synok, ne davaj emy nervy tebe trepat.*"

Son, don't let that scum get the best of you.

I looked in Scamz's eyes. "*On prosto suka. Svoloch.*"

He's a fucking bitch.

The moment Scamz had raised his gun at me, Shotgun had returned the favor.

Scamz was about to die the same way his old man had died, at the wrong end of a shotgun. He knew he had stepped out of his league.

We didn't bluff.

We didn't con.

We killed.

And we did it without conversation or hesitation.

Scamz knew who we were and wasn't afraid.

This just wasn't in his favor. It would be continued at another time.

He lowered his gun.

Then he nodded, put the gun down, and reached for his backpack again.

Shotgun lowered his weapon but didn't move his attention.

I scowled at Scamz. Then I walked away. I went to his woman.

Arizona was in severe pain. When the light in the room hit her, I saw more damage.

I groaned and my heart caught fire.

The right side of her face was scarred from forehead to chin and she had deep cuts in her jaw. On the same side of her face, it looked like sections of her hair had been pulled out. Her leg was wrapped in a makeshift splint, wasn't sure if it was broken or just needed to be stabilized.

It looked like they had been at ground zero of a suicide bomb attack.

Debris was in her wet, mangled hair. Thousands of small pebbles polluted her long mane like glitter that had lost its shine. Pebbles dropped from her hair as more gravel and asphalt rained from her clothing. The rain that had saturated what she wore drained like piss. Particles from explosions had left rips, tears, and holes in her once-fine clothing, which now clung to her frame. She looked like a poster child for the Salvation Army.

Her face and body bruised, Arizona held her stomach, the veins like thick spiderwebs.

She was dying before my eyes.

Scamz hurried.

He dug inside his backpack again. First he dug out a laptop, flipped it open and hit the POWER button. Then he went back inside the backpack, took out a glass bottle big enough to hold five hundred milliliters of fluid. He sat on the bed next to Arizona while we watched.

It looked like the veins in her stomach were swollen, as if they were about to break.

Shotgun watched Scamz struggle to open the bottle and said, "Let me try that."

Scamz looked at the big man, hesitated, then handed him the bottle.

Shotgun opened it like it was nothing. He handed the bottle back to Scamz.

Scamz shook the bottle, shook it hard, mixed up the contents.

Shotgun moved to the window, returned to looking out for the next wave of trouble.

Konstantin stood next to me, his hand on my shoulder, making sure I didn't snap again.

Arizona moaned.

Across the street, the jazz kicked up louder, the trumpet leading the way.

Scamz stood over Arizona like he was a doctor, the opened bottle in his hand. He tilted the bottle, and a green solution that smelled like Pine-Sol and spoiled chicken was poured onto Arizona's wounded flesh. He poured the fluid directly on the spots where the blood was leaking.

I snapped, "What you doing?"

Konstantin pulled me back.

Arizona's bruised skin loosened and wrinkled like it had aged fifty years. Scamz moved around her and poured more of the green liquid around the circumference of her swollen belly.

Blood dripped from Arizona's head as she gripped the edges of the bed. Scamz poured more fluid and Arizona pulled at the mattress, but had to stop. Both of her hands were bloody and in severe pain. Teeth clenched and breathing hard, inhaling through her nose, exhaling through her mouth, short spurts, like she was doing her best to sprint away from her agony. But her agony had the stronger pace.

The skin stretched to its limit, then snapped back, snapped back hard.

Her yell was drowned by a Billie Holiday number that played across the street.

Deep red fluids seeped out of Arizona's broken flesh.

Arizona panted like she was about to explode.

Her stomach.

Her flesh remained wrinkled, became filled with veins, like a thousand stretch marks.

Then.

Her belly wobbled, shifted positions like it was possessed, moved to the side.

It was as if the baby she had inside her body was kicking and trying to break free.

Her unborn child moved again, shifted until its weight eased toward her ribs.

It looked unreal.

Then Scamz grabbed Arizona's belly and pulled.

The stretched skin began to buckle, crumpled from being strained.

Scamz pulled again.

Arizona's flesh stretched for eight inches, then stretched for ten inches.

And snapped back.

Arizona grunted with its impact.

She was in too much pain to scream.

Then Scamz got a firm grim, held Arizona's swollen belly and pulled again, stretched Arizona's stomach almost a foot. Her flesh separated in sections, sections that were no more than a sixteenth of an inch wide, sections that collapsed and left threads of flesh hanging on to her swollen belly. Those threads of flesh snapped one at a time, popped like guitar strings that had been strained.

The remaining skin came loose, like a scab being peeled away from skin.

Sweat drained from Arizona's face as her swollen belly tumbled to her side.

Her skin was macerated. As if that belly had been attached to her flesh for weeks. Or months.

Across the street, the drummer kicked into a wicked solo.

Shotgun's mouth had dropped open. He said, "What the fuck kinda mess is that?"

Konstantin said the same thing in Russian.

What Arizona carried rolled from her body and landed on the mattress, the edges soaked with redness the color of blood and liquids that had the consistency of embryonic fluids. Strings of strained flesh hung from both the detached pregnancy and Arizona's reddened skin.

Scamz yelled, "Bring the other package. Bring me the one you recovered."

I hurried to the front room and came back with the briefcase.

By the time I returned, Scamz had a knife and was making an incision into the part of round and swollen flesh that had fallen away from Arizona's wounded body. He cut like he was a surgeon doing a C-section, careful like he was trying not to harm a premature baby, cut like he was trying not to hit a vital organ. Scamz made a slit and dug his hands inside, like a doctor being careful as he removed a baby. Hands covered in goo that looked like coagulated blood and afterbirth, he pulled out a small black case, one that was no larger than a hardback book. It was thin. Its height, width, and depth was less than two inches by seven inches by nine inches. Scamz used the edge of his hand to move more of the goo, then found the edge of the case, ripped a plastic covering away. The case was bright red. Looked like a mini laptop. It had a green flashing light on top and a red digital readout. That had to be the sensor and GPS.

I didn't understand what it was or how it worked. And I didn't care.

Most of the spilled blood was from inside the faux pregnancy. It had been a work of art. Detached, it still looked real. Had been designed for a con woman by someone who knew their craft. It had weight and texture to match her flesh and was insulated with bloodlike fluids.

Arizona rolled away, was on her side.

I was five feet away, and she was almost unrecognizable. She still looked like she had been flogged and thrown into the center of an earthquake.

The pregnancy was fake, but her injures were real. The rest of the damage to her was real. Scamz took the package and got out of the way, and I moved closer to Arizona. I looked her over. She was in bad shape, still shifted and made faces like she was in labor, but none of her wounds was life threatening.

Konstantin said, "Her stomach saved her from being crushed."

I held her hand.

The woman who had earned the moniker Queen Scamz.

A seasoned con woman who always worked a grift from an unexpected angle.

One of the packages had been attached to her body all along.

While Scamz worked at a frantic pace, I leaned down beside Arizona.

She said, "You . . . look . . . bad."

"You don't look too good yourself."

"I'm embarrassed."

"You don't have to be."

"I messed . . . on myself."

It was hard to look at her face. Damn hard. Was hard to not feel uncontrollable rage.

I asked, "Where is your brother?"

It took her a moment, but she managed to whisper, "He's . . . gone. They . . . killed him."

"Shit. I'm sorry."

"His body. It's in . . . in . . . the car."

I cursed, then I swallowed. "Sierra?"

Arizona trembled, closed her eyes, gritted her teeth like she was being attacked by a wave of pain. She struggled to breathe. Like she was fighting some form of PTSD.

She was in a bed of sticky fluids that had been released when her stomach was removed and cut open. It mixed with her piss and bowel movement.

I was about to pick her up, wanted to carry her to the bathroom, clean her up.

But Shotgun called out, "We got some company. A whole lot of company."

I hurried to the window. Four vehicles had stopped outside between this building and the strip of businesses and apartments across the street. They were getting out of cars right in front of Thelonious Monk jazz club.

Konstantin was at the window too. The Russian said, "Looks like Germans. Albanians. French. And it looks like they're doing something unexpected. They're working together."

I cursed.

Shotgun said, "We're almost outta ammo."

Konstantin cursed.

The package had been delivered. We could walk away.

That was the professional thing to do.

I would love to leave bitch-ass Scamz to fend for himself.

Would love to watch a con man fight to survive in the land of assassins.

Would love for him to die here, a few hours from the End of the World.

Then I looked at Arizona.

She'd never make it out of here alive. This building would be her tomb.

I snapped, "We need to move from here."

Scamz snapped back, "We've invested a year in this bloody project."

"It's time to walk away."

"We have lost millions of dollars."

"Leave it all. We can get away if we leave now."

He snapped like he was about to go insane. "Just let me do what I'm doing. Arizona, tell me what to do. This bloody thing was set up without a bloody instruction book."

He didn't have a clue what to do next.

Eyes closed, mouth bloodied, lips puffed and split, Arizona coughed, struggled to get her breathing to even out. "Look for . . . pop-out connector . . . on both packages."

"Then what?"

"I told you . . . connect them . . . daisy chain. Small package . . . is the brains. It's a computer. Connect them . . . then . . . it pops open."

"Then what?"

"Connect to computer. Hit CONTROL, ESCAPE, and F2. Special program . . . embedded . . . that activates firmware . . . will run on its own. Wireless card . . . make sure it's connected."

She panted, cursed in Tagalog, then told Scamz that he had to log on to a site used to bounce the Internet signal and make it hard to trace, then the laptops would communicate through firmware and use Web sites that, once activated, would only be good for ten minutes.

She said, "Pray we . . . have . . . signal. Pray . . . it works."

I asked, "How long will that take?"

"After setup . . . program runs . . . takes . . . five . . . minutes."

That was forever.

I told Shotgun and Konstantin to leave, told them to take the stairs, get to the streets.

They refused to leave without me. And I refused to leave without Arizona.

And I couldn't carry Arizona. Wasn't sure her body could take being carried.

We were trapped.

The sidewalks remained crowded.

The jazz played louder, with unbridled enthusiasm.

I counted fifteen men I hadn't seen before. Fifteen healthy, well-armed men who had weapons hidden underneath their coats. Well-rested and fresh men with serious faces.

At least three held trackers.

The three men with the trackers moved up and down the street.

They eliminated the jazz club. Then they eliminated that side of the street.

They all turned and faced the apartments on this side.

All fifteen looked this way.

My body couldn't handle another fight. Konstantin's expression said he was in the same condition. We didn't have what it took to be in another brute-force, no-holds-barred shoot-out.

As assassins stood on a crowded street and had no idea what was going on, their three leaders nodded.

Scamz sweated and cursed, his British accent grating on my nerves.

Debris fell from his soaking-wet frame as he struggled with both packages.

Nine men came toward this building.

They left six outside, one holding a sensor.

Smart move.

If we managed to exit the building, we would do so under a hail of gunfire.

One of them moved a car and blocked the exit of the building.

That meant we would have to leave on foot.

Across the street, the band began playing a Lionel Richie song.

The one about dancing on a goddamn ceiling.

The last song all of us might ever hear on a cold night in South America.

Shotgun made sure his weapon was loaded.

Konstantin did his best to hold a gun.

I clenched my teeth and readied myself as best I could.

But no matter how a man prepared, he was never ready for Death.

Scamz remained frantic as Arizona continued her suffering, doing her best to give Scamz instructions, instructions that she had no doubt kept to herself. There wasn't as much trust on that team as I had assumed. Arizona told him the parts had to be there. Scamz flipped the packages around, searched like a madman. The smaller package that had been inside Arizona had a pop-out connecter made for a USB port, a well-hidden pop-out connector that blended into the case like a secret room. It was a male connector that fit into a female connector on the larger black briefcase, the one we had taken from the *villa*. That connector was easier to find. Then there was a third connection that went to the laptop. That cable was already attached to the laptop.

That cable ran back to the smaller package.

Scamz struggled, rushed, and daisy-chained them together.

Arizona told him passwords.

There were three levels of goddamn passwords.

The first two were phrases in Latin.

The first was *Faber est suae quisque fortunae.*

Konstantin whispered what that meant. "Every man is the artisan of his own fortune."

The second was *Audaces fortuna iuvat.*

I whispered, "Fortune favors the bold."

But it was the third password that made Scamz pause.

The final password was Gideon.

Scamz paused. "Gideon."

Arizona repeated my name. Told him to type in Gideon.

It was as if she had moaned my name while they were in the throes of passion.

His pause didn't last long. Not as long as my muted surprise.

Scamz played the piano like he was a pro, but his typing was shit.

I stood near the door. Shoes moved like marching ants. I heard them.

I guessed this was what it felt like to be on death row. About to walk that green mile.

Shotgun's heart beat like the drums across the street.

I said, "How are you liking South America?"

He nodded. "At least I got to see winter in the summertime. Got to see a few pretty women. Even the ugly women down here are pretty. Seeing them was worth the trip."

I smiled at my buddy.

Then I nodded at Konstantin.

He said, "Always thought it would be the cancer that took me off my feet."

I said, "You have your white shoes back on."

"Of course. Put them on in the car."

He smiled. I did the same.

I glanced back at Arizona.

She wallowed in fluids, was as helpless as a newborn child.

Arizona made another painful sound, then said, "Gun."

I shook my head.

Sweat ran down her swollen face. She grimaced said, "Give me . . . a goddamn gun."

I handed her a nine, the one that Scamz had brought in with him and pointed at me.

Arizona raised up on her elbow, positioned herself the best she could.

For a moment she looked like the innocent girl I had met in North Hollywood. I imagined that would be my last time looking at her, my last vision of her would be with her face like that.

Not that my damaged mug looked any better.

The look on her face said that before she died, she'd take at least one with her.

Through my undamaged eye, grating my teeth, I frowned at Scamz. I watched him sweat, struggle, and race to complete a task Arizona would have mastered in seconds.

My life was in his hands. Once again he controlled the plastic bag over my head.

Eighteen footsteps came down the opposite end of the hallway.

They were like tigers moving through the bush and approaching their prey.

Wounded prey, thin on ammunition, guns in hands with broken claws.

The slow footsteps of nine heavily armed men sounded like a cavalry.

Nine guns that would explode like a civil war.

Capítulo 46

la próxima guerra

Medianoche thought he heard gunfire in the distance.

He sat in an armless chair, lights off, facing his bedroom window.

Alone.

Naked.

Angry.

He held a gun in each bandaged hand. Had his knees wrapped and packed in ice.

His feet were flat against the wooden floor, toes flexing and releasing like a boxer's fists.

The sensor was in front of him.

No green or yellow or red light. Not one iota of illumination.

He stared, waiting for a blip.

Anything. A faint light. Anything that signaled there was a pulse.

But there was nothing.

Nothing.

It had flatlined.

Medianoche sat motionless in his darkened apartment on the seventeenth floor.

Eighteen floors above Buenos Aires, a vertical city that never went to bed.

An empty queen-sized bed was behind him.

The scents of four women fading from his sullied sheets.

Fading like the light had faded not too long ago.

Body in pain, a throbbing pain that he ignored, his mind on other things.

He moved his tongue around his inflamed mouth, still tasted blood.

He tried to figure it out. The signal had been there. The goddamn signal had been there. It was strong when the pregnant woman named Arizona stood before them at the monument.

The Four Horsemen had defeated those also-rans and had obtained the package.

They had the portal to hundreds of millions of U.S. dollars.

Maybe a billion.

Even the best-laid plans of mice and men often go awry.

When they returned to the stolen van on that ragged road on the outskirts of the shantytown, when their grueling run had ended near Avenida Gendarmería Nacional, as they stood in the rain, battered with the stench of a foul war dripping from their clothing and clinging to their skin, as they looked like they had crawled through trenches lined with the inner lining of a South American nightmare, The Beast had frowned and held up the sensor.

He was outside the van, armed, fuming, drooling, distressed.

He had stood up, crawled out of the van, weapon in hand, in severe pain, his face telling that it hurt like hell to breathe, blood seeping from his wound, down his leg, into his right shoe.

The Beast was able to stand but unable to run, and barely able to take two steps.

That blade had barely missed The Beast's spine. Had just missed major arteries.

The package was behind The Beast, on its side, next to Draco's dead body, sitting in the dead soldier's blood. The Beast had been left guarding the package.

Russians. Slavs. Germans. Serbs. More Jamaicans.

They all had trackers. Soon well-armed hostiles were expected to rear their ugly heads.

But no hostiles had come in search of the key to the pot of gold.

That should have been the first clue.

When they had made it to the van, The Beast growled that the goddamn signal was no longer green. The goddamn signal had gone yellow. Like the package was moving away.

Impossible.

Fucking impossible.

Medianoche had picked up the briefcase. Shook it like something might be loose.

Then the impossible gave way to what was possible.

Señorita Raven stood at his side and screamed into the rain.

The briefcase they had obtained was a phony. Rigged to look like the second package.

Medianoche refused to believe it was over. Not when he knew the war was only beginning. But the signal. The way it had reacted to the package when they were at the foot of the monument. When they were at the monument, the signal was strong and bright as high noon.

Medianoche nodded.

He replayed the firefight at the monument in his mind. The same conclusion each time.

The fucking signal had been strong.

When Arizona stood in his face, briefcase in hand, the signal was strong.

Before they had left those tangos dead and dying in the middle of beautiful explosions at the base of General Justo José de Urquiza, the signal had declared them as being victorious.

At the monument.

The beeps were accurate, had sounded the bull's-eye tone when Arizona had stood inches away with the package. When the briefcase was in front of then, the goddamn sensor responded, had sung that the battle had ended and the war had been won.

The victory had been as false as the one the second President Bush declared when he landed on the aircraft carrier *Abraham Lincoln* and said the war with Iraq was over.

Back when that war had barely begun.

Victory was a fluid, misused word. It took many victories to win any war.

Medianoche ran ice across his swollen face. Rubbed his aching temples.

Then he cursed and spat against the white wall. His mouth hurt. He cursed again. And again. Knocked a clock and lamp off his nightstand. Threw books. Broke pictures.

Scamz hadn't been a man, hadn't stepped into the line of fire and brought the package.

Nor had the other man, the sonofabitch who looked like Cary Grant.

Or the other young woman, the other slant-eyed Asian they had gunned down.

Arizona had wobbled from the wreckage, came into the freezing rain, and offered up the package. The safe one. The pregnant one. The one they thought they wouldn't put down.

The one who played with knives.

He played it again and again. Eliminated everything extra. Erased the impossible.

The package had to be within two feet to yield that response from the sensor.

Two feet. Twenty-four inches.

In his mind, Medianoche saw Arizona, standing at arm's length, briefcase in hand.

But the signal said that it was all a lie. The sensor wasn't faulty. It had been verified.

When a man eliminated what was impossible, what was left was the truth.

He followed irrefutable logic and removed the briefcase from the equation.

The only thing left within two feet was the pregnant woman.

Medianoche nodded again.

He whispered a quotation by Sun Tzu, "All warfare is based on deception."

There was our perception of reality. And then there was reality.

There was what we thought was true. And then there was the truth.

Arizona. Smart bitch. Slick bitch. Had to be a dead bitch.

After they sped away from the slums, they'd fought traffic, driven back to the roundabout. They went back to the base of General Justo José de Urquiza, returned to see if the package had been buried underneath the destruction they had left behind. Then they had picked up the signal and raced toward Avenida Santa Fe, sped into Barrio Norte. Then the signal vanished.

Now he stared at the goddamn sensor the same way he had stared at it then.

When it had gone dark.

It remained as dark as the hole in his head, that cavern where an eye used to be.

Before North Carolina. Before that snot-nosed Guacho.

Before Gideon. Before that sonofawhore. Son of a dead whore.

Medianoche dressed. Put in his glass eye. Put on another Colombian-made suit.

He grabbed another fedora, then put the useless sensor inside his coat pocket.

He opened his small container, put white powder on his fingertip, sniffed.

He loaded both of his nine millimeters. He put on his black gloves.

He was going to see The Beast.

Capítulo 47

engaño

The Beast.

The man with plenary power over The Four Horsemen.

He was dressed in a long white robe made of cotton with golden stitching.

A glass of scotch in one hand. Cuban cigar in the other.

Lips tight. Face so tense his eyebrows almost touched.

His face was painted with disappointment as pain emanated from his lower back.

Medianoche watched him as he moved slowly. The Beast cursed, said that he didn't want to move at all, but he had to go to the bathroom. Had to get cleaned up. Had to shower.

Medianoche sat at the dining table. A *Buenos Aires Herald* was on the table. Turned to the front page. Brazil's president blamed white people with blue eyes for the world economic crisis and said it was wrong that developing countries should pay for mistakes made in richer countries.

Medianoche put both guns down, business end pointed away.

He faced The Beast. The man who had come to North Carolina to rescue him.

The sensor rested between them.

Medianoche said, "Time to talk."

The Beast sipped his scotch. "I picked up chatter. At least three fucking teams showed up since the battle at the *villas*. Three different organizations. All with guns. All with sensors."

"Not that. No need to talk about that. Not now. Something else."

"At this point, what is there?"

"North Carolina."

"That."

"That."

The Beast nodded. "What do you remember?"

"It's doesn't fucking matter what I *remember*. It's about what you *know*."

The Beast sipped his scotch. "Here as a friend or as a foe?"

"I've never been your foe. And, hopefully, you've never been mine."

The Beast puffed his Cuban cigar. "We're running on fumes. Battle weary."

Medianoche said, "And we should close this out now."

The Beast took his time, puffed his cigar again. "This is about Gideon."

"This feels bigger than that."

"First you see a young woman that reminds you of Thelma. That stirs you up in La Boca." The Beast nodded. "Then this Gideon thing. Said he was your kid."

"He can say whatever he wants. He's not mine."

The Beast shrugged. "I wouldn't care one way or the other. An enemy is an enemy."

"No one cares about the son of a whore. Not even a whore."

"Señorita Raven said he was convinced he was your kid."

Medianoche said, "From the mouth of a manipulative bitch. She said I raped her."

The Beast puffed his cigar again. "Liar."

"Damn good liar. The shrapnel-faced slag almost convinced me, and I know the truth."

"You fucked her."

"I fucked her."

The Beast smiled. "That Indian pussy any good?"

"Not like it was brand-new."

"You fucked her, then wanted to put her six feet under."

"Enemies closer. That's what you told me. I followed orders."

"You've always been a good soldier."

A moment went by. The wind whistled against the window.

Cold outside. Warm inside The Beast's apartment.

Almost as warm as the islands.

The Beast sipped his scotch.

Medianoche watched him and nodded. "My father."

"What about that loser?"

"Smelling your scotch brought back a few memories. He crossed my mind right now. That strict, pious, alcoholic, abusive, crazy sonofabitch, war veteran was a cockhound."

The Beast nodded. "Like father, like son."

Medianoche said, "Your mother took me and my old man in after that flood back in sixty-three."

"My mother loved your old man. No matter how he treated her."

"Your mother hated me. She beat me every chance she got."

The Beast said, "Your old man was equally abusive."

"He was a piece of work."

"My crazy mother and your alcoholic father."

"Match made in Hell. Couldn't wait to get old enough to join the military."

The Beast said, "You followed me into service."

"I followed you. Went to serve my country, as every man should."

That was something that was not in the files.

They weren't brothers. But had been closer than siblings.

Medianoche tapped the wooden table for emphasis and said, "Montego Bay."

"Back to that."

"What do you remember? No. What did I forget, tell me that."

"Thelma."

"Thelma and anything else I need to know."

"We both had Thelma. In Montego Bay, we had her and other women, but we had her the most. We drank and smoked. Sometimes we tag-teamed. Sometimes we had her at the same time. She did it all. Some days you went there, had her to yourself."

"I take it you did the same."

The Beast said, "She was good. To be so young, she was good."

Medianoche nodded. "So we both had her."

The Beast nodded.

Medianoche looked at his wrapped hands, licked the inside of his mouth and tasted blood, felt the ache in his kidneys and ribs, then glanced at his guns.

The Beast said, "You took me to dozens of whorehouses."

"As therapy."

"Wasn't my thing. But it was yours."

Medianoche said, "For your problem."

"But you had the bigger problem. The way you loved the whores."

"I enjoy women. The military didn't find anything dishonorable about that."

The Beast leaned back, made a face that said he'd had a surge of pain.

Either that or Medianoche's words had hit him deep.

The Beast recovered and said, "You loved whores."

"Never loved a whore. Never would. I loved the women I married."

"Your wife in Montserrat almost got you to retire and live the boring island life."

"Loved her. Most of all. And all for naught."

"I loved my wife. And in the end, love is a currency that loses its value, like the peso." The Beast shook his head. "But marriage never stopped a man from exercising his vices."

"Or his demons."

"But not like you, Medianoche. You went through women like they were . . . whores."

"Not with my third wife."

The Beast said, "Gracelyn."

"Yeah. Gracelyn. I could be with a thousand whores, and not one could move me like one kiss from Gracelyn. She could kiss all night long. I'd never liked kissing, but I loved kissing Gracelyn. I was going to go back. Was going to say fuck it and go back to Montserrat."

"What happened?"

"You called. The man who had saved my life called."

"There was more work for The Four Horsemen."

"And like a good soldier, I answered the call. Never went back to Montserrat."

"Might not be too late."

"It's too late. Way too late for that."

Medianoche looked around the pristine apartment.

He said, "Draco."

"He was loyal and honorable. Will be missed."

Medianoche nodded, opened and closed his hands. "His body?"

The Beast said, "I'll handle the disposal of his remains."

Medianoche licked his swollen lips. "I left three beautiful Latin women in Rodríguez's apartment."

"They're still there?"

"They're in the soldier's apartment. I heard them laughing."

The Beast nodded. "They're waiting for him to come back."

"Or the next customer. Looks like you're going to need some assistance."

"Back hurts so bad it's impossible to bend over and wipe my ass."

"You'll be incapacitated a few days."

"With this injury, yeah. Will be difficult to walk around. With Draco gone, until I can find a replacement, I'll have to clean up and prepare my own meals."

"The three whores could do all of that for you. Plus other things, if you needed."

"Send them over. I will need nurses."

"Like I needed a nurse in North Carolina."

"Back to that again."

Medianoche paused. "Tell me what I don't remember."

The Beast took in air. He sipped his scotch.

Medianoche said, "You were outside. When I was shot, you were there."

The Beast nodded. Then he puffed his Cuban cigar.

A moment passed before Medianoche said, "You lied."

"I invoked creativity in a situation where creativity was needed."

Medianoche repeated, "You lied."

"The hospital. The police. You were in a coma long enough for the heat to die down. There would have been too many questions. I gave you information on a need-to-know basis."

"Like the government."

The Beast nodded. "Like the government."

"The biggest liars of them all."

"I've always looked out for your best interests."

Medianoche said, "You told me that you were in another country when that happened."

"I said that I was in another country when you came out of your coma."

"You lied by omission. So, in other words, when it happened, you were there."

"Memory returns."

"Some. Only the edges."

"I see. What sparked it?"

"Doesn't matter."

The Beast said, "She threatened us."

"Why?"

"Margaret. Do you remember her?"

"I know that name. It's in my mind. But means nothing."

"She was Thelma's friend. A Slav who was working the red-light areas in America."

"What about her?"

"You found her in a small shit town in Alabama. You left her body in a Dumpster."

"Why did I go to a small shit town in Alabama and hunt her down?"

"She tried to blackmail you. She knew about a few jobs you had done. You were with her and Thelma. Same time. They worked as a team for a while. You had gotten comfortable. Said too much. You killed Margaret, then you went back to take care of Thelma."

"Then what happened?"

"Thelma was gone. It took a few years, but you eventually found that she was in Charlotte. You found her and had me go to North Carolina with you."

"Enough."

The Beast nodded.

Medianoche said, "Your story has holes in it."

The Beast sipped his scotch. "I suggest you leave that part of your past alone."

Medianoche put his hand on his loaded guns.

He asked, "Señorita Raven?"

"In her room."

"She suspect anything?"

"Nothing at all."

The Beast went into his bedroom. When the door opened, Medianoche saw Draco's corpse was on the bed, laid out in a military uniform, an American flag across his body.

The bedroom door closed.

When it opened again, The Beast was dressed in a Colombian-made suit. He held the wall to keep his balance, his jaw tight and brows furrowed with an agony he denied.

Medianoche said, "I can do this on my own."

The Beast straightened up as best he could. "We eliminate the extras together."

Medianoche nodded.

The Beast took a breath. "The signal?"

"Still dead. Not coming back to life."

"Then that means one of the teams that arrived has obtained the real package."

"Both packages."

"My guess is they killed whoever was left alive on Scamz's team."

"And obtained both goddamn packages."

"Game over."

Medianoche thought about Arizona being within arm's length.

They had played with their perceptions. They had corrupted reality. Like magicians.

Medianoche went to the window, opened it, dropped the sensor, let it fall eighteen floors.

Outside, the dark skies were turning gray. The rain had started again.

Medianoche said, "We still have other jobs we need to wrap up."

The Beast sipped the last of his scotch, nodded. "Señorita Raven is of no use to us now."

"She never was."

"Let's make this quick. I'm on pain pills and scotch."

"Then let's get moving."

Locked and loaded, they went toward Señorita Raven's apartment.

The Beast led the way to the event that would end in the death of another Horseman. His steps were slow and painful. He held his gun in his right hand, slightly behind him. Medianoche stayed a step behind. Stayed to The Beast's right side.

The Beast's right-hand man.

The Beast's lapdog. That was what Señorita Raven had called him.

A fucking lapdog.

They stood in front of Señorita Raven's door. They listened for a moment.

They wouldn't kick the door in.

They wouldn't use stun and flash as they closed in for the kill.

There was a friendly knock.

The Beast called out, "Señorita Raven."

"Yes, sir."

"Open up. I'm coming to check on you before we leave for Alemán Hospital."

"Everything okay, sir?"

"Medianoche insists I should have my injury looked at."

The door opened and Señorita Raven stood there, weary, face scarred, eyes bloodshot.

Amaravati Panchali Ganeshes.

Face filled with shrapnel. She had eyes that took Medianoche back to another country.

She was a damaged woman. She was damaged art.

From every angle, she looked like Madhuri Shankar Dixit with shrapnel peppering her once-beautiful face. Thick eyebrows that stood over brown eyes like caterpillars.

The arrogant soldier was barefoot and had on skinny jeans that hugged her figure in a way that was obscene. She had a yellow-and-blue sweater, tight over her full breasts, and her Ono Moda watch. Medianoche took in everything she wore in a heartbeat, for a reason.

She didn't have on any Colombian-made gear. She wasn't bulletproof.

As rain fell and the temperature dropped toward freezing, she didn't expect anything.

All edges and angles and an attitude that was as sharp as a razor.

As sharp as the razor she had used to cut her wrists during her attempt to check out.

But Medianoche saw past what that lying slag allowed to show. Battle exhaustion had the best of her. She was shell-shocked and fatigued, avoiding sleep to delay nightmares.

He felt the same way.

The Beast led the way into Señorita Raven's apartment.

The Punjabi bitch took a few steps back. Not too close, still point-blank.

Medianoche noticed that there were no wisecracks about his missing eye.

No feministic insults or penis-envious macho posturing.

She pulled her lips in, so much anger in her body language as she asked, "No signal?"

No one answered. The question had sounded more rhetorical than desperate.

The Beast looked at the bullet holes in the wall. At the disarray that had gone untouched.

Her expensive tango shoes were on her floor. So was her come-stained dress.

He looked at Señorita Raven, anger and disgust bubbling beneath his tight lips.

She frowned at him, a look of disdain and hate on her marked face.

The Beast said, "It's been a long, trying day."

"Yes, sir."

"We'll make this quick, soldier."

"Yes, sir."

The Beast raised his silenced gun and aimed at Señorita Raven.

Her eyes widened with surprise.

Just as every other nonessential Horseman had done in the end.

Medianoche raised his gun, raised his faster than The Beast had raised his.

That back injury had slowed The Beast down.

Medianoche fired first.

He fired the same way the snot-nose kid had fired at him.

Medianoche's shot sent brain matter flying against stark white walls.

Chapter 48

the long con

We remained secreted across from the Thelonious Monk club.

It was close to seven in the morning. The club was winding down.

Buses. Taxis. Hundreds of people filed out into the damp and cold streets.

The jazz had died. But we were alive.

Trapped inside a small apartment. Sweating. Hearts beating loud and strong.

The packages had been connected. And once connected, the signal died.

That transmission had stopped with nine assassins standing right outside our door.

Had died as we kept our weapons aimed at the door.

Had died and left the three team members who had the sensors baffled.

The nine assassins had done an about-face and raced down the hall-way. We heard them outside the door, walking from apartment door to apartment door, confused, their chatter in three languages. They called their leaders and told them there was no signal, then asked for instructions. Minutes later, they had bolted down the stairway, exited the building, and reconvened outside the club. The three men with three sensors came together.

The leaders had a meeting. Like they were three wise men.

They looked at each other, cursed, looked at the buildings.

There was no signal. Three sensors had gone dead at the same moment.

Four, if the Horsemen were out there somewhere.

Downstairs, frustrations mounted. Looked like they were accusing each other of treachery. Each team looked like they thought they had been double-crossed.

It looked like they were about to start gunning each other down.

We remained in the window. We remained locked and loaded.

It wasn't over.

We were still trapped in Buenos Aires. Anything could happen.

Behind us, Arizona remained in agony.

What they had, they wanted so bad they were willing to skip immediate medical attention.

But having three international teams outside was too risky.

The three teams of assassins separated, moved back to their fleet of cars.

The signal was supposed to be as dead as a ghost, but they weren't leaving, and I didn't know why.

Arizona moaned, said the signal wasn't supposed to get reactivated.

The way that it was set up, once the money began transferring, the signal ceased.

Konstantin asked her if she was 100 percent sure.

She wasn't. Her information had come from Hopkins. A man who had conned her.

We stayed in the windows, peeping down at the streets while the assassins made phone calls and waited for the signal to reappear.

Jazz remained loud throughout the night. Each beautiful note striking a tender nerve.

Three hours later, the assassins got back inside their cars.

Ten minutes after that, they left the street. They circled the block at least a dozen times.

I wouldn't be surprised if they had left representatives lurking in the shadows.

The room we were in had become a cave. A cave that stank to high heaven.

Shotgun still had sewage on his clothes and shoes, from the run through the *villa*. And my shit-smelling clothes were in the bathroom.

The stench covered us. Suffocated us.

An hour passed before Konstantin took the keys to the Peugeot and left too.

Konstantin wouldn't stand out like me. Or Shotgun.

We needed food, water, medical supplies, and toilet paper.

An hour after that, I went to Scamz. He was with Arizona. He had taken her to the bathroom. Her leg was messed up, bruised. Face swollen like she had had too much plastic surgery. He closed the door and cleaned her up with what was in the cabinets.

While he did that, I took the soiled sheets off the bed, flipped the mattress, then found more sheets and made the bed as best I could. Was hard to do with swollen hands.

I said, "Everything was accomplished."

Scamz said, "We bloody failed."

"How did you fail?"

"It's not as much money as we thought would be there."

"Not our problem."

He was angry. "Hopkins fucked us over."

I dug inside my pocket and took out the Rolex I'd bought in Puerto Rico.

The Rolex had cost twenty thousand dollars.

A Patek Philippe Sky Moon Tourbillon cost one point five million. A Vacheron Constantin Tour de I'lle cost about two point five. A Hublot Black Caviar Bang was one million and a Louis Moinet Magistralis or a Blancpain 1735 cost about one hundred to two hundred thousand dollars less. A Girard-Perregaux Opera Three cost three hundred thousand.

Compared with those watches, a Rolex didn't get honorable mention. By those standards, a Rolex wasn't an expensive watch, it was a common watch. Not the priciest in the world.

Low-class, opportunistic, undereducated rappers wore them. That said a lot right there.

The Rolex had been in my pocket while I battled my way out of the *villa*.

I looked at a twenty-thousand-dollar cliché.

Then I looked at Scamz. He was nothing more than a cliché.

I said, "Maybe this will offset some of your expenses."

I tossed him the Rolex.

He caught the watch, looked at it, then tossed it back.

He had been insulted.

I smiled.

He wiped his hands on his torn clothing.

I said, "Just make sure our funds are transferred, Scamzito. Make sure we get paid."

Scamz maintained eye contact.

My face swollen, one eye black-and-blue, I did the same.

I said, "Problem, Scamzito?"

That was Spanish for Little Scamz.

My insult got to him. He made fists like he was ready to run at me.

We stopped bulldogging when there was a tap at the door.

Konstantin had returned with a dozen bags.

Three of those bags were filled with fruit, water, croissants, and *medialunas*.

Everything we needed plus fresh clothes.

The clothes were ill fitting and modest. But they were clean.

Shotgun left with me.

We loaded up our guns, mixed with the pedestrians, and flagged down a Radio Taxi.

Our next stop was Village Recoleta. Had to get there before the day was crowded.

I was early and walked the block carrying an umbrella. I took in the area before I waited outside Cúspide Libros, a swank bookstore sitting between a two-level McDonald's and Cine Recoleta, their high-end movie theater. Nine millimeter resting in my waistband, I took in the crowd congregated near the Sahara Restaurant and Café. I expected Medianoche to reappear. Then I checked out the people walking along the back wall of the Recoleta Cemetery. I looked up. The tops of the mausoleums stood higher than the twelve-foot-tall brick wall. The architecture was astounding, so staring up there wouldn't draw any attention. I was looking for a shooter. That wall was high enough to give a sniper the perfect advantage.

I didn't trust anyone who wasn't on my team.

Shotgun was down on the corner of Presidente José E. Uriburu and Vicente Lopez, sitting on a metal bench in front of Locos Por El Fútbol, a sports bar that had at least twenty flat-screens facing the streets. He sat down so he wouldn't look so large in the land of little people.

A thin middle-aged man in jeans and a beige coat walked up to me. He said, "Gideon?"

I nodded. "*Soy Gideon.*"

He looked me up and down and handed me a set of keys.

I said, "*¿Vos sos el medico?*"

He nodded. "Yes, I'm the doctor. I speak English. I lived in New York for ten years."

I said, "How are things?"

"Everything will be okay until you can get the proper care."

"Do you have time to see Arizona?"

He shook his head. "I am scheduled for surgery. Many surgeries."

I had a feeling that those surgeries were due to the destruction that had been laid on Buenos Aires over the past forty-eight hours. More than Arizona's brother had died.

Many more. And I had no idea how many more were injured.

I nodded, then handed him a roll of U.S. dollars. All hundred-dollar bills.

He told me where to go to retrieve the final package.

He said, "Tell Scamz to follow my instructions. I left them written in the vehicle. And there are two boxes that have antibiotics, antiseptics, morphine, a leg splint, and bandages. If any one of you needs stitches, that is included too. Just sew the injury like you're sewing clothes."

Then he pulled up his gloves, opened his umbrella, and walked away.

He turned right at McDonald's, waved down a Radio Taxi, and vanished.

I headed past Monaco Café. Shotgun joined me as I passed the fountains. We hurried by Pagana Disco Bar, Porte Zuelo wine bar, crossed Azcuénaga, and hurried past more bars and a museum. Down near the corner, in front of a fruit store and flower stand, was where the doctor had left a small white van. He had parked next to the curb and walked two blocks to meet me.

We hurried and got inside the van.

Shotgun said, "That woman in the crowd looked just like Catherine."

"Where?"

"She's gone now. She was crossing the street with some more people."

I looked back at the cargo. She was on a makeshift bed with an IV in her arm.

Her face was swollen. Left arm broken. Bullets removed. Her body stitched up.

It was Sierra. Her hair was matted. Her lips dry and chapped. Her face was battered and bruised, lips and cheeks swollen like her sister's. Her gunshot wounds had been treated, her body given the proper care. She was in no shape to get on an airplane.

She'd almost died.

She looked at me, wordless. Emotionless. As cold as the world she had grown up in. She was drugged up. And shivering. She needed more blankets. And we didn't have any.

Her world had to be like being under water, water filled with ice cubes.

I said, "Your brother is dead. But Arizona is okay."

I don't know why I said that. Felt like I had to say something.

Even though she had never spoken a word to me, I had to say something.

I wanted to ask those fuckers if this shit was worth it.

Sierra shivered. Her teeth chattered, and she stared at me the same way she had stared at me in Amsterdam. I was the man who had been sent to Holland to kill her, once upon a time.

Now I was the man who had been sent to Recoleta to save her.

She closed her eyes. Tears fell. Wasn't sure if those were tears of pain or grief.

We met Konstantin in Puerto Madero on Calle Victoria Ocampo. We bundled up, moved through air that felt like ice, and boarded a private yacht at the Puerto Madero Yacht Club. No sign of trouble. But it was too soon to relax. We were out in the open, just outside the Reserva Ecológica. Scamz and Arizona had already been loaded. Once again, we needed Shotgun's power to help carry Sierra and her makeshift bed, to get her loaded onto the yacht. Then we went back to the Peugeot. We opened the trunk and looked down at a dead man.

We carried that dead man onto the yacht, put him in the same section with his wounded sisters. Arizona cried. Her expression told me that this had cost more than she had expected.

I went up top. We were where the waters from the Atlantic Ocean flooded the cul-de-sac between Argentina and Uruguay and created Río de la Plata.

After that, we took to the brown waters that divided the two countries.

It was a one-hundred-and-thirty-mile journey across water as brown as the Mississippi River. An ugly ride that had Shotgun on deck with his head hanging over the railing.

But we made it to Uruguay and docked at a pier in Colonia del Sacramento. Two men were waiting on us. Both doctors. The men hurried on board. One for each woman.

I tended to my team, looked at Konstantin's wounded arm, at Shotgun's injuries.

We patched each other up, closed up stitches, cleaned up our mess.

I climbed off the yacht, had to get my feet on solid ground.

I felt nauseated. My head ached. I was dehydrated.

Konstantin came down and stood next to me, his left arm in a sling.

Shotgun left the yacht, stood in the crisp air next to Konstantin.

Shotgun asked, "We done or we got more work to do in this country too?"

Konstantin said, "We're done."

Shotgun looked around at the winding cobble streets and the stucco homes and buildings. There were large hostels, churches, restaurants, military cannons, lighthouses, and parks in the distance.

He asked, "Where are we now?"

"Colonia del Sacramento, Uruguay. This used to be a smuggler's city."

Shotgun asked, "We safe now?"

Konstantin shook his head. "Once you get into this business, you're never safe."

Shotgun nodded. "Kinda figured that."

I took a deep breath.

Konstantin said, "We're at the old port. We can catch a bus about two miles from here. Buses run every hour until about ten tonight, and it's a three-hour ride to get into Montevideo. We could get some rest in another safe house, but I'd suggest we keep moving and rest on the bus. The passports we have already have visas, so we might be able to catch a small plane into Brazil. From there we either connect through São Paulo or fly directly back into the States."

Shotgun asked, "How long will that take?"

"At least twenty-four hours."

"Was a lot quicker getting down here than going back."

I took out my iPhone. Wanted to pull up the cameras in Powder Springs.

There was no signal. That meant I couldn't call them right now.

Catherine and I would have to talk about Medianoche, the man she knew as Midnight.

If she knew he was alive, she'd need to come clean.

If she didn't know, she needed to be warned.

Konstantin asked, "You want to go back on board and say good-bye to Arizona?"

A few cold raindrops splattered against my wounded face as I looked back at the yacht.

Scamz was on deck, dressed in dark colors and a darker coat, looking down at us.

I'd gone to the End of the World and put his grandfather and uncle into the ground.

One day he might end up on my hit list. One day some sponsor might ring my phone because they had a contract on him. That day would be like Christmas morning.

I was my own man. I had my own name.

And I didn't need to go back and look down on his woman.

I shook my head and told Konstantin I didn't need to go say good-bye.

The nights I'd had with Arizona, she'd always left before sunrise.

She'd never said good-bye before she left me. Not even a kiss.

Arizona was with the man she had chosen in the end.

I'd been with her twice. He'd been with her the past year.

And a few hours ago, I'd said some harsh things. Things that couldn't be unsaid.

So the ugly truth had been told, and every word had fallen on Arizona's ears.

That was unprofessional. This was business.

She had already given me the information I needed.

I'd kept my promise to Scamz.

I was done.

Arizona had come up short on the con.

She had that problem, a dead brother at her side, and a wounded sister to worry about.

I needed to lead my team back home. That was my responsibility.

Three hired guns walked down the docks, all three of us limping in some way. We made our way through a laid-back city that had old street lanterns and cobblestone streets, some of the walls covered with beautiful flowers. The old cars made it seem like we had gone back in time. We passed women working at Whiskerías and Casas de Masajes, saw a few people smoking pot.

We moved deeper into an old city that was a mixture of Spanish and Portuguese.

There were old cannons, but there was no gunfire mixed with the rain that had begun to fall.

I'd jumped out of moving trains, fallen from buildings, been shot at with grenades.

Had battled the low-life scum of a man who might've had a hand in creating me.

My body felt it all. The waves of pain were unending.

Agony must've shown on my face, because Shotgun dug in his pocket and handed me another BC Powder. I nodded my thanks. He took one. Then passed a packet to Konstantin.

Not long after, we were on a crowded bus heading toward Montevideo.

I sat in the window, looked out at the rain, my mind on Catherine and the boys.

Hawks was on my mind too. I was glad she wasn't swimming in this cesspool of danger.

The information Arizona had given me, I had already passed it on to Hawks. I had sent it to her as soon as it was given to me. She'd been in the background working for me.

Dark clouds shadowed every thought. This job was done, but I still had another two-point-five-million-dollar problem that had weight and its own rapidly approaching deadline.

I shared the same information I'd sent to Hawks with Konstantin.

He asked, "No word from her?"

"No word. Not yet."

While Konstantin looked the information over, I had a long conversation with Shotgun.

He was in this fraternity now.

I told him what Konstantin already knew, told him about a man they had called Midnight.

I told him who Medianoche was. Or might be. I told him about that day in North Carolina.

I told him that Catherine used to be a whore named Thelma. I told him how we had lived on the run most of our lives. I told him I had gone to kill Catherine when she was Thelma, had wanted to kill the woman who taught me to kill, told him that I had gone to assassinate her more than once but never did. I told him about the DNA results that had been inside the FedEx box.

I told him how I got the name Gideon. I told him about a cold night in Detroit.

I told him who I really was. I told him the good, the bad, and the ugly.

Most of it was ugly.

The big man was left speechless.

Capítulo 49

el desaparecido

The Beast was no more.

The man with plenary power over The Four Horsemen was dead.

Gun in hand, Medianoche stood over his leader's body. Half of The Beast's face was gone. There would be no coma. There would be no coming back. There would be no lies.

They had been like brothers. So this ending was biblical in Medianoche's eyes.

Señorita Raven remained across the apartment, unarmed, awaiting her fate.

Señorita Raven asked, "What just happened here?"

"He's dead. You're not. That's all that matters."

"Why did you kill him?"

"Because enemies should only be allowed to get so close."

Señorita Raven looked at the gun in Medianoche's hand. He saw her trying to decide if she could move fast enough to run inside her bedroom.

He saw her expression say that she didn't stand a chance in hell.

She asked, "Now what? You're going to kill me too?"

"I could kill you and throw your body out the window just to see it fall."

That paused her. "Are you?"

"That depends on you."

"What do you mean, depends on me?"

"Decide what you want to do. I'll be back soon."

"What are my options?"

"Be here or be gone. You can go back to East Saint Louis."

"I'll never go back to East Saint Louis."

"Like I said, depends on you."

She asked, "You're going after the package?"

"That's done. I'm leaving. Lot on my mind. Shit to do. And don't follow me."

"You killed The Beast."

"He was about to kill you."

"Is that why you killed him?"

Medianoche didn't answer.

He told Señorita Raven, "If you stay on board, I have an assignment for you. But if you leave, I can give you another assignment. A final assignment. The pay will be doubled either way."

"But I can stay."

"You can stay."

"If I stay, that makes me second in command."

"It does."

"And I get to help pick the next members."

"You do. But I have final word."

She paused. "Do I have to sleep with you?"

"You don't have to."

She nodded. "What is the assignment?"

"It's a job in Montserrat. A woman named Gracelyn."

"Your ex-wife. The one that broke your heart."

"Do it however you want to do it. As long as it gets done."

"What about The Beast and Draco?"

Medianoche looked down at his dead friend.

It was time for a changing of the guard.

Then he looked back at Señorita Raven.

He said, "Call the cleaner. Tell them there are two bodies. Have them cremated."

"Sir, I want Señor Rodríguez's body taken from the morgue. He's in the morgue toe-tagged as a John Doe. We can say he was on the train and was an innocent bystander. I'll go to the morgue. Nobody saw me on that train, so I'll say I was his girlfriend and I will claim his body. One thing, sir. I want his body sent home to his family. And I want you to pay for it. He died saving your life, and I want you to show some goddamn appreciation and pay for it."

"You one-eyed fuck."

"What?"

"You usually end it with 'you one-eyed fuck.'"

"Oh. Right. Well. Not this time. I got tired of saying that."

"Good. Because I'm not in the mood."

"Regardless of your mood, I want you to show some respect for a dead soldier."

"I could put a hole in your head right now."

"You could. But you won't."

Medianoche frowned at her. "You've got balls."

"Big balls, sir. When it comes to looking after my comrades, gigantic balls. I looked after him. And I offered to look after you. But you took that the wrong way. You took it as a threat."

He nodded. "Make it so. Go get him from the morgue. Ship him back to his family."

"The three girls next door?"

"Send those whores home."

"Can I throw money in their faces first?"

He stared at Señorita Raven.

He asked, "Can I trust you?"

"Depends. Can I trust you?"

"Don't lie to me."

"Don't disrespect me."

He nodded.

She did the same.

Until this mission was over, it would remain friends close, enemies closer.

He asked, "Anything else in his files I should know about?"

"Yeah."

"What?"

Señorita Raven said, "She's alive."

"Who's alive?"

"Thelma. She's alive. The woman who got your eye shot out. She's around."

"Gideon said she died last year."

"The Beast was in contact with her a few years ago."

"You sure about that?"

"If I read his records properly, and he kept electronic journals, he saw her in Amsterdam somewhere between eight and eleven years ago. He saw her in Germany too. And based on his records, he was in contact with her when she was in London, by phone, then in contact with her about two months ago. So somebody's lying. The Beast e-mailed her, but that e-mail address she used is no longer in use. Looks like he was protecting her. She was in Georgia."

"Georgia? She's alive and in Eurasia?"

"Not the country Georgia. The state in the Bible Belt section of the United States."

"Big state. Which city?"

"The files didn't say where. Just said she was in Georgia. And get this. The files said that Thelma had another son. A little boy named Sven."

"The whore had another son." Medianoche grunted. "Can't blame that one on me."

"She wouldn't have to. It was The Beast's kid."

He looked down at his friend's dead body. Lies had been told and the truth had been taken to the grave.

Medianoche said, "You sure he had a child with her?"

"One hundred percent."

"In their communications, what was said about me?"

"No chatter about you at all. Based on what I read, she thinks you're dead."

A lot was known, but a lot was missing.

Medianoche told Señorita Raven, "I want you to go through all of his files."

"I can't. After he knew I had hijacked his Wi-Fi and peeped inside the files, he deleted everything, then ran a program that writes meaningless shit over the memory a thousand times. My guess was he had Draco do that. The Beast wasn't computer literate. I guess when I lost it on the elevator and said that I'd read some files, he became paranoid and erased everything. He erased before I told him about the Wi-Fi hijacking. If the files were transferred to some other location, I don't know. But I'm sure he did transfer the files somewhere."

"That's why he wanted you dead."

"You knew he wanted me dead."

"I knew."

"How long did you know?"

"Long enough." He looked at her. "Call the cleaner. Have the bodies burned."

"What about the ashes?"

"Walk the streets and sprinkle their ashes on the dog shit, for all I care."

Medianoche took to the elevator. Pushed the button.

Señorita Raven stuck her head out in the hallway.

She said, "Sir?"

"Yeah."

"Can I at least get an apology?"

"I didn't rape you."

"For throwing the money in my face. That really hurt my feelings. That hurt me more than anything that happened after. I've put my life on the line for many men. Over and over."

Medianoche nodded. "I apologize."

"Apology accepted."

Then he walked onto the elevator. As it descended, he thought about Gideon. The sonofawhore and the whore were out there.

It hadn't ended.

It was only beginning.

Meidanoche took the crowded subte.

He rode the B line to Leandro N. Alem, the end of the line in that direction.

He made his way to the escalator, passed by kiosks with vendors selling scarves, came out at Luna Park. The rain had stopped. He walked through a crowd of Muslims, Jews, Catholics, and atheists who were marching in protest, all waving signs that read BASTA DE INSEGURIDAD.

He hurried toward the Santillana Group Building.

The Four Horsemen had failed. Faulty leadership was to blame.

He would have to build a better, stronger group.

Medianoche held a cup of coffee in his hand.

He went inside the building, found his way to an office on the twentieth floor, and handed the coffee to an old businessman, an old man who had helped thirty thousand people vanish.

An hour later, Medianoche was walking inside Galerías Pacífico. It was one of Buenos Aires' plushest downtown malls. It had also been the site of an abandoned torture center, the truth uncovered accidentally during a movie shoot. Tiffany's, Polo Ralph Lauren, Christian Lacroix, and hundreds of other stores stood sparkling on the wretched ground where the First Army Corps had imprisoned people in the bowels of the mall. Down below all the fine shopping, the prison walls had been marked with the final desperate words carved by its dying prisoners.

Medianoche shook his head. They had been so close to fortune.

He walked through the sweet smells of perfume and took the escalator to the downstairs food court. The area was crowded. Lots of mothers and children. Medianoche bought a cup of coffee and sat in the section near the Coffee Store, closer to the end by Sony Style.

An older Latin man came downstairs. He had four small children with him.

Those were the old man's grandchildren. All between the ages of eight and twelve.

The old man sat down and sent his grandchildren to get in line at Burger King.

Medianoche seasoned the coffee, just as he had done earlier.

As soon as the children left, Medianoche sat down in front of the smiling old man.

The old man took one look at Medianoche and said, "You are a soldier."

"I was."

"Soldiers recognize soldiers."

Medianoche nodded. "That we do."

"Bad men recognize bad men."

"We have an aura."

The old man crossed his legs. "You have killed many."

"More than I can count. For country and for profit."

"You are no different from me."

"I'd like to think I am."

The old man nodded. "And I take it that you are here for me."

"You always come back to see your grandchildren. You always bring them here."

"Our habits are what make us human. The same habits take us to the grave."

Medianoche showed the old man a folder. Pictures of the old man in military uniform. Pictures of the vanished. Medianoche had photos of the old man's family. Addresses.

The old man was an old warrior whose better days had gone by.

He said, "I only followed orders. I did nothing wrong. I had orders."

"Like a good soldier."

"Arrest me. Let me stand trial with the others."

"Afraid not."

"And if I refuse to go quietly?"

Medianoche motioned at the old man's grandchildren.

That was a real threat. The old man knew that.

This could be done the hard way. Or this could be done the easy way.

Then Medianoche handed the old man the cup of coffee.

Medianoche told the old man, "Drink. It tastes better if you drink it hot."

The old man said, "After all I did for Argentina, you give me poison."

"Caprica Ortiz. She wanted you to hear her name before you die."

"I do not know her."

"She wanted you to die in increments. But I don't have time. So yours will be a quick death. Quicker than the death you and your soldiers rendered to those you tortured."

"My grandchildren. What about my innocent grandchildren?"

"Think of the ones who never got to have grandchildren. Think of the grandchildren who didn't get this much time with their grandparents. She told me to tell you that you've been lucky."

"Please. Allow me to make one phone call. I need someone to come get them."

"Sorry. No phone calls. Tell me the number and I will call when this is done."

"This is irony."

"It is. This is irony. You will see your end here, in a building where the military junta used to torture Argentina's missing citizens. I bet the ghosts of those you killed are applauding."

The old man looked back at his grandchildren, saw them standing in line, patient and well-behaved. Kids who wanted to spend the day with their grandfather and eat fast food.

Medianoche watched the old man's hands shake as he drank the coffee.

He drank it all, took the top off the cup and showed Medianoche that it was empty.

The old man smiled.

Medianoche said, "You have enough time to go hug your grandkids."

"No. I will sit here. It is better this way. If they don't see me go."

"Your call."

"See you in Hell."

"Save me a seat by the furnace."

"I shall."

Medianoche walked away.

They were naked inside the bathroom of a suite in the Four Seasons.

Her gray hair was down, framing her beautiful face. Medianoche thought she looked better than Sophia Loren did back in the '40s, and vintage Sophia Loren was hard to top.

Caprica Ortiz held the marble counter and stared at Medianoche's reflection in the mirror. He slipped his erection inside her, took her from behind, held her waist and moved in slow motion, watched the sinful expression swell in her face. He crawled inside her a little at a time.

She whispered, "Go slow this time. Please, Medianoche, go slower."

"I will."

He went deeper and she closed her eyes, her mouth open in an orgasmic expression.

It was like making love to a virgin on her wedding night.

Caprica Ortiz was married, loved her husband, but said she hadn't had sex in almost five years. She moaned a lot but didn't move much, just held the counter and made wonderful sounds.

Medianoche backed up and sat on the toilet, kept that same position. He held her hips, made her move up and down. She relaxed into him, accepted as much of him as she could, then leaned back into him and gave him her tongue. Her kisses were good. Were magical. Felt like they had healing power. He turned her around, opened her legs, and made her straddle him.

"You are a well-endowed man. Much larger than my husband."

"You are a beautiful woman."

"Not as beautiful as I once was."

"And I don't get as hard as I used to."

Her gray hair. The lines around her eyes. Her beautiful, pouty breasts.

She looked fifty. A beautiful and confident fifty.

She sat on him with her mouth open, her gray hair framing her face as her lips parted in ecstasy, her sensual gaze deep and piercing, a stare that was as frightening as it was seductive.

Medianoche held her close, kissed her, focused on his breathing, focused on the sensations. Making love to a mature woman was much better than fucking a young woman.

Experience was where it mattered.

Caprica Ortiz reached over to the marble counter, picked up her *mate*, sipped through the metal straw, then put the metal straw to Medianoche's lips, let him sip, then she put the *mate* back on the counter. Medianoche sucked her breasts for a while. The soft and sweet breasts of a mother. He gave her shallow penetration, slow movements, felt her holding on, heard her breathing get ragged as he worked his way deeper. She held the marble counter with one hand while her other hand pressed down on Medianoche's leg.

She began taking all of him. She moaned and took all he had to offer.

Medianoche had killed his commander. He needed to numb his pain.

She put her mouth on his, made her tongue dance inside his mouth as she moved up and down. Each up and down strengthened Medianoche, made physical wounds heal.

He needed to destress.

Then Medianoche took her back to the bed, but she wouldn't let him put her on the bed.

Caprica Ortiz snatched the comforter off the bed and threw it over the carpet.

She said, "Sit."

Medianoche sat on the floor and she eased down on him, looked in his eyes, gave him a basilisk stare and squatted over him, surrounded him with heat and dampness. She got comfortable and wrapped her legs around him, rocked awhile, then straddled him again, moving up and down. She never took her eyes away from Medianoche.

Caprica Ortiz jerked, moaned, lost her rhythm, her orgasm taking control of her.

Medianoche lifted her up, put her on the bed facedown, had her body flat on the mattress. He moved in and out of her. She reached back and grabbed her ankles, pulled her feet up to the middle of her back. Caprica Ortiz trembled and came again.

And when her orgasm had settled, he turned her over.

He said, "You're very flexible."

"Yoga. Pilates. I do both. It helps with stress."

He held her in missionary position, her legs wrapped around his, fucked her until he came.

He fell away from her, his heart beating as fast as it had beat in the *villas*.

She looked at his face. Looked at the cuts and swellings. She tended to his wounds like a battlefield nurse. He took pain pills and drank scotch, but nothing helped like sex.

He rested on one side of the bed, on his back, hands behind his head, staring at the ceiling. He had killed his best friend. He had killed a liar. He wasn't sure if he had done what was right, but he had done what he felt like he had to do. He was nobody's lapdog.

Caprica Ortiz was on her side, facing him, her wedding ring sparkling in the light.

She asked, "Was I okay? Was the sex with me okay?"

"You were great."

"I'm a little nervous. You're my first."

"Your first?"

"My first affair. Does this make me a bad person?"

"All great women have affairs."

"True. They said Evita had many extramarital affairs. They said she was with Aristotle Onassis, Tyrone Power, Errol Flynn, Warren Beatty, Otto Skorzeny, many others. Powerful and beautiful men wanted her. And some say she had whatever man she saw fit to have. She used them all as stepping-stones to ensure she achieved what she needed to achieve."

Medianoche wasn't listening. Her voice had been a drone. Background noise.

He frowned and felt a pain in his heart.

He had killed his friend. It could not be undone.

Caprica Ortiz traced her fingers over his chest. "The four men on my list, they're dead."

Medianoche ran his fingers through her hair. "The men on your list are dead."

"I will find more. I will find as many as I can."

Medianoche looked at the clock. He had fucked her for more than an hour.

She had been softened up. Now he could get to what the mission was all about.

He said, "I gave you what you needed. Now I need to use your resources."

"What help do you need, Medianoche?"

"You have been able to track and find people that the government have been unable to find. Point-blank, I need to find someone. Some-one I need to kill. An assassin named Gideon."

"Is it personal?"

"Very."

"I will help you find Gideon." She nodded. "I have to go back home to my husband soon."

"Too bad you're married."

"And if I wasn't?"

"You'd become my fourth wife."

Medianoche touched his swollen face. Ran his tongue over his tender lips.

She said, "Right now I will do anything for you."

"Anything?"

"Except damage my family. I find it incredibly difficult to resist you. I am very attracted to you. You looked at me, and my clothes melted away. The night we met, you could've had me."

"You could've had me too."

She moved her gray hair from her face and smiled. "Tell me what you need."

He said, "Use your resources to find Gideon."

"Anything else?"

"Open that pretty mouth of yours and give me a blow job before you go."

"What?"

"I want you to take me inside your pretty mouth."

She paused, then laughed a little. "I haven't done that in a long time."

"You can go slow."

"I want to make you feel as good as you've made me feel."

"I want what you want."

He wanted to fill her mouth. He wanted her to stop talking.

He didn't want to be alone, but he didn't want to engage in any conversation.

He needed to think.

He stared at the ceiling while she took him inside her mouth.

She was good.

Damn good.

Medianoche pulled Caprica Ortiz up to his face, kissed her, then turned her over.

He put her on her back.

She opened her legs like he was her brand-new husband.

Beautiful gray hair.

As stunning as Sophia Loren when she was the sex kitten of the world.

A body that time hadn't damaged.

He mounted Caprica Ortiz, kissed her like she was his wife.

Medianoche eased inside her again.

He moved slowly.

Took his time.

He was thinking about killing a whore from Yerres.

He would kill her and both of her sons.

Chapter 50

build my gallows high

By the time we made it halfway to Montevideo, Shotgun and Konstantin were both sleeping. I stayed awake. Medianoche was on my mind and wouldn't leave me alone.

My cellular vibrated and surpised me. It was a text message: FUNDS TRANSFERRED.

My business with Scamz was done.

We were moving through an area where I could get a signal.

I kept my iPhone in my hand and went online.

I looked in on Powder Springs. Catherine had given up looking for the cameras.

She and the boys were fine.

It hit me then. I had a brother. Steven was my brother.

My phone rang. Hawks was calling. I answered.

She said, "I have your little problem sitting right in front of me."

The information that I had gotten from Arizona had been sent to Hawks the moment it was in my hands. Arizona had been efficient. And Hawks was reliable. She'd left London on British Airways and flown back to Atlanta, then hopped on a Delta flight and gone to Memphis, Tennessee. With the information I had gotten from Arizona, Hawks had found my blackmailers.

There were two. They were holed up not too far from the Mississippi River at a boutique luxury hotel, the Madison. Hawks had knocked on the door and said she was from the front desk.

And the fools had opened the door and come face-to-face with a loaded nine.

Hawks said they knew. The moment they saw the gun, they knew what it was about.

Hawks had put them in chairs, used duct tape to tie them down.

And they started talking. But now it was time for them to talk to me.

Hawks put them on speakerphone.

I said, "You're the guy I met at Starbucks."

"I am . . . yeah."

"Nicolas Jacoby. The guy with two fake IDs."

"Uh. Yeah."

"The guy I took in the bathroom."

"You beat me up. That really wasn't necessary. I'm a pacifist. I detest violence."

"Jacoby. That's not your real name."

"No. It's not my real name."

"Who are you?"

"Todd Parker. My name is Todd Parker."

"What's your job? You're not in the wet-works business. Are you con men?"

The young man said, "We're cyberpunks."

"And that means?"

"We're hackers, that's all. Just computer hackers trying to make it big."

"Opportunistic computer hackers."

"Well, yeah. You could say that. We're not on the level with hackers like Kevin Mitnick and Adrian Lamo, but we're in the same business. We're the best hackers in the area."

"Why are you in Memphis?"

Todd said, "I went to Rhodes College."

"What was your major?"

"Biology."

I said, "You majored in biology and you want to bribe me for two-point-five-million dollars."

The girl spoke up, "We're sorry. We're really sorry."

"Who are you?"

"Nasheeta. My name is Nasheeta Rizk Tannous."

I said, "You're Lebanese."

She said, "Yes."

"You were at the Starbucks in Florida."

"Yes."

"You are the girl who had on the pink blouse and all the tattoos."

"Yes."

"You left Starbucks and Todd stayed."

"Yes."

"Why did you leave?"

"Because I was afraid. I didn't want to do it. I told him not to do it."

"He's your boyfriend."

"Yes."

I asked, "How did you two get information on me?"

Nasheeta did the talking. "I used to work for the mayor in Detroit. I did some work on her computers. After she was killed in Antigua, I decrypted her files. Her workers had erased her hard drive. That was in her instructions. If anything happened to her, they were to immediately erase the files on her personal computers and burn other files she had hidden in her home and office. They didn't destroy her laptop. So, after they were done, I bought her laptop when they auctioned her belongings. I ran a program, a mirror file, and decrypted what was on her hard drive. She kept detailed information on everyone. She had phone logs. She had records. And she had information that she had gathered on Gideon. She had hired you to kill her husband."

"And you and Todd decided to blackmail me."

Todd said, "Well. Yes. It seemed like it would be . . . easy. It's easy in the movies."

"Todd, let's not bullshit. Tell me the truth."

Nasheeta said, "That is the truth."

I paused, "Todd, who do you work for?"

"No one."

I said, "Todd, you were at Starbucks *before* I made it to Starbucks. You knew I was going to be at Starbucks. Last time, tell me who you're working for."

He didn't answer.

I said, "Is that how you want to play it?"

He stuttered, "We . . . we don't work for anyone."

I paused for a moment. "Okay. Then we're done."

Nasheeta said, "Wait. I'll tell you who we work for."

Todd snapped, "Shut up, Nasheeta."

She said, "I don't know who the man is, but Todd knows. Todd met with him in Florida. That is why we went to Florida, to meet with him. He only met Todd. I am just the computer person. I promise. That's all I did. I told Todd that this was dangerous. I didn't want to do it."

I waited a few seconds, then said, "Todd?"

He didn't say anything.

Nasheeta cried, "Todd . . . please . . . tell them . . . please Todd."

Todd said nothing.

I said, "You threatened me. You threatened to ruin my life and send what you had to Scotland Yard. Interpol. CIA. FBI. NTSB. DHS. You said you'd send information about me to every law-enforcement agency in the islands and Canada. To every social networking site. Said you would do all of that with one click."

Todd remained silent as Nasheeta begged for her life.

I whispered, "We're done."

Todd said, "Wait."

I said, "Okay."

"I have a question."

"Okay."

"Were you ever going to pay?"

"Of course not. I would've tracked you down and done a blackout."

"What is that?"

"I would've killed you and everybody in your family."

"Jesus."

"You'll see him soon."

Hawks took them off speakerphone.

She was a ruthless killer and a passionate woman.

Today she'd be a ruthless killer.

I asked, "What do you have?"

"Gun and no silencer. But I brought duct tape and Glad plastic wrap."

I said, "You're one creative woman."

"Doesn't cost much to do a job. Two dollars is all you need to do a job."

"Yeah."

"I can do this job with a sharp number-two pencil. Or a hotel ink pen."

"No blood."

Hawks said, "I'll cover their heads in Glad plastic and wrap them up with duct tape."

"You have an exit?"

"Mapped it out before I came up the stairs to the room. I'll be out of here and walking down Beale Street in the next five minutes. Will be across from the Peabody and eating ribs at the Rendezvous in ten. Two hours after that I'll be walking through Graceland. Can't come to Memphis and not see Elvis."

I paused. "They're kids. They're in the wrong business."

"They stepped into the major leagues."

"They know too much."

"I know. Damn shame. But what has to be done has to be done."

"Make sure it looks like a hit."

Hawks said, "Sounds like you're sending a message."

"I am sending a message."

"To whom?"

"He knows. I can't prove it. Evidence is circumstantial at best. But he knows."

Hawks asked, "You want to stay on the line and listen in until I'm done."

"No. I'll let you do your thing."

Hawks said, "I'm going to be on the road, have to do a job in Chargoggagoggmanchauggagoggchaubunagungama, but I hope I see you soon."

"Same here."

"Miss you."

"Same here."

"Hey. Got your text. My contact will have information on those names in the morning."

"Jeremy Bentham in Smyrna, Georgia, and Nathalie Marie Masreliez from Yerres, France."

"Until then, take it easy. And tell *mi jefe* I said *hola*."

"Will do, Hawks. Will do."

Hawks hung up the phone. I did the same.

I didn't care about Jeremy Bentham from Smyrna or Nathalie-Marie Masreliez from Yerres right now.

I'd address those issues tomorrow.

Right now my mind remained on Todd Parker and Nasheeta Rizk Tannous.

There was one problem with their story.

The details about Detroit were on point. And maybe they did access her laptop.

The big problem was that they had arrived at Starbucks before I got there.

They were waiting on me. They didn't follow me there.

They knew I was going to meet Arizona there.

Todd Parker had said Arizona's name. He had stood in my face and said Arizona's name. I'd bet that only one other person knew where I was meeting Arizona.

And that would've been Scamz.

He was a man who could arrange the kind of fake IDs Todd Parker had had.

I doubted if Arizona would've tried to con me out of two-point-five million.

But I think that somewhere along the line, she knew that Scamz was running that con.

Or maybe she didn't. If she did, the stakes were too high to let that be known.

When we were in Florida sitting at Starbucks, I remembered how Arizona had taken out all of her toys, how she had taken out her electronic devices that kept our conversation from being monitored. I wondered if that was because of Scamz. I knew stealing the credit card information was for Arizona, that was her thing, but she had told me to turn my iPhone off.

She wasn't trying to rob me like she robbed everyone else.

No matter how I turned around in that maze of thoughts, it always ended at Scamz.

Maybe because I didn't like him.

It went back to the man Arizona didn't trust with the passwords to their big scheme.

There was a lot I didn't know. And there was a lot I didn't care to know.

But I was sure about one thing. Konstantin was right.

In Arizona's business, family meant nothing.

A grifter's world was all about the grift.

I closed my eyes. I saw two naked men. Men stripped of all identification.

I saw a father and son shivering, icebergs and mountains in the distance.

I heard the mercy that came from a silenced nine millimeter.

Then I saw frozen blood in the land of fire.

Do the job. Take the money. Keep it moving.

I always did the job. I always took the money. It was time to keep it moving.

I looked out at the rain as we pulled up into the capital of Uruguay.

My injuries told me that this hadn't been a bad dream.

Medianoche was alive. Midnight was out there in the world.

Just as sure as I had bullets and a gun, I knew we'd meet again.

acknowledgments

Hola! ¿Como está, usted? ¿Todo bien? Cuatro Chiclets, por favor.

Okay, that's all the Spanish I know.

Sorry.

Guess I'll have to crack open that Rosetta Stone Spanish One tutorial I bought at the airport back in 2001.

LOL.

I went to Argentina for the first time back in September of 2008. It was a random trip in search of another international location for a novel. I had never been there, didn't know anyone who had been there. That was enough for me. I was going to try to fly to Venezuela, but their prez was tripping at the time, trying to kick people out of the American embassy and saying some pretty harsh things about the United States, and not knowing how the rest of the citizens felt about North Americans who lived in the lower forty-nine, I canceled that trip and ended up going to Argentina.

On a winter day in September, I stepped off the plane into a brand-new world and had no idea what to expect. As soon as I exited the plane, I was immediately overwhelmed, in a good way. Filled with both beauty and danger, I knew Buenos Aires was going to be a great location, a country with a history both powerful and touching.

Eduardo Windhausen! My favorite *remis*! Thanks for picking me up from the airport! I was as lost as the people on *Lost*!

As we left the airport, I looked around and thought, What if?

That is the foundation of all storytelling.

What if?

Camera in one hand, video recorder in the other, I looked at everything and imagined.

What if . . . what if . . . what if. . . .

No matter what type of story I chose to work on, Buenos Aires had many wonderful locations.

And Argentina has a history that is astounding.

So far as the story, I knew I wanted something dark and gritty, populated with wonderful, damaged characters who weren't politically correct. That's what I like about writing, the troubled characters who operate outside the box. It has nothing to do with romance. They might have passing romantic moments, but they are (fictional) humans and they have to eat, meaning that at times their lust must be fed. And I'm not shy about giving up the details. Because there is always something else going on. Even when they have sex, there is darkness. In the classic noir stories, the women are as much bad news for men as men are bad news for women.

Orgasm is the great deceiver and they know that.

If not, the characters will learn that lesson before the book ends.

What I like about the characters the most, maybe, is that they have their own rules and own sense of morality. If they have any morality at all. The unpredictable are always the most interesting. I love the characters in the graphic novels *The Dead and the Dying*, *Coward*, *Lawless*, *100 Bullets*, *Batman: Year One*, and *The Punisher*. Some of my favorite writers in that genre are Garth Ennis, Frank Miller, Ed Brubaker, and Brian Azzarello. Those guys can throw down, no holds barred. It doesn't matter if the character is a super-assassin or a softhearted guy who happens to be at the wrong place and at the wrong time, the characters they create are untouchable. My hat is off to those writers. I want to join that club when I grow up.

And I hope I can bring Gideon, Shotgun, Driver, and Dante along. They belong in that medium.

Anyway, back to chatting about the thick book you have in your hand.

Initially I had started writing a few scenes with Gideon already on a job down in Buenos Aires, something divorced from his other dealings, maybe a prequel to his first appearance in *Sleeping with Strangers*, but after a month or so, that wasn't working; the scenes didn't impress me, and I needed a new approach.

Gideon had to remain connected to his other adventures. It had to remain ongoing.

I hit reset and started over. First I created Medianoche, then decided he wasn't enough, not for what I had in mind. Then I looked back at some old, unused chapters from my previous works, in particular one scene I had created for *Dying for Revenge*, but had cut halfway through that project. It was the scene with Arizona walking into Starbucks in Aventura. It was a good scene, but it didn't fit into *Dying for Revenge*.

I thought, Yeah. Perfect. Arizona. Great entrance. Great characters have to have great entrances. I think I learned that in Theater 101. Or I could've been having a conversation with an inebriated relative. All that to say I was convinced that it was time for Arizona to come back and make an appearance in the series. And once I agreed that she could have a big part in this one, Arizona loosened her grip and moved the knife from my throat and let me breathe. She was pissed that she wasn't hired for the last book. Now that I think about it, her ass had been pissed since London. Something about getting her hair wet in the filthy Thames. And she had read *D4R*, stormed into my office, and slapped me upside my head with the book, sent my locks flying all over my head, then stood over me and demanded to know who the hell Hawks was. I smiled a little. Arizona can be a bit jealous. Anyway. Once my pulse slowed down and I saw Arizona was in the corner, waiting, knife in hand, I wiped the blood from my lip and realized that the initial idea I had for her could still work, once modified to fit the new story.

So I sipped my *mate*, then took the ball and ran with that idea.

I didn't like Medianoche working solo. I liked the character, an aged soldier who was being haunted by his past. He needed some company. So I created The Four Horsemen. Right off the bat, I liked that league of assassins. It had a balance of old soldiers and new warriors. The group had the diversity I enjoy writing about.

Cool.

And now you're holding the end result of a few ideas that started back in September '08 as I sat in a rented apartment in Palermo. Oh, yeah. I rented my temporary living space from a beautiful woman named Lucia. I had landed in Argentina and had no accommodations, but Eduardo took me to a rental office in Palermo. We popped online, and as fate would have it, Lucia's place was available. She is a wonderful woman. She had me situated in a matter of hours. She is fantastic. She made sure I had what was most important—my Internet connection. LOL. And she made sure I was able to get around in an intimidating country.

Anyway, where was I? That head injury Arizona gave me causes me to ramble.

Oh, yeah. I was on the seventeenth floor looking out the window at gray skies and rain, heater on high. I convinced myself that the location I had rented would be the perfect spot for Medianoche and his crew to have as their hideout. Every hero and villain needs a place to sleep at night. Of course I played What if? with the space. I was at Lucia's rental for three weeks; then went back to the E.E.U.U. I took all of my notes and worked on the front end of the novel, focused on Gideon and his world. Then when I was back in the Paris of the South in February of 2009, I redid a lot with Medianoche and his crew. On that trip I stayed at the Melia, in the area called Recoleta. I spent a lot of time on subtes, riding city buses. Rode trains from Retiro to the end; took in tango shows in Capital City; observed protests at the docks; went to Palermo parks on the weekends; took a side trip to Uruguay and walked around Colonia; came back to Buenos Aires; visited museum after museum; rode a bicycle along the dirty river that people say isn't dirty; ate grilled chicken on the boardwalk in Recoleta; read the local papers and met the locals; got a better understanding of both the city and the country.

Whew.

For a guy who can't speak Spanish, I think I did okay.

My wallet and camera were stolen, but hey, shit happens.

Well, long story short, another novel is in the can.

Drumroll please. Time to thank my crew.

Thanks to my wonderful agent, Sara Camilli. This was another intense project for me. Bouncing back and forth to Buenos Aires to make this book happen was both exhausting and fun. I learned a lot about another country, and I learned a little about how they see the E.E.U.U. in return. This one clocked in at more than four hundred pages. I have to write a smaller book next time. This one is about the size of the first two.

But Gideon rocks!

How many more books do I have left to do? Are we there yet?

And a thousand thanks to Stephen Camilli. Dude, you rock. Thanks for taking the time out of your schedule to show me some of BsAs. The talk on the history of Argentina was fantastic. The parade was amazing. And the concert was great. I'll have to catch the Frisbee tournament next time. And most of all, thanks for all of the translations. *Mi español* sucks. Sorry I had Gideon come down to BsAs and pretty much tear up everything from Retiro to Palermo. LOL. ☺ I'll send down a friend and a roll of duct tape. I promise to have the city repaired faster than you can read this sentence. See? Done. Everything is back as it was. Including the *villas*.

Now, off to the E.E.U.U.

Maria Pentkovski in San Francisco, once again thanks for the Russian translations! I'm trying to get Konstantin more stage time. LOL. Hope to see you again. I owe you a cup of grande coffee and an overpriced doughnut from . . . you know where.

Tiffany Pace over in Las Vegas, thanks for the initial edits. Holla!

John Paine, thanks for the first round of notes and input as this project was trying to get its legs. As usual, your insight is invaluable and your work is the best.

To my new editor, Erika Imranyi, you are awesome! Thanks thanks thanks! We finally got this one done.

Brian Tart, Kara Welsh, and everyone hard at work in publicity, thanks for everything!

To my buddies over in the United Kingdom, Kayode Disu and Monique Pendleton, thanks for reading these chapters over and over and over. LOL. Writing is rewriting. The best part of the entire process is when it's just us, chatting and getting into the book. That's the part I love the most. When the book is still raw, when it's untitled, and no other eyes have seen it. Because we get it. We know it from the inside out. It felt like I took both of you to Argentina with me. LOL. You guys are great. You stuck around for months. And never complained. Thanks a lot. I mean that from the heart. No wonder Gideon started his adventures in London. I can't wait to swim back across the pond and sneak by the people in Customs so I can hang out with Kamu and the gang at Poetry in Motion. That event rocks! And I have to check out Spanish Harlem!

Denea Marcel McBroom, once again, thanks for reading this and all the changes. I know you're Arizona's number-one fan. LOL. NOT!

Asami King in Chi-town, once again, thanks for the English-to-Japanese translation.

I have to thank the staff at the Melia Recoleta Plaza Boutique Hotel in Recoleta, my home for close to three months. All of you were absolutely wonderful. Thanks for making a stranger in a strange land feel at home. It was like being with extended family. The Friday night jazz was awesome and the room was fantastic. I enjoyed the Antigua Jazz Band. "40 Años a la Antigua."

And big thanks to the overnight staff at the front desk for bringing their "resident writer" fruit and coffee at three a.m.; that was priceless. Peace and love and many blessing to all of you and your families.

Now, in case I left anyone out, here is your chance to shine.

I want to thank _____ for all of his/her help while I was all over the United States and down in Buenos Aires working on this project. Without your help, insight, and wisdom, I would've written the book anyway, because that is what I do, dammit. ☺ But go ahead and pen your name in so you can feel special.

And now for my people who speak Spanish!

Quiero agradecerle a _____ por toda su ayuda mientras estuve en E.E.U.U. y en Buenos Aires completando este proyecto. Sin tu ayuda, sabiduría, y visión, hubiera escrito el libro igual, porque eso es lo que hago. ☺ Pero, dale, escribí tu nombre allí, así te sentís especial.

Worn, blue Adidas sweats with that trademark white stripe, blue and gray LIFE IS GOOD T-shirt, bottle of Arrowhead mountain spring water at my side.

See ya!

Eric Jerome Dickey
15June09
7:12:46 a.m.
Latitude 34° 3' 8" N, Longitude 118° 14' 34" W
67°F. Overcast. Wind: N at 0 mph. Humidity: 75%

www.ericjeromedickey.com
www.myspace.com/ericjeromedickey
www.facebook.com

http://www.youtube.com/watch?v=c7IE7r7mQxk
http://www.youtube.com/watch?v=2shR99NnwCA
http://www.youtube.com/watch?v=e7Ns1U0OnE8
http://www.youtube.com/watch?v=dt1E0-i4Fcs&feature=related

about the author

Originally from Memphis, Tennessee, Eric Jerome Dickey is the *New York Times* bestselling author of seventeen novels. He is also the author of a six-issue miniseries of comic books for Marvel Enterprises featuring Storm (*X-Men*) and the Black Panther. He lives on the road and rests in whatever hotel will have him.

049459044